THE FATHOMLESS FIRE

THOMAS WHARTON is an award-winning writer for adults and younger readers whose work has been translated into several languages. *The Fathomless Fire* is the second book in The Perilous Realm series, which began with *The Shadow of Malabron*. The author says of the Perilous Realm, "It is not just a world with stories in it. This world is Story. It is the place that all the tales in our world come from. Whatever you might find in a story, you will find here. Adventures, strange encounters, riddles. Heroes and monsters. Bravery, goodness, and terrible evil. And many other things that have yet no name in our world. And you are here now, and that means you are in a story, too."

The author is a professor of English at the University of Alberta, and lives in Edmonton with his wife and three children.

The Fathomless Fire

The Perilous Realm
Book Two

THOMAS WHARTON

Doubleday Canada

Library and Archives Canada Cataloguing in Publication

Wharton, Thomas, 1963–
The fathomless fire / Thomas Wharton.

Issued also in an electronic format.
ISBN 978-0-385-66458-5

I. Title.

PS8595.H28F37 2012 jC813'.54 C2011-900105-5

This book is a work of fiction. Names, characters, places and incidents are products of the author's imagination or are used fictitiously. Any resemblance to actual events or locales or persons, living or dead, is entirely coincidental.

Cover design by Walker Books Ltd.
Cover illustration © 2012 Ciruelo Cabral
Printed and bound in the USA

Published in Canada by Doubleday Canada,
a division of Random House of Canada Limited

www.randomhouse.ca

10 9 8 7 6 5 4 3 2 1

For Conor

Not so long ago, or very far away . . .

WILL LIGHTFOOT, a boy from our world, ran away from his family and stumbled into the Perilous Realm, the world of Story. There he was stalked by terrifying spectres called fetches, but was rescued by Rowen, a girl from the city of Fable. Her grandfather, Nicholas Pendrake, a toymaker and master of lore, feared that Will was being hunted by Malabron, the Night King, who wished to destroy all stories but his own. At the library of Fable, Will accidentally awoke Shade, a talking wolf who became Will's protector and loyal friend. Determined to find a way home before Malabron's dread servant, the Angel, tracked him down, Will set out from Fable with Rowen, Pendrake, and Shade, as well as Finn Madoc, a young knight in training, and Moth, a mysterious archer whose companion was a raven named Morrigan. With his new friends, Will travelled far and faced many dangers before he finally found the way back to his own world. In the end, however, it was revealed that the Angel had been sent to capture not Will but Rowen, who discovered she had hidden powers of her own, and a destiny greater than she had ever imagined . . .

1

And so Will Lightfoot went home to his own world beyond the Realm, and you might think that was the end of the story, but it was really only the beginning.

– Tales from the Golden Goose

HE WAS LEAVING TONIGHT. He couldn't wait any longer.

Will stuffed the bottle of water into his pack with the apple and the energy bars. He looked around his tiny, low-ceilinged bedroom, wondering if there was anything else he should bring. It all depended, he thought, on how long he would be gone. And that was something he didn't know.

From the floor below came a clatter of pots and pans. Dad was making dinner, and apparently destroying the kitchen in the process. The noise was surprisingly loud, as if Dad was in the same room with him. Will wasn't used to the way sound carried in this new house, but then he wasn't used to a lot about it yet. His family had moved in only a few weeks ago, after travelling across the country from the town that Will had lived in all his life. He hadn't wanted to move in the first place, and when they'd first pulled up in front of this ramshackle little two-storey house, with its peeling paint and unmown lawn, his heart had sunk. But now, despite the unfamiliar smells and the cramped quarters, made worse by all their still-unpacked boxes, he had to admit there was something he liked about the place. It was at the edge of town, on a quiet, tree-shaded road lined with other houses of the same age and state of repair. There wasn't much traffic. It was a place where you could come and go without many people around to notice.

Looking out of his window now he could see trees and a few scattered rooftops. The house, he thought, stood between two worlds, the city and the country. And that was it. The house was like him. Between worlds.

"What are you doing?"

Will jumped and turned to the door. His little sister Jess stood there, a doll tucked under one arm and a wide-eyed look of curiosity on her face.

"Nothing," Will said quickly.

"Are you going somewhere?"

She was eyeing the pack he was still holding in his hand. Since they'd moved in Jess had been coming into his room without warning, as if the house was so new to her she was still figuring out the living arrangements. He shouldn't have left his door open.

"For a hike, maybe," Will said, tossing the pack onto his bed with what he hoped looked like a casual gesture. "Tomorrow, if it's a nice day."

He expected her to ask if she could come along. She was always tagging along behind him whenever he went anywhere. But to his surprise she only watched him silently, with an odd expression he couldn't intrepret.

"Dad wants you downstairs," she said as she turned suddenly and walked away, leaving Will with the uneasy feeling that his plans were not as secret as he had thought. But how could Jess know anything about them? She and Dad had no idea what had happened to him during the trip to their new home. They didn't know he'd gone on a journey of his own, to a place far stranger than this unfamiliar house.

And now he was going back. He had no choice. Not after what had happened last night.

Last night, Will talked to a shadow . . .

It was a warm summer evening and he couldn't sleep. The house made strange noises at night, soft little creaks and odd knockings. He lay awake in his bed for a long time, listening to these sounds and trying to guess what was making them. After a while he gave up on sleep, climbed out of bed and started unpacking some of the boxes in his room labelled *Will's stuff*.

To his surprise he realized that one of the boxes wasn't from the move. On the lid was his name, written in his mother's neat, graceful hand. This was a box of his things that she had packed away long ago.

He opened the box and began to unpack it, and each thing he lifted out brought memories with it. His old stuffed animals. Plastic figures of superheroes and monsters. Crayon drawings of his from years ago. And at the bottom, books.

He lifted the books out one at a time and turned the pages, remembering. There were his favourite storybooks when he was very young. *The Wolf and the Three Little Pigs. Jack and the Beanstalk. Little Red Riding Hood.* The bindings were loose and the pages tattered and torn. Some pages had his childish crayon scrawls on them. He hadn't treated books very well back then.

His mother had read him these stories at bedtime. He had asked for them over and over. And when they both got tired of the storybooks, she told him stories that she made up herself. Most of her own stories were about a boy who *could run faster than a hare and leap higher than a deer, so the people called him Light-of-foot, or Lightfoot for short ...*

Will's mother had died three years ago, not long after Will's eleventh birthday, but he could still hear her voice, as clearly as if she was here beside him, telling him about Lightfoot's adventures. At first Will believed the stories were true, and he was thrilled to have the same name as this boy hero of long ago, who was always outwitting monsters and menaces of every kind. *He was not only fast on his feet, he was clever, too, and it was quick thinking that got him out of more than one tight spot, like the time he stood up to Captain Stormcloud and his Lightning Warriors ...*

It didn't take Will long to realize his mother was making it all up as she went along. But he still loved to hear about Lightfoot and asked her for another of his adventures almost every night. He tried to recall how the story of Lightfoot and the one-eyed Captain Stormcloud had ended, but he couldn't, and then he remembered why. His mother had never finished it. It was a long story with lots of surprising twists and turns: she had been telling it to him over many nights, and then she had fallen ill, and went to the hospital. There were no more stories after that. He never found out how Lightfoot defeated Stormcloud and his warriors.

He remembered how every time she finished one of her stories and was tucking him in, he would ask her for just one more. And she would tilt her head, and smile, and say ...

A gust of wind swept in through the open window, sending Will's drawings flying and knocking over the reading lamp on the table beside his bed. Before he could catch it, the lamp landed on the rug and the shade sprang off the bulb. Will lunged, rescuing the shade before it rolled under the bed. As he was about to put it back on the lamp, he heard a sound behind him. A very distinct and unmistakable cough. The kind of cough someone makes when they're trying politely to get your attention.

He whirled around.

There was no one else in the room. The door was closed. All he saw was his own looming shadow, thrown by the bare bulb onto the far wall.

But there was another shadow, standing next to his.

Another person-shape, where there shouldn't be one. Will turned his head slowly to the side, his heart pounding. There was no one beside him casting that other shadow.

"Hello," said a voice.

Will raced for the door.

"Wait!" said the voice, although it was not quite a voice. More like the hollow echo of a voice. "Why do they always run away?" it muttered.

Much to his own surprise, Will didn't flee out of the door and down the stairs. Instead he stopped, turned and faced the shadow. He wasn't sure why, but it was at least partly the certainty, deep down, that this impossible thing had come from that other world he had visited, and was hoping to return to.

His dad's voice boomed from the living room below: "What's going on up there?"

"Sorry," Will shouted. "Just dropped something."

The shadow of someone who wasn't there moved away from Will's own shadow, towards the corner of the room. An old saggy armchair stood there, on which Will piled his clothes at the end of the day. The shadow-person raised a shadow-hand and gestured to the shadow of the chair.

"May I?" the voice asked. How a shadow could be speaking to him, Will didn't know, but the voice sounded . . .

right somehow. A shadow should sound like that, he thought, like the *edges* of a voice with everything in the middle taken away.

Will nodded his head slowly.

The shadow of someone settled into the shadow-chair with a long sigh.

"That's better," it said, patting the arms of the chair. "It wasn't easy getting here, believe me. I'm a bit out of breath. The truth is I've never had to travel this far before to carry out my task."

"Where are you from?" Will asked.

There was a moment of silence.

"You don't really need me to answer that," the shadow replied, with the slightest tinge of sarcasm.

"No, I guess not. What are . . . *who* are you?"

"That's a better question. Unfortunately, the answer is that I'm not anybody. I'm a shadow."

"A shadow of who?"

"Just a shadow. No *who*."

"But every shadow has to be a shadow of *something*."

"Perhaps, but that's not important right now. I've got a task to perform, so I'd better get to it before my time is up. I'm here to bring you a message."

"What message?"

The shadow seemed to lean forward in the shadow of the chair.

"A stone will speak," it said slowly. "The sky will come to earth. And a friend will fall."

"What are you talking about?" Will said. "I don't understand. Who sent this message?"

"No one sent it. But here it is. A stone will speak, the sky will come to earth, and a friend will fall."

Will couldn't make sense of the first two things the

shadow had said, but the third was disturbing. A friend will fall. He thought of Rowen, her grandfather the loremaster, and Shade, the wolf, and fear shot through him like an electric shock.

"What do you mean, a friend will fall. Is someone going to die?"

The shadow sat back again in its shadow-chair.

"I know only what I've told you."

"My friends were fine when I left," Will said. "Do you know what's happening to them?"

"I've told you all I can tell you. Now I'm just going to catch my breath, if you don't mind, then I'll be on my way."

Will's mouth went dry. He stared at the shadow, frustrated by the fact that it had no face. There was no*body* to look at. Which made everything it said doubtful. This could be the shadow of anyone.

"Who sent you?" Will demanded. "*Tell me.*"

"I've already told you, no one sent me. I'm here because it's what must be."

"Well, who told you a friend is going to fall?"

The shadow had no eyes, but Will had the odd feeling that if it had, it would have been rolling them in annoyance.

"*No one* told me. I serve nobody. I'm just here, simple as that, with a message for you about what will be. I'll repeat it again if you like: a stone will speak, the sky—"

"Is that all you can say?" Will broke in, his alarm turning to anger.

"That's all I can say."

"Meaning you don't know anything more, or you won't tell me?"

The shadow sat for a moment in silence, then hoisted itself out of the shadow-armchair with a grunt of effort.

"That's a comfortable chair. Now if you'll excuse me—"

"No, wait. If you know more, you *have to* tell me. Are these things happening now, or are they going to happen soon . . . ?"

"As I said, I've done what I came to do. I am not able to give out any further information. The laws forbid it."

The shadow seemed to dim slightly, and Will was suddenly afraid it would disappear.

"What laws?" he asked quickly. "Please, I'm not from your world. I don't understand."

"The laws of Story, if you must know. I exist because of those laws. Or I suppose you could say I am one of the laws."

"But there's more you could tell me, isn't there? It sounds like you know more than you're saying."

The shadow sighed.

"I am a shadow of things to come. Things that haven't happened yet. My task is to bring people warnings or hints about what's on the way. Hints that many choose to ignore, unfortunately, but that's their problem, not mine. All I'm meant to do is to cast a shadow back from the *will be* to the *now*, and what I do is what I am. And that is all."

"But you could say more if you wanted to, couldn't you?"

"A shadow has no wants," it said mechanically, as if reciting something it had repeated many times. "A shadow does not give directions, explanations or advice. A shadow is its task and nothing more."

"But you've already broken the law," Will said eagerly, the idea forming even as he spoke. "You told me what you are and what you do. So you have given me an explanation."

The shadow went still, as if it was startled by what Will had said. Then it scratched its head slowly.

"I've bent the rules, haven't I?" the shadow said in a dazed murmur. "I never did that before. It must be because I'm so far from home. I've never had to travel out *here* to deliver a message. This is all highly irregular and ..."

"Well, you might as well go ahead and tell me more," Will said with a shrug. "Now that you've already started. What difference will it make?"

The shadow didn't answer straight away. It wavered and bobbed, as if it was being cast now by a flickering candle flame.

"I must not," the shadow said with what sounded to Will like a note of fear in its voice. "I'm ... I'm a shadow of things to come. That's all I am. And my time is almost up. I have to ..."

"Wait, please. I need to know what friend you're talking about. Maybe there's some way I can warn them, before it's too late."

The shadow grew even more dim and wavery.

"I can't tell you what my message means or who it refers to," the shadow said, its voice already sounding far away, "because I really do not know." The shadow had almost faded away to nothing. "All I know is that somehow you left the story, you vanished into this ... wherever this is, which has never happened before to my knowledge. And now you're needed back in the story."

"You mean . . . maybe I can change what's going to happen?"

"I didn't say that. But I do know that I'm here only because the story wants you back."

"But how do I get back?"

"The same way you left," the shadow's voice said, but from where, Will couldn't tell, because it had already vanished.

In a daze Will looked around his room, as if he might find the shadow still lurking somewhere. He saw the fallen lamp, picked it up and set it back on the table. Then his eyes fell on the box of old books. He remembered that just before the shadow appeared he'd been thinking about what his mother always told him when he asked for one more story at bedtime.

Don't worry, she would say. *The story will wait for us.*

He wondered now about the story the shadow had spoken of, the one he had been a part of and wanted more than anything to return to. Would it wait for him?

2

When the hour came for his departure he took counsel with his hosts, and they told him of the several roads he might take, and the dangers of each. And when he had heard them out he made ready to leave, but he would not tell them his thought, nor speak of the path he had chosen.

– Legends of the Errantry

IN THE KITCHEN things were close to a state of chaos. Dad had pots overflowing on the stove, lasagna bubbling away in the oven, and the various ingredients of a salad scattered widely over the counter.

"Well, howdy, stranger," Dad drawled at Will over his shoulder as he chopped celery. Since they'd moved out west, Dad had been pretending he was a cowboy. The joke was already stale. "I asked you to set the table half an hour ago."

"I was busy," Will said, hearing the annoyance in his own voice. The shadow's warnings and Jess's odd behaviour were still troubling him, and he was letting it show. If Jess suspected something and told Dad, things would get a lot more difficult.

Dad stopped chopping, and stared at Will.

"What's up with you?"

"Sorry."

"You can set out the mashed potatoes, too. Use one of Mum's nice bowls."

"Have they been unpacked yet?"

"Right, never mind the nice bowls."

As Will was just finishing setting out the plates and cutlery, the front doorbell rang.

"I'll get it!" came a shout from upstairs, and a moment later Jess bounded down the stairs. Will met her at the door just as she was flinging it open.

Aunt Carrie stood on the step, smiling and holding a flat white box.

"Auntie Carrie!" Jess shouted.

"Hi, sweetie," she said, holding the box aloft with one hand and hugging Jess tightly with her other arm. "Mmm, smells like dinner's cooking."

"Dad's making lasagna and mashed potatoes," Jess said.

"Is he?" Aunt Carrie said. "Interesting combination. Come here, Will." She gave him a hug, too, and handed him the box. "Apple pie for dessert. In case dinner doesn't turn out quite as planned."

"I heard that," Dad shouted from the kitchen. They all laughed, even Will, despite his thoughts being elsewhere. He had always liked his Dad's lively younger sister. The fact that she lived in this town was one of the reasons Dad had decided they should move here, and Will had to admit it had been good for all of them to have her nearby. She'd made the move to a strange town a little easier, and she had the knack of bringing out the seldom-seen fun side in Will's father. Jess loved her, too. Over the past few weeks his little sister, who had been so quiet and withdrawn since their mother died, had begun to talk more and even laughed a little again, and Will knew it was mostly thanks to Aunt

Carrie. All of which made him feel somewhat less guilty about what he had to do.

"We're going to have a great weekend, pumpkin," Aunt Carrie said to Jess, giving her another squeeze. "You're more than welcome to join us, Will." Aunt Carrie was taking Jess to stay with her for a couple of days while Dad went out of town on a construction job. Dad had wanted Will to go with them, but after much discussion, and a lot of chores done without too much complaint, Will had managed to convince the adults that he would be fine on his own at home.

"Thanks," Will said to Aunt Carrie. "I've got things to do here."

He couldn't help glancing at Jess. She was giving him that odd look again. He turned away quickly.

"Your schedule's full, is it?" Aunt Carrie said with a wink.

"Chow's ready, cowpokes," Dad announced, striding to the table with the lasagna pan held on high. "Prepare to feast."

"This looks wonderful," Aunt Carrie said, gazing over the spread laid out on the tablecloth. "But looks can be deceiving."

"Gee thanks, sis."

They sat down and tucked in eagerly. As the dishes were passed around so were the funny family stories. Most of them were told by Aunt Carrie about their dad when he was a boy, and there were a few surprises.

"Did you know that your dad used to do nothing but read?"

Will and Jess shook their heads in disbelief. Dad's bedside shelf held maybe half a dozen books, if that.

"He was such a bookworm, he rarely saw the light of day. If we did something bad our parents punished us by sending me to my room, and your dad *outside*."

"All that changed when I got my first motorbike," Dad said, grinning.

"No kidding," said Aunt Carrie, rolling her eyes. "After that we hardly ever saw you."

Will listened to the stories eagerly, and told some of his own, but he couldn't keep from glancing at the clock on the wall, secretly willing the hands to move faster. With all the stories and the laughter, no one else paid attention to the time. Finally, Will had to speak up.

"Don't you have to leave soon?" he asked Dad, nodding his head towards the clock.

"Oops, you're right!" Dad shouted, jumping up from the table. "We didn't even get to the pie."

"We'll bake a new one for your return," Aunt Carrie said. "You'd better get going."

Dad hurried to his room and came back lugging his beaten-up duffelbag. He threw on his old leather jacket, then kissed Jess and put his arm around Will.

"Be good, you two," he said, then turned to Will. "Be safe."

As before he gave Will an uneasy glance, as if he wanted to say something more. But instead he hurried out and a moment later they heard his truck roar away.

They had a slice of apple pie, then Will and Jess cleared the table. Aunt Carrie wanted to help, but they told her Dad had insisted they do the work themselves. Grudgingly she gave in and had a cup of coffee while Will and Jess washed up. They didn't talk as they worked, and Will was acutely aware of the tense silence. As they were putting away the last of the dishes, Jess turned to him. In a barely audible voice she said, "Are you going tonight?"

Will shut the cutlery drawer with great care.

"I already told you," he said, trying to keep his voice casual, "I might go for a hike tomorrow."

Her unwavering look cut right through his lie.

"I mean, are you going *back*," she said. "You know, back *there*."

Will stared at her.

"How do you . . . ?" he began in a strained whisper.

Aunt Carrie came into the kitchen with her coffee cup.

"Time to make tracks, pumpkin," she said to Jess.

Will waited impatiently while Aunt Carrie helped Jess get her things ready. He hoped his eagerness for them to leave wasn't too obvious, and more than that he was worried Jess would say something to Aunt Carrie. But when Jess came to the front door with her suitcase, the look she gave Will told him that she would keep his secret.

"You sure about this, Will?" Aunt Carrie asked him as he saw them off at the front door. "I don't know if I'd want to spend the night by myself in this creaky old place."

"I'll be fine," Will said, with a twinge of guilt. He wasn't happy about lying, especially not to Aunt Carrie. If only he could tell her, it would take a lot of the weight off. He had the feeling she would actually listen. Maybe she would even be on his side about leaving. But it was too late for that now.

A few moments later Aunt Carrie's car drove off down the street. Will let out a long breath and shut the front door. He was on his own at last.

He hurried up the stairs to his room and checked the contents of his pack one more time. He was bringing enough food and water, he thought, for at least a day or maybe two. He hoped it wouldn't take him anywhere near that long to find the place he meant to go.

On the journey to their new home Will had taken his dad's prized antique motorcycle without asking and crashed it, knocking himself out. When he came to, he'd found himself in another world, a strange and frightening place called the Perilous Realm. He hadn't been looking for it, he hadn't wanted to be there, but not for a moment since returning from the Realm had he been able to forget it.

In the Realm he had met Pendrake, the kindly old toymaker who was really a master of ancient lore, and Finn Madoc, a brave young knight-apprentice. Shade, a talking wolf, had become his good friend.

And Rowen.

Rowen of Blue Hill, Pendrake's granddaughter.

Together they had gone on a long, dangerous quest to find Will a way home. They were joined by Moth, an archer of the Fair Folk, or the Tain Shee as they called themselves, and Morrigan, his sister. Will had been pursued by mindless spectres called fetches, and nearly eaten by hogmen, and had even met an ice dragon. So much had happened to him, to them all, and then he'd returned to his own world. Now he no longer knew for certain where he belonged. He had never felt about anyone the way he felt about Rowen, and being apart from her had made those feelings even stronger. He knew she cared about him as a friend, but whether she felt anything more for him he didn't know. Even if she didn't, he was determined to see her again. He had to get back to the Realm, he had to help her if there was any way he could.

Malabron, the Night King, sought to destroy the countless stories of the Perilous Realm, leaving only one, his own, an endless story of darkness and despair. According to Pendrake, Will had a special gift for finding lost and hidden things, and Malabron, so it had seemed, wanted to use that gift for his own purpose. So Will had set out from the city of Fable where Pendrake and Rowen lived, to find a way home before Malabron's most terrible servant, the dreaded

Angel, tracked him down. But it had turned out in the end that Rowen was the one Malabron really sought, not Will, as everyone had believed. He was not the Night King's prey, she was. And that was even worse.

What was happening to her right now, to Shade and the others? Even before the shadow's visit, Will had been thinking about little other than them. Helping his family move into the new house, he'd felt as though he was watching someone else from a distance. His old familiar life seemed strange to him, and all he wanted was to return to the Realm, to Rowen. But he couldn't just leave his family, he couldn't run away again. He'd had to wait until the chance came to get away without anyone noticing, and that chance had finally come. But what troubled him most now was that he knew from his own experience that time passed differently in the Realm. He had spent weeks with Rowen and the others, but when he got back to his own world he discovered he'd been missing only a few hours. Since then, for him, a few weeks had gone by, but for Rowen maybe much more time had passed. Maybe months, or even years. What if the things the shadow had warned him of had already happened, and he was too late?

His eyes burned.

A friend will fall.

He glanced out of his bedroom window, which overlooked the weed-choked, uncut jungle of the back yard. The late summer sun was setting and the garden was already in shadow, but the trees beyond were flooded with a warm golden light.

How do I get back?

The same way you left.

He had returned from the Realm that first time by walking through a forest. This scrubby patch of woods at the edge of town wasn't really a forest, but it was the closest thing to one around here. It would have to do.

Will hurried back downstairs, took one last quick look around, then turned off the light in the front room. For a moment he stood still in the dark, silent house, aware more than ever of its unfamiliarity. It wasn't his home. Not yet. Maybe it never would be. Maybe his real home was the place he was hoping to get back to.

As he passed through the kitchen on his way to the back door, the light came on. Will froze. Dad was sitting at the table, his finger on the light switch.

"Sit down, son," Dad said, patting the chair beside his. Will hesitated a moment, then obeyed. He thought for an instant about making up some story about going for a late-night walk, but the look in Dad's eyes warned him not to bother.

"Aren't you supposed to be . . . ?" Will began, and trailed off.

"I got a ways down the road but I turned back. I don't have your mum's uncanny sixth sense about you kids, but I had a . . . *feeling*. I've had it for a long time, really. Ever since we moved in here. I guess it was accurate."

So Jess hadn't told him anything, Will thought. Which didn't explain how *she* knew.

"Tell me what's going on, Will."

"It's a long story," Will said, his shoulders slumping, then he laughed in spite of himself. "A really long story."

"This has something to do with what happened on the trip, doesn't it?"

Will nodded. He was almost relieved it had come to this. They hadn't really talked about the incident with the motorcycle, but as far as his dad knew, Will had simply been missing for a few hours then had just suddenly turned up, safe and sound. All Will had said was that he'd got lost, which was the truth, or some of it at least. Now he wasn't sure what to say.

"When you crashed the bike and disappeared, I was worried sick," Dad said. "Mad as heck, too, but mostly worried. Then when you came back, Will, I saw something had changed. I mean you had changed. I know it doesn't make sense but it was like you'd been . . . very far away. Like you'd gone through something that mattered a lot more than a motorcycle. You weren't the same kid who'd ridden off all angry with the move, with me, with . . . the way things turned out. It's crazy, but it was like in a couple of hours you'd grown up."

Dad reached over and put a hand on Will's shoulder.

"So I've been watching you," he went on. "These past few weeks, you've been in another world. When you look at someone you look past them, to some other place no one can see."

Will glanced away. This was how Jess had figured it out, too, he realized. They may not have known where he'd gone, but he hadn't been able to disguise what he'd been through, or the fact that he meant to return. He wasn't finished with the Realm, or it wasn't finished with him. The urge came now to tell Dad everything, but he didn't know where to start, or what would happen if he did. It was almost too much to think about, let alone speak of.

Dad studied Will in silence for a while, then he laughed softly.

"We're not all that different, you know, Will. Hard as that is to believe. When I was your age, I wanted so much to be part of something bigger than the world I knew. All those books I read as a kid, about fantastic adventures in faraway lands, I really believed those things could happen to me. They never did, of course. But you, I don't know how but I know you've become part of something like that, something larger than ... *this*. Can't you tell me what that something is?"

Will turned to look at Dad. Slowly he stood up.

"I can't," he said. "I have to go now, before it's too late."

"If your mother was here, she'd kill me if I let you walk out that door," Dad said, and Will heard the pain in his voice. "How can I let you go?"

"Dad, please. I ... need you to trust me. This is something I have to do."

Dad stood and faced him with a look in his eyes Will had seen only once before, when his mother had died. For the first time he understood just how much his father needed him, and feared for him. A lump formed in his throat. He swallowed hard.

"I do trust you, Will," Dad said. "I ... just can't lose you, too."

"You won't," Will said. "I'll come back, I promise."

"Don't do this, Will," Dad said, but there was no warning in his voice, only sadness.

Will looked at Dad for a long moment, then he picked up his pack. He felt empty inside, and all his eagerness to leave had vanished. He turned away quickly, fighting back tears.

"Will," Dad said, his voice a cracked whisper.

Will opened the back door and hurried down the steps. At the end of the garden there was a gate in the rickety, falling-down wooden fence. Will lifted the latch and pushed. The gate swung open with a shriek of rusty springs.

Will looked back. Dad was standing on the back porch. The light was behind him and Will couldn't see his face, but he stood there with his arms at his sides like someone lost.

Will stepped through the gate. With another shriek it

swung shut behind him and rattled loudly, as if angry at being disturbed.

Under the trees the shadows of twilight closed over him. Suddenly he was aware of the trees whispering and creaking in the wind, and other sounds: faint clicks, knockings, all the small, unidentifiable noises of the woods at dusk. He walked on, quickening his pace as his eyes grew accustomed to the gloom, all his senses on alert.

After he'd gone a short distance he paused to look back the way he'd come. The light over the kitchen door was already a tiny flicker, like a star in the empty reaches of space. He walked a little further, then looked back again. The light was gone.

3

The Far Lands of the Realm, little known to us here in the Bourne, are by all reports strange and wondrous. Roaming Alicantrax is an entire country on the back of a giant elephant. The inhabitants of Zazamanc live for only a day. In the desert of Surth is a lake of blood that heals all wounds. Yet it is said that the further you go from the Bourne and the stranger folk become, the more everything reminds you of home.

– Redquill's Atlas and Gazetteer of the Perilous Realm

ROWEN WOKE SUDDENLY in darkness. For a moment she had no idea where she was, and she sat up in fear. Then she saw the glow of embers, and felt a warm woollen blanket over her shoulders, and she remembered. She and her grandfather were in a snug, in the Forest of Eldark. They were on the way home to Fable.

"Rowen?" Her grandfather's voice came from somewhere nearby. She thought she could just make out, beside the fireplace, the shape of his cloak, the pale grey of his beard.

"What's the matter?" he asked her.

"I had a bad dream," she said.

She could see him better now, seated in one of the rocking chairs by the fire. She wondered if he had slept at all or whether he had sat through the whole night, keeping watch. They had found the snug at sunset the previous evening.

A snug was a mysterious but always welcome refuge on a long journey through the wild. It was a hidden shelter, concealed from all passers-by but those who knew where and how to look for them. If you found one there was always a bright, welcoming fire inside, a pot of stew bubbling on the hearth, and soft, warm featherbeds, even though you never saw or heard whoever it was that had prepared all of this for your arrival.

"What did you dream, Rowen?" her grandfather asked her now.

"I don't remember much of it. It's not important. Just a dream." Though it was warm in the snug, she shivered and drew her blanket around her like a cloak. She did remember the dream, but she wasn't ready to talk about it just yet. The dream had been so real. Fable in flames. The walls and houses tumbling like children's blocks. She had been standing in a high place, looking down upon the destruction, unable to move or turn away. Then she was surrounded by a circle of dim, silent figures in armour. One of them had approached her, and to her terror and confusion it had knelt before her. The figure wore a blank mask of polished metal with no features where a face should have been, so that she saw only her own dark reflection. The figure reached up a gauntleted hand and took off the mask, and there was nothing inside. No one. She turned to run but she couldn't move, she couldn't escape, and then someone took her hand. It was Will Lightfoot, the boy who had come from the Untold, the world beyond the Realm.

In the dream he was just as she remembered him, his unruly dark hair that she'd always wanted to brush back from his face, his warm brown eyes. He had taken her hand, spoken to her as he led her out of the circle of faceless figures. What had he said?

Now she was awake and he wasn't there, and she wanted him to be, more than anything.

She took a deep shuddering breath, drew her arms close around herself.

"What's wrong, Rowen?" her grandfather asked softly.

"Nothing," she said, not wanting to add to his worries. "I'm just cold."

It was a year ago now that Rowen and her grandfather had gone with Will on his journey to find a way home, with Finn Madoc of the Errantry, Shade the wolf, and Moth and Morrigan of the Fair Folk. They had travelled far, through lands Rowen had never known existed. They'd faced many dangers together and made new friends, like Freya Ragnarsdaughter of Skald, a young woman who had joined them on their journey and who Rowen was sure had fallen a little in love with Finn Madoc. She wondered if Freya and Finn would ever see each other again. Skald was so far from Fable.

Rowen and Will had become good friends themselves. Perhaps more than friends. She remembered how Will had looked at her before he left, how fast her heart began to beat when she understood what she felt for him. She wondered where he was now and whether he was thinking about her this very moment, as she was about him. He'd said he would come back some day and find her. According to Grandfather, it was very rare for anyone to cross over from Will's world to the Perilous Realm, but Will had done it once. Surely he could find the way again. If he still wanted to. Maybe he was glad to have escaped the terrors of her world and didn't want to come back. Maybe now that he was with his family again, living his own life, he'd already begun to forget her.

In her dream Will had taken her hand, said something to her. What was it?

She couldn't remember. All that was left of the dream

was the burning, the metal mask coming away to reveal . . . nothing.

Fighting a wave of dizziness she climbed out of bed, slipped on her cloak and opened the door a little way. She needed to breathe fresh air. Outside the snug the forest was still dark, but gazing up into the treetops she saw a faint pale light.

A soft sigh of breath came from nearby. Briar, the horse that pulled their wagon, was stirring. The Fair Folk had given them Briar, and the sturdy, brightly painted wagon when they had parted a few days ago.

"Morning's almost here," Pendrake said, rising to stand beside her. In one hand he held his waylight, a small lantern that pulsed softly with a faint blue light. Sputter, the tiny messenger wisp that lived in the lantern, was going to sleep, as he usually did in the daylight. He was nothing more than a tiny spark of light, but he could carry their messages many miles, or light their way in the darkest night.

They hurried through a breakfast of porridge and tea, then packed up their things. Grandfather took his walking staff that was leaning against the wall and tapped it once on the floor, as he always did when they were about to set out.

"If we make good time today," he said, "we should be at the border of the Bourne by nightfall. From there it won't be long before we're home."

Home, Rowen thought as she followed him out of the snug door. Did she still have a home any more?

The journey with Will had led to the revelation that Rowen was a descendant of the Stewards, the first weavers of Story in the dawn of the Realm. They had stood against Malabron, the Night King, in the long-ago war of the Great Unweaving, when the Realm was torn asunder and many stories were lost. Then they had vanished, though traces of their power still remained in the Realm. And in *her*. That she was in some way related to the ancient shapers of Story she still found difficult to believe, or speak of. The thought was too large, like a towering wave that threatened to sweep away everything she knew.

But it was true. And it was why the Night King had sent his dread servant, the Angel, after Rowen, while she was travelling with Will. Because she had the power of the Stewards within her, the power to shape Story, though as yet she had barely begun learning how to use it. The Angel had caught her, too, and would have taken her a captive to Malabron if she hadn't been rescued by Will and Moth the Shee archer. Moth had died destroying his ancient enemy, but he had freed his sister Morrigan from the curse that had turned her into a raven. Then the Tain Shee, the Fair Folk, had found them, and Rowen had felt safe for a while. And Will had found a way back home to his own world.

After Will was gone, Rowen and her grandfather had stayed with the Fair Folk, making the long journey home with them in their travelling court. The Tain Shee were so skilled at concealment and silence that very few had ever seen their court, and most people knew them as the Shee n'ashoon, the Hidden Folk. Her grandfather's hope was that by staying with the Shee, Rowen would be concealed from their common enemy until she was safely back home in Fable.

Rowen had been glad to spend time in the company of the Fair Folk. Their plain, peaceful life, their tales and songs had cheered her after the terrible things she had been through. She had listened and learned much from them about the history and lore of the Realm. They spoke of the great tree on the hill where they had met with the Stewards at midsummer each year, a tree whose blossoms sent forth seeds of light. Each day with them had felt like many bright, untroubled days flowing together, as if within the court of the Shee there was a power to slow the passing of time.

Rowen had most often sought out Morrigan, Moth's sister. After the Angel was destroyed she had returned to her true shape as a young woman, but her grief for her brother was still etched in her pale face, and she went always in black, and rarely smiled. When the court set up camp in the evenings Rowen would find Morrigan, or Morrigan would find her, and they would walk together through the woods. Rowen would ask her about the long-ago days of her people, when the Shee were not wandering exiles but had lived in a beautiful city on the shore of the Western Sea. Morrigan seemed less sad and troubled when she spoke of those times, but it wasn't long before the light would fade again from her eyes. Then she would leave Rowen and go away on her own.

Then one night Morrigan had come to Rowen's tent to tell her she was leaving. To Rowen's astonishment she was wearing the white cloak that had belonged to the Angel. Rowen knew the cloak was a living thing called a shrowde, but she had thought it was destroyed along with the Angel during his battle with Moth.

"Yes, the shrowde is still alive," Morrigan had replied, to Rowen's unasked question. "It is not evil in itself but was forced to serve the Angel. The shrowde has learned to trust me now. We will travel together."

"Why do you have to go?" Rowen had asked. "This is your home."

Morrigan shook her head.

"This court was never my home," she said with a bitter smile. "My home was lost ages ago. And then I was lost, too, for a long time, in the darkness. Too long. That darkness is inside me now and I've brought it among my people. I cannot stay."

"Where will you go?"

Morrigan looked out of the tent door into the dark. Her eyes were lost, empty.

"I don't know," she said.

"Aren't you going to say goodbye to anyone?"

"It's better this way. Would you tell them, Rowen, that I have gone, and why I could not stay?"

"I'll tell them, yes. But Morrigan, will I see you again?"

Morrigan looked at her with pain in her eyes.

"For your sake I hope you will not," she said.

So Morrigan had left that night, and the Tain Shee missed her, and Rowen did, too. They travelled on, and not many days afterwards came to the shore of a small lake nestled among wooded hills, its surface as still and smooth as a mirror. That evening the Lady of the Shee summoned Rowen and her grandfather to walk with her along the lake shore. She told them they were not far from the edge of the Forest of Eldark, beyond which lay the country of the Bourne, Rowen's home.

"We must part now, my friends," the Lady had said. "The Shee have been the Hidden Folk for a long time. Perhaps too long. That time is over now. All across the Realm stories are darkening, disappearing. We must reveal ourselves at last, and either defeat our enemy or perish. It is better that you are not with us when that day comes."

"Are you going to search for Morrigan?" Rowen had asked.

"She is far from us now. It has been a long time."

"But she left only a few days ago," Rowen said.

"Days here in the Green Court pass slowly, though not as slowly as they once did. Even here the tapestry begins to fray. But for now, in the world outside, time still flows more swiftly than it does here. You have been with us longer than it may seem. You have grown much in that time, Rowen, and I think you are ready now for what awaits you."

The Lady turned and gazed out across the still waters of the lake.

"There are few places left like this," she said sadly, "where time stops altogether."

So Rowen and her grandfather left the Fair Folk, to finish the journey home on their own, and they found that it was as the Lady had said: as soon as the court had vanished, so did their power to slow time. Rowen felt within her flesh and bones the many days and nights that had passed, and the changes of season. It was summer again in the Realm, as it had been when they'd first set out with Will, which now seemed a very long time ago. Her own fourteenth birthday had gone by without her even knowing it. She and her grandfather had been travelling with the Fair Folk for a year.

Maybe, she thought, enough time had gone by that they would be safe now, that the Night King had forgotten them. She hoped it was so, though she felt that hope as a small, fluttering flame that at any moment might be snuffed out.

As dawn broke they loaded the wagon, hitched up Briar, and rode for several hours through woods that were damp and cheerless. It was late summer, the trees were green, but there was a heaviness in the air. A feeling of foreboding had been growing in Rowen all the way through the forest. She wondered if it was the dream, still lingering in her thoughts. She felt a great, painful longing for home, as if all the time that had really passed while she was with the Fair Folk had just now caught up with her. She hadn't seen Edweth, their housekeeper, or any of her friends in the Errantry for so long. And Will. Where was he? Had he returned to the Realm while she was gone? If he had, and found she wasn't in Fable, would he come looking for her?

At midday they came out into a clearing. The sudden wind struck cold and sharp, bringing tears to Rowen's eyes. The grass in this open space was dry and withered-looking, as if some blight had fallen here. Without warning Pendrake brought Briar to a halt, climbed quickly down from the wagon and gazed around the clearing. Rowen was about to ask him what he was doing when he suddenly set off at a fast clip towards a nearby hill. She followed, surprised at this unexpected burst of activity after he had been so weary and subdued all morning.

Pendrake climbed the steep slope with Rowen at his heels. It was not a high hill and they soon reached the top. Rowen guessed that her grandfather wanted a view of the surrounding countryside, but instead he knelt and prodded the hilltop's thatch of dry grass with the end of his staff.

"No, it *was* here," he murmured to himself. "I'm sure of it."

"What was here?" Rowen asked.

"Do you remember," Pendrake said, climbing stiffly to his feet, "when we were here in the forest with Will and he found that first knot-path?"

Rowen nodded, smiling at the memory. On their journey Will had stumbled on one of the mysterious, hidden paths that could take you in a few moments to another far-off part of the Realm.

"He came running back scared because he'd seen a giant," she said, "only he wouldn't call it a giant."

Pendrake gestured to the hill beneath them.

"Here he is."

Rowen frowned.

"Here *who* is?" Then she understood and looked down in alarm at her feet. They were standing right on top of . . .

Rowen froze.

"What happened to him?" she breathed, not daring to move.

"I was hoping you could tell me," Pendrake said.

With a sinking heart, Rowen knew what he was asking of her. The power of the Stewards had given her a strange kind of second sight. Sometimes when she was close to people she would *see*, like pictures unfolding in her mind, the story that was their lives: she caught glimpses of their past, or she saw the choices that lay before them like so many paths through a forest, and sometimes she could tell which path was the right one for them to take. And if there had once been Story in a place, or in an object, even if all outward signs of it had vanished, she could sense it. Events that had happened long ago would appear to her, visions that only she could see but could do nothing to stop. Sometimes the visions were so vivid they seemed almost stronger than her own memories. More often they were dim or fleeting, hard to understand. Her grandfather had called this sense of Story a gift, but she didn't see it that way.

A gift was something you could refuse.

Now she went still, calmed her breathing, and waited. Often the visions rose up unbidden, without any effort on her part. That's how it had been the first time, on the journey with Will. She had seen dim, ghostlike shapes of people that no one else could see. It had terrified her, until her grandfather had revealed to her what the shapes really were: traces left by the past, by old stories that were no more. But not every vision was like that. Sometimes it took effort and time. She had to *try*. It was a strange kind of trying, though. She had to keep still and calm, letting her thoughts come and go without hanging on to any of them or letting them lead her elsewhere, as they so often did. Thoughts were tricky things. Once you had one, it was so easy to have another one, and another, and before you knew it, you were off somewhere else, imagining your next dinner or remembering something that happened years ago . . . To find the story hidden in things, she had to keep her own stories, the ones she was always spinning in her own head, from getting in the way. She had to let things be as they were, here and now, and the here-and-now, she had learned to her surprise, was a very difficult place to stay.

But standing on the hill in the cold wind, she stayed with things as they were as well as she could, and the story came, and she saw what had once been the here-and-now.

"He was in a great war, a long time ago," she said, telling it to herself as much as to her grandfather as it unfolded before her. "He didn't want to go, he wanted to be left alone, but in the end he went. He fought on the side of good, and there was a great and terrible battle which they only won because of him. So they gave him a reward. They gave him this meadow to live in. By himself, as he wished, for ever."

"Yes, that's the tale he told me once," Pendrake whispered. "Do you see anything else?"

Rowen shook her head.

"Nothing."

"Nothing?"

"It just . . . stops," she said.

Rowen took a deep breath and blinked back tears.

"Are you all right?" Pendrake asked, placing a hand on her shoulder. She nodded. The sad and frightening stories were bad enough, but now she wondered if the happy ones were worse. That's what the giant's story had been here, in this clearing. Happy. There had been warm sunlight here then. Flowers and birdsong. She wished she could climb inside the giant's peaceful, sleepy story, where bees buzzed among the blossoms and clouds drifted lazily across a perfect blue sky, and just stay there, leaving everything behind: the feeling of being hunted, the trial her grandfather had hinted she must soon face to become a loremaster, the *not knowing* how things were going to end.

"It *stops,*" Pendrake murmured, gazing around the quiet clearing. "I wonder . . . He was usually napping whenever I visited him. He *was* getting very hill-like. Maybe this time he's gone all the way."

"Gone where?"

"Sometimes the story just goes out of a place. The giant becomes a hill. The dragon becomes a river. It's the way of things in this world. But . . ."

He paused, and pursed his lips.

"But you don't think that's it," Rowen said.

"Sometimes a story withers and dies before its time, like some of those we've seen, because another story is growing stronger."

"You mean Malabron's?"

Pendrake nodded.

"Like an invading weed, choking the life out of other plants."

He leaned wearily on his staff, and Rowen thought again how much older and more tired he had seemed these last few weeks. As if whatever was happening to the Realm was also happening to him . . . She thrust the terrifying thought from her mind.

"Will the giant come back?" she asked.

"That could happen, yes, in the natural course of things. If stories are needed again they sometimes return from the

Weaving, where they came from in the first place. But if one story grows too powerful, others will be swallowed up by it and forgotten." He gazed around at the clearing spread out below them and pulled his cloak closer around him. "Let's not linger here. We need to get back to Fable."

They walked slowly back down the hill to the wagon, Rowen pondering her grandfather's frightening words.

He had already taught her a little about the Weaving, the mysterious, hidden realm-within-the-Realm that was the source of all stories. As far as she'd been able to understand, the Weaving was something like the place you went to when you dreamed, that ghostly, ungraspable world where anything could happen. Everything possible and impossible, everything the Realm was made from, flowed out of the Weaving, like water bubbling from a hidden spring. When Rowen had seen the giant's story as it had once been she was touching the Weaving, because the past was contained in it, and the future, as well as everything that might have been or never was.

But a loremaster could do more than just catch these fleeting glimpses of the Weaving. One could tap into it, like drawing water from a well. What one drew out was a kind of power or living spirit that the Stewards had called *innumith.* Her grandfather called it the fathomless fire. The stuff of Story.

He had shown her something of what a loremaster could do with this power. He could kindle a fire in damp wood, and mend torn clothing just by running his fingers over the tear. Once when they were caught in a sudden storm he kept the rain from falling on them, even though it went on falling everywhere else.

"You start with what's already in front of you," he'd explained to her when she asked how he could do these things. "You take what is, and you . . . nudge it a little, with what might be." These were useful little tricks, he'd added when he taught her to do them, but some day she would accomplish far greater things. It was said the loremasters of old could perform wonders like walking on air, or moving mountains, or stepping through the Weaving into other worlds.

"But that's not what really matters," he'd cautioned her. "What matters is what you learn about yourself. About what you can be. And that's something I can't teach you."

After they had parted from the Fair Folk, he would no longer let her practise the so-called tricks he'd taught her. There was a very good reason: every such drawing upon the Weaving, no matter how slight, was like a tug on one of the countless interwoven threads of Story that bound the realm together. And Malabron in his realm of shadow, like a spider lurking in its web, could sense the movements of these threads. They already knew that he was aware of them and probably also had some idea of where they had come from. The Bourne had always been a quiet, unimportant place, and often Rowen had wished she lived somewhere more exciting, more in the middle of things. But now, as they climbed onto the wagon and set off again for home, she found herself wishing that the Bourne could go on being a quiet, unimportant place for ever, even though she knew with dread in her heart that those days were over.

4

I started out as Nothing and then I became a Something, yet I must be more than a Something because plainly I am a part of Everything. But I cannot be Everything because then Nothing would be left out.

– The Enigmatist's Handbook

LATE THAT AFTERNOON they stopped to rest by the side of a narrow, stony stream. Pendrake looked around approvingly and said that they were very close to the western border of the Bourne. Rowen was glad to hear it. In a few days they would be home.

"Should we send Sputter with a message to Edweth?"

"I think we should wait," her grandfather said. "We don't know what we may find when we return."

Rowen's brighter mood dimmed as she considered what her grandfather's words implied. He would only be this cautious if he was afraid that the wisp's message to the housekeeper might be intercepted by someone hostile to them. That meant he was no longer certain that even the toyshop was safe.

Gloomily she sat down near Briar, who was munching contentedly on the lush grass at the edge of the stream. Pendrake sat quietly for a while, too, then he reached into the tall grass in front of him and lifted out a short stick of dry wood. He turned it over in his hands, studying it. When he had looked the stick all over several times, he began to whittle it with his pocket knife. Rowen had seen him do this often on their travels. He was always picking up odds and ends with which to make toys, even though he hadn't made any for a long time now.

"How did you become a toymaker, Grandfather?" Rowen asked him.

"I was always carving as a boy," he said with the flicker of a smile. "It was my favourite pastime back then. But I left that all behind when I began my training as a loremaster. I wandered far and wide, seeking knowledge, seeking understanding, and I forgot about carving, forgot about making toys. Then I met your grandmother, and I knew that my wandering days were over."

Rowen knew little about Maya, her grandmother. She had been a loremaster too, from a land far to the east, a place Rowen had never been. And she had been a weaver, like Morrigan of the Tain Shee. She had woven many of the tapestries that hung in the toyshop, including the one in Rowen's room that depicted her own mother and father. Rowen did not remember her. All she knew was that her grandmother had somehow gone *into* the Weaving and had never come back.

"We were on our way home to Fable after a long journey," Pendrake went on, "and one night we took lodgings at an inn. That night Maya told me the baby was coming, so I fetched a midwife, and she sent me down to the common room to wait. I don't mind telling you, the thought of becoming a father was terrifying to me. What trade could I live by, to feed my family? The few coins I got from telling stories were hardly enough for the two of us, and now we were going to be *three*. Well, there was a travelling minstrel in the common room that night. He sang an old song from your grandmother's homeland, about a weaver woman who weaves a tiger on her loom with such skill that the tiger comes to life, so then she has to weave a jungle for the tiger to live in, and before long, the woman has woven a whole world. While I waited and worried about the future, I took a scrap from the woodpile by the fire and I carved a tiger. That night your mother, Gildred, was born, and I knew what trade I could live by."

He held up the stick he'd been whittling.

"Not sure what this one will be yet," her grandfather said, appraising his handiwork.

Rowen smiled. She was about to ask him a question about her grandmother when she saw that the look in his eyes had changed. She had seen this before and she knew that he had sensed something out of the ordinary. Slowly, so as not to appear suspicious, she glanced around. There was nothing but what she had seen for days now as they passed through the great forest: trees, flickering sunlight, leafy shadows.

Pendrake noticed her glance. He nodded slowly.

"Someone or something is watching us," he said in an undertone. "Keep on your guard."

They climbed back onto the seat of the wagon, and Briar reluctantly started across the shallow stream. The pots and pans hanging from the wagon's boards made their usual tinny clatter, but to Rowen the noise now sounded ten times as loud. On the other side the path began to climb a densely wooded rise, and Briar plodded along even more slowly. At the top of the rise the path went around a huge mossy boulder that leaned out over the trail.

On the other side of the boulder Briar stopped abruptly. She snorted and pawed the ground with her hoof.

In the path before them stood a large grey wolf.

"Shade!" cried Rowen. Before Pendrake could stop her, she jumped from the wagon. She ran a few steps towards the wolf, then halted. The eyes. There was something wrong with the wolf's eyes. They were large and luminous, like the eyes of an owl. These were not a wolf's eyes.

Rowen backed away. This was not Shade, the wolf that had been Will's companion and protector during their journey together. She was not even certain this creature really was a wolf.

"You're a long way from home," Pendrake said to the wolf in a calm, quiet voice. He had climbed from the wagon and was standing beside Rowen.

"Don't come any closer," the wolf snarled in a voice like rough stones scraping together. "I'll eat you."

"There's no need for that kind of talk," the old man said. "We both know you won't do anything of the sort. I just want to know why you've been following us."

Grandfather's met this creature before, Rowen thought to herself. Then, as she watched in astonishment, something happened to the wolf that was even more strange. It turned and bounded away, but as it ran its shaggy wolfish shape seemed to waver, as if one was seeing it through a haze of rippling heat. Rowen kept her eyes on it, but in the next moment there was no wolf, only a patch of dappled green shadows. She blinked, startled, with an eerie feeling that the wolf had never been there at all, as if the creature had only been a trick of the light. But that couldn't be . . .

They waited, but when the wolf did not reappear, they climbed back onto the seat of the wagon. It took a few words of encouragement to get Briar moving again.

"Did you see the eyes?" Pendrake asked Rowen.

"Yes."

"We've seen those eyes before."

At that, Rowen remembered. On their way through the Forest of Eldark with Will they had been waylaid by a strange, mad being who could change his shape. He had lured them to a maze-like grove from which not even Shade could find the way out. The being had wanted them to solve a riddle, and when Pendrake gave the right answer, he had grudgingly let them go. Her grandfather said that some called him the Woodwraith. He was a creature of Story without a story.

"His grove is a long way from here, though," Pendrake mused. "I wonder what brought him out of it."

No more riddles, whispered a voice so close that it made them both start. Briar huffed nervously and tossed her head. Pendrake pulled up on the reins. He climbed down from the wagon and Rowen joined him.

"Where are you?" Pendrake shouted, looking this way and that. "Show yourself."

No more riddles, the eerie, whispery voice repeated. *Someone's house is gone. No more house. No more riddles.*

There was a stirring of shadows and leaves around them. Rowen glanced from place to place. Every time her eyes fell on something that looked like a shape, a creature, *something*, it was suddenly not there, as if her very act of seeing had made it vanish.

"Has something happened to the place where you lived?" Pendrake asked. Rowen remembered that the creature called his strange bare grove in the forest his house.

The one who is not, said the voice. *He happened. The one who was following you. It's your fault. You brought that one. To our house.*

"He means the Angel," Rowen said. She felt a cold chill at the memory of Malabron's terrible servant, who had almost succeeded in taking her away to the Shadow Realm.

"The one who is not, he came to your house?" Pendrake asked.

You asked someone to play the riddle game with that one, but that one would not play. He tore down someone's house. He broke everything. Everything broken. Then he found . . . he found . . .

"What did he find?"

USssss! the voice hissed, becoming a shriek like wind rising to a gale.

"What did he do to you?" Rowen asked when the piercing noise had faded again to silence.

There was no answer.

"Show yourself to us, please," Pendrake said. "Let's talk face to face."

Whose face? We have every face. No face. Any face.

"Well, choose one. We want to see you."

The wind rose to a roar. Leaves skittered and whirled around the wagon. The dappled shadows that Rowen had seen darting among the branches seemed to gather in one place in the midst of the spinning whirl of leaves. Then a huge brown bear stood there, teetering on its short hind legs. Like the wolf, it had large yellow eyes that glimmered as if the shifting light and shadow of the forest was within them as well as without.

Briar whinnied and backed away, rocking the wagon. Rowen caught her reins and held tight.

"We could hurt you," the bear said in a low, rumbling voice that seemed to rise up from the earth itself. "Punish you for bringing the one who is not."

"You could do that," Pendrake said, "but I don't think you would. It's not who you are."

The bear gave a deep, menacing growl. Then it dropped onto all fours as if defeated. It swung its head from side to side and let out a low, mournful bleat.

Then it was not there.

Who you are, came the Woodwraith's voice from all around them, echoing Pendrake's words.

Who. You. Are.

"Maybe you can find a new home," Rowen called, peering into the shadows. "Is there anywhere else you could go?"

Going, the voice moaned. *We're going away. A little at a time. Every day, a little more nothing. That should be funny. What is more of nothing? But it isn't funny. Where there was something, every day, harder to be anything. Soon there will be no one at all. Then we will never find out who we really are.*

"We're sorry that the Angel—the one who is not—hurt you," Rowen said. "We didn't mean for that to happen."

They waited. There was no reply.

"Maybe we can help you," Rowen said. "Find you a new place to live. Couldn't we, Grandfather?"

"I really don't know, Rowen," Pendrake said, with what she thought was a trace of annoyance in his voice. "We can't linger here in the forest, and if the Woodwraith—"

That is not our name, the voice hissed. *That is a name others gave to us because they could not tell us what we were.*

"Well, what is your name?" Rowen snapped, refusing to be intimidated. "Are we supposed to call you *someone*?"

Riddle, the voice said after a brief silence. *Call us Riddle.*

"You could come with us, Riddle," Rowen said, and she saw Pendrake frown. He was clearly not happy with the suggestion, and she wondered why. They could help this poor creature. They owed it to him. And more than that, she saw now. She could sense the threads of Story weaving into place around her, and she knew that bringing Riddle with them was something that had to be.

"We're going to a city called Fable," she went on, determined. "Do you know what that is?"

There was no answer.

"A city is a place with many people," Pendrake said. "People everywhere, day and night. And many things that would be strange to you. There are no woods to hide in. And you have lived alone in this forest for a very long time."

Suddenly there before them stood the wolf.

"Someone . . . Riddle would be with *you*," it said. "Riddle would stay close to you. Like the wolf did with the boy. We could be like that. Always with you. Then maybe we would not disappear."

Riddle's voice was so tight with fear that Rowen felt fear clutch at her, too. She remembered how lost and frightened she had been when the story-visions first began happening to her. Everything she had known and hoped for, her dream of becoming a knight of the Errantry like her mother, had been swept away. But now she thought that with a creature like Riddle beside her, as Shade had been with Will, she might not feel quite so lost and alone.

"Could he come with us, Grandfather?" she asked, trying to hide the tremor in her voice.

Pendrake sighed.

"I don't know how much time we'll have in Fable," he said. "We may have to leave quickly and travel fast."

Now Rowen thought she understood his reluctance to have the Woodwraith come with them. If Rowen was still being hunted, they might only be bringing this creature with them into further danger. But that had to be better than leaving him here, alone and terrified. And she had *seen*. For an instant. Whatever path she was on, Riddle was meant to be with her.

"Besides," Pendrake added before Rowen could speak up, "people in Fable were not very pleased when we had Shade walking around in the streets."

"Others would not . . . like us?" the wolf asked.

"Some would be afraid. These days Bournefolk are less tolerant of the unfamiliar."

"You can take any shape you want, can't you, Riddle?" Rowen asked.

"This is what we do," the voice said eagerly. "Any shape. Anything."

The wolf was suddenly not there. In a tree limb above the place where it had been standing, a tawny mountain lion was hunkered back on its hind legs as if ready to pounce on them. Rowen stepped back in spite of herself, uncertain for a moment whether this was still Riddle. Then she noticed the lion's luminous, owl-like eyes.

"I'm not sure that would solve the problem," Pendrake said.

"How about something like that but smaller," Rowen suggested.

An instant later, a smaller cat crouched where the mountain lion had been. It had a tawny striped coat, long white whiskers and large furry paws. The same eerie, shining eyes gazed at them from its face, but on this animal they did not seem so alarmingly strange.

"A wildcat," Pendrake said.

"This one is the best in the forest at hiding," the cat said, in a soft, silvery voice that made Rowen think of moonlight. "When he doesn't want to be seen, he is not seen."

"This could work," Rowen said, nodding approvingly. "People will think you're our pet cat. Maybe."

"But you must promise to stay in that shape," Pendrake said, "at least when other people are around. And no talking unless we're alone. No sudden vanishing would be a good idea, too, come to think of it. I can't say for certain, but it might be that staying in one shape, and staying *here*, with us I mean, may help keep you from disappearing for good."

"We promise," the cat said solemnly. "Riddle will stay, like this. Close to the girl. No going away. The grey-bearded one makes the rules for us, too."

"My name is Pendrake. This is my granddaughter, Rowen."

"Pendrake. And Rowen."

"And Riddle," Pendrake said. "And now we must be off. We still have a long way to travel before we reach home."

With amazing speed the cat bounded down the trunk of the tree and came to a halt in front of them. Rowen and her grandfather climbed back onto the wagon's front seat. After a long hesitation, during which Rowen wondered if Riddle might just disappear again, the cat sprang onto the seat and slipped into the space between them. Alarmed by his sudden movements, Rowen almost pushed Riddle away, but stopped herself in time.

Pendrake flicked the reins and Briar started forward. Rowen glanced warily out of the corner of her eye at Riddle. He sat gazing straight ahead, without moving, like a statue. He was such a strange, unpredictable creature, she thought, but she had done the right thing. He would just take a lot of getting used to.

It wasn't long before the trees began to thin out and Rowen caught flickering glimpses of meadows and fields beyond the leafy woods, flooded with the hazy, golden light of a late summer afternoon. The Bourne.

As they left the forest, Riddle's eyes were wider than Rowen had yet seen them. He sat perfectly still, gazing at this strange new world, but she could feel his excitement.

She should have been excited, too. They would be in Fable soon. She would see Edweth and her friends. Maybe even Will, if he came back to the Realm as he said he would. Then she remembered that even Fable was perhaps not safe any more. She felt her small, dim hope flicker within her, as if at any moment it might go out.

5

Maybe you've heard the tale differently from the way I've told it. That wouldn't be surprising, for these stories have been passed around many a fire on many a night. The tales travel, from mouth to ear, east to west, near and far, and one thing is certain: nobody can say there is only one way to tell them.

– Tales from the Golden Goose

THERE WERE NO MORE TREES.

After he had walked a long time the woods had come to an end, and Will had found himself on an open stretch of bare, cracked earth. A few large stones were scattered here and there, but the world beyond this patch of barren ground had vanished in a pale grey haze. The air was bone-dry and cold.

The haze was dust, Will realized. He could feel it in his eyes as he walked, and tasted it on his tongue: it had a faintly bitter, metallic tang.

Will turned in a slow circle. Night was coming on, he was already tired from his long walk through the woods, and he didn't know where he was. If he was really on the right path to the Realm, he thought he should have known for sure by now. The first time he had come to the Realm he'd been lost and confused, but he had known one thing for certain: the world had changed. Or he had changed worlds. This time he felt only that he was lost.

He walked for a while, but the dust did not clear. Another of the large stones loomed up out of the haze. Will sat down on it to rest a moment. It might be better to turn back and set out again in the morning, he told himself. But he wondered with a pang of fear whether he could even find his way home through this haze.

A friend will fall. No, he couldn't turn back.

Almost without thinking he slipped his hand down the collar of his shirt and pulled out a silver chain that hung around his neck. On the chain was a small triangular piece of mirrored glass. He clutched it tightly in his closed fist.

Before he left the Realm the last time, the Lady of the Shee had given him a shard of the ancient Mirror Samaya, which had been shattered in the war against the Night King. The shard had helped Will find his way home. When he'd looked into it he was startled to see his own reflection disappear, but then suddenly he *knew* what he had to do. Maybe that's what the shadow had been trying to tell him. *The same way you left*. Maybe he could use the shard the other way, too. To get back to the Realm.

Will opened his palm and looked into the shard. There was his face, reflected in the mirror. He stared into the glass, trying to summon the same certainty he'd felt the first time, but this time his face remained, looking back at him with a frown.

The stone moved under him.

Will jumped up with a shout. The stone was not a stone. It was a man. No, larger than a man. Someone or something huge, climbing to its feet and sloughing off the thick dust that had covered it so that Will had mistaken it for a stone.

Will backed away. The huge figure shook itself all over so that great clouds of dust billowed off it, and Will saw what he had been sitting on.

A creature shaped like a man, but there the resemblance ended. Under a mane of dark, shaggy hair was an ugly, beastlike face that brought to mind a cross between a lion and an ill-tempered pug dog.

Will stumbled backwards and fell.

"Wait," the man-thing said. "Who are . . . ?"

The man-thing's voice was so low and booming, the sound of it thrummed in Will's chest like the rumble of a kettledrum. Then he remembered the words of the shadow: *A stone will speak.*

Will picked himself up and was about to run for his life, but the man-thing's stillness made him hesitate.

"I don't know . . ." the man-thing said haltingly, ". . . where I am."

There was such fear and confusion in his voice that Will paused, then took a step closer.

"I don't know either," he said.

"My name . . . " the man-thing said. "My name is . . . Balor Gruff. That's it. Yes."

His eyes wandered about the dim landscape, then fixed on Will.

"I don't know how I got here," he said, shaking his head as if to clear it of the dust that surrounded them. "And I don't know who you are."

There was no threat in the man-thing's voice, Will realized. And the first part of the shadow's message, it seemed, had come to pass. But did the first part have anything to do with the friend who would fall? Would whatever he did now make any difference? Will thought quickly and decided to trust his instincts about the man-thing.

"I'm Will. Will Lightfoot," he said. "You were asleep on the ground. The dust had covered you and I thought you were a stone, so I sat down on you. I'm sorry about that, really."

The man-thing's brow furrowed. Then to Will's astonishment he shook himself all over once more, like a great shaggy bear waking from its winter slumber.

"What happened to me?" he roared. "I was on night patrol in the Wood and then all of a sudden here I am, which is I don't know where, and here you are, and . . . what did you say your name was?"

"Will Lightfoot. I'm on my way to—"

He broke off, having glimpsed the pin on the man-thing's cloak: a small white five-petalled flower that he recognized. Finn Madoc, he remembered, had a similar flower on his cloak.

"You're from the Errantry," Will said eagerly.

"I am," the man-thing said, in a tone of certainty. "Yes, I am. And what's it to you?"

"I know Finn Madoc, the knight-apprentice. He's my friend. I was trying to find my way to Fable and then—"

"Wait, wait," the man-thing broke in, "did you say your name was Will Lightfoot?"

"Yes."

"You're *the* Will Lightfoot?"

The man-thing eyed him up and down, as if he couldn't believe what he was hearing. Will was stung, though he had no idea why he should feel that way.

"It's an honour to meet you, Master Lightfoot," the man-thing said, breaking into a toothy grin. Evidently he had decided to believe Will. "My name is Balor Gruff. Oh, yes, I've already told you that. Finn is a good friend of mine, too, though he's not an apprentice any more. Earned his knighthood a while back. But more to the point, if you're Will Lightfoot, then I believe my luck has changed for the better."

Will didn't know what to say to that.

"I was on patrol near Fable," Balor Gruff said, "when this . . . *dust* came up out of nowhere. I kept walking, expecting it to lift eventually, but it didn't. So then I . . . well, I don't know what happened exactly. I couldn't have fallen asleep. I never fall asleep on duty."

"So we're not far from Fable, then?"

"Well, I don't believe so. But as to which way to go to get there, I may need some time to work it out."

"You mean you're lost."

"Balor Gruff never gets lost," the man-thing rumbled. "Never. I'll find my way out of this place eventually, no fear of that. But now you're here, Will Lightfoot, the pathfinder. There's no reason we can't work together, and maybe get home sooner."

"The *what*?"

"Pardon?"

"You called me a . . ."

"Pathfinder. It's what they call someone with your gift. You're famous for it in Fable. Will Lightfoot, the great pathfinder, slayer of trolls, friend of wolf and raven."

"Slayer of trolls? I never—"

"You're a legend, lad. It's all the knight-apprentices talk about these days."

"How . . . how long have they been talking about me?"

"I don't know. Ages. I first heard about you when Finn got back to Fable from his travels with you and the loremaster . . . must have been, let's see, well nigh a year ago now."

Will was relieved to hear that Finn had reached home safely, but Balor's words also confirmed his fear: much more time had gone by for his friends than for him. Which meant that maybe the shadow's warning was about something that had already happened, and he was too late.

"What's the matter?" Balor asked.

"Have you seen Finn recently? Is he all right?"

"I saw him just before I left on patrol. He was fine. Why?"

Will took a deep breath. Here was some good news, at last.

"Do you know Master Pendrake?" he asked.

"I've met him a few times," Balor said. "Kindly old fellow. Gave me a toy horse once when I was just an ogreling, I mean when . . . *hmph.* He and his granddaughter went with you on your journey, didn't they?"

"They did. Do you know if they're back in Fable?"

Balor shrugged.

"Couldn't say, lad. Haven't seen Pendrake in a long time, come to think of it."

"I have to get to Fable," Will said. "I think my friends might be in trouble."

"Well let's not waste any more time gabbing," Balor said, then he frowned. "But, the thing is, I don't recognize this . . . ground."

He raised his head and sniffed.

"Nothing here even *smells* familiar." He cleared his throat. "The fact is, I'm not . . . hmm . . . entirely sure where in the Realm we are."

"We're not in the Realm," Will said.

"*What?*"

"At least I don't think so. Not exactly."

"Well then where in blazes are we?"

Will shook his head.

"I don't know. But maybe . . . maybe I can get us out of here."

He took hold of the mirror shard again, but didn't look into it. He would worry about the strange things this Balor Gruff had been saying later, once he'd found his friends and made sure they were safe. His thoughts needed to be calm, *he* needed to be calm, and he wasn't. Time was passing while he was lost here, and who knew what was happening to Rowen, and Shade . . .

He closed his eyes, took a slow, deep breath, settled himself. How had it worked for him the last time?

"Is that some kind of compass?" Balor Gruff asked in a hoarse whisper, eyeing the shard. Will shook his head, irritated at the interruption. But the question suddenly made something clear. So clear it was like a voice in his head, telling him what he needed to do.

Get out of your own way.

"No, it's not a compass," he said.

The secret wasn't really in the shard, he realized now. It had worked for him the first time only when he'd stopped *trying* to make it work. Its power was to make clear what was already inside him, what he already knew. He just had to trust that. He had to get out of his own way.

Will slipped the shard back into his shirt, took a deep breath, and started walking.

"That's it?" Balor Gruff said, following him. "You know where you're going?"

Will didn't answer. He walked on at a steady pace, and the dust seemed to gather more thickly around him as he walked, falling upon his skin and eyelashes, but he didn't stop. He kept on, with Balor Gruff's heavy footfalls just behind him.

"By the way," the man-thing said as they walked, "I'm a wildman."

"What?"

"You must've been wondering about that. Everyone does when they first meet me. I'm a wildman. That's the generally accepted name for my folk. Though ignorant people sometimes mistake me for a woodwose or an . . . " He mumbled a word that Will didn't catch.

"Pardon?"

"I said *ogre,*" Balor muttered between his teeth.

Will stared.

"I never thought you were—"

"I'm a *wildman,*" Balor said loudly, as if announcing it to anyone else who might be nearby. "Let's be clear on that point. I was found by a band of knight-errants when I was a baby, sleeping in a bed of moss in the middle of a forest that's a known haunt of wildmen, *not* of ogres. Lost or abandoned, nobody knows, but there I was. *Gruff* was the only sound I could make back then, so it stuck. The knights brought me to Fable and I was raised by the Errantry and they taught me to read and fight and ride. Wasn't really keen on the reading, but I took to the fighting and riding like a pig to slops. And I learned the Errantry code, to defend the weak and not set oneself above others. And while ogres are usually nearsighted and hopelessly stupid, I happen to have eagle eyes, an uncanny nose, and a matchless sense of direction. And that's why I'm the Errantry's best tracker, so . . . "

He paused and cleared his throat. It occurred to Will that here was the Errantry's best tracker, following someone else.

"And so," Balor finished in a somewhat more subdued voice, "I'm a wildman."

A few moments later Will slowed down, then stopped and stood still.

"What is it?" Balor whispered.

Will didn't answer. He had no words for the strange sensation that had just passed through him. It wasn't anything he could see, or smell, or feel in the air. It was more like a pull on his body, as if he had begun to walk downhill, even though the ground here was perfectly level. He had felt something like it once before. One summer when he was little, Will had visited the seashore with his family. He'd waded out a long way into the water, which came up only to his waist. Then suddenly he felt the sandy bottom drop away beneath his feet. He had come to the edge of the deep. The *ocean*. Terrified, he'd thrashed his way back to the safety of the shallows.

Now he had come to an edge like that. What lay beyond was *deeper* somehow than where he had just been walking, though not in a way that could be seen. There was no slope here, no sudden dropping away of the ground beneath his feet. He could simply *feel* a whole world tugging at him. He was on the edge of the Realm and its vast ocean of stories.

Instead of pulling back in fear, he plunged forward, walking more quickly than before.

"What is it?" Balor whispered again, hurrying to catch up.

"We're almost there," Will said.

Balor took a deep sniff of air. He nodded eagerly.

"Yes. I think you're—*we're* on the right track. We found it."

They walked on more quickly now. The dust began to thin out, until they could see further ahead. There were shapes now . . . trees, bushes, mossy boulders swam up out of the yellow haze.

"There!" Balor cried.

They hurried forward and suddenly before them, on a hill at the far end of a wide green valley dotted with a patchwork of fields, was the city of Fable.

Will let out his breath. It felt as though he hadn't since he started walking. He took in the city's familiar walls of motley-coloured stone, the slender towers, the mysterious gleam of the city's innumerable blue lamps shining in the dusk like stars. At the height of the city he could just make out the great cloudy plume of trees that surrounded Appleyard, the home of the Errantry, the company of knights whose duty was the defence of the Bourne.

"We've done it," Balor exclaimed. Then he turned to Will and clapped a huge hand on his shoulder. "No, you did it, Will Lightfoot. You have my thanks, and my vow as a knight-errant that if there is ever any way I can be of service to you, I will."

Will nodded. Rowen had wanted to become a knight of the Errantry, he remembered, like her mother. But after what she had learned about her ancestry and powers, it seemed unlikely she would be given the chance to fulfil that dream. At the thought of Rowen, Will felt a rush of eagerness. She might be here, in Fable, only moments away.

A short time later they were approaching the gates. So much was coming back to Will now, memories that seemed to have almost faded away, as if he'd been gone for years instead of a few weeks. Fable was home to a people known as Wayfarers, descendants of travellers from Will's world, which people here called the Untold. A few Wayfarers had come to the Perilous Realm on purpose, but most, like Will, had found this world by accident. Of those, some had chosen to stay in the Realm, like Rowen's father. He had met Rowen's mother and had never gone back to the Untold. When Rowen was a small child her parents had died in a raid by Nightbane, vicious creatures from the dark side of Story who served Malabron. Rowen had grown up in the care of her grandfather, Nicholas Pendrake, the loremaster.

Balor raised a hand and shouted something that Will

guessed was a password. A moment later the tall wooden doors braced with iron swung slowly open. Will glimpsed sentries just inside, and more on the parapet above the turreted gatehouse. He was surprised to see the gates guarded like this. When he came to Fable the first time, they were open for travellers and countryfolk to pass in and out, even at night. He knew from something Rowen had hinted at that the gate was watched or protected in some mysterious way, but whatever that protection was, clearly the people of Fable no longer thought it enough.

Two of the sentries approached the wildman with astonished looks on their faces.

"Balor Gruff?" the younger of the two said hesitantly.

"Gared Bamble," the wildman replied. "What are you gaping at?"

"Nothing," the sentry stammered. "I mean, you've been missing for three days, Balor. Nobody had any idea what had happened to you."

"Three days," the wildman echoed. He looked stunned for a moment, then gave Will an uneasy glance.

"Finn Madoc and some of the other knights are out looking for you right now," the sentry said. "They've been searching everywhere."

Balor glowered at the sentry. "If you're trying to pull one over on me, Gared Bamble . . ."

"It's the truth, Balor, I swear."

"Well, I'd better report in at Appleyard," Balor said grimly. "And this young lad is coming with me."

"Who is he?" the older sentry asked.

"You've heard of Will Lightfoot, pathfinder, wolf-friend, vanquisher of Nightbane, haven't you?"

"We've heard of him," the older sentry said.

"Well here he is, in the flesh."

The sentries exchanged a doubtful glance.

"I don't know, Balor . . ." the younger one said. "We'll have to get permission from Appleyard first. You know Captain Thorne's new orders. No strangers allowed past the gate without his approval."

"Well, I will go and get his approval," Balor snapped. "And to save time I'll take Will with me."

They left the sentries staring after them and hastened up the long curve of the main street.

"Will you get in trouble for this?" Will asked.

"The captain of the guard—Captain Thorne—has been much more strict about these things lately," Balor said, then he winked. "Don't worry about me. I may be peeling potatoes for a while but it won't be the first time. And not likely the last."

The hour was late but even so, Will was surprised at how quiet and empty the streets were. The first time he'd come to Fable the city had been crowded and busy at night, with shops open selling food and drink, mostly to folk who had come to Fable from far away. Tonight he saw only a few people hurrying through the streets, and the occasional messenger wisp zinging overhead. And one other sight that was unfamiliar: sentries on almost every corner.

"Curfew," Balor explained. "Another of Captain Thorne's new orders. Strange folk have been seen in and around Fable lately. Storyfolk passing through on their way elsewhere, a lot more than usual. The whole Realm seems to be restless."

When they neared the gates of Appleyard, Will stopped.

"The toyshop is this way," he said, nodding towards the narrow lane. "I have to see if Rowen and her grandfather are at home."

Balor sighed.

"According to the rules, which I do try to follow on

occasion, I should take you to my superior officer. But I know you're worried about your friends. Go on, then."

"Thank you, Balor."

"Ah, wait, one more thing."

He drew a short sword from a scabbard on his belt and held it over Will's head, then brought the flat of the blade down slowly on one of Will's shoulders and then the other.

"Will Lightfoot," the wildman boomed, "for thy valour and skill in the field, I do appoint thee a knight-apprentice of the Errantry."

Will couldn't help but laugh at Balor's jest, despite his troubled thoughts.

"We'll meet again soon," the wildman said with a grin, and strode away.

A few moments later Will was at the door of Nicholas Pendrake's toyshop in Pluvius Lane. The old man was a mage of great power and a master of ancient lore, but his daily living came from making children's toys. For all that most folk in Fable knew, this was all he did, and that was the way he preferred it. For the loremaster had long kept a secret, even from Rowen, about her ancestry, and her own powers.

Will knocked loudly at the door and after a wait that seemed too long, it was opened by Edweth, Pendrake's tiny but intimidating housekeeper. She peered out suspiciously at first, then her ruddy face beamed with delight when she recognized Will.

"Bless us, look who it is," she said, throwing the door open wide. "Will Lightfoot. I wondered if I'd ever see you again, my dear. My goodness, come in, come in."

"Are they here, Edweth?" Will asked.

"Oh, the Master and Rowen," she sighed. "How I wish. But come in and sit down. I'll make you a little something to eat and you can tell me how you got here and what's brought you all this way."

Brimming with questions, Will kept silent for the moment and followed the housekeeper through the front hall. The shelves were crowded with toys of all descriptions, just as he remembered. In the spick and span kitchen, Will took a seat at the dining table while Edweth busied herself with cups and plates. She asked him what had brought him back to Fable, but he didn't want to alarm her straight away, not until he had received some answers himself, so he avoided answering.

"So the loremaster and Rowen haven't returned yet from the journey we went on?" he asked instead.

"No. I did get a message from them, months ago it was. Brought by Sputter. Plucky fellow. Who knows how many miles he'd flown to bring it to me. Anyway, the message said you'd gone home safely, Will, and that the Master and Rowen were staying with the Hidden Folk for a time and that he didn't know when they'd be back. I haven't heard anything from them since. *Months*. Hmph. That child has been away from home far too long and I'm worried to death about her. Travelling with these *Fair Folk* is all very well, I suppose, but there's no better place for Rowen than her own home."

"And Shade . . . ?"

The housekeeper shook her head.

"I've not heard anything about your wolf friend since the day you left here, I'm afraid."

Will looked down, struggling with his disappointment. He had found his way back to the Realm, to Fable, and as far as he knew, Rowen was safe with the Fair Folk. But still, she wasn't here, and there was no way to warn her about the shadow's message. And Shade could be anywhere. When they parted, the wolf had said he was going in search of other Speaking Creatures like himself. Where was he now? A lump formed in Will's throat. If it hadn't been for Shade, he would never have made it home. It was the wolf's keen senses and unerring instinct, he knew, far more than his own gift, that had brought him safely through danger. Shade had saved his life more than once, at the risk of his own. The wolf had become the best friend Will had ever had. Saying goodbye to him had been as difficult as leaving Rowen. How he wished Shade was here with him now.

A friend will fall. He shook his head, banishing terrible thoughts.

"So the message didn't say where they were or when they'd be back?" he asked Edweth.

"It didn't say," the housekeeper said with a frown as she set a tray loaded with cheese, bread and various kinds of cakes on the table. "That was too much caution, to my mind. I've never told anyone anything that wasn't their business, as he well knows. But tale be told, Will, you're back in Fable and at least you're safe and sound."

She shook her head, as if amazed that he was actually here.

"They've talked so much about you since you left," she said, gazing at him with teary eyes, though whether the look was one of admiration or concern, Will could not tell. Neither choice appealed to him.

"Who's been talking about me?"

"Everyone. The tale of how you defeated that horrible Angel of Malabron and saved Rowen is one of the favourites around the fire at the Golden Goose and every other tavern in town. When I go to market I sometimes see the little urchins playing your adventures with the fetches and the dragon and—"

"My *adventures*?"

"I'm sure they have it all scrambled and blown up into something far worse than it was. At least I hope so. I don't need more to worry about."

"But how did the story get out, Edweth? Who would have told it?"

Edweth shook her head.

"This *is* the City of Stories, after all. All I know is, Rowen's young friends in the Errantry have kept the story alive. They come here regularly to see if Rowen is back and all they can talk about is you. They've been hoping for your return, too. And now at last here you are."

"*At last*," Will echoed, and took a deep breath. "Balor Gruff says I've been gone a year."

"That's about right. That's how your story's had time to grow while you've been away. They're calling you a great . . . now what was the word again?"

Will sighed.

"Pathfinder," he said. But if it was true, he thought now, then maybe there was a chance he could find his friends before it was too late.

6

. . . I hear the voices of the fisherfolk calling
singing of the long-lost sea . . .

– The Kantar

NEAR THE EAVES OF the Forest of Eldark, just inside the Bourne, lies the little village of Molly's Arm. It looks much the same as any other village in the Bourne, except that on closer inspection it doesn't. For the cottages and bungalows of Molly's Arm are all shaped like boats. Some have gangplanks instead of steps leading up to the front doors. A few even have masts, not for sails but for hanging the family washing. Despite the fact that there is no sea anywhere nearby, nor even a good-sized lake, a first-time visitor to Molly's Arm could be forgiven for thinking a giant wave had just swept through the area and tossed an entire fishing fleet onto dry land.

The village sits perched on a high ridge overlooking a vast sweep of the forest. On gusty days the rush of the wind across the miles of the treetops resembles the waves of a great restless body of water, and that is happiness to the people of Molly's Arm. Long ago they were proud and hardy fisherfolk who lived far away on the shore of a cold, misty sea. In those days the fat gleaming fish filled their nets to the brim, and all was well. But then the fat gleaming fish became thinner, and fewer, and harder to catch, until at last the nets were coming up empty out of the icy, indifferent waves. So the people turned from the sea and packed up their belongings and went in search of another ocean. After many long years of wandering they came to the Perilous Realm, and at last to the quiet woods and fields of the Bourne. They camped one night at the top of a bare ridge pointed like a ship's prow at the deep dark forest, and when they heard the roar of the wind over the trees like a mighty surf, their weary hearts were filled once more with contentment.

They decided to stay. Why they called the place Molly's Arm is anyone's guess.

Rowen, Pendrake and Riddle, in the shape of a cat, arrived in the village on a cold, blustery evening. Rowen was glad to see the lights of the houses glimmering in the dark. Her grandfather had been unable to find a snug for them to take shelter in, and as night fell the forest had seemed unusually dark and foreboding. So she was relieved when he decided they would spend the night in Molly's Arm, if there was a room to be had at the local inn.

As they approached the village, Rowen glanced often at Riddle. This would be his first time in the presence of other people. They had already warned the cat not to speak or change form, and he had promised to behave, but a quick glance Rowen shared with her grandfather told her he harboured the same doubts she did. They simply didn't know whether this strange being could really be trusted to keep his word, or his shape.

Pendrake had visited Molly's Arm before, but Rowen had not. As Briar plodded up the steep main street of the village, she stared in surprise at the squat, cone-shaped lampposts bobbing in tubs of water like buoys, their bells clanging mournfully in the wind. No one seemed to be about, though that was hardly surprising given the weather. Riddle kept close to Rowen and flinched at every unfamiliar sound.

"Is this Rowen's city?" he asked her, his eerie eyes wider than usual.

"No, we're not there yet."

"This is a strange place."

"I agree."

They came to an inn that Pendrake knew from his previous visits, a long low building that in the dim light could have easily been mistaken for a barge. They would stop in here to get warm and see if the place had any beds to spare for the night. A sign swinging above the door read *The Tipsy Mermaid,* under a poorly drawn image of, unsurprisingly, a mermaid tilted at an odd angle and raising a tall tankard of something frothy.

They climbed from the wagon and tied Briar to the hitching rail.

"She'll be cold out here," Rowen said, patting the horse.

"They have a stable at the back," Pendrake said. "We'll get them to see to her."

They ducked through a low doorway, along a short, cramped passage and into the common room of the inn. It was filled with a crowd of people that Rowen could not see very well at first, because the air was so smoky it stung her eyes to tears. But the room was warm and there was a cheerful blaze crackling in the fireplace, and the strong smell of things toasting and simmering. All of which would have made Rowen feel cosy and safe if it wasn't for the fact that when she and her grandfather appeared in the doorway, all conversation died to a murmur. Every eye in the house, it seemed, was on them.

"Nicholas Pendrake!" cried a large, buxom, round-faced woman standing behind a counter cluttered with mugs and glasses. "Stay where you be 'til I come where you're at!"

She squeezed herself through the countertop flap-door and charged through the throng of drinkers, which parted hastily at her approach. She was a very *round* woman, Rowen marvelled, half expecting her to break into a roll on the way.

"Bless my days, Nicholas, it's been a long time."

"It has, Kate. Far too long."

"And how are you getting on in the world?"

"Well enough, thank you. And you?"

The woman sighed.

"Near stove in and taking on water, as always. But can't complain, for all the good it does. And this pretty barnacle sticking close to you . . . ?"

"My granddaughter, Rowen."

"Granddaughter!" the woman exclaimed, her eyebrows shooting up. "Thundering damp, how the years fly. Well, in you get now and find a seat. I'll fix you something hot. You know you're always welcome at the Mermaid, Nicholas."

She was turning away when she caught sight of Riddle, twined around Rowen's leg, his eyes fixed on the tavern-keeper with the petrified stare of a cornered rabbit. For a moment Kate's beaming face was crossed with a look of puzzlement, then she broke into a wide grin.

"A fine pair you *three* are. I'm sure we can trawl up a saucer of something nice for kitty as well."

"We have a horse outside, too—" Rowen began.

"To be sure," Kate said, and in an alarmingly loud voice she bellowed, "Jib! See to their equipage!" A sleepy looking lad bobbed up out of the crowd and hurried out of the door. Kate charged back to the bar, but stopped half-way there, set her hands on her hips and glared around the room. The assembly took the hint. From every corner loud conversations started up again.

Pendrake and Rowen found an empty table and sat down. Riddle crept under the table to settle between Rowen's feet. One or two grizzled-looking older men nodded to Pendrake, raised their glasses. He nodded back.

"They seem friendly here," Rowen said cautiously. People had gone back to their talk and drink, but she sensed she and her grandfather were still under scrutiny out of the corners of eyes and the edges of ears.

"They're warm-hearted folk," her grandfather said. "It wouldn't hurt us to be more like them in Fable. But they live at the edge of the forest, and that makes them, well, edgy. Newcomers have to earn their trust."

Kate returned with mugs of hot cider for Pendrake and Rowen, and a saucer of cream for Riddle. When she placed the saucer on the floor near the cat he sniffed at it, took an exploratory lick, then drew his head back suddenly. For one alarming instant Rowen saw the cat-shape shimmer and thin out, as if he was about to vanish. He solidified again, but stayed away from the cream.

Kate eyed Riddle with a look that said she wasn't sure what she had just seen, but was pretty certain she didn't like it.

"Never met a kitty as didn't love the cream," she muttered.

"Riddle isn't used to such things," Rowen said hurriedly. "Thanks very much, though."

Someone across the room called for the hostess. After another dubious glance at Riddle, Kate bustled away.

Rowen leaned down to Riddle.

"You mustn't do that," she whispered.

"Don't like it here," Riddle whined. "Too many others. Too many voices."

"There's nothing to be afraid of. Trust me. No one's going to hurt you."

"Riddle wants to go back. Back under the trees."

"Just keep quiet, all right? And no disappearing."

"Won't drink this stuff."

"Then don't."

"What does Rowen get to drink?"

"Sshhh!"

The cat gave a feline whimper but said nothing more. Rowen and her grandfather drank their cider in silence and listened to the conversations around them, which were mostly about the weather, the crops, and how the forest looked today. The general consensus about that was *unsettled.* After a while Rowen felt the warmth working on her. Her eyelids drooped and she began to slide down by degrees in her chair. She shook herself awake, then looked across the table to see that her grandfather, too, was nodding off.

She remembered the hill of the sleeping giant. *Sometimes a story withers and dies . . .*

"Grandfather," she whispered urgently.

Pendrake stirred and looked around in surprise.

"I must have dozed off," he said, frowning. Then he eyed his mug and gave a soft laugh. "I wonder what Kate put in this cider . . ."

"I'd like to hear more about Grandmother," Rowen said. "You told me she went into the Weaving, but you didn't say what happened to her."

Pendrake nodded.

"It's something all loremasters must do, sooner or later.

The Weaving is the source of our power and the storehouse of all wisdom. Maya, your grandmother, hoped to recover the ancient lore of the Stewards. To restore at least some of what was lost in the Great Unweaving."

He gazed down at the table and drew a deep breath.

"I begged her not to try," he said. "But she was determined. This was after Gildred—after your mother and father died, and you were still a little child, but Maya knew, somehow she knew that you were . . . different. That your Untold heritage would be a gift and a burden no loremaster had known before. She wanted you to have all the knowledge you might need some day. So she went. But she never returned."

Rowen swallowed. Tears stung her eyes.

"But she didn't *die* . . ."

Pendrake looked at her a long moment before answering. She could see how much he wished to tell her something hopeful.

"I searched the Weaving myself," he said slowly, "as deeply as I dared, but I never found her. The longer one stays there, the more difficult it is to come back."

"But what *is* the Weaving, Grandfather? I still don't understand."

"That's one of the reasons we're going home, Rowen. You have to see for yourself, and Fable is the only place you can do that."

"You want me to go into the Weaving?"

"It's not that I want you to, Rowen. You *have to*."

"Why?"

Pendrake was about to answer, then his gaze shifted suddenly to something behind Rowen.

"Come out of the Deep, have you?" a thin, scrapy sort of voice rasped in her ear. She nearly jumped out of her chair.

An old man with long, snow-white hair stood behind her, glaring at her. A white scar ran down one side of his long, leathery face, from the tip of one eyebrow to the corner of his mouth.

"Pardon?" Rowen stammered, her heart thumping.

"The *Deep*," intoned the old man. "Is that where you've come from, friends?"

"He means the forest, Rowen," Pendrake said. "And yes, we were in the Deep, if you must know."

The old man nodded knowingly, as if this information explained a great deal.

"And where might you be headed?" he asked, his eyes narrowing.

Pendrake didn't answer, and the quick glance he gave Rowen warned her not to speak up either.

"Well," said the old man with a shrug, "it's a good thing you stopped in for the night. It's a steep dark one out there. Not good for decent folk to be travelling."

"Yes, it is dark," Pendrake said. "And cold, too."

"Aye, a coat and two scarves colder than yesternight. Mighty odd weather for this season."

"You're right about that."

The old man pointedly eyed one of the empty chairs at the table. It was clear he was hoping to be invited to sit. When that didn't happen, he lowered himself quickly into the chair anyway, then leaned across the table. His next words came in a whisper.

"Odd times all around. Odd things happening, odd creatures prowling the edge of the Deep as were never seen before by these old eyes."

He glanced down at Riddle, then fixed his disconcerting gaze on Pendrake.

"Never seen before," he repeated.

"What have you seen?" Pendrake asked.

"Ohhhh," the old man breathed, shaking his head ominously, "things as should know their place and keep to it. Old things, from the oldest tales. And strangers washing up here, like flotsam from some faraway shipwreck. All manner of strangers. Where do *you* hail from?"

"We're from the Bourne," Pendrake said curtly.

"Aye, I knew that, by the look of you. You're Fable folk, I'm thinking."

Pendrake said nothing.

"Ah, well," the old man shrugged, "there's one thing I know for certain, and you can take the news home with you for free. Something on the worse side of bad is brewing out there in the world, and the waves of it are lapping at our shores."

Pendrake nodded.

"I believe you," he said.

The old man stared at Pendrake as if he wasn't sure he'd heard right.

"You *do*?" he whispered, then cleared his throat. "I mean, of *course* you do. These fools don't see that it's already on our doorsteps, but those of us with sharp eyes, with brains—"

"Seamus Gudgeon," Kate shouted from the bar, "are you plaguing my guests with your farragoes of doom and gloom?"

The old man stood up suddenly and glared at the tavernkeeper, one eye twitching. It was clear he was about to reply with heated words, when suddenly the door flew open. Everyone turned to look at the new arrival, a short, stout man with immense sideburns, a walking stick under one arm. He stamped his feet on the mat and rubbed his pudgy hands together.

"Cold as a gravedigger's backside this night, boys," he

announced to the room. "Nearly froze helping the wife furl the bed-sheets."

"Thanks for the breaking news, Gilly Sprat," Kate shouted. "Now shut the door with yourself on this side of it."

The man nodded eagerly, turned and gave a shrill whistle. As he was pulling the door closed, a dog came loping in after him.

Only very large dogs can lope. This was a very large dog, Rowen saw first. Then she saw that the dog had caught sight of Riddle. And Riddle had seen the dog.

From there things went badly, fast.

The dog made straight for the cat, but then Riddle was not there and the dog was under Rowen's chair, barking and snapping at her heels, but that wasn't the worst of it, because something that hadn't been in the room a moment before was high up in a corner by the fireplace, something like a very large, scaly bat with outspread wings, shrieking and hissing. And now people were yelling and scrambling over each other to get out of that suddenly unpopular corner, and glasses were shattering and crockery smashing, and Rowen was knocked out of her chair by the dog, and the table went over too, and as she was picking herself up out of a puddle of cream she saw that the bat-thing was gone and the dog was whimpering with terror and scrambling backwards across the floor, because now there was a black horse in the middle of the rapidly emptying room, snorting gouts of red fire from its mouth and nostrils and pawing at the air with its hooves.

She had to do something.

The next thing she knew she was standing in front of the frantic, mad-eyed horse, a hot wind in her face, speaking to it in as calm a voice as she could muster through her own fear.

"It's all right, Riddle, it's all right..."

The horse's huge eyes rolled about in terror then seemed

to see her, focus on her. Parts of its body began to bob and flicker, like shadows cast by a flame wavering in a gust of wind. Then the horse was gone, or it *was* only bobbing shadows of people and things cast by the fluttering candles along the walls. A disembodied tongue of fire hung in the air a moment, then went out suddenly with a *pop*.

There was a brief hush, in which Rowen could hear her own panting breath.

People began to pick themselves up off the floor and each other. Kate's round head rose slowly from behind the counter like the moon, and nearly as pale. The dog and its master were one quivering huddled thing by the door.

And here was Riddle, a tawny cat again, sitting quietly at Rowen's side as if he'd never been anywhere else. He licked one of his paws, in a rather unconvincing attempt to look feline. It didn't help, given that he still had a horse's ears. After a moment he seemed to realize this. With a blurry flicker, the proper cat's ears took their place.

He might have trampled me, Rowen thought with a shudder, as if only now could she let herself feel the terror of what had just happened. *But he didn't. He listened.*

Then she thought, *Grandfather*. She turned, seeking him out in the jumble of bodies and overturned furniture, and saw him picking himself up off the floor, a grimace of pain on his face.

"Grandfather!"

"I'm fine, Rowen," he said, but she heard the strain in his voice and wondered how bad a fall he had taken.

"Didn't I tell the lot of you?" croaked Seamus, climbing unsteadily out from under a table. "Didn't I say mind now, the Deep is vomiting up its evil on our shingle, but you all told me I was cracked, you did . . ."

"I'll crack you all right if you don't hush your gob," Kate

warned him, patting down her apron with shaky hands as she came out from behind the bar. "It's Nicholas Pendrake that I'd be hearing from right now."

Rowen's grandfather came to her side, limping slightly. He gave her a quick smile that said, *You did very well.* For some reason she couldn't quite get at, she felt tears rise. Then she saw the shadow of pain still on his face and understood. In moments like this she had always counted on him to take charge and make things right. This time she'd done it herself, without a second thought. As if deep down she had begun to doubt he could.

"This is Riddle," Pendrake said, gesturing to the cat, who had put on a convincingly feline expression of *who, me?* "He's a creature of the forest, the Deep, it's true, but he's harmless. He was lost and alone, and needed our help, so my granddaughter and I brought him with us."

"And what else did you bring with you?" Seamus croaked. "Decent folk don't be prowling around in the Deep these days. It's unnatural. We were never meant to swim in those waters, and anyone who does is not to be trusted, I say."

"And didn't I say mind your mouth, old man," Kate snapped.

"I'll go one better than that," Seamus said with a scowl, and he strode for the door. "I'll take my custom elsewhere, while I still can. And if any of you have a crumb of brains, you'll join me."

"Well if you're going, then be off with you," Kate said, waving him away with a hand.

The door rattled behind the old man as he stalked out. No one else moved, not because they didn't want to, Rowen realized, but because they were afraid to take their eyes off Riddle, even for a moment.

Kate snatched a tumbler from one of her customers, who

was letting the contents spill unnoticed down his shirt-front as he stared slack-jawed at Riddle. "Now, Nicholas," she said, "we're old friends, we are, but I just don't know about this . . . this . . . *that.*"

She pointed a trembling finger at Riddle, who had slunk behind Rowen's legs. Rowen reached down and scooped him up in her arms. To her surprise, he didn't resist. He was lighter than she had expected, too, and there was something else surprising about him, she now discovered: she had held cats before who purred, but Riddle *hummed.* That was the only word for the strange feeling he gave off, of something vibrating with life. It didn't make her feel calm and sleepy like a cat's purr could, but more awake. It was like holding a bag full of bees.

"I understand, Kate," Pendrake said. "I assure you there's no danger. Riddle won't harm anyone. He's just not used to being around so many people."

"It isn't so many *now.*"

"You're right and I'm sorry about that too. We've done enough damage here for one night, so we'll be on our way."

Rowen was only too glad to be leaving, but they had taken only a few steps towards the door when it burst open and Seamus came staggering in, his long haggard face contorted in fear. He clutched Pendrake's sleeve and wheezed out a string of words Rowen couldn't catch.

"What is it, Seamus?" Kate cried.

"The D—D—Deep," the old man managed to gasp out. "The Deep is . . ."

He couldn't summon the words.

"Show us," Kate said.

Everyone who was still in the room after Riddle's shape-changing episode hurried out into the street after the old man. The wind had died down, but there was a heaviness in the air, Rowen thought, like you sometimes felt before a thunderstorm. Dogs were barking their heads off all over the village. Lamps were lighting up in windows, and people in nightshirts were peering out their doors. Some joined the procession, asking anxiously what was going on. Up the street the growing crowd went, following Seamus. In a short time they came to an elevated spot where they could all gather, near the edge of the ridge the village was perched on, and look out over the forest.

Only now they didn't have to look out quite as far as usual.

"Do you see?" croaked Seamus, stabbing a bony finger, as if anyone needed further directions. Despite the clouded night, it was clear as day.

"The Deep is rising."

For as long as anyone in Molly's Arm could remember, the eaves of the Forest of Eldark had nestled at the foot of the ridge. Near, but safely far at the same time. Now there were trees growing more than halfway up the slope, looking ancient and deeply rooted, as if they had always been there. The tops of a few of the tallest trees even rose above the rim of the ridge. Somehow, in the short time since Rowen and her grandfather had left the forest, it had *come closer.* Or had the trees grown larger, Rowen wondered. Or both? And what was just as frightening was that there was no sound. The forest was absolutely still. Not a breath of wind stirred the leaves. Not a chirp, a hoot or a rustle could be heard. If the forest was a sea, it was under an eerie calm.

"It's even higher now than when I first left the Mermaid," the old man moaned.

"It *is* rising," someone wailed. "What'll we do?"

"Powers preserve us," somebody else cried. "We'll be inundated."

Rowen felt a ripple of panic pass through the crowd. Some looked fearfully at Riddle as if they thought he might be the cause of this latest eruption of the unknown and terrifying into their quiet lives. The cat was aware of the glances directed at him and he burrowed himself even further into the shelter of Rowen's arms.

"What does it mean, Nicholas?" Kate breathed, clutching at Pendrake's sleeve.

"You know this forest as the Deep," he said. "It's also the Dark. That's what's rising now."

There was a brief silence as the assembled villagers took in what the loremaster had said.

"Then this is the end," someone wailed. "Our homes, our farms . . . everything will be lost."

A clamour of distress rose. Pendrake turned to Rowen, his face grim.

"We have to help them," he said to her, then he sighed. "This is going to give the threads a good tug."

He raised his hands for quiet, but no one paid him any notice. They were too busy panicking, Rowen realized. Then Kate stepped out of the crowd and stood beside Pendrake.

"Stop your jabbering and pay attention!" the innkeeper roared. "Nicholas can help us!"

The clamour subsided, and most of those who had already begun hurrying back to the village returned.

"Thank you, Kate," Pendrake said.

He turned to face the forest, then took the last few steps that brought him to the very brink of the ridge. The night wind caught his long grey hair and tossed it about. He really did look, Rowen thought, like someone standing at the edge of the sea. Then he gripped his staff in both hands and lifted it slowly into the air.

"Is that a magic staff?" asked a young boy, his eyes wide.

Pendrake turned and smiled at him. "It's a stick," he said.

Rowen's heart lightened to see the gleam of amusement in her grandfather's eyes. She thought he looked more like his old self than he had in days.

Pendrake turned his attention back to the staff, which he lifted higher.

"This must be a beautiful spot on a sunny day," he murmured, as if speaking to himself.

"It is," Kate said, glancing at Rowen with a puzzled expression. "A lovely spot entirely."

"I can imagine," Pendrake said.

To Rowen's surprise her grandfather began to prod the staff at the empty air, as if there was something in the darkness itself he was searching for, or trying to dislodge.

"There it is," he said at last.

With that he swept the staff in a long arc over his head, and the darkness opened.

That was how it looked to Rowen. The darkness opened like a seam and a shaft of bright golden light poured through. It was if the night air was the roof of a tent and her grandfather had torn through it to let in a sliver of day. The top of the ridge was bathed in brilliant sunshine.

There were gasps from the crowd, and one terrified shriek followed by a chorus of shushing. Riddle moaned in fear. The opening her grandfather had made continued to widen on its own, and in moments it stretched across the entire length of the ridge. Rowen couldn't take her eyes off that unaccountable brightness in the midst of the dark. Then someone shouted, *"Look at the trees!"*, and she turned her gaze downwards and blinked in surprise.

The trees had fallen back. She stared, certain the forest's edge was now further from the top of the ridge than it had been when she'd looked at it only moments ago. The light was falling upon the leaves and trunks of the outermost trees and the forest, she thought, looked peaceful and almost inviting.

Pendrake lowered his staff. He turned to face the awe-struck villagers.

"There," he said to Kate, who had backed away with a stunned look in her eyes. "That should hold it for a while. You've gained a little time, but still you need to be ready to leave Molly's Arm at a moment's notice. The forest will rise again, make no mistake about it. We can only hope the true cause of this threat can be dealt with before your village is lost."

After assigning three young men to keep a watch on the trees, Pendrake turned away from his handiwork and sought out Rowen. He gave her a wink and took her arm, and they walked back down the hill to the village. She thought of what he had said earlier, that each time they reached into the Weaving they tugged upon the threads of Story.

"What about the Night King?" she asked. "Haven't we just . . . told him where we are?"

"It had to be done," Pendrake said heavily. "That's part of being a loremaster, too."

Kate came up alongside them.

"I'm sorry for doubting you, Nicholas," she said with a contrite expression. "I can't think what would have become of us if you hadn't been here tonight. Of course you're still welcome to stay at the Mermaid. No charge. You and your granddaughter, and even the cat, or whatever it is."

"Thank you, Kate," Pendrake said. "But we'll be carrying on to Fable tonight. After what's happened here, there is clearly no longer any time to lose."

Rowen glanced back up the hill. Some of the crowd had followed them back down into the village, but many were still gathered on the ridge, gazing up at the light. It was like a beacon, she thought with a shiver of dread, a beacon that would be seen from a long way off.

Many miles from the village of Molly's Arm, something awoke.

In a desolate marsh near the edge of the Bourne stood a solitary dead tree, its bare, blackened limbs reaching like claws to the sky. Among the tangled branches countless generations of spiders had woven so many webs that the tree seemed to be draped in tattered veils. Among these webs was one that hadn't been woven by any spider, at least not the kind that crawled on eight legs and caught flies for its meals. Anyone who passed this way (though few ever did) and stopped to marvel at this strange tree might have noticed that this particular web was much larger than any of the others, and made of much thinner, nearly invisible thread, almost as if it wasn't there at all. When the wind blew through the branches, all the other webs stirred and trembled, except this one. It had not been made for catching the usual sort of prey, either, for whenever a fly or a beetle on the wing strayed into its threads the insect would pass right through, unharmed.

This web was only one of many like it that had been strung throughout this part of the Realm, in out-of-the-way places like the marsh. They had been spun and linked together with invisible threads like secret tripwires, to catch one thing only: a presence.

At the same moment that Pendrake stood on the ridge above the forest and cut a hole in the darkness, the threads of this particular web quivered for the first time.

The prey had returned.

The web's trembling threads did not bring a spider

scuttling out of its lair to investigate the catch. Instead, the web began to quiver more strongly. Slow ripples and undulations crossed its surface, then ridges and hollows appeared, stretching and warping the web as if it was a gossamer-thin cocoon with something inside trying to tear its way out. But there was no inside to the cocoon: there was only the web, shaping itself around nothing to create a something. After a while the shapes of limbs could be made out, straining and reaching, then something that might have been a head appeared, slowly turning from side to side as if seeking an elusive sight or sound.

At last the web that was now a web-*thing* tore itself free from the branches. The human-like shape fell to the wet, slimy earth and lay still. After a while it stirred, climbed slowly to its feet, and began shuffling forward through the marsh.

The thing had no eyes. It felt its way as a spider feels the tremors of a fly's struggle through the strands of its web. It sensed the drawing of power from the Weaving and it moved now towards the prey that had used that power, as though towards a long-awaited meal.

The web-thing was still whitish-grey and almost transparent, but as it walked it grew more solid and opaque, and its human-like features became more distinct. It passed through a cloud of mosquitoes and a slit opened in the head, widening to a gaping maw. There was a sound of indrawn breath and the insects were sucked helplessly inside. The mouth swiftly ravelled shut. Not long afterwards it opened again and a thin, high-pitched whine came out. It was like the whine of a cloud of mosquitoes, if mosquitoes ever tried to form words. *Aaaiiiii . . . aaammmm . . . ooooo . . . nnnnnng* . . . the web-thing whined over and over. Eventually the whine fell in pitch, deepening and growing louder, until it resembled something more like a human voice. *iiiiii . . . aammm . . .*

The web-thing was practising speech. It would need speech later on, when it came to the places where humans dwelt. It would have to pass for one of them, at least until it found the prey.

iiiii amm looookinnng . . . for rowennnnnn . . .

The thing made of spider's web had no mind of its own. It was not alive, unless one thinks of words as having life. It was a being spun from words, a walking, breathing spell known as a thrawl. *Rowen* was one of the words that the thrawl had been woven from. Another word was *find.* And another word was the thrawl's own secret name, given to it by the lord of the Shadow Realm. It would speak that name only when it had found the one it sought. Then the spell would be unleashed, and the prey would be caught at last.

In the old days, if you owned a decent sword and a reasonably good horse, you could call yourself a knight-errant and off you'd go, defending the weak, slaying monsters, searching for lost magical relics . . . just generally doing as you pleased. The problem was that many of these so-called knights would blunder into worse trouble than they could handle, and if they weren't killed outright, they would beat a hasty retreat back to Fable, usually bringing the trouble home with them, hot on their heels. Eventually it was decided that some sort of training was in order for these young, would-be adventurers, to help keep them alive a little longer, and to protect Fable from their mistakes. And so the Errantry was born . . .

— The Recollections of Grimshaw the Elder

WILL SLEPT IN HIS OLD ROOM at the toyshop that night, and early the next morning, after a quick breakfast with Edweth, he hurried to Appleyard. The Errantry had a network of scouts and riders all over the Bourne and in other lands, too, and his hope was that someone might have brought back news of the loremaster or Shade. As he climbed the rising stone path to the Gathering House, however, he found the same curious and hopeful looks directed at him from passing members of the Errantry as he'd had the night before.

He was nearing the steps of the Gathering House, a huge structure flanked on all sides by great trees with spreading branches, when a tall boy about his own age called his name and rushed over to him.

"It's really you," the boy said breathlessly. "They said you were back. I'm Peter, a friend of Rowen's."

Will remembered him now. He'd met Peter when Rowen had shown him around Appleyard not long after he'd first arrived in Fable.

"I was actually on my way to Master Pendrake's shop to find you," Peter said. "You saved me the trouble."

"Find me?"

"It's the Marshal. He wants to speak to you."

Will nodded. He had known this would be coming. Last night Balor Gruff had no doubt reported directly to Lord Caliburn, the Marshal of the Errantry, who found out about everything going on in Fable, sooner or later. Will had met him before, and found him to be cold and unfriendly. He had wanted Will to stay in Fable rather than search for a way home, not because he feared for Will's safety, it seemed, but because he had hoped Will's gift for finding what was lost and hidden could be put to use in defence of the Bourne. Will didn't relish the thought of seeing him again.

"Thanks," Will said glumly. He started to move away.

"Will?" Peter said.

"Yes?"

"I'm glad you came back. We all are."

Will nodded again, too flustered to reply. He hurried on and climbed the steps to the Gathering House, giving his name to the guards at the door, then made his way through the busy corridors, keeping his head down in the hope of not attracting any attention. But as he passed the hall that led to the dormitories, a girl appeared out of nowhere and stood in his path. She was small and round-faced, and breathing heavily as if she'd just been running.

"Are you Will Lightfoot?" she asked in a near-whisper.

"Yes."

"You find lost things, don't you?" she said, her brown eyes fixed solemnly on him.

Will sighed.

"Listen, I don't know what you've heard about me but—"

"My name's Mairi," the girl said quickly. "My ferret, his name's Dart, he got out of his cage this morning when I was feeding him a piece of roast beef I'd saved from last night's supper. I've looked everywhere but—"

"Look, I'm sorry," Will interrupted. "There's nothing I can do."

"But if the prefect finds him before I do he'll take him away," the girl pleaded more urgently now. "We're not supposed to have pets in the dormitory. Please, you're the only one who can help me. You find what's lost. You saved Balor Gruff. You're a hero."

"Don't believe everything you hear," Will said, blushing and annoyed at himself for it.

"But the other apprentices say you—"

"Ferrets live in holes, don't they?" Will said angrily, stepping around the girl. "Look for a hole."

Lord Caliburn stood leaning over his desk, a large map unrolled before him. Someone else was with him, on the other side of the desk, so that his back was to Will. There was a feeling in the room, Will thought, as if a thunderstorm had just passed through. He knew that the Marshal and this other man had been arguing.

Will cleared his throat to announce his presence. The other man turned. He was middle-aged, very tall and broad-shouldered, almost as large as Balor Gruff. His face was craggy and weather-beaten, his eyes cold and piercing under thick black brows. It was a memorable face, but Will didn't recognize him.

"Will Lightfoot," the Marshal said. "Welcome back to Fable." His voice was as clipped and emotionless as Will remembered it, but the man had changed in some way, he thought. The look in his eyes was one of weariness, or perhaps even pain.

"Thank you, sir," Will replied.

"This is Captain Thorne," the Marshal said, introducing the man who stood at the desk.

This was the captain of the guard who had given the new orders about strangers in Fable, Will remembered. Thorne nodded curtly to Will.

"We owe you our thanks," the Marshal said stiffly. "If not for you, our best tracker might never have made it home. I've sent scouts to find out where this dust cloud has drifted to, but it seems to have vanished. Which is good, but still, I don't like mysteries. You don't have any thoughts to offer, do you?"

"It wasn't a dust cloud," Will said. "It was a *place*. Or no place. I don't know how to describe it. All I know is, we weren't in the Realm. I don't know where we were."

"Balor Gruff tells me you've returned to the Realm to look for your friends. So this time your coming here wasn't an accident."

"That's right."

"I'd like to hear the whole tale of why and how you returned, if you don't mind."

Before he began his story Will glanced at the captain. Thorne was studying him with a cold, suspicious look that flustered him, then made him angry. Quickly, he told of his meeting with the shadow and the warnings it had given, then how he had set out to return to the Realm and encountered Balor. Caliburn listened without making any comment.

When Will was finished, the Marshal and Thorne exchanged a quick glance.

"But your friends aren't here," Caliburn said. "Even Finn is still away, searching for Balor Gruff. So what are your plans?"

"I was hoping someone in Fable could tell me where the loremaster might be, but I doubt that anyone knows. The same with Shade. So I'm going to find them myself, somehow. After all, people are calling me—"

He broke off, not wanting to bring up the fact that he was being hailed as a returning hero. But Captain Thorne nodded eagerly, as if he'd been waiting for this very subject.

"The Marshal and I have heard the rumours," he said in a low, hoarse voice, "or perhaps they're better called legends—being told about you in Fable. About your journey with the loremaster and the others. They say you're a hero."

"People have got the story wrong," Will said hotly. "I wasn't a . . . *hero*. We only made it through because of Master Pendrake, and Moth, and Finn Madoc."

At the mention of Finn's name, the Marshal's face seemed to darken a moment.

"I am glad to hear that a member of the Errantry did his duty," he said. "I would expect no less of him. And I am sorry about the archer of the Tain Shee. I know that he was a valiant warrior."

"But now they're saying that the great pathfinder, Will Lightfoot, has returned to us in our hour of need," the captain said, with what seemed to be a trace of a sneer in his voice.

"I don't know anything about that," Will said. "I just came to find my friends. To help them, if I can."

"Well, one thing is certain, this *is* an hour of need," the Marshal said grimly. "Storyfolk are flocking to the Bourne, fleeing war and disaster, and bringing alarming tidings of the world beyond our borders. Storylands all over the Realm, it seems, are vanishing. Drying up. Crumbling away. And as the stories die, Nightbane have been on the move in great numbers. Burning and destroying what remains."

Will remembered what the Lady of the Tain Shee had told him and the others before he returned home. She had warned that they had only a brief time of peace before the enemy's forces would rise like a tide across the Realm. While he had been gone, it was clear that the time of peace had passed.

"But why are Storyfolk coming *here*, to Fable?" he asked.

"That's a question best left for the loremaster," the Marshal said. "I only hope he returns soon. What concerns me is the safety of the Bourne."

"That is my concern, too, sir," Thorne said. "And although I'm not pleased about the way this boy was recruited without proper approval, this does seem an opportunity to—"

"*Recruited*?" Will broke in.

Thorne frowned.

"Balor appointed you his knight-apprentice," the captain said. "Do you mean to say you didn't know? He didn't even tell you?"

"He did," Will said, his thoughts whirling, "but . . . I thought he was joking."

A faint flicker of a smile passed across the Marshal's face.

"It isn't always easy to tell with Balor Gruff. But in this case he was serious. No matter how impulsively it was done, he made you his apprentice."

"In which case," Captain Thorne said, "you're now a member of the Errantry, Will Lightfoot. With all of the duties and obligations that entails."

"But I didn't ask Balor to do it," Will protested. "I can't

join the Errantry. That's not why I came back. I'm not staying in Fable."

"So you're planning to search for your friends?" the Marshal asked.

"I am."

"On your own?" Thorne said. "Tell me, where will you go? Which direction? What if the loremaster and his granddaughter, or the wolf, are hundreds of miles away?"

Will clenched his fists and said nothing. The captain's questions had gone right to the heart of his own fears. It had been one thing to set out into the unknown with companions like Shade and the loremaster, but to do so by himself was reckless and dangerous, and he knew it. He remembered that the Angel had tracked down Rowen only because he had been able to invade Will's dreams and seek for her that way. Will had been a danger to Rowen without knowing it. If he charged off now on his own and got captured by Malabron's servants, they might turn his gift to their own use. He could endanger his friends again. But what choice did he have? He couldn't just stay here and do nothing.

Lord Caliburn sighed, and Will looked up to see concern and even sadness in his eyes.

"I must ask you to reconsider your plans, Will," he said. "To go alone into the wilds, especially now, would be folly. You would be placing *yourself* in great danger, without any certainty of helping your friends. You must understand that."

"I do, but I can't just wait here," Will said desperately. "I have to get a warning to the loremaster, and to Shade, if there's any way. I need to know they're all right."

"You can be ordered not to leave Fable," Thorne said. "An order that the guards at the gate will see is obeyed. After all, you're a knight-apprentice of the Errantry now, and are bound by our rules."

"Will cannot be held accountable to Balor's rash act," the Marshal said, with an angry wave of his hand. "He didn't truly give his consent."

"The boy's apprenticeship is binding if you order it so, Lord."

There followed a strained silence in which the two men glared at one another without a word. Now Will understood what they had been arguing about. The Marshal was on his side, but against his leaving, while Captain Thorne wanted to keep him here as a knight-apprentice.

"You have valuable knowledge and experience that none of our recruits have," the captain went on, addressing Will now. "The way I see it, you could be of the most help to your friends right here in Fable, by training with the Errantry and learning to develop your gift—"

"I once made the same argument," Lord Caliburn broke in. "It was wrong of me then, and it would be wrong now. You may leave Fable if you wish, Will, even though I would prefer you remained here for your own sake and my peace of mind. I ask only one thing of you. Stay in Fable just one more day. After what happened to Balor, there's no telling what other threats or traps might be lurking close by. Give my scouts time to return with their reports, which should be the day after tomorrow. Will you at least stay here until then?"

Will pursed his lips. He was about to refuse, but something in the Marshal's voice or manner reminded him of his own father. With a pang he remembered his last sight of his dad, standing on the back steps under the porch light.

He took a deep breath.

"I'll stay," he said with a nod, though his heart was sinking. "One more day."

* * *

As Will came out onto the steps of the Gathering House, downcast and uncertain what to do with himself, a voice hailed him.

He looked up. Running across the lawn towards him was the girl who'd lost her ferret.

"It's Mairi," she said shyly when she reached him, brushing back her wind-tangled hair. "I found Dart, just where you said he'd be."

"What do you mean? I didn't tell you where to look."

"Yes, you did. You said to look in a hole and I did and there he was," the girl gushed, beaming. "In an old rat hole in the wall behind my bed. I don't know how he fitted into it but he was in there all right, just like you said."

"Well, that's great—"

"I got him to come out with another piece of roast beef. He's back in his cage now and the prefect never found out. Thank you."

She was standing very close, her big brown eyes gazing up at him with admiration. She was a pretty girl, he realized, and he felt suddenly uncomfortable.

"You're welcome," he said.

"I can't wait to tell everyone about what you did. You really are the pathfinder."

"I hope so," Will said under his breath, and walked quickly away.

Will returned to the toyshop to tell Edweth what had happened, and that he was leaving the day after tomorrow, no matter what. She tried with various arguments to convince him not to go at all, but he wouldn't let himself be budged by her entreaties.

He spent the rest of the day wandering through Fable in a fruitless quest for clues as to where Rowen and her grandfather might be. He found some more of Rowen's friends, but none of them knew anything that could help him. Late in the afternoon he returned dejectedly to the toyshop, and with Edweth's permission, searched through Pendrake's workshop on the top floor.

The room was not as cluttered as he remembered it, and he suspected that Edweth had been unable to resist tidying up a little while the Master was gone. There were no papers or maps on Pendrake's desk, and the many books piled and stacked around the room told him nothing. He lingered in the workshop for a while, though, remembering the first time he had come here, and how confused and terrified he'd been when the loremaster told him he was in a story now and he would have to find his own way out of it.

In the evening Will visited the Golden Goose, the inn on the bridge over the stream that ran in a stone canal through the city. Fable folk mingled here in the evenings with travellers from far-flung lands of the Realm, to hear and tell stories. There was a chance, he thought, that one of the inn's guests might have met Pendrake and Rowen, or perhaps Shade, on their travels.

When he slipped into the crowded, noisy common room, Will was glad to see that no one seemed to recognize him. It wasn't surprising, since most of the folk gathered here this evening weren't from the Bourne, let alone from Fable. They were Storyfolk from far-off lands, and many of them looked it. There were people here of every shape and size, and some whose strange and even alarming features made him wonder whether the word *people* applied to them.

Will found a seat in one corner and listened while a succession of Storyfolk spun tales of their adventures, stories that were sometimes so wondrous or terrible that he had a hard time believing everything he heard, even after all that he himself had seen and done on his own journey. And too many of the tales, he thought with dismay, were about dark and wicked things encroaching on lands that had long been peaceful and safe. He listened carefully to every story, however, and even asked a few of the tellers afterwards if they had met a toymaker and his granddaughter, or a talking wolf, on their travels. He tried to be as unspecific as he could about who the loremaster and Rowen were, while still providing details that might jog someone's memory, because he wasn't sure it was wise to reveal too much about them to these strangers. But no one had seen any of his friends.

Will returned to the toyshop late that night, restless and heartsick, wondering why the shadow had urged him to return, had told him he was *needed*, when he wasn't accomplishing anything.

Before sunrise the next day, Will hurried back to Appleyard to find out if the scouts had reported in. He was climbing the steps of the Gathering House when a huge hand fell on his shoulder. He turned to see Balor beaming down at him.

"There you are," the wildman boomed. "I thought I'd already lost my new apprentice. That would have been rather embarrassing."

"I'm not your apprentice," Will said, trying to hide his annoyance. Balor's face fell.

"Well, yes, I imagine you're angry about that . . ." he muttered, looking away. "Sorry."

"It doesn't matter," Will said. "The Marshal says what you did isn't binding. I can leave Fable if I want to. And that's what I'm going to do."

"Well, I suppose you must," Balor said with a shrug. "It's just that if you *were* my apprentice, we could probably get permission to take a short ride out of Fable, just the two of us, for a few days, to teach you some of the basic scouting skills, and who knows, maybe along the way we can do a little searching for the loremaster and your wolf friend."

Will gaped at him.

"You mean you'd come with me," he said. "You'd help me look for them."

"For a while at least. But, since you're not my apprentice . . ."

"When can we leave?" Will asked eagerly. Going on horseback, and with Balor, seemed to him a much better way to travel than on foot and alone. They could cover much more ground that way, and Balor would know the roads and lands around the Bourne. And the dangers that lay beyond.

"Like you, I'll have to wait until the scouts report in," Balor said. "But with luck we can set out tomorrow and—" He paused, as if another thought had just occurred to him. "You have ridden a horse before, haven't you?"

"Yes," Will said, though he thought to himself that a ride on a pony at the fair when he was seven probably didn't count.

Balor eyed him dubiously, then grinned.

"Well, that's good. Very good."

His spirits lifted, Will reported to the quartermaster, as Balor suggested, to collect the travelling gear he would need. When he had everything ready—a cloak, boots that fit snugly, a rucksack and the supplies that went in it—he sought out the wildman again. They spent the rest of the day together. Balor took Will around Appleyard, and was clearly enjoying showing off his new apprentice, the famous Will Lightfoot, to everyone they met. Later they looked over some maps in the Gathering House library. Will traced the route he had taken on his journey, and pointed out the place, as near as he could, where they had met the Fair Folk and Will had parted from his friends. He and Balor agreed it would make sense to begin their own search in that direction, but it would mean facing the daunting vastness of the Deep Dark Forest. Finally Balor told Will to go home to the toyshop and get a good sleep.

"By the book, you should be staying here in the dormitory with the other apprentices," the wildman said. "But you'll be pestered with questions half the night if you do that."

Will agreed and took his leave, promising to return at dawn. But he didn't go straight back to the toyshop. Instead he returned once more to the Inn of the Golden Goose.

He found a place on a bench along the back wall. There were several conversations going on around him all at once, and at first he wasn't able to pick anything out of the noise. After a while, though, he noticed that one voice was louder than the rest. It was coming from the nook near the fireplace, where a very short, stocky, bearded man was holding forth to a small crowd. Then Will looked more closely at the speaker. He was certain he had seen him before, but couldn't remember where.

The bearded man was drinking heavily from a huge metal tankard. Between long gulps he would wipe the glistening foam from his moustache and go on with an involved, meandering tale about the silver mine he had once owned with his brothers. The story didn't sound particularly interesting, but Will listened as well as he could over the hubbub, curious now about why this man looked so familiar.

" . . . and so off she went, on the arm of that tall, ridiculously good-looking king's son," the man said in a low, gravelly voice. "Oh, she promised to return and visit us often, but we never did see her again. Well, I don't blame her.

So young and sweet she was. As fresh as a spring rain. Really now, what kind of life was it for her, cooking and cleaning for seven quarrelsome, untidy men, and all of us as handsome as tree stumps? No, I was glad for her, truly I was. But after she was gone, I found my heart just wasn't in the mining any more, even though we were digging out more good ore than we ever had. To come home and see the house all dark and shut up, when you were expecting warm light and her sweet voice singing to greet you . . . No, it was never the same afterwards. So I sold my share to my brothers, and I set off to see the world. And I did see it. A great deal of it. More than I might've wished to . . . "

As the man went on with his tale, Will remembered where he had seen him before. He was a dwarf, and he knew Rowen. The first time Will had met him, which was here at the Golden Goose, the dwarf had been arguing with someone who wanted him to join some sort of quest. Rowen had advised the dwarf to go, and to Will's surprise, he had changed his mind and agreed immediately. It turned out, Will had learned then, that Rowen had a gift for helping Storyfolk, which was one of the signs that she was meant to be a loremaster.

"Of course I remember you," the dwarf bellowed after his tale had wrapped up and Will approached him with a cautious greeting. "My memory's like a flawless crystal. Let me see . . . it was the last time I saw the lady Rowen of Blue Hill, wasn't it? Yes, it was. You were there with her. What's your name, lad?"

"Will Lightfoot."

"Lightfoot, is it? I've got some distant cousins near Mount Moonfang named Flintfoot. And there's a half-dwarven clan in the Forlorn Hills by the name of Shalefoot. You don't have any Dwarf in your ancestry, do you, boy? Maybe a little Kobold?"

"Not that I know of."

"That's a shame. But I won't hold it against you. That's not the dwarvish way. I am Mimling Hammersong, of the Hammersongs of Stonesthrow Mine. Take a seat, my boy. Did the lass tell you the tale of how we met?"

"She didn't," Will said, pulling up a chair.

"Ah, well, when I first arrived in Fable I was down to my last few coins and looking for any work I could get. I came here to the Goose one night, hoping to get hired for some quest or other. Dwarves have always been in demand for quests. It's a tradition, a good luck sort of thing. If you want a successful quest, get a dwarf. Well, sure enough there was a band of adventurers at the inn that night, looking for someone with tunnelling experience to help on a treasure-seeking expedition to a dragon's lair. I didn't like the look of this bunch, real shifty characters I thought, and the job sounded a little too . . . adventurous for my taste. I had been a miner up to that point, you see. I'd only ever swung my hammer at seams of ore, not goblin skulls. I was about to turn them down, when this little voice pipes up, 'You should go, Mister Dwarf.' It was Rowen, of course. She was there with her grandfather, who'd been telling some of his marvellous tales. Only a wee chip off the rock she was then, even nearer to the ground than me, but already so sure of herself. The toymaker tried to shush her, but she wouldn't be shushed, not that one."

The dwarf gave a low chuckle. His iron-grey eyes glittered in the firelight.

"I thought it was funny at first," he went on, "but there's a way of looking at you she has. I can't explain it. Almost in spite of myself I agreed I would go on the expedition. It was a long, hard journey, and there was adventure sure enough, and blood and fire, but in the end we came away with treasure. Not a king's ransom, but enough to pay the bills and then some. And I'd crushed a few goblin skulls along the way, and discovered I liked it. A lot. After that I was in demand as a professional quester, and I never looked back. I'd really found my calling. And I owe it all to Rowen."

Mimling smiled as if at fond memories, then he blinked and glanced around the room.

"In fact, I was hoping I might see her here tonight. I just got back from the last quest she sent me on, and I wanted to thank her for convincing me to go. Do you happen to know if my lady is in town?"

"Rowen's not here," Will said. "Neither is Master Pendrake."

"Ah, that's a pity."

"That's why I came to the inn, to find out if anyone's seen them."

To Will's surprise, the dwarf reached out and patted his shoulder.

"I understand, lad. You love the girl."

To his consternation, Will felt himself blushing. He fumbled for words.

"Of course you do," the dwarf said thickly, wiping a tear from his eye. "And so do I. Everyone who meets my lady Rowen falls head over heels for her. She's a treasure, that one. A gem. A spark of fire."

It occurred to Will that Mimling had probably had more than a few tankards of ale.

"I guess . . . you haven't seen Rowen, then?"

"Not since I was last here. And that was a year ago now if it was a day."

Will's spirits fell. He sat in silence while the dwarf slurped down the foamy dregs of his tankard and shouted for another one.

"Did it work out for you," Will finally asked, "the quest Rowen sent you on?"

"What? Oh, that little jaunt to the Caverns of Nethergrim. Well, it's a strange tale. We never actually made it to the caverns."

He paused, and his ruddy face knotted up with a look of perplexity.

"I tell you, Will Lightfoot, the world is changing, for the worse. Folk aren't as trusting or hopeful as they used to be. It's like something is chipping away at them. Everywhere I go now there's this foreboding, as if everyone feels that terrible things are coming. And the land itself is . . . not itself. The Realm has always been tricky, changeable, but it's getting worse. There's almost nothing you can place trust in any more. The rivers, hills, trees, even the stones . . . "

The dwarf lifted the new tankard that had just been set before him, gazed past it with a puzzled, far-off look, and put it back down again.

"One thing I *knew* was stone," he said slowly. "Stone is reliable. It stays in one place and doesn't wander off. Or it didn't used to. But now the old landmarks, even entire *mountains*, they're either somewhere they're not supposed to be, or they're just gone."

"Gone?"

"Gone. We were following a treasure map, one of those ancient traveller's maps guaranteed by the Cartographers' Guild, but we kept running into things that weren't supposed to be there, or not running into things that *were*. I'd been in those lands before, and nothing was the way I remembered it. The map wasn't wrong, the *world* was. And so we . . . Ah, I told the whole story before you came over to say hello. I won't burden you with it. The point is, there was no Nethergrim to be found, but after wandering around looking for it we did stumble across treasure. Lots of it. A musty old dragon-hoard in the middle of a swamp, guarded by three bog trolls who fought hard to keep it."

The dwarf winced and slowly rubbed his thigh.

"I didn't come away from that battle unscathed," he said, "but we did take the treasure from the trolls, in the end. I guess we wanted it more."

"So it turned out all right, then," Will said. "Rowen's advice was good."

Mimling stroked his long beard, in which droplets of ale glistened.

"True enough, I suppose. But the strange thing was, when I looked at my share of the coins and jewels, I found I just didn't care. That greedy old dragon had dried to bones sitting on this heap of . . . of *stuff*, the trolls had died defending it, and for what? And here I was, just like them. All the wandering about, the goblin-bashing . . . I knew right then that I'd had enough. I finally admitted to myself how much I missed the quiet life I'd had with my brothers, mining and minding our own affairs. I'd been missing it for a long time, really, but it took this trip, and all that treasure, to make me see it."

The dwarf had a faraway look in his eyes again, then he hoisted the tankard, took a long, long gulp, and slammed it back down on the table.

"So I gave my companions most of my share, which they were quite happy to take, and I left. Just walked away. Since by then I was already quite far north I decided to seek out a dwarven tribe who dwelt in those parts, or so it was said. The Elders, or the Ironwise we call them, the greatest smiths and metalcrafters in the Realm. As a wee dwarfling I'd thrilled to the tales of the wondrous things they forged in ancient times, in their city of Adamant. Jewelled crowns, weapons of magic power, even flying ships . . . I'd always hoped to meet them one day, learn from them. It was time to revive that old dream. So I set out to find them, the Ironwise, if only to satisfy myself that they were more than just a legend. But I didn't get far. The leg, you see. It's rough country up there at the best of times, and this was the dead of winter. In the end I was forced to turn back without finding what I sought. I started on the long road home to Stonesthrow Mine, but I thought I'd stop at Fable on the way, to see my lady Rowen and thank her for sending me on this quest. And it was then, on my way here, that I had a very strange encounter."

The dwarf paused for another quaff. Will refrained from asking about this very strange encounter, not wanting the dwarf to launch into another long-winded tale. Now that he knew Mimling couldn't help him, he was eager to question some of the other travellers in the common room. He was about to make an excuse and leave, when the dwarf nudged him with his tankard.

"It was the oddest thing I'd met with on the entire trip. I was crossing the great trackless plains north of the Bourne. It's the land of the Horse Folk. Do you know of them, Will? They live in tents of animal skins and ride swift steeds to hunt the wisent, the great horned beasts of the plain. Anyhow, they are not known to be terribly welcoming to strangers, so I was on my guard. One night a storm came up. There was a mighty ruckus of lightning and thunder, but oddly, no rain. Still, I thought I'd better find shelter, so I climbed down into a narrow gully. I found a shallow cave, but as I was crawling in, there was a growl and something told me to keep my distance. Then, in a flash of lightning I saw what was in the cave. A wolf. A wolf who could talk."

Will stared at the dwarf. His heart started to pound.

"A talking wolf?"

"A big handsome fellow he was," Mimling said with a

nod, "and the sight of him nearly made me jump out of my boots. But he was in no condition to attack me, I saw right away. He was just lying there, panting, barely able to raise his head."

"Did the wolf say what his name was?"

The dwarf shook his head.

"He didn't. But by the look on your face I'm thinking you might know this creature."

"It could be . . . I have a friend, a wolf named Shade. I haven't seen him since I was here last."

"Coat all silver-grey?"

"Yes."

"Yellow-gold eyes that make you stop in your tracks?"

"Yes. And a voice like—"

"Like running water, and the wind . . . "

" . . . in the trees, yes."

"It must be him, then," the dwarf said, sitting back in his chair with a wide-eyed look of amazement.

Will swallowed hard, holding back tears.

"You said he was dying . . . ?"

"It looked that way to me, lad. He'd been badly burned, and he was feverish." The dwarf's eyes grew watery. "A terrible thing to see a fellow creature suffering so. And he was such a noble beast. He told me he was being hunted, and that I should get away from this place because those who were hunting him were close by. I asked him how he'd been burned, and he said he'd been struck by lightning, of all things."

Will stood up.

"Where did you say this was? North of here? How long ago?"

"Wait, lad, wait. There's more I have to tell you."

Will sat back down. He gripped the edge of the table to keep his hands from shaking.

"I told him I would go for help," the dwarf continued, "though I didn't know where help might be found in that wilderness. He asked me then how far it was to the Bourne, and I told him my guess was a week or more and that I was on my way there. I said I would stay with him, help him along on the way to the Bourne, but he insisted I leave him. He asked me to get to Fable as quickly as I could and find someone named Finn Madoc of the Errantry."

"I know Finn," Will said. "He was with us on my journey home. Shade must have been on his way to Fable. He was trying to get help."

"But then why wouldn't the wolf have asked me to find *you*?"

Will considered this for a moment.

"Because I wasn't here," he said at last. "Shade knew that. He knew I'd gone home to . . . where I come from. Mimling, I have to go to Appleyard and tell the Errantry what's happened. When you left Shade, was he . . . ?"

"He was alive, lad, barely. But that was nine days ago. Who knows what may have happened since?"

"He's still alive," Will said. "He has to be. Will you come with me to Appleyard, Mimling? You can tell them where you saw Shade. They'll know how to find the place."

"But I was lost, lad. I'm not sure where in the Realm I was. Not long after I left the wolf I came to the ford of the Wandering River, and that's when I got my bearings. So I can't say for certain . . . "

"But if you just come with me, you can tell them what you told me and—"

The dwarf made an apologetic grimace.

"As soon as I got here, I went to the Errantry myself, to find this Madoc fellow and bring him the news. But he wasn't there. And my leg was smarting from the climb to

Appleyard, so I came here to see if a sip or two might ease the pain, and now . . . "

"Will you wait here, Mimling?" Will said. "I'll go to Appleyard and bring someone back. Just don't go anywhere, please."

The dwarf snorted.

"No fear of that, lad. I'm well-rooted now."

Will raced back up the winding streets, his thoughts whirling. Shade was badly hurt. He might be dying, if he wasn't already dead. Will pushed away that thought. Shade was more than an ordinary wolf. He had been a friend of the Stewards long ago: they had brought him back from death and given him great strength and long life. If their power was still in him then maybe he could survive even this. *Burned by lightning.*

Lightning. Suddenly Will heard his mother's voice in his head, telling him one of her stories about the boy hero, Lightfoot. *There was the time he stood up to Captain Stormcloud and his Lightning Warriors . . .*

Will shook his head. That was just a story his mother had made up. It couldn't have anything to do with what had happened to Shade. He had only thought of that bedtime story because of the old books he'd found before leaving home.

Will quickened his pace, thinking now that he would seek out Balor. The wildman had said he would help him if he ever needed it. As he hurried up the street, rain began to fall, and the cobbles became slippery. Will fell once on the steep street, picked himself up and ran on. As he approached the gates of Appleyard, he saw a rider ahead of him, in a stained travel cloak with the hood up against the drizzle. Probably someone returning from a scouting patrol outside the city. On an impulse Will ran up to the rider, who had climbed from his mount and was handing the reins to a groom.

"Excuse me," Will said to the cloaked rider. "I need to speak to someone in the Errantry. It's very important."

The rider turned and drew back his hood. It was Finn Madoc.

Late that night the Deep Dark Forest reached the top of the rise. A towering wall of trees loomed over Molly's Arm, but there it stopped, just on the far side of the shaft of golden light. The young men who had been assigned to keep watch during the day after Pendrake's departure reported back every quarter hour at the Mermaid, which had become a makeshift headquarters for all the planning and preparations under way in the village.

A few of the villagers had already packed up their carts and wagons and left town, not wanting to stay around to see if the loremaster's barrier would hold. Most of the others were doing as Pendrake had advised: gathering their possessions and their livestock ready for sudden flight. A stubborn few, like old Seamus Gudgeon, were loudly determined to stay no matter what.

Kate, the innkeeper, had decided she was staying, too. She had run the Mermaid for years now by herself, ever since her dear husband George had departed for the farthest shore. She had helmed the inn through good times and bad. This was her home, her ark on the stormy sea of life, and besides, travellers coming to Fable from far countries would still need a warm mug and a berth. She would stay until the last moment, and even beyond, she thought. The Deep would have to scuttle and capsize her inn first.

It was very late, and her fellow planners had all left, as had her last few customers, the most loyal or the most in need of fortification before they set off on the road out of the village. Her servant Jib had gone home to help his old and ailing mother pack her bags. Kate was alone.

The door opened and someone came in.

"We're closing up," Kate said from behind the bar where she was putting away the mugs and glasses. There was no reply.

She turned and eyed the stranger suspiciously. He was wearing a floppy hat that shaded his face, a weather-stained cloak and gloves that looked too long for him, so that the fingers drooped like a scarecrow's. She was all too familiar with shifty characters who stole clothes off people's washing lines and skulked about, pretending to be decent folk so they could get a hand in the money drawer when you weren't looking.

The stranger's face was pale, almost bone-white. His skin was creased and somehow *stretched*-looking, as if he hadn't grown inside it like everyone else but had been wrapped in it. His eyes, thin black slits, bothered her the most and she wasn't sure why, until she realized that he never blinked. He stood at the doorway, making no move to take a seat.

"I said we're closing up. By which I mean the taps are shut off and the mugs put away." She paused, and shivered. "And there are no beds left," she added. This wasn't true—the rooms were all empty, but she knew at that moment she didn't want this . . . *person* under the same roof with her for longer than it took her to send him on his way.

"Looking for someone," said the stranger, in an oddly *buzzing* voice, as if he were mouthing the words through a piece of wax paper. "Looking for Rowen of Blue Hill . . ."

"I don't know anyone by that name," Kate said, slowly reaching a hand below the counter where she kept the stout oak stick handy in case of trouble.

"She was here," said the stranger, without a trace of doubt in his voice.

"Well if she was, she's not here now. So why don't you move along."

The stranger stared at her a long moment, and Kate had the distressing feeling that she was being studied as if she might be something good to eat. Then the stranger turned without a word and left. The moment he was gone, Kate hurried over from the bar and did something she hadn't done since she and her dear George had first opened the Mermaid for business thirty years ago: she bolted the door.

8

Another of Will's companions on the journey was the young knight-apprentice, Finn Madoc, who soon proved his courage and resourcefulness. Many said of Finn that he followed the code of the Errantry with almost fanatic devotion because of the shadow in his past, the shadow of his brother Corr, who hated all that the Errantry stood for and had fled the Bourne with the foul stain of murder on his hands.

– Tales from the Golden Goose

"NORTH OF THE WANDERING RIVER?" Finn asked. "How far?"

They were sitting by the fire in the common room of the Golden Goose, which was even busier than it had been when Will left for Appleyard. The noisy crowd meant Mimling had had to repeat parts of his story to Finn several times.

"As I've already told you, I'm not sure how far. The land was . . . strange. And that was nine days ago now. Would've taken me even longer to get to Fable but I hitched a ride part of the way with a merchant caravan. The point is, by now the wolf . . ."

He broke off and darted a glance at Will from under his bushy brows.

"You say this was Horse Folk land?" Finn asked.

"I think so."

"They don't usually come this far south to hunt the wisent. That's strange."

Will was relieved that Finn was here, and glad to see him again. On their journey together he had come to admire the young man's calm, decisive character: he usually said very little, but when it was time to act, he did so without hesitation. Will hoped he himself might learn to be like the young knight-errant some day.

"Strange indeed," mused the dwarf. "Like everything else these days."

To Will's surprise Mimling chuckled, a sound like gravel being shaken in a bag. "It's curious, though, isn't it, when you think about it," he said. "I mean, you have to wonder if this was meant to be. The three of us here now . . . "

"What do you mean?" Finn asked.

"Well, I've been puzzling it over . . . " He sighed, as if the effort of puzzling had exhausted him. "Why did my lady Rowen advise me to go on this last quest, I wonder?"

"She thought it would be good for you," Will offered.

"I suppose she did," the dwarf said, nodding. "But this time, it wasn't about treasure or adventure. This time was different. I went all that way, and brought back nothing . . . nothing except words *you* needed to hear, young Master Lightfoot. I wonder now . . . maybe the purpose of it all . . . my purpose . . . was to bring you those words."

He shook his head.

"Too much thinking, Hammersong," he muttered to himself. "Not your strong point . . . "

His head drooped. Finn took the tankard that was just slipping out of the dwarf's fingers and set it on the table.

"I've been north of the ford," Finn said to Will. "I know that country. Only a four- or five-day ride from here on swift horses . . . "

"If I can find a knot-path, we can get there even faster," Will said.

To Will's surprise, Finn didn't say anything in response to this. He and Will stood and thanked Mimling, who suddenly sat up, looking alert and sober.

"When you see my lady Rowen again," he rumbled, "tell her that Mimling Hammersong will repay all that he owes to her."

"I will."

"Even though you haven't said so, I can tell you're worried about her, Will. You fear for her. And I'm guessing that whatever's threatening Rowen has something to do with everything else that's going wrong with the Realm."

Will nodded, surprised at how much the dwarf had understood.

"It's true," he said. "At least I think so. I need to find her."

"You will, I have no doubt of it. And when you do, you tell her, Master Will, that Mimling Hammersong will not forget, and that if there's a way he can help her, by the bones of the earth he will."

Will and Finn left the inn and set off for Appleyard. With Finn at his side, Will's spirits lifted and he felt a surge of hope that they would find Shade before it was too late. During their earlier journey together, Finn had seemed cold and aloof until Will got to know him better. He'd learned that Finn had once been a runaway, like him, and even a thief, living by his wits in the streets of Fable. When Finn was a boy, his older brother Corr had left Fable under a cloud. Will didn't know the whole story, but he knew that Corr had taken fifty men with him, to hunt down Nightbane raiders who had attacked the Bourne, but neither Corr nor any of his men had ever returned. Finn confided in Will that he probably would have ended up like his brother, angry and rebellious, if he hadn't met Pendrake. The loremaster had taken him in and shown him there was another path he might choose than the hopeless one he had started down. The Errantry had given Finn a new life. Other than his hope of finding Corr some day, nothing mattered to Finn more than fulfilling his oath as a knight-errant.

"How soon can we leave?" Will asked now.

Finn turned to him with a troubled look.

"Things have changed in the Realm, Will," he said. "For the worse. The wild lands outside the Bourne have become even more dangerous than they were the last time you were here. I can take a swift horse and with luck find Shade where Mimling left him."

"You mean you don't want me coming along."

Finn shook his head.

"I'm afraid not. I'll be travelling fast, through pathless country, and I know you haven't done much riding. It might be difficult for you to keep up. And what's more, whoever hurt Shade might still be out there hunting him. We don't know who that is or what they're capable of."

"But Finn, Shade may be dying. I can't just—"

"We have good healers in the Errantry, Will. I know one who'll come with me if I ask him. He can help Shade, if anyone can."

"But what if you can't find Shade? You might need me then."

"Will, you're not coming along and that's final," Finn said sharply, and Will stared at him, stung by the cold finality in his voice.

After a long silence, Finn spoke again, his voice softer.

"Will, if you hadn't gone to the Golden Goose we might never have found out what happened to Shade. You've already helped him. The best thing you can do now is stay here in Fable, in case Rowen returns. If I can bring Shade back, I will. I promise you."

"I hear you've been looking for me, Madoc," a deep voice boomed. Will and Finn whirled to see Balor Gruff lumbering towards them. With the news about Shade, and the return of Finn, Will had forgotten that he and the wildman had already planned to ride out on a search expedition tomorrow.

"Balor!" Finn exclaimed. "I've been searching for you for three days."

"You'd think someone my size would be hard to miss. Good thing our pathfinder came along when he did."

Will grinned in spite of himself.

"Did I hear the two of you talking about Shade?" Balor asked. "I hope you've had some news, Will?"

Quickly Will related Mimling's story to Balor. The wildman listened with a scowl of concentration.

"Well, that settles it," he said firmly when Will had finished. "We'll find your wolf-friend, I promise you. And anyhow, you might need a *real* tracker on this expedition, Madoc."

Finn nodded.

"I'd be happy to have you along, Balor," he said.

"Oh, and I'll be bringing my new apprentice," the wildman added.

"I didn't know you had one at the moment. Who is it?"

Balor grinned at Will. Finn looked puzzled, then he glanced from the wildman to Will and back again. His mouth dropped open a moment before he recovered himself and shook his head.

"No," he said. "No, Will hasn't had any of the proper . . . I won't allow this, Balor."

"It's not up to you, lad," Balor said darkly, folding his arms across his chest. "If it wasn't for Will, I'd probably still be blundering around in some blasted dust cloud. It seems to me that if the world has grown that treacherous, we'd be wise to have Will Lightfoot watching out for us."

"The Marshal will tell you the same thing," Finn said with a rare anger in his voice, "that your apprentice hasn't been trained."

"My apprentice has already made it through worse things than most trainees ever see. Caliburn knows that. And *you* know that, Finn, better than I do. You were there when it all happened."

Finn shook his head again. Then he sighed, and turned to Will.

"So be it. You can come with us for as long as I deem it safe, Will. But if I order you to return to Fable, you will do so with Balor. There will be no debate on that point. Are we understood?"

"Understood," Will said.

Finn turned to the wildman and raised his eyebrows.

"Very well," Balor grumbled.

"Good, then," Finn said. "We ride out at daybreak tomorrow. Will, you'd best stay here at Appleyard tonight so we can be off as quickly as possible tomorrow. Be ready at the dawn bell. We'll meet at the stables and find you a horse."

Will went to see Edweth, to tell her he was leaving. She fussed over him and all but ordered him to stay in Fable, but when she saw the determined look in his eyes, she gave in. She wouldn't let him out of the door, however, until she'd filled his pack with food for the journey, muttering that the Errantry kept its recruits disgracefully underfed.

Will returned at last to Appleyard and made his way to the dormitory to get some sleep, but he soon discovered that wouldn't be easy. Moments after he arrived in the long room in search of a bed the other apprentices were crowded around him, eager to speak with *the* Will Lightfoot, the famous pathfinder, and hear first hand about his adventures. Once the prefect had ordered them all to keep quiet, Will found sleep wouldn't come anyway. The thought of Shade kept him awake. He was still awake when the dawn bell rang.

Will hurried to the stables, his weariness forgotten now that they would finally be setting out. Balor met him on the way to tell him that the Marshal had refused permission for their expedition to leave.

"Why would he do that?" Will fumed.

"He won't let us go until he's questioned Mimling for himself," Balor explained. "He and Captain Thorne are restricting travel after what happened to me."

"But Mimling told me he'd be heading home this morning," Will said. "He could be miles from Fable by now. And the last time I was here, the Marshal didn't keep me from leaving."

"That's because Master Pendrake was pleading your case. This time the loremaster isn't here to speak up for you. And with Finn and I coming along, this is an Errantry matter now. So we will have to wait."

As it turned out, Mimling hadn't left Fable yet. The copious amounts of ale he'd drunk to ease his leg had necessitated a long sleep-in, and at noon the dwarf was just packing up his things when messengers from Appleyard found him at the Golden Goose. He was not happy about having to climb the hill and tell his story all over again, but in the end he consented. The Marshal kept him waiting hours, however, before he finally questioned Mimling and let him go on his way.

At last, late in the afternoon, the Marshal gave his consent for the search party to leave the following morning. When Finn brought the news, Will seethed with anger. It was a whole day wasted.

"It's as if Lord Caliburn doesn't want us going on this mission," he said.

"He doesn't want anyone leaving the city needlessly," Finn said. "For him, a knight's overriding duty is to protect Fable. That's what started all the trouble between him and Corr—"

He broke off suddenly, as if he'd said more than he meant to.

"Listen, Will," he said, "why don't you go to the stables and find a horse for the morning. The head groom's name is Arden. Tell her I sent you. She'll help you pick out a good, reliable mount."

Will wanted to ask Finn about his brother, but with a nod he silently agreed. He crossed the grounds to the stables, and after some searching and making inquiries, found Arden the head groom, a cheerful-looking older woman. She walked up and down the stalls with him, musing out loud about several of the horses. She seemed to have worked out straight away that Will was no rider.

"I wish I could give you Briar," she said. "She's a horse of the Hidden Folk, I'm told. I don't know about that, but she's a fine animal sure enough. Just brought to Fable today, from a very long journey, and I'd say she's earned a rest."

Will looked over the railing at the dappled grey and white horse calmly munching hay. She lifted her head a moment, giving Will no more than a passing glance, as if she, like Arden, had immediately sized up his riding experience.

"She's been on the road for months, and none the worse for it, by the look of things," Arden went on. "That doesn't surprise me, since it was the toymaker she was with. He cares for animals, you can tell. And they trust him."

"The toymaker?" Will said, his heart beginning to beat faster. "You mean Master Pendrake?"

"Of course. He and his granddaughter got home just a while ago. Why do you ask?"

He ran.

He made it to the corner of Pluvius Lane more quickly than he ever had before, but there he was forced to slow down, to catch his breath, but also because the street was busy with people going about their business. As he pushed through the crowd, ignoring the angry glances levelled at him, he caught sight of a red cloak on someone hurrying past him up the road to Appleyard. He stopped, and the person in the red cloak stopped too.

Rowen.

They pushed through the crowd towards each other. It *was* her, though he could scarcely believe it. She was beaming at the sight of him, calling his name, but he could barely hear her above the noise of the bustling street. She had grown taller, he saw right away, and something else had changed about her, though he couldn't say what it was. They met and for a moment he stood stunned at the sight of her, until she spoke.

"Will. You're here. You're really here."

They embraced. Will held her tightly. She was safe in his arms.

"I didn't know you'd come back—" he began.

"Edweth told me you were at Appleyard—" she said at the same time. They laughed and stepped apart.

"You first," Will said.

"Grandfather and I got home just now. Edweth said you'd arrived in Fable a few days ago. She said you were leaving to look for Shade. I was hoping you hadn't left yet."

"We leave in the morning."

Neither of them spoke for a long moment: they were still looking at each other as if not quite believing they were together again. For Will it had been less than a month since he'd seen her, but for Rowen, he remembered, a whole year had gone by. He saw the girl he'd known, in her eager smile and her bright, animated eyes, but he saw a young woman, too: she was taller, less wiry and more sure of herself in the way she moved. He felt suddenly as if she had left him behind.

He realized he was staring, and looked down.

At Rowen's feet was a cat. A cat with large yellow eyes that were fixed on him with an unsettling directness. It was as if this strange animal knew who he was.

"That's Riddle," Rowen said. "He used to live in the Forest of Eldark."

"Riddle," Will repeated, then he remembered where he had seen those odd eyes before.

"You mean, that's . . . ?"

"Yes. I'll explain later. Edweth told us about the warning the shadow gave you, that brought you back. She said that Shade . . ."

Will told her Mimling's story. When he came to the part about Shade being burned by lightning, Rowen put her hand over her mouth.

"Who would do such a thing?" she breathed, tears sliding down her face. "Find him, Will, please find him. We can't let him die out there somewhere, alone . . ."

"I'm going to find him," Will said.

Rowen wiped her eyes and tried to smile.

"I've missed you, Will," she said. "I hoped so much you would come back."

"I had to. I... had to make sure you were all right."

He knew what he really wanted to tell her, but he couldn't bring himself to speak the words. For all he knew, she thought of him only as a good friend. If he told her his true feelings he might drive her away and lose her friendship. He couldn't bear that thought.

"I'm fine," Rowen said. "Just tired. But happy to be back home."

Will wanted to believe her, but he could see in her eyes that everything was not well.

A short time later they were sitting in the ground-floor library at the toyshop, a cosy, book-lined room with comfortable chairs and a fireplace, and Will was telling the story of his return to Master Pendrake, who was listening eagerly to all he had to say. Edweth had come in and out several times already, beaming and fussing over them, asking them repeatedly if they wanted anything to eat and bringing Rowen blankets in case she was cold. Every time the housekeeper came in or went out she glanced suspiciously at Riddle. The cat sat on the hearth rug, stretched out like a sphinx and watching all of this intently with his eerie eyes.

Finn was with them, too: he had heard the news of the loremaster's return and had come from Appleyard not long after Will. There was much to talk about. The loremaster wanted to hear from Will about the shadow of things to come, and everything that had happened to him on his way back to Fable.

"The shadow must've been telling the truth," Will finished, "because of what's happened to Shade."

Pendrake's keen grey eyes became distant a moment.

"I've encountered these shadows of things to come," he

said. "It would be a very rare thing, if not impossible, for one of them to lie. In fact, I think they're incapable of it."

"Where do they come from?" Will asked.

"I've wondered that myself, but all I can tell you is that they simply turn up when they're needed. In any case, the warning did bring you here, and with luck you'll be able to help Shade. What's most unusual is that the shadow crossed over into your world, Will. The Untold. I've never heard of such a thing happening before."

"What do you think that means?" Will asked.

"I'm not sure, but clearly you're needed here, Will, in what's going to happen."

"And what is that?" Finn asked.

The loremaster's gaze fixed each of them in turn.

"It seems the shadow told Will that a friend is in danger, but the truth is, we all are," he finally said. "And we have been for a long time, as the Fair Folk have always known and as the Lady warned us. Only now the danger is much closer to home."

The loremaster had his own troubling story to tell, about the Deep Dark Forest drawing closer to Molly's Arm.

"And there's that strange dust that trapped Balor," Finn added when Pendrake had finished his tale. "No one in the Errantry has encountered such a thing before."

"No one who escaped to tell about it, at any rate," Pendrake said.

"What do you think it was?" Will asked.

"Do you remember the Bog of Mool?" Pendrake asked Will. "The fragment of story we stumbled into there?"

"Of course," Will said. "The storyshard. We kept repeating the same things over and over."

"And we almost didn't make it out, until we found the golem," Rowen added.

"Balor was trapped by something much like that, I suspect," Pendrake said. "An un-place, a hole in the fabric of the Realm where nothing happens, where one forgets oneself and falls into a slumber like death. The Night King's rise is changing the Realm, tearing rifts in the Weaving that holds it all together. The stronger Malabron grows, the more of these rifts and storyshards there will be."

"Can the rifts be sealed up again?" Finn asked. "Or is there a way to avoid them?"

Pendrake gazed into his teacup, then looked up at Finn.

"To both your questions I have no certain answer. I do know that the Realm *can* heal itself. It did so after the first war against Malabron, when the threads of the Weaving were torn asunder and many stories were broken and scattered. So maybe the rifts will repair themselves in time. But after the Great Unweaving, much of the Realm never returned to what it once was. Much was . . . warped beyond repair, or lost for ever. It may be the same now. As for avoiding the rifts, usually you don't realize you're inside one until it's too late, like the storyshard in the bog. The best one can do is to be watchful and alert at all times."

While the old man spoke, Will studied him. He was much the same as Will remembered him, keen-eyed and seemingly stern, but with a smile never far away. During the conversation he kept glancing at Rowen with a look of concern. Will knew about Rowen's link to the Stewards, though he didn't really understand what this meant for her. He guessed now that Pendrake's look had something to do with that, and he wondered fearfully what lay ahead for Rowen. Her eyes met his, and he knew she was thinking much the same thoughts.

"Tomorrow I will search for the rift that trapped Balor," Pendrake concluded. "I will try to seal it if I can. But mending a few holes in the Weaving won't be enough to stop the

Night King. We are likely to find more such dangers close to home, I'm afraid, unless the Tain Shee are victorious."

No one spoke after this, as if they were afraid to air the fear they all felt. Then Finn rose from his chair and excused himself, saying he still had preparations to make for the journey. Will thought that he should go with Finn, back to Appleyard, but he wasn't ready to leave Rowen just yet, so he said nothing. Then Finn glanced at him, and Will saw in the quick smile that crossed the young man's face that Finn understood.

Pendrake stood and embraced Finn.

"Go carefully, my son," the old man said to him. "And come back safely."

Finn thanked the loremaster, then with a reminder to Will to be ready at dawn, he took his leave. After he'd gone, Pendrake turned to Will.

"There is much to think about, and to do," he said. "I must speak with the Marshal yet this evening, before I finally get a long-awaited sleep in my own bed. But . . . there's something I should have told you a long time ago, Will. I've been thinking about when you first came to the Realm. You thought you were meant to be the hero of the story you had stumbled into, and you didn't want to be. You didn't think of yourself as a hero. And when you found out that you weren't the hero, that the story was really about Rowen, do you remember what happened then?"

Will shook his head, uncertain what the loremaster was getting at.

"The Angel took Rowen and you went after him, and helped Moth destroy him," the loremaster said. "If you hadn't been there, Rowen might not be here now. You acted as a hero would."

Will shook his head.

"I didn't think about what I was doing," he said. "I just did what I had to."

"Exactly. And I wanted to tell you how proud I am of you. No matter what happens, no matter what role each of us plays in the story we're all part of now, that will never change."

Will lowered his head, his heart too full to speak.

"Now, let's you and I get to Appleyard before it gets any later," Pendrake said, reaching for his staff.

"I'd like to go too, Grandfather," Rowen said.

The old man frowned.

"I'd prefer it if you stayed here, Rowen. The toyshop is really the safest place for you to be."

A spasm of anger crossed Rowen's face for the briefest moment.

"You keep telling me that," she said, "but you won't say why."

"I will explain everything when there's time for it," Pendrake said, then he sighed and tapped his staff once on the floor. "Very well, then. Get your cloak."

While the loremaster went to speak with Lord Caliburn in his chambers, Will and Rowen climbed the hill above the Gathering House. The path of flat stones wound up through the groves of apple trees to a bare summit, where a beacon tower stood. Along the rim of the hill, facing towards the city, lay the sunken, moss-covered remains of what might have been a wall or the ancient foundation of a building.

The lighted windows and streetlamps of the city glimmered below them in the dusk. Further away, a few scattered lights from farmhouses shone, like the lights of ships on a dark sea. Beyond was a dim immensity. Will knew he and Rowen were in the well-defended city of Fable, in the heart of the Bourne, but he felt as if they were standing on an exposed rock before the whole vast, unknown Realm.

"So I guess I've caught up with you in age," Rowen said.

Will nodded, though he was thinking that she had always seemed older than him, not in years but in other ways.

"And now you're a legend," she said with a smile. "The great—"

"Please don't say it," Will muttered, and they both laughed.

"It's so strange," Rowen said after a moment. "We've been apart for a year, but for both of us it was only a few days. Well, for you it was. For me it seemed that way."

"It was a long few days for me," Will said, and before he knew what he was doing he plunged on. "I couldn't stop thinking about you, about where you were and what might be happening to you."

He fell silent and looked away. Again he had not said everything he really wanted to. He would have to be someone else, someone with a gift for words, to do that. And what if he was just fooling himself that she thought of him as more than a friend? What if he told her how he really felt and she looked at him with pity, or even laughed at him? It was better this way, better that she didn't know. Then he wouldn't lose her.

"I thought about you, too," Rowen said, after a long silence. "I was hoping you'd be here when I came back to Fable. If I'm going to be a loremaster, there's something I have to do. Something I can only do here, and I'm . . . I don't know what's going to happen."

He listened, frowning with concentration while she told him what she had learned about the Weaving, and how she would have to go there, wherever *there* was, as part of her training to become a loremaster. Will nodded, but didn't say anything. He knew that she had her grandfather's gift, but what that meant was mostly a mystery to him. He only knew she was going on a journey, too, though he didn't understand where or how.

"Is this Weaving dangerous?" he finally asked.

"I don't really know. Grandfather talks about it as if it is. But he won't say much."

"Maybe you shouldn't go, then."

To his surprise she turned suddenly and walked away from him. After a few steps she stopped.

"As if I have a choice," she said bitterly. Then she sighed and turned to him again.

"On our journey home I had a frightening dream," she said. "That was probably about the same time you came to the Realm."

"What happened in the dream?"

"I was standing high up, in a place like this," she said, looking out at the city below them, "and Fable was burning. And there were these silent figures all around, like knights in armour, but their helmets had no eye-slits, no visors. They were just blank masks."

She hesitated, deciding she couldn't tell him how one of the knights or whatever they were had knelt before her. That had terrified her more than anything.

"One of them took off its mask and there was nothing inside," she went on. "I tried to run away but I couldn't, and then you were there with me. You said something to me."

"What did I say?"

"I don't remember."

"I know what I said to you."

Rowen stared at him.

"You do?"

"I told you it was just a dream and not to worry."

Rowen laughed, then grew serious again.

"I used to read Grandfather's books and look at his maps and wish I could be part of all those stories out there. Now I wish things could just go back to the way they were. Or I could go back to the way I was: not knowing anything about the Night King, or the Stewards, or any of it. I thought Fable wasn't really part of the world. I thought nothing would ever happen here."

Rowen sat on the low moss-covered wall at the brow of the hill and after a moment Will sat down beside her. Just being here with her, close to her, filled him with happiness and fear and the desire to protect her. He wanted so much to keep her safe, even from her own destiny as a loremaster, which he feared might take her further from him than he could ever follow. Here on this windswept hilltop all the darkness and threat of the Realm seemed to be gathering around them and his heart went cold with dread and hopelessness. How could someone like him protect her from a whole world?

Rowen shivered, as if his fear had passed to her. Then she stirred against him and slid her arm through his. Their hands met and their fingers entwined. Will felt his heart begin to beat again, as if her touch had brought him back to life. He knew then that she felt for him what he did for her, and all he wanted from this moment on was never to be parted from her.

"I don't want tomorrow to come," Rowen said.

"Neither do I."

He put his arm around her and drew her closer. He drank in her nearness, the scent of her hair. He would do anything for her. He would brave any danger.

"I don't want to lose you," he whispered. "Not after I just found you again."

She took a deep, shaking breath. He felt the fire that was her life, how fragile it was against the cold and dark that surrounded them.

"We shouldn't be saying goodbye already," she said. "Why does it have to be that way?"

Will couldn't answer. He looked into Rowen's eyes and leaned towards her. She closed her eyes and raised her face to his. Their lips touched.

There was a rustle of leaves close by, and Rowen suddenly pulled away.

"Riddle . . ." she said warningly, gazing into the dark bushes near the wall. Something stirred there. Then the strange cat appeared out of the leafy shadows and padded slowly towards them, his eyes gleaming eerily in the dark.

"Didn't think you could see us," the cat said, and Will started at the voice. Riddle hadn't spoken at all while they'd been at the toyshop.

"How long have you been here, Riddle?" Rowen asked.

The cat sat on his haunches and stared at them.

"We followed Rowen. Didn't want to stay at the toyshop. Don't like the small, loud one who cleans things all the time. She scowls at us."

"Give Edweth time. She'll come around."

"How did you get past the sentries at Appleyard Gate?" Will asked. "They don't let so much as a mouse through without permission."

"We . . . changed shape," Riddle murmured, looking away.

"Into what?" Rowen asked.

"Hrmm . . ."

"What shape did you take, Riddle?"

"The small, loud one," the cat said, and gave a soft harrumph that sounded exactly like Edweth when she was about to give someone a piece of her mind.

"You're not supposed to do that," Rowen exclaimed, rising from her seat on the wall. "You said you would stay a cat while we were here. If Edweth ever found out you were walking around pretending to be her . . ."

"It was a good game. Everyone smiled at Riddle. They didn't know."

"It's not a game."

"Don't tell the toymaker. Don't get Riddle into trouble."

"Then Riddle had better get back to the toyshop right now."

"Can't we stay here with you, Rowen? We like this place. Reminds us of our house in the forest."

"Well, that's nice for you, I suppose. Maybe you and I can come back here some other time. But now Will and I would like to be alone."

"But if you're here with each other, you won't be alone."

"Yes. That's just what I mean. Just the two of us, *alone*."

The cat's eyes lit up and his mouth curved into an eerie feline smile.

"A riddle," he breathed. "Wait. Let us think. Riddle will riddle out the answer."

"Well, go and do your riddling out at the toyshop, or I'll tell Grandfather what you've been up to."

Riddle stared at them for another moment, then turned abruptly and slipped away into the shadows. Rowen sat back down on the wall and sighed.

"Riddle's home was destroyed by the Angel," she said, "and now he says he's disappearing, a little at a time. We let him come with us, as long as he promised to stay in one shape. So far that hasn't worked out very well."

From below came the ringing of the curfew bell, calling knight-apprentices back to the Gathering House.

"It's time, isn't it?" Rowen said bleakly.

Will took her hand in both of his.

"Once you're done with the Weaving," he asked her, "will you be leaving Fable again?"

"Maybe," Rowen said. "I think it depends on what happens while I'm here."

They walked together down the path to the Gathering House. Pendrake stood near the front steps, silhouetted against the light from within.

Before they reached him, Will stopped.

"I don't think I should leave you," Will said, shaking his head slowly. "Maybe I should just let Finn and Balor go on their own, so I don't slow them down..."

Rowen moved closer to him.

"Will, you have to go. It's Shade."

Will nodded, his heart torn.

"I know," he said heavily.

"Don't worry about me," Rowen said. "I'll be all right."

She wouldn't look at him when she said it, and Will knew she was trying to hide her own fears from him. If only there was some way he could know that she was safe while he was gone... Then he thought of the mirror shard. He took it from beneath his shirt, slipped the chain off his neck, and held the shard out to her in his palm.

"I want you to have this," he said.

"The Lady gave you that," Rowen said, her eyes wide. "I can't take it from you."

"I thought I needed it to find my way to the Realm, but I didn't. It's supposed to protect the wearer from harm. That's what the Lord of the Shee said. Please, Rowen, just take it."

She shook her head.

"I won't," she said.

Will frowned. He wrapped the shard in the loose folds of his shirt, gripped it in his fingers, and pressed hard with both thumbs. It broke with a muffled snap.

"What have you done?" Rowen gasped.

Will stared at the two pieces of the shard that lay in his hands. His own shocked face stared back at him. It had actually broken. He hadn't really expected it to. With an uneasy feeling, as though he had just committed a crime, he held out the half of the shard that was still attached to the chain.

"Now there's some for both of us," he said.

Rowen looked pained, and even afraid, but she took the shard.

"Be careful, Will," she said, her voice trembling, then she threw her arms around him one more time. "Come back to me."

"I will come back. No matter what."

They held on to one another for a long time. Will could feel Rowen's heart beating close to his and for a moment he couldn't tell them apart. Then she pulled away from him, and ran to her grandfather. They waved one last time, then turned and walked towards the gates of Appleyard. Will watched them until they were out of sight, and even then he stood a long time on the path, unwilling to turn away.

"His name's Cutter," said Arden as she patted the small, dappled horse affectionately on the flank.

"Cutter?" Will asked nervously, not sure he liked the sound of that.

"Because he's sharp and quick like a knife," the groom explained. "When you're not riding him, keep him tied. He likes to run."

Will eyed the horse uneasily.

"You're sure I can't take Briar?" he asked.

Arden laughed.

"If you want to be in the saddle a few extra days, sure," she said.

Under Arden's watchful eye, Will saddled the horse, grateful that Cutter put up with his fumbling without any outward signs of annoyance other than an impatient snort.

At last he was ready, with his bedroll and pack slung behind the saddle. Nervously he led Cutter out of the stable, into the cold grey light of early morning, to where Finn and Balor stood waiting with their own horses. There was someone else with them, a dark-skinned man with close-cropped hair and spectacles. Will remembered that Finn had said he knew a healer who might be able to help Shade.

"Alazar," the man said, clasping Will's hand in a tight grip.

"Doctor Alazar here," Balor boomed, "in addition to being a Knight Hospitaller of the Errantry and former Royal Physician to Shakya, Lord of the Sunlands, is a scholar. Do you know what a scholar is, Master Lightfoot?"

Will shrugged. "It means he studies things—"

"Right," Balor interrupted. "He studies *things.* He collects rare plants, and looks at the stars, and draws pictures of birds and mushrooms in his journal. All of which makes me wonder what he's doing here with us *real* knights."

Balor said this so scornfully that Will expected an angry response from the doctor, but he only smiled.

"Remind me, now, Balor," he said quietly, "which expedition was it where you ate those berries I warned you not to eat? The berries that made you break out in itchy blue spots?"

Balor looked sheepish for a moment, then he laughed and clapped Alazar on the shoulder. Will was surprised the smaller man wasn't sent hurtling across the yard.

"'Zar is one of our best healers and bonesetters," the wildman said to Will. "He specializes in Storyfolk ailments. You know, princes turned into frogs, dancing shoes that won't come off, the unpleasant results of poorly thought-out wishes, that sort of thing."

"Have you treated animals?" Will asked, then regretted the question, which made it sound as if he doubted the doctor's skill.

"A few," Alazar said, tilting his head meaningfully at Balor.

"That's rich," the wildman muttered.

Finn had stood by, wrapped in his usual calm silence while this banter went on, then he presented Will with a short sword and scabbard from the armoury. Will buckled the weapon to his belt, and glanced expectantly at Finn. When he was here the first time, Finn had given him a knife that had been forged to protect against creatures no ordinary blade could harm. Finn saw Will's look and shook his head.

"Just an ordinary sword this time," he said. "The Marshal has tightened the restrictions around weaponry. Anything with special powers is to remain in Fable in case of need."

Will nodded, trying to hide his disappointment.

"Magic weapons," Balor snorted. "They only make a knight lazy. If you can't defend yourself with a good blade or your bare hands, you ought not to get into the fight in the first place."

"It's not like you always have a choice," Finn said.

When everything was ready, the four rode out of the gates of Appleyard, out of Fable, down the road to the crossroads, and from there turned north. Will took one long look back at the towers of Fable. He wondered how long it would be until he saw them again, or Rowen. Or if he ever would.

9

—I pray you, old man, the princess said, *tell me of this Other World and what I will find there.*

—My lady, the old man said, *I am forbidden to speak of its wonders. But still, I may show you where it lies, if you follow me of your own free will and promise to speak to no one of what you see there.*

—Tales from the Golden Goose

ROWEN SLEPT VERY LITTLE that night. She kept waking from uneasy dreams. Then she would think of Will, wondering if he was still awake, too.

Long before the sun rose she gave up on sleep and got dressed. Before going downstairs she took a long look around her room. Everything seemed so strange and so familiar to her at the same time. On the wall above her bed hung the tapestry her grandmother had woven, an image of Rowen's mother and father. It had been there ever since she could remember. Like the toy castle her grandfather had made for her when she was little, which stood in its corner, faithfully dusted by Edweth every day even though Rowen hadn't played with it in years. All of the painted little wooden figurines stood in a row on the castle ramparts: the king and queen, the jester, the handsome prince, the friendly dragon, and the red-haired princess, with her tiny tiara and glass slippers. Her grandfather used to act out stories for her with the figurines, until she was old enough to do it herself. Then she would spend hours alone, dreaming up long, involved adventures for the toys to have. Adventures that always ended happily for the little red-haired princess.

She turned away suddenly and went down to the kitchen. Edweth was already there, making her favourite breakfast, porridge with apple slices, as if she had known that Rowen would be getting up early this morning. But then Edweth almost always seemed to know what Rowen was going to do before she did it. Rowen sat and ate without talking, which was unusual for her. She was keenly aware that Edweth kept glancing at her as she bustled about the kitchen.

When she had finished her breakfast, Rowen sat for a while, still in silence. She barely noticed when Edweth began to braid her tangled hair.

"The girl doesn't know what a brush is," muttered the housekeeper, and Rowen couldn't help smiling. Edweth always braided her hair when she was worried about her.

"Edweth, you knew my grandmother," she finally said.

"I *know* her, if that's what you mean."

Rowen turned and looked at the housekeeper.

"Then you think she's not . . . ?"

"If there is any way in the world for her to get back to her beloved grandchild, she will find it," Edweth said, then she cleared her throat. "That's what I know about the matter."

Riddle slunk into the kitchen with a guilty look and nudged at the food Edweth had set out for him in a bowl. It looked as though he was either still afraid that Rowen was going to tell her grandfather what he had done the evening before, or he had already committed some other breach of his promise. Rowen suspected it was the latter, but she wasn't in the mood to question him about it. Instead she asked something that had been at the back of her mind for a long time.

"Did you always live in the forest, Riddle?"

"In the forest," the cat echoed. "Riddle lived in the forest. In our house in the forest, playing the riddle game."

"Yes, but before that . . . "

"Before that?"

"You know, I mean did you come from somewhere else before you lived in the forest?"

"Yes, we . . . I did that. Came from somewhere else."

"Where?"

"Somewhere else."

"Yes, I know, but where was this somewhere else?"

"Not here. Not there."

Rowen sighed and was searching for another way to approach the question when her grandfather appeared in the doorway. He had his staff, and was wearing his cloak for outdoors. It was stained with mud at the bottom and Rowen knew he had been out already today, probably long before the sun had come up. The grim look on his face made Rowen's stomach churn.

"I found the rift that trapped Balor," he said. "Or what was left of it. The tear in the weave was nearly gone. I don't know how that could have happened. Usually once a rift forms it only grows larger, unless . . ." He stroked his beard.

"Unless what?" Rowen asked.

"Unless someone else was there before me and mended the rift."

"Who else could have done that?"

"No one that I know. There must be another explanation. But anyway, the rift is no longer a danger to anyone."

"That's good, isn't it?" Rowen said eagerly, frightened by the grim weariness in her grandfather's voice.

"When I came back to the city, there was a message waiting from Lord Caliburn," he said. "Another knight-errant has gone missing. Gared Bamble."

"I've met him," Rowen said. "Could he be lost like Balor was, in another of those rifts?"

"Gared was last seen on sentry duty, on the city wall. He was in Fable, not on patrol outside the city like Balor."

"He disappeared *in Fable*?" Edweth said incredulously. Pendrake nodded.

"What could have happened?" Rowen asked.

"I don't really know," Pendrake said. "I doubt that it could be a rift. Not in Fable. It hasn't come to that yet, and let us hope it never will. But . . . there may be enemies in the city."

"Servants of Malabron?"

"Quite possibly. Which means it's all the more urgent we carry on with what we have to do today."

Rowen swallowed hard.

"Aren't you going to eat something, Grandfather?" she asked, then she was angry with herself for such an obvious attempt at stalling.

"Later," he said.

She glanced at Edweth, who gave her what was clearly meant as an encouraging smile, though it only made her heart sink lower. She rose from the table and followed her grandfather out of the kitchen. He handed Rowen her cloak and she put it on, but to her surprise he didn't go to the door of the shop. Instead he led her to the stairs, and she followed. They climbed slowly to the top floor of the house and stopped in front of a narrow door that was made of rough, unvarnished wood. An insignificant-looking door you would probably not look at twice.

Of course, Rowen thought. *The raincabinet. I should have guessed.*

She gazed at the rough-hewn door, deeply set into the stone wall. She had grown up in this house and had always wondered about the faint, occasional noises of rain and thunder that came from behind this door. She'd opened the door herself when she was very young and had found what you'd expect on the other side of such a door: an ordinary broom cupboard containing only a broom, a mop and a wooden pail, with a puddle of water on the stone floor. But she had known even then that there was something more here than met the eye. Then Will Lightfoot had come to the toyshop and opened the door, and there was no broom cupboard here then—only rain and darkness. Rowen had always meant to ask her grandfather about that, but at the time there had been too many other matters to worry about.

"So the Weaving is in here?" she asked.

"The Weaving is everywhere, but this is a doorway into it," Pendrake said. "The only one that I know of. Loremasters have kept it hidden for generations."

"From Malabron."

Pendrake nodded.

"Then why don't you keep it locked?"

"If you put a lock on a door," Pendrake said, "the curious will assume there's something inside you don't want them to find. Better to have them believe there's nothing worth finding. No one gets excited about mops and brooms. Well, no one other than Edweth."

Rowen smiled in spite of her fears.

"Our little land is more important than anyone imagines," the loremaster went on. "More important than I've ever let anyone know, even you. Fable has always been considered a crossroads, a place where Storyfolk from everywhere in the Realm come to share their tales. But it is a crossroads in a far deeper sense. When you heard a story did you ever wonder what comes after 'the end,' or before 'once upon a time'? That's where Fable is. It lies just on the edge of every tale, the place one passes through to get to where the story happens. And yet at the same time Fable is the heart of all Story, because of what lies behind this door."

"Would Malabron destroy Fable if he knew about the raincabinet?"

"Better to say he would use the raincabinet to destroy. Through the ages he has been so bent on conquering storylands themselves that he's ignored the Bourne as unimportant, an out-of-the-way place with no story of its own. Then he became aware of your thread in the weave, so unlike any other, and he sent the Angel and the fetches to find you. He knows now what part of the Realm you come from and he will not have given up searching for you, of that I'm certain. I fear he may already suspect that this out-of-the-way little place holds a great secret. If he were to discover that here in Fable is a doorway to all of the Weaving, we would be in the gravest danger. If Malabron found this doorway, if he made it his own, with a moment's thought he could unweave the entire Realm. He could make his story the only one, an Un-story of despair and darkness without end."

Rowen took a deep breath. She turned to the raincabinet.

"Then maybe we should just keep it closed," she said.

"We cannot do that, Rowen. You must open this door now. If you're going to stand any chance against the Night King, you need to see where the power to do that comes from."

She nodded bleakly, without any real hope or belief in what he had said, then she reached for the handle and tugged it. After a moment when she thought it wouldn't give, the door swung open easily. A gust of cold, damp air struck her face. Inside, rain was falling, the wind-whipped droplets flickering in the light from the corridor.

Pendrake raised his hand.

"Behold," he said, with a teasing smile Rowen hadn't seen in far too long. She would have laughed if she'd been able to, but she was too uneasy, and now too curious as well. She leaned forward, rising on the tips of her toes, trying to see into the darkness of the cabinet without actually stepping inside.

"How can this be here?" she asked in a whisper. "What happened to the broom cupboard?"

"What you see depends a lot on what you expect to see."

"But where does this room lead to?"

"Nowhere," Pendrake said. "Some houses have mice or termites in the walls. This house has rain."

"I don't understand. You mean it's raining . . . *inside the walls*?"

Pendrake nodded.

"The loremasters of old built the house that way. When you walk outside in a real rain, things far away become blurry and hard to see. It's like that with this rain. Anyone searching for us through the threads of Story will find only a tale of rain here, if they don't look too closely. It's like a curtain, or a veil."

"The rain keeps us hidden," Rowen exclaimed, suddenly understanding. "So the Night King doesn't find us."

"That's it. We loremasters have kept this rain falling and this portal into the Weaving concealed through many generations. We've hidden ourselves here, too, whenever the Night King's servants hunted us. And that's why I've tried to keep you close to the toyshop all these years. I thought that only here would you be safe from harm."

There was such regret in his voice that Rowen felt tears start in her eyes. She swallowed hard, then looked again into the raincabinet.

"I still don't understand, Grandfather," she said. "What *is* the Weaving?"

Pendrake was about to answer, then he smiled and shook his head.

"Don't you ever get tired of an old man's talk?" he asked. "I know I do. It's better you see for yourself."

He tipped his staff towards the doorway. "Go on."

Rowen looked at him.

"Aren't you . . . ?" she faltered.

"I'll be right beside you."

"Where are we going?" said a voice from behind them. The cat was sitting placidly in the middle of the corridor as if he had always been there.

"Riddle, what are you doing here?" Rowen hissed, secretly pleased at the interruption. The cat peered into the raincabinet, sniffed, then looked up at Rowen.

"It's raining in there," he said.

"Yes it is."

"Riddle likes rain," the cat said, his ears perking up. "We're coming with Rowen."

"I'm afraid not, Riddle," the loremaster said. "Where we're going is not a good place for you to be."

"Why not?"

"It's difficult to explain. It would be frightening for you in there. Things are always becoming . . . other things."

The cat's eyes brightened.

"Just like Riddle."

Pendrake's bushy brows knitted. He gazed curiously at the cat.

"Yes, just like Riddle," he said slowly. Rowen studied him. She knew that look: her grandfather had had a sudden new idea, and as usual, she didn't know what it was.

"Then can Riddle come with you?" the cat asked eagerly.

Pendrake stroked his beard thoughtfully, as if he was considering it. Then he shook his head.

"Listen to me, Riddle," he said softly. "You promised that if we let you come home with us you would do as we asked. And I'm asking you to stay here. You can keep watch outside the door."

"Watch for what?"

"Just stay here, by the door. Please."

The cat gazed at Pendrake a moment with its eerie eyes, and Rowen shivered in spite of herself. There was a power in him, she thought now, that he himself wasn't truly aware of. Why did this creature listen to them at all when he didn't have to? But then the cat looked away and commenced licking his paws, as if coming with them was the last thing on his mind. He was very good at being a cat, Rowen thought. Maybe that's what he was really meant to be.

"Right, then," Pendrake said, and cleared his throat. "Let's get on with this."

Rowen turned back to the raincabinet. There was a quick, dim flicker of light from somewhere within, like lightning seen through thick clouds. Rowen pulled her hood up, lowered her head, and stepped quickly through the doorway.

She was standing in a sunny green meadow under a bright blue sky.

The air was warm and filled with birdsong. Near her a stream rushed, burbling through tall grass. Rowen pulled back her hood and squinted in the bright light. On a distant hilltop three, no, four white horses were calmly grazing.

She turned to her grandfather, her eyes wide with wonder. To her surprise he wasn't behind her but seated on a large stone a short distance away, watching her.

"Grandfather?" she said, hurrying towards him.

"Yes, it's me, Rowen. I'm here. We're both here."

"Where is here?"

"This is the Weaving."

She turned quickly. There was no doorway to be seen.

"Where's the way out?" she asked with a pang of dread. She heard the fear in her voice and tried to calm herself. "What happened to the rain?"

"The doorway is closer than you think."

"But I can't see it. How do we find the way back?"

"We *tell* our way back. But not yet."

"So this . . . *this* is the Weaving?"

"There is far more to it, believe me. I wove this lovely quiet meadow around us so that your first moments here wouldn't be too strange. It won't last long, though. Nothing in the Weaving ever does. But for a little while we can stay, as you get used to the way things are here."

"Good," she said dizzily, and sat down on the stone beside him.

As she gazed around she noticed something odd about the world. Whatever she looked at—the horses, the grass, the trees and the puffy white clouds in the sky—stood out sharp and clear, but as soon as she looked away from something it became blurred, shimmering, the way a stone pavement seen from a distance seemed to ripple like water on a hot day. When she wasn't looking directly at them, things seemed to be flowing into other things, like different colours of paint running together. Nearby was an immense, gnarled oak that looked as though it had stood rooted in this one spot for hundreds of years. But as its huge trunk and vast leafy canopy passed from her gaze, she saw it waver and melt into a shimmer of *maybe*, as if it might choose to become some other tree, or a stone, or anything else. Then she looked straight at the tree again and it was *there*, ancient and undeniable. It was a little like walking underwater.

On a sudden impulse she stood up and stamped her foot. The earth under her shoes seemed solid enough, though it, too, wavered doubtfully at the edges of her sight.

This would take some getting used to.

She looked again for the horses on the hill. They were not there any more, but in the sky above the hilltop four feathery white clouds that were somewhat horse-shaped drifted slowly across the blue.

"Everything here looks . . . unsure of itself," she said.

"What are *you* sure of right now?"

"Not very much."

"Then the Weaving is unsure, too. It's like the world of dreams, remember. A dream may seem to just *happen*, but the truth is you're shaping it, too, with your thoughts and feelings. The Weaving responds to our presence. Just the fact that we're here is changing what we see."

"What is everything here made of?"

"What are stories made of? Dreams, memories, fantasies. There is great power in this storystuff, but you must be very careful how you use it. A true loremaster only draws from the Weaving for good reasons, never to cause harm or dominate others. If you try too hard to grasp *innumith* and bend it to your will, it erupts into werefire, the devouring flame of madness that destroys those who try to control it."

"Werefire . . . That's what happened to Freya's city."

"Yes. The mages of Skald let loose a force they couldn't understand or subdue."

"You said the Weaving contains the threads of everyone's story. Does that mean we could find out where Shade is, by finding his thread?"

"In the Weaving one can see that all the threads of story are connected to one another. But it's not easy to find and follow one single thread among the many. I searched for Shade's last night, after everyone left."

"You did? And... you found him?"

"I was able to trace some of his journey. He is somewhere north of the Bourne, as Mimling said, but beyond that, I could not see clearly. There is much disturbance in the Realm where Shade is. Stories clashing with each other. I searched as long as I could but eventually I had to give up. One can only go so far into the Weaving before there's a danger of becoming lost and not finding the way back. This morning, after I got the Marshal's message, I searched the Weaving for clues as to what might have become of Gared Bamble. He never left Fable, I'm sure of that much, but..."

Pendrake's brow furrowed.

"What did you see, Grandfather?"

"When you find the thread of someone's story in the Weaving, it's not the person himself, it's more like the trace he's left in the weave of things. Like the print of feet in wet sand. You can see where someone has been, or where he's going. But Gared's thread... it's as if someone or something else is walking in his footprints. Covering them up."

"What does that mean?"

"I wish I knew, but I doubt that it's anything good."

Rowen bowed her head for a moment, then looked up.

"Will I be able to follow these threads like you?"

"In time. Today there's something else you need to see."

He bent down and plucked a flower from the grass. A small flower with white petals that he held up before her.

"Here," he said. "Take it."

She took the flower. As soon as she held the thin, fragile stem between her fingers, to her shock she felt the same humming, vibrant *aliveness* she'd felt when she held Riddle in her arms. Everything here was like that, she understood as it pulsed through her, too.

"Grandfather," she said quickly. "I think Riddle must have come from here. From the Weaving."

Pendrake nodded.

"I've suspected that for some time."

"We should bring him here. He might be able to remember who he is."

"We will, when the time is right. I kept him away because I didn't know what he was likely to do. It might be too much for him. Too sudden. I wanted you to see the Weaving first without any distractions. Now, breathe on the flower."

"Grandfather?"

"Breathe on it."

She raised the flower to her mouth and blew a gentle breath over it. To her surprise the flower began to break up and scatter into tiny grains of light, like shining dandelion seeds. Rowen held out her hand to catch the grains of light as they slowly fell. They gathered in her palm and shimmered there.

"What's happening?" Rowen whispered.

"This is the deep truth of the Weaving, in your hand. All stories flow into one another. Things change into other things. The Weaving is nothing but that change. Who knows what else this flower might become? A teacup, an apple . . ."

She gave a little gasp. In her palm was a glass slipper.

"Did *you* make it do that?" she asked.

"I think you did, actually. You and the Weaving together."

"But I wasn't thinking about glass slippers. Why did the flower turn into this and not something else?"

He gave her a strange, almost sad look.

"There are some very ancient, very powerful stories in the Weaving," he said. "They're like strong currents in a river that can pull you under. You'll have to be watchful."

He tapped his staff on the earth.

"I must go now, Rowen," he said.

"Grandfather?"

"To really come to know your gifts, you must find your own path out of the Weaving. All loremasters have gone through this trial. I did myself, when I was your age, and I had to do it alone, as you will. I cannot help you now, because what you must learn in the Weaving is not some magical power, it is the power that comes from knowing who you really are. And only you can discover that."

"You're . . . leaving me here?"

"I won't be far away. Trust me. And trust yourself."

"What's going to happen when you're gone?"

"This meadow will disappear, but what will take its place I cannot say for certain. But if you keep your wits, and *remember*, you will find the way back."

"Remember? Remember what?"

"Who you are. Everything here is like a dream, but you can always wake up from a dream. You always have that choice. And I already know that you will be a far greater loremaster than I ever was. We will see each other again soon."

He seemed about to say more, then he paused and peered up into the blue.

"What is it?" Rowen asked. She followed his gaze, and stifled a gasp.

The sky was falling.

The bright blue dome was cracking, breaking away in large and small fragments, like bits of eggshell, which whirled and fell through the darkening air. And behind the blue was the starless black of night. The earth beneath her began to tremble and when she looked down she saw small round stones rising everywhere among the grass, like goose bumps on skin.

"What's happening to ..." she began, but when she looked again at where he had been, her grandfather was gone.

A shadow fell over the bright meadow, like an eclipse of the sun. Rowen felt the air chill, as if she had just stepped into cold water. Everywhere bits of blue sky were plummeting to the earth, and as they neared it their colour faded to a dark grey and they thickened, taking on solidity and depth. They were becoming slabs of stone, and as they reached the earth they began to pile up on one another, making walls that rose higher and higher. Then the walls grew windows and doors, and streetlamps sprang up one after another beside these sudden buildings like swiftly growing ferns. Rowen looked down and saw that the meadow had been paved over with cobblestones.

She was alone on a deserted street, with the glass slipper in her hand. From somewhere far off a bell began to toll. And then she was running, though she didn't know why, or from what.

10

. . . the wind always knows where it is going . . .

– The Kantar

WILL AND HIS COMPANIONS rode hard that first day, north from Fable along the high road that wound up through wooded hills. They passed through several villages, but Finn only let them stop once briefly, for a quick noonday meal and to water the horses. Cutter was a steady and reliable mount, as Arden the groom had said, and during the ride Will lost any illusions he might have entertained about who was really in charge. He had quickly given up trying to control the horse's movements and had merely hung on while Cutter followed Finn's horse. As long as they found Shade in time, it didn't matter to him how poor a figure he cut in the saddle.

At dusk on the second day of their ride they reached the citadel of Annen Bawn, the Errantry outpost on the northern border of the Bourne. The rocky valley they had been riding through for the last hour narrowed suddenly, and sheer cliffs rose on either side. A narrow, stony stream rushed through the middle of the valley, beside the road. Up ahead, Will saw what at first he took to be a natural arch of stone that crossed from one side of the valley to the other. As they approached, he saw that the arch was in fact a constructed thing, made of huge blocks of hewn stone. This was Annen Bawn itself, he realized. He could see lights in windows and on high ramparts. Below, on the level of the road, a wall ran from one base of the arch to the other, leaving a gateway that the road went through. A portcullis hung above, that could be lowered to seal off the gateway when needed. There were winches and stacked timbers on either side, which suggested to Will that the wall and the portcullis were new additions to the citadel's defences and had probably just been finished.

As they approached Annen Bawn a horn blew somewhere above them, and a cloaked sentry stepped out of the roadside shadows with a lantern and ordered them to halt. Finn handed him the letter of commission from Lord Caliburn. The sentry, an older man with a scarred face, took it and read it by the light of his lantern. When he was finished, he looked up at Finn. His eyes seemed to have gone cold.

"Your party may stay the night," he said without expression. "We have fodder and stabling for your horses."

"That won't be required," Finn said stiffly. "We'll be riding further tonight."

The sentry nodded and stepped aside to let them pass. As eager as he was to find Shade, Will's heart sank. They wouldn't be stopping at the citadel. He was bone-weary and sore, and wondered how much longer he'd be able to stay in the saddle before he toppled over from exhaustion. But Finn said nothing to him or the others. He just spurred his horse and rode on ahead.

As they followed him, Will glanced at Balor with a questioning look.

"It's about his brother, Corr," the wildman said in a low voice. He glanced at Finn, who hadn't slowed his pace and was now some distance ahead of them. Then he sighed and turned to Will.

"I don't know how much you've heard about Corr Madoc."

"Not much. Just what Finn told me."

"Even as a boy, Corr was strong, and skilled at fighting. It seemed he would be accepted into the Errantry as a matter of course, but it didn't happen. He went to Appleyard to try out as an apprentice, but a few days later he was sent home. It turned out he'd nearly killed another boy on the practice grounds. Then, when he was old enough, he formed his own band of mounted fighters, and trained them himself, to protect the outlying farms and villages from Nightbane raids. He claimed the Errantry only cared about protecting Fable. He called himself the protector of the rest of the Bourne."

"His band did some good, that has to be admitted," the doctor added, "but before long they were waylaying Errantry patrols and taking their weapons and horses. After that he was little better than an outlaw in the Bourne."

"True," Balor said, "but none of the country folk would turn him in, because he brought them food and other supplies when they were needy. Then came the worst Nightbane raid of them all. The enemy attacked in such numbers, and so suddenly, that the Errantry was surprised and overwhelmed. And Corr's band was too small to be everywhere they were needed."

"Was that the raid where Rowen's mother and father were killed?" Will asked.

"Yes, and many others, too. Mostly farmers in the

borderlands, which Corr saw as proof that he was right: that the Errantry thought only of Fable. So he gathered his band with the intent of pursuing the raiders and hunting them down. A number of knights-errant who also wanted vengeance joined him. When Corr and his men rode out of the Bourne, they stopped here at Annen Bawn. They didn't have enough horses to carry themselves and all the gear they needed for a long journey. So they broke into the pasture where the citadel's horses were grazing, and made off with a few. There was a young man keeping watch on the herd that day. A knight-apprentice not much older than you. He rode after Corr, to stop him from taking the horses, and Corr struck him down."

Will stared in shock.

"The young man died the next day. His name was Donal Caliburn."

"The Marshal's son . . ." Will said, in a shocked whisper.

Balor nodded.

"His only son. It's hard to say if Corr even knew who he was. When Finn joined the Errantry years later, the Marshal made him swear an oath that if Finn ever found his brother, he would bring him back to Fable to face judgement. Still, I don't think Caliburn has ever fully trusted Finn. He's always made things difficult for him. And so has Captain Thorne, for that matter. Lord Caliburn's son was his apprentice."

"And that sentry just now . . . ?"

"Captain Thorne was garrison commander here when Corr killed the boy. They've never forgiven or forgotten at Annen Bawn."

Balor was about to say more, when Finn called to them.

"We'll camp there," he said, pointing to a stand of tall pines not far off the road. They nudged their horses and followed him.

* * *

They soon had a fire going and sat around it eating their—to Will—meagre dinner. The horses were tethered nearby, where there was a stream and lush grass for them to feed on. Will tucked into his dinner eagerly, remembering how hungry he had always felt on his first journey through the Realm. There had never seemed to be quite enough to eat then, and he assumed it would be the same now. The Errantry travelled light, carrying only what was absolutely necessary, and that included food.

When he had all too quickly finished his meal, Will noticed that no one was speaking, not even Balor. The incident at Annen Bawn had apparently dampened everyone's spirits. The doctor was writing in his journal and the wildman was picking his teeth with a sliver of wood. Will shivered and realized how cold it had become since night had fallen.

"Get some rest," Finn said. Will glanced at him. The young knight-errant had barely said a word since they made camp and Will had avoided speaking to him.

"We'll stay until the fire dies down," Finn said quietly. "Then the moon should be well up and we'll move on."

Will nodded. He laid out his bedroll and used his pack as a pillow. He lay down and closed his eyes, but his head was too full of thoughts for sleep. Shade was out here somewhere in this seemingly endless land, and Rowen was now far from him, too.

Turning on to his side, he took his half of the mirror shard out of his pocket. Why had he broken it? What if he'd destroyed whatever power it might have? Then it wouldn't do him or Rowen any good at all.

He held the shard tightly in his hand and closed his eyes. Although he had doubted that he would get any sleep, he was startled to find himself, what seemed only moments later, being nudged awake by Doctor Alazar. A hazy half-moon glowed through clouds in the dark sky.

"Rise and shine, Will," the doctor said, in a kindly tone. "Such is life in the Errantry."

Will sat up groggily. He realized now he'd been more tired by the previous day's ride than he'd admitted to himself. He'd fallen asleep deeply enough to have a dream, a strange dream in which he had been trying to catch up with someone who was walking ahead of him on a dark plain under the stars. He thought it was Rowen, but when he got closer the figure ahead of him turned, as if to wait for him, and he saw it was a man he didn't recognize, an older man with long, braided grey hair. The man's eyes were milky-white, unseeing. In the dream Will had been about to catch up with the man when the doctor woke him.

He remembered how the Angel had appeared in his dreams, coming closer to him each time he'd dreamed of him. And it had turned out that these were more than just strange dreams: the Angel had been searching for him through Will's own dreams, in order to find Rowen. But if this blind man was someone like that, not just a figment of his mind but someone walking in his dreams, Will wondered why he felt no sense of fear or danger.

He packed away his bedroll and looked around blearily. The fire was down to smouldering embers. Finn and Balor were not there.

"Balor finally convinced Finn to ride back to Annen Bawn, for news of the road ahead," the doctor said, noticing Will's wondering look. He handed Will a mug of steaming tea, which he took gladly. "They should be back soon. In the meantime, if it's not a bother, I wanted to ask you about something that happened the last time you came to the Realm. On your journey home, you passed through the

Bog of Mool, I understand, and met a strange being there..."

Will nodded.

"It's hard to explain," he began. "We stumbled into a storyshard, a fragment of story that made us repeat the same things, over and over, until we realized what was happening to us. Something like what happened to Balor. We might have been stuck there for ever, then Shade found a golem, a man made of clay, trapped in the shard with us."

"A golem," the doctor echoed, his eyes gleaming with wonder behind his spectacles. "I've never encountered one of those."

"The golem was building this tower of stones that was sinking into the swamp. He could never finish it. Master Pendrake thought that if we stopped the golem from carrying out his task, it might free us all from his endless story. So he prised this... thing out of the golem's forehead, a sort of wax disc, I think. It was what made the golem come to life. There was a word on the disc that was the golem's name, Ord. That didn't work, though—the golem just stopped dead, and we started slowing down, as though we were going to stop moving for ever, too."

The doctor had taken out his leather-bound journal and was writing in it with the stub of a pencil.

"Go on, please," he said.

"So then Finn put the stone from his brother Corr's ring into the hole in the golem's forehead, and it—he—took off, walking north. We followed him for a while, though we couldn't keep up in the bog, and he disappeared. But we were free of the storyshard."

The doctor nodded, his eyes wide.

"So Finn thought that the stone from his ring had given the golem a new task?"

"To find the owner of the ring," Will said. "So now Finn

believes that means Corr must still be alive, and probably somewhere in the north."

"That's why he has been asking for scouting missions in that direction. I wondered about that. But as far as I know, he's heard nothing new about Corr. There are said to be strange things happening in the far north these days, though. Like great storms that bring lightning and thunder but no rain."

The doctor bent over his journal and went on writing.

"Lightning," Will said under his breath.

The doctor looked up.

"What's that?"

Will didn't answer. He was remembering what Mimling had said about how Shade was injured. Lightning. He'd been burned by lightning thrown by someone or something from the sky. And again he remembered his mother's stories of Lightfoot and his battle with the furious and cruel Captain Stormcloud.

The Lightning Warriors swooped down in their flying ships, hurtling great stabbing bolts of white fire at him. Lightfoot ran and dodged and ducked, but finally one of the bolts struck him . . .

He was considering whether to tell Alazar what he was thinking when Finn and Balor returned.

"Did they have any news?" the doctor asked as they climbed from their horses.

"Not much we haven't already heard in Fable," Finn replied. "Vague reports of trouble in the north. Storms. Folk fleeing Nightbane armed with weapons of *gaal*."

Will remembered hearing that word before. *Gaal* was a poisonous metal. Fever iron, some called it, deadly to the Fair Folk and with the power to drive anyone else who touched it into fury and madness. Moth the Shee warrior had a sword of *gaal* he'd carried with him. It was the only weapon that could destroy his enemy, the Angel, but it had also been slowly killing him.

"Well, if we're only going a short way north of the Wandering River, none of that will concern us," Balor said.

"Not for the moment," Alazar said.

The night sky began to pale with approaching dawn not long after they set off. That morning's ride took them out of the Bourne and into the wilder country beyond. They followed the high road through rolling woodlands until, at the top of a windy rise, it forked into two narrower paths running east and west. To the west, not far away, stood a slender, many-turreted white castle on a hill, with the steeples and roofs of a city clustered at its foot. Further west rose the towers of another castle on a hill, surrounded by another city below it. Looking east, Will saw two, no, three more distant castles on hills.

"The Little Kingdoms," Balor said, with what sounded like affection in his voice.

"We'll head straight across country from here," Finn said. "It may slow us down to leave the road, but it's better to avoid the Kingdoms."

"That makes sense," Balor said, but to Will he sounded disappointed.

"Are they dangerous?" Will asked the wildman, as they left the road and descended the north side of the hill.

"The Little Kingdoms?" Balor said. "Not really. It's just that you can't visit them without *something* happening. It's where we send knight-apprentices on their first solitary quests. They're guaranteed to have some kind of adventure, and it usually turns out all right. It's a law or something, I think. There's always supposed to be a happily-ever-after in the Little Kingdoms, and if there isn't you can apparently lodge a complaint somewhere. Anyhow, if we'd had more time for your training, I would've sent you off to one of them." He pointed to one of the nearer castles, with blue and silver pennants fluttering from its towers. "Probably that one. It has the stupidest ogres, but the prettiest damsels in distress."

Once they had left the road, the country grew hillier and more dense with trees and underbrush. For a while Finn took them beside a stream, until it lost itself in wet marshy ground, then he led the way up a rocky hillside and out into more open, drier ground, where they let the horses run at full speed. Will hung on, terrified, as Cutter raced across the hard turf, his hooves thundering, but soon he relaxed and began to enjoy the speed and the wind in his face.

After a few miles the horses slowed and went along at an easier pace. They passed through woods again, then crossed a shallow stream, where they rested briefly and watered the horses. On the other side of the stream Finn led them in another all-out gallop. So went the ride, at faster and slower paces, through the morning and into the afternoon. A chill wind came up and the sky clouded over ominously, as if a rainstorm might be on the way, but they rode on. From time to time, Balor whistled melodies and sang verses from old ballads. His singing was more of an off-key bellowing and he kept forgetting the words, but the others couldn't help being cheered by his high spirits.

"This is where a knight-errant belongs," he said to Will. "Out here in the big wide world, with no idea what you're going to meet over the next hill."

As if to prove his point, Balor spurred his horse up the slope of the grassy hill they were climbing, and Will did the same with Cutter. *Shade would love this,* Will thought. In a few moments they had crested the hill and reined in their horses.

Below them lay a long, deep hollow ringed by wooded

ridges. The hollow was filled, or *choked,* Will thought, with a thick tangle of reeds and bracken. Bare black trunks of dead trees stuck out here and there like withered arms.

"This wasn't here before," Finn said, rising in his saddle to gaze down into the hollow.

"You're right," the doctor said. "There was a lake here, teeming with fish, and a village at the far end, with a watermill. A place called Edgewater."

"I came this way only weeks ago, and stopped at their inn for ale," Balor said. "What could have happened?"

"There were tall grasses and marsh reeds at one end of the lake, I remember," the doctor said. "But things couldn't have become this overgrown so quickly . . ."

"It must be what the loremaster warned us of," Finn said. "The land here is changing, like the forest near Molly's Arm. I was going to take us through the hollow, but I think we should go around, along the eastern ridge. I don't like the look of this place at all. Better if we avoid it all together."

"No," Will said, and they all turned to look at him. "No, we need to ride through the hollow."

"Will?" Finn asked.

"It's a knot-path," Will said, and he was certain of it as he spoke the words. The grassy hollow was a shortcut to another, faraway part of the Realm, like those he had stumbled across on his first journey.

"I've heard rumour of such things," Balor said in a sceptical tone. "Never been through one."

"I have," Finn said. "Will, are you sure this path will take us closer to Shade?"

Will closed his eyes and breathed deeply. It was almost as if he could see the sun blazing in a vault of cloudless blue sky, and hear the wind moving across miles and miles of tall, waving grasses.

. . . and Lightfoot rode north on his pony Great Heart, and they crossed the silent empty prairie and came at last to the Hill of the Teeth . . .

His mother's story again. More of it had come back to him now. Will remembered how her words had conjured so vividly for him that great sea of grass bowing and waving in the wind, the vast bowl of the sky dotted with white clouds, and in the distance, a row of sharp-pointed hills like fangs . . .

He opened his eyes. The gloomy, weed-choked hollow lay before him, under a cloudy sky. But he was sure of what he had sensed, as if that vast sunlit land was somehow inside him. Somewhere beyond this hollow he would find Shade.

"The great plain," he said. "This path will take us there in a short time."

Balor shrugged and eyed the hollow darkly.

"If there's anything left of the lake under all that green, then the ground is probably boggy and treacherous," he said. "We could waste hours floundering around in there."

Finn appeared to be weighing Balor's words. Then he turned to Will again.

"We'll go through the hollow," he said. "Will, you'll lead us."

Will nodded. He nudged Cutter's flank sharply with his heel.

"Come on," he said to the horse. "We're going down there."

Cutter tossed his head a moment, as if objecting like Balor, but then he began slowly to descend. Finn and the others followed. In a few moments they had reached the bottom of the hill and were wading into the reeds, which came up to their horses' shoulders.

Cutter whinnied, though whether from fear or annoyance Will couldn't tell. He stared forward into the wall of reeds, shielding his eyes from the sharp stalks that slid across his legs. There was no trail, as far as he could see. They had to force their way through, and the thick reeds bent before them unwillingly, as if trying to keep them out, then sprang up again once they'd passed. The ground was boggy, as Balor had predicted, and squelched under the horses' hooves. The further they penetrated into the hollow, the taller the reeds grew, until they rose well over their horses' heads and not even Balor could see the ridges on either side of the hollow any more.

Near him was a tangle of reeds that had twined and twisted around each other, and in their clutches was a wooden chair. The stalks had grown through the spindles that formed the back and had wrapped themselves around its legs. It looked as if the reeds had caught the chair in a living green cage.

"Odd," Balor said.

They kept on, and a short distance ahead they came across a barrel tangled in reeds much like the chair had been. There were stalks growing through the barrel's loose slats, as if it was slowly being taken apart. And near the barrel they also found the reed-snarled remains of a small boat.

"If this is what's left of Edgewater," Balor said, "what happened to the people?"

"We can only hope they escaped," Finn said. "Strange that there was no word of this at Annen Bawn, though."

Balor gave Will a dubious glance.

"Maybe they didn't escape," he said.

Will lowered his head and urged Cutter forward.

Now they pressed on as quickly as they could, but the further they went, the more thick and tangled the reeds became. Finally they were forced to dismount and lead the horses while hacking through the stalks with their swords.

It was hard work, and often they had to stop to catch their breath. Despite his weariness, Will pushed on, hacking with one arm and leading Cutter by the reins with the other. He hadn't been wrong about this place being a knot-path, he was still sure of that, despite Balor's doubts. And he was not going to let anything, especially not a lot of tall grass, keep him from reaching Shade.

He cut and slashed with the sword and shouldered his way forward until the sweat was running into his eyes and blinding him. He shook his head angrily and kept on, and finally he felt the reeds thinning out, resisting him less. He paused to wipe his eyes and then, to his excitement, he glimpsed the flicker of bright daylight. He was almost there. Cutter realized it too. The horse gave a whinny and plunged forward. Now he was the one tugging Will along.

"That's it," Will encouraged him. "You can get us out of here faster than I can."

He turned his head to call back to the others about what he'd found. To his shock, there was nothing behind him but a wall of reeds. His companions had vanished.

"Finn!" he shouted. "Balor!"

"Will!" came Balor's reply, but his voice sounded distant. Will wondered how he could possibly have gone so far ahead of the others so quickly.

"Will," Balor shouted again. "Don't turn back. Keep going!"

There was a desperate warning in his voice that filled Will with dread. Something had happened. But Cutter was tugging at the reins, pulling him to the end of the path.

Will dropped the reins.

"Go," he said to the horse. Cutter tossed his head and lunged away towards the light.

Will turned and struggled back the way he had come. He

shouted his friends' names, heard their voices calling him from what seemed like even further away, warning him to stay away. He pushed on, back along the slashed trail he had made, surprised to see that it was almost gone already, as if the cut stalks had healed themselves or new ones had grown in their place. Very soon all traces of the trail ended and he was surrounded again by a high wall of reeds. He raised his sword to cut a way through, but he was exhausted now, his arm burning and weak, and his blade seemed almost to glance off the thickly massed stalks.

"Finn!" he shouted. "I can't get through!"

There was no reply. Will went still and listened. He heard only the hiss of the wind in the reeds.

11

Fox wanted all of that cool, sparkling clear water for himself, he didn't want to share any of it with anyone. And so he drank and drank until the spring was dry.

—Tales from the Golden Goose

THE BELL IN THE PALACE clock tower was tolling midnight. She ran in her ragged dress through the streets of the sleeping town, her bare feet cold on the stones. In her hand she clutched a glass slipper. Every so often she would stop to catch her breath and glance back furtively at the palace on the hill, its many windows still brightly lit despite the late hour. Even from here, faint sounds of music and revelry were carried to her on the still night air. How she longed to go back there, to step into that bright, happy world again. But she had been warned. The brief, wonderful dream she'd been granted would suddenly vanish on the stroke of midnight. It wasn't meant to last.

"Nothing here lasts very long," she said to herself, then wondered why she had said it.

Someone had spoken those words to her, not long

ago, though she couldn't remember who or why.

As the last ringing tones of the final stroke of midnight died away, she held up her hand. There was no glass slipper in her palm any more, only a worn and dirty cloth shoe. She wondered if the same thing had happened to the other slipper, the one that had come off as she'd fled down the steps of the palace in her hurry to escape.

"A glass slipper," she said, gazing at the shoe and remembering that someone had spoken to her about this, too. "A teacup. An apple . . ."

The shoe was still a shoe. Why did she think it should be something else . . . ?

She took one last long look at the palace on the hill, then ran on. When she reached her house, she slipped in through the servants' entrance at the side just as her stepmother's carriage was pulling into the curving front driveway. She ran up to her garret room, tied on her apron and tucked the cloth shoe into its pocket. Before rushing out of the door she paused to smooth her tangled hair in front of the mirror.

Her reflection looked back at her with a puzzled expression, like the face of a stranger seen through a window.

"What is your name?" she asked the face she saw in the mirror, and a cold wave of dread rolled through her. Something was very wrong. But there was no time. No time.

She hurried down to the kitchen to make tea, knowing it would be called for when the others got home.

A few moments later, as she knew it would, the front parlour bell rang furiously. She carried the silver and fine china tea things on a gilded tray to her stepmother and her two stepsisters. They were lounging on the gilt-embroidered sofas, talking about the beautiful, mysterious young woman who had danced with the prince all evening and had suddenly run off into the night without a word.

The girl set the tray down, trying to keep her hands from shaking. As usual her stepmother and stepsisters barely noticed her. She filled their cups with tea. The stepsisters were miserable about the evening, which was supposed to have been their great opportunity to be noticed by the prince, to have him fall in love with them in their expensive gowns and jewels. But he had danced with no one else after the mysterious, masked young woman appeared. And when she vanished he was inconsolable.

"They say he found one of her glass slippers," the older stepsister said.

"I heard he's planning to search the whole kingdom until he finds her," the younger stepsister said, pouting.

"Yes," their mother said, taking a sip of her tea. "He will. Which means he will come here to our house sooner or later."

The sugar spoon clattered against the teacups. The girl scrambled to retrieve it.

"You clumsy idiot!" the younger stepsister snapped at her. "Watch what you're doing!"

She lowered her head and stepped back.

The stepmother paid no notice to what had happened. She was stroking her chin with a far-off look.

"What are you thinking, Mother?" the older stepsister asked.

The stepmother smiled her icy, loveless smile.

"When the prince comes here, searching for the foot that fits that glass slipper, we will make certain that he doesn't leave without finding a bride."

"Really?" the younger sister squealed, clapping her hands. "It should be me, Mamma."

"But what if the slipper doesn't fit either of us?" the older stepsister asked.

"We will find a way," the stepmother mused. "There's

always a way. After all, the young woman could be anyone."

The stepmother turned then, slowly, and looked hard at the girl. It was as if she was seeing her stepdaughter for the first time. The look on her face changed slowly from suspicion to dawning understanding, and at last to cold hatred.

"Anyone," her stepmother repeated. "Don't you think so, daughter?"

The stepsisters gaped in amazement. Their mother hardly ever addressed a word to the girl, let alone called her *daughter.*

"Why are you asking *her*, Mamma?" the younger stepsister said. "She doesn't know anything."

"I'm curious to hear what she thinks about all of this," the stepmother said. "I really am. I wonder if she has any thoughts on who this mysterious girl might be. Well, do you? *Speak.*"

The girl looked at the three of them sitting before her. The incredulous, sour faces of her stepsisters. The pitiless gleam in her stepmother's eyes. But she didn't know these faces. She didn't know this house. It was supposed to be her father's house. He had died and left her with this woman and her daughters. That's what she'd told herself. That's what *they* believed. But none of it was true. This was not her life.

This was not her story.

"Do you . . ." she said. "Do you know who I am?"

They stared blankly at her, then the sisters burst into harsh laughter.

"She doesn't even know her name, Mamma," the younger sister exclaimed. "Oh, this is too much. Just when I thought she couldn't get any stupider."

"No, you don't know me," the girl said, and turned away from the three of them. She gazed around the room. There was somewhere else she was supposed to be. There was *someone* else she was supposed to be. Not this. This wasn't real.

Remember.

She reached into the pocket of her apron, took out the dirty cloth shoe.

"What is that?" the younger stepsister demanded.

The shoe became a flower.

The stepsisters gasped.

An apple.

Fear flickered in the stepmother's eyes.

A glass slipper.

The girl remembered. She knew where she was. *Everything here is like a dream.* All she had to do was wake up.

"Look, Mamma," the younger stepsister shrieked. "She has the . . . "

"How dare you?" the older stepsister said, rising from her chair. "How dare you keep this from us? Bring me that slipper this instant."

The slipper had shrunk to a tiny grain of light. Her hand closed around it and she took a deep breath. *There are some very old, very powerful stories . . .* It was time for her to leave this one.

"Where is it?" the older stepsister demanded, her face flushed crimson with rage. "What have you done with it?"

"Send her to her room, Mamma," the younger stepsister cried. "Don't let her out. Never let her out, ever again."

The stepmother had risen slowly from her seat. She was gazing at the one she had thought to be her stepdaughter, and she opened her mouth to speak when there came a loud knock at the front door.

The younger stepsister gave a shriek and covered her mouth.

"Who could that be at this hour?" the older stepsister asked, then her face went white. "Do you think . . . already . . . ?"

"Yes," the stepmother said, glancing out of the window. "My daughters, it's the prince's coach and four." She turned to the girl with a look of hatred, then pointed to the stairs. "Go to your room. Stay there until I call for you. Do *not* come downstairs, do you hear me?"

But it had always been the stepdaughter's task to answer the door. And for now, until she found her way out, she would finish what had been started. So she went towards the door.

"Wait," her stepmother cried. "What are you doing?" But it was too late. She had already turned the handle and swung the door wide.

It was raining. There was nothing to see but the slashing rain, falling in darkness.

She stepped into the rain with her hands outstretched.

"Where are you going?" a fading voice shouted behind her. "How dare you? You can't leave!"

The voice died away. She saw a light ahead, flickering through the rain. There. That was the way out. She began to walk faster. The light grew, took on the shape of a doorway.

She broke into a run. She had found the way back. She knew her name.

On the other side of the doorway, Rowen pitched forward, sobbing, into her grandfather's arms.

"I forgot everything," Rowen said. "I forgot all of you."

She was sitting up in her bed and Pendrake was seated beside her with his hand on hers. Edweth was nearby, folding clothes and casting a stern look at the loremaster that he was choosing to ignore. Riddle sat perched on the end of the bed, silent and watchful.

She gripped the edge of the blanket. This was real. This was where she belonged.

"The same thing happened to me the first time I entered the Weaving," Pendrake said. "I was lost and frightened, everything was changing, and then I stumbled into a story. A familiar story that kept me from being afraid, for a while."

"It was so real," Rowen said, remembering the glittering chandeliers in the palace, the music, the prince's warm eyes and kind smile. The story had been hurrying to its happy ending, and she had been glad to go along with it. Ever after.

She had even forgotten Will.

"I could've stayed there . . ." she whispered in horror. Then she was angry at herself, and ashamed, as if she had betrayed them all, Grandfather, Edweth, Will. Her eyes burned. She was glad Will wasn't here now to see this, but at the same time she felt a fierce longing for him. She vowed she would never tell him what had happened to her today.

"You did very well," her grandfather said softly. "You found your way back much more quickly than I did during my first time in the Weaving. As I knew you would. Otherwise I could never have let you go. What you've learned today about the power of the Weaving you will need in order to stand against the Night King, should it come to that. His story is even stronger than the one you fell into just now. It will be much harder to resist, to remember who you are."

Rowen wiped her eyes. A new thought occurred to her. She hesitated to ask about it, but couldn't help herself.

"Did Grandmother get lost like that?" she asked, then was sorry for the question when she saw the look of pain that crossed her grandfather's face.

"I don't believe that's what happened," Pendrake said after a moment. "She had travelled through the Weaving many times. She knew its dangers and secrets far better than anyone. Your grandmother is the most powerful loremaster I know."

Rowen stared at him in surprise.

"It's true," he said. "That's the only reason I was able to let her go."

"Why can't we find her in there?"

"So far, where you and I have walked in the Weaving is only the shallows. There are depths far beyond the shifting, dreamlike regions you have seen. That's where she went, to search for the ancient lore of the Stewards."

"But we *could* find her, by following her thread, couldn't we? Just like you did Shade's."

"I have tried many times over the years, Rowen, believe me. Sometimes I felt I was close. But I knew that if I kept on, if I went any deeper, I might never return, and then you would have been left alone, with no one to teach you what you needed to learn. I couldn't let that happen."

His hand gripped hers.

"I understand," she said, and then an idea came to her, one she would keep to herself for now. But he was studying her with fear in his eyes and she knew he had guessed what she was thinking.

"You mustn't rush this," he said at last. "There is still much for you to learn."

"But I—"

"Promise me, Rowen. Promise me you won't go back into the Weaving without me. We will find her, some day, but we will do it together."

Rowen looked away. She had been lost in a story but she had found her way out again. By herself. She knew in time she could master the Weaving, learn to wield the fathomless fire and make it serve her. And when she was able to seek those deeper places he'd spoken of, she could find her grandmother and bring her home.

But if she was wrong, if she went alone in search of her

grandmother and didn't return, her grandfather would have lost everyone. His wife, his daughter, and her. He would be alone. She couldn't do that to him, just as he hadn't been able to leave her. She would have to wait until she was ready. Until she had learned enough.

She took a deep breath, and turned to her grandfather.

"I promise," she said.

Her grandfather nodded.

"Get some rest," he said, patting her knee as he rose from the side of the bed. "We'll go again soon. One step at a time."

"Excuse me, but *again*?" Edweth blurted out. "Do you think it's a good idea for Rowen to go back to this Weaving place at all, Master Nicholas? I know I don't understand these things, but from what you're saying it sounds to me like she was nearly lost in there for ever, and I don't . . ." The housekeeper broke off, her eyes welling with tears. "I don't want that to happen to *her* too."

"She may be lost *here* if she doesn't learn what she needs to know," Pendrake replied in a cold voice. The housekeeper pursed her lips, and went back to her work in a bristling silence that Rowen could feel from across the room.

Although Edweth insisted Rowen stay where she was for the rest of that day, she relented in the afternoon, and let her get out of bed and get dressed. Rowen was eager to revisit the Weaving, but her grandfather had gone to Appleyard for a meeting of the Council.

She paced, and looked into books, and talked with Edweth. She hadn't seen any of her friends since she'd returned home, except Will. For a while she stood looking out of her bedroom window, from which she could just glimpse the edge of the wall of Appleyard. She understood now why her grandfather had kept her close to the toyshop all these years, but it still felt a little like being a prisoner. She thought of Will, somewhere out in the wild lands beyond the Bourne with Finn, Balor and the doctor. Even the dangers they might be facing seemed preferable to being cooped up here, unable to do anything to help. She was safe here, supposedly, but if no one else was, it wasn't right.

Then she thought of the mirror shard on the chain around her neck.

She drew out the shard and held it so that she could see her reflection. Will had the other half, though she remembered that both pieces were only fragments of a much larger mirror, one that the Fair Folk had used, her grandfather had told her, to see what was happening in distant parts of the Realm. Did these broken pieces still have that power? Or was it a power that the one gazing into the mirror must have?

Her reflection looked back at her with no answers. She slipped the mirror shard back beneath her shirt.

She drifted through the house, wrapped in her thoughts, and eventually found herself in front of the raincabinet. When she realized where she was she stopped, went still, and listened. The faint, hollow sound of rain came from behind the door.

The storystuff was everywhere, Grandfather had said. Just waiting to be drawn out of things . . .

She held out her hand in front of her, palm upwards, and took a deep breath. Could she make something appear out of thin air, she wondered, or did she need something already *here*? What had her grandfather told her? Start with what is . . . and nudge it a little, with what might be.

"What is Rowen doing?"

Rowen jumped. Riddle stood behind her. He'd come up so quietly she hadn't heard a sound. "Nothing," she snapped, then sighed and leaned against the raincabinet door.

"Is Rowen going to visit the rain again?"

"Not today."

"Riddle wonders what you found in there."

"I thought you might. It's very strange, Riddle. Like Grandfather said, it's a place where things are always becoming other things."

"Yes, like Riddle."

"True. And the next time we go, Grandfather says you're coming with us. We think maybe—"

She didn't finish because the cat's ears twitched and every part of him seemed to become tense and alert.

"Someone's here," he said.

"Where?"

"With the toymaker. Someone's come to see him."

Rowen listened and heard the muffled sound of voices from downstairs. She hurried down to the main floor with Riddle at her heels, and found her grandfather in the library, the room they always used when they had guests. He was sitting near the fireplace but he was not alone. Another man sat in the chair opposite his. A man younger than her grandfather, though his long dark hair was greying at the temples. He had a flat, sallow face and thin lips that were curved in a slight smile. The long burgundy coat he wore looked well-made and expensive.

"Rowen," her grandfather said. "This is Ammon Brax, a mage from Kyning Rore."

The mage rose and bowed to Rowen.

"A pleasure to make your acquaintance, young lady," the mage said.

Rowen nodded but made no reply. She was on her guard, having sensed from the moment she entered the room that all was not well. Her grandfather's polite, forced smile was more proof of that.

"Did your grandfather tell you that I was once his pupil?" Brax asked, resuming his seat by the fire.

"He didn't," Rowen said. She had heard of Kyning Rore. It was a famous school for mages on an island in the Eastern Sea, an island of white stone carved in the shape of a great spiralling seashell. Her grandfather had taught there for a time, many years ago, but when he spoke of the place, which was rarely, it was always with a hint of disapproval.

"Master Pendrake was kind enough to share some of his wisdom with eager young scholars like me," Brax said to Rowen. "He taught me much. I can only hope I've put what I learned to good use."

"You've certainly been busy, Ammon," Pendrake said. "I've heard your name here and there over the years, even in an out-of-the-way place like the Bourne. Head of the Council of Mages already, at your age. That is quite something."

Brax inclined his head at the compliment. His thin-lipped smile widened slightly.

"One of the dangers of this strange profession of ours," he said. "But being in demand does take one far and wide, and that's how I was finally able to track down my old master. I have to say, though, I never thought to find you . . . here."

"I was hardly your master, Ammon," Pendrake said with a frown. "And I'd like to think that back then I wasn't so old, either."

Brax laughed.

"And back then how desperately I wished I wasn't so young," the mage said. "But really, I have to wonder what keeps you in Fable, Master Nicholas. It's a quiet haven in a troubled world, to be sure. I can understand the attraction of that, believe me. But you, you're the great Nicholas Pendrake, and *this*, well . . . Fable is so far from where things are happening that truly matter. The places where mages and masters of lore are desperately needed in these dark times. Do you remember old Professor Wodden?"

"A good man," Pendrake said with a nod.

"Remember what he used to say about magecraft? 'In your hands lies the power to shake the thrones of the mighty.'"

"I remember. He also used to warn his students not to get too cosy around the thrones of the mighty."

"But neither should one hide one's gifts under a rock."

When Pendrake didn't reply the mage turned to Rowen.

"I hope he's been passing his wisdom on to you at least, my dear."

Rowen glanced at her grandfather. She sensed now that this man was fishing for something and she needed to be careful how she answered.

"I'm not really interested in that stuff," she said with a shrug. "I want to be a knight of the Errantry." She was trying to sound indifferent and even a little dull, and the condescending smile the mage gave her seemed to suggest it had worked.

"An admirable goal," Brax said to her, but his gaze had already slid away as if she was no longer worth considering. "This peaceful little land should remain peaceful, and for that it will need defenders. I'm sure you're making your grandfather very proud."

There was no hint of scorn in his tone, but Rowen knew both she and the Errantry were being looked down upon. She decided she did not like this Ammon Brax, and hoped he would leave soon.

Riddle had come into the room after Rowen and was crouching at her feet. The mage noticed the cat now, and his eyes gleamed with interest.

"An unusual-looking animal," he said. "Where in the Realm did you find it?"

"If you want to know what keeps me in Fable, here she is," Pendrake broke in suddenly, gesturing to Rowen. "I have looked after my granddaughter since her parents died. This is our home."

The mage lowered his head.

"I am truly sorry for your loss," he said. "And for my rudeness. Forgive me."

"There is nothing to forgive. But tell me now, Ammon, what has brought you here to our out-of-the-way part of the world?"

"Trouble, I'm afraid. I don't know how much you've heard of what's happening out there in the great kingdoms of the Realm, but there is much turmoil and fear. Nightbane have been gathering and raiding in places they've never been seen before. Storyfolk are arming themselves for war, or leaving their homes and farms and taking to the roads with all their possessions piled on carts. Embassies from some of the afflicted lands have come to Kyning Rore over the last year, demanding advice and help from the Council. I thought it best to see for myself rather than depend on rumours and tales, so I've been travelling. Visiting towns and villages, speaking with folk, learning what I can. I'm on my way back to the Rore now, and I wasn't even planning to stop in Fable, but then I heard that the elusive Nicholas Pendrake was living here. It has been a long time, master."

"It has, Ammon, and I appreciate your taking the time from such urgent matters to visit me. You must be eager to return home."

The mage rose from his chair.

"I do have a long journey ahead," he said, bowing slightly. "But I have decided to stay in Fable a few more days. Your Marshal wishes to consult me, as does the Guild of Enigmatists. Such is the price of fame. So I hope I may visit again, if it isn't a bother?"

Pendrake stood, and Rowen did likewise.

"Not at all," her grandfather said with a strained smile. "You are most welcome."

When the mage had been seen to the door, Pendrake returned to the library with Rowen close behind. She could see that he was troubled, and she had her own unfavourable impression of the mage, but she waited for her grandfather to speak.

He stirred the fire with a poker.

"Ammon Brax," he muttered to himself. "This is not the best time."

"Was he really your student?" Rowen asked.

"He wished to be. He was determined, I'll say that for him, and very clever. I almost considered taking him on as an apprentice. Almost. He had studied hard, it's true, and had already learned a great deal when I first met him, but I soon realized the only thing he really cared about was Ammon Brax. He was too consumed by dreams of fame and power. I suppose he finally got what he was after."

"I think he was after something today," Rowen said, and her grandfather glanced up at her and grinned.

"Your answer to him was just right, Rowen. You sounded so uninterested in what we were talking about you almost had me fooled."

"What do you think he wants?"

"I'm not sure he himself knows. But it's clear he's not convinced that I've settled in Fable only for the quiet life. Of course he suspects there's more here than meets the eye, that Fable is somehow deeply involved in what's happening in the wider world. He wouldn't be a mage if he didn't have a nose for such things. So now I imagine he's planning to stay as long as he can and see what he can uncover. But Rowen, he mustn't find out anything."

"Does he know about the Weaving?"

"He knows it exists. Like all mages he can draw the fire from it, to make what credulous folk call magic. He can dazzle crowds, and sway kings and rulers with a show of spellcraft. But he doesn't truly know the Weaving. Few mages do, because they derive their power from prising things apart. They pluck out a piece of the world and think they've understood all of it. That is why they so often do harm, even when they believe they're doing good. As yet I think Brax doesn't suspect just how important Fable really is, and we must keep it that way. That kind of knowledge in the hands of someone like him would be disastrous. For now I'm afraid we had better stay out of the raincabinet."

12

...food and fire are needful
to one who comes from the mountains
with winter at his heels...

– The Kantar

THE NEXT MORNING THE LOREMASTER was called again to Appleyard. Left to herself, Rowen sought out Riddle, who had disappeared from her room the previous day and had been making himself hard to find, for some reason. She found him at last, as she guessed she would, sitting at the door of the raincabinet. The cat turned and looked at her as she approached.

"Today?" he asked.

"It doesn't look like it."

They left the raincabinet and without really thinking, Rowen wandered into her grandfather's workshop. She had been in here many times, but to Riddle it was all new. He padded around the room, peering at the odd things in glass bottles and the various skeletons and stuffed creatures. At one point Rowen caught him taking the shape of a crow, like the stuffed bird of the same kind on one of the shelves. This reminded her of Morrigan and the Tain Shee. Rowen wondered where they were now. Had the Fair Folk already gone into battle with the Night King? Had they defeated him? And if they had, or hadn't, how would she and her grandfather find out?

Just then Rowen heard a high-pitched humming and turned to one of the open windows, where a messenger wisp suddenly appeared. The tiny, pulsing star of white light sped into the room and hovered above Riddle's head, emitting crackling sounds, like a lit sparkler. The cat swiped at it with a claw, but the wisp darted away and stopped in front of Rowen, bobbing as if with excitement.

"What is it?" she asked. This wasn't Sputter, their own wisp, but another one she didn't recognize.

The wisp landed on a sheet of parchment on her grandfather's desk, danced over it quickly, leaving the image of a horse rearing on its hind legs.

"That's Captain Thorne's sign," Rowen said aloud. "The captain of the guard. He hardly ever calls for Grandfather's help."

The wisp was already leaving another image: that of an arched gateway, and within the gate, a hammer and anvil. Then the wisp rose from the parchment and dropped with a tiny hiss into a nearby bottle of ink.

Someone's come to the main gate, Rowen thought, and she felt a rush of excitement. The hammer and anvil gave her an idea of who it might be, and why the captain had called for Pendrake. She dipped a pen in the ink bottle, wrote a quick note to her grandfather on another sheet of parchment and tossed it into the embers in the fireplace. An instant later the wisp reappeared out of the flames and zinged away out of the window again, carrying her message. Then Rowen hurried downstairs to the kitchen, where Edweth was making bread.

"Grandfather sent for me," she said, trying to sound breathless and in a hurry, to hide her unease at lying.

Edweth slapped down a cake of dough. Flour billowed up around her.

"I thought you were going to help me with this," the housekeeper said.

"When I get back," Rowen called, already halfway out of the door.

A party of over two dozen men and women had arrived at the gates bearing weapons and dressed in mail and leather helmets. Watchmen had challenged them, and one of them stepped forward and answered, a tall, ruddy-faced young woman with long blonde hair in braids. She announced that she and her companions were folk of the city of Skald, in the mountains west of the great forest, and that she herself was a friend of Nicholas Pendrake the toymaker.

Freya Ragnarsdaughter and the other Skaldings were still standing outside the walls of the city when Rowen arrived. Captain Thorne was there, on horseback, with a contingent of city guards.

"Where is Master Pendrake?" the captain asked with an impatient glare at Rowen.

"He's on his way," Rowen said.

"This woman says she knows you and your grandfather," the captain said doubtfully, as Freya hurried to Rowen.

"Freya," said Rowen excitedly. "Grandfather will be so happy to see you."

"Not when he's heard my news," Freya said. She had broken into a beaming smile when she first saw Rowen, but now she was frowning as if troubled. "Something happened in Skald that Father Nicholas must know about. But the captain won't let us into the city. You can tell him who we are, Rowen."

Rowen turned to Thorne, who seemed to be waiting for her to speak. She remembered how, on her journey with Will, they had unwillingly taken refuge from their pursuers in the fortress-city of Skald, whose folk were said to be untrustworthy and warlike. But they had found the people of Skald to be kind, generous and brave, especially Freya and her family. And Freya had come with them on the rest of their journey and had shared all of their hardships and dangers.

"Freya Ragnarsdaughter is a friend," Rowen said, speaking as loudly as she could to keep the trembling out of her voice. "These are good, honest folk. You should trust them and let them in."

"Thank you," Thorne said to her in an acid tone. "We'll be sure to consult you on all such matters from now on."

There were low chuckles from some of his men. Freya stepped forward.

"Master Nicholas said that Skald and Fable should become friends and allies," Freya said to the captain in a louder voice. "We're here in the hope of beginning that friendship."

The captain smiled coldly.

"It takes twenty-four or -five warriors armed to the teeth to deliver a gesture of friendship?"

"I would have come alone, but my father insisted I travel with others. The roads between here and Skald are dangerous."

"True enough. All manner of suspicious characters travel them these days, usually in armed gangs. If you have a message for the loremaster, you may give it to me and I'll see that he gets it."

"There's no need for that," a voice said, and Rowen turned gladly to see her grandfather making his way through the crowd that had gathered to see what kind of trouble was happening at the gates. Rowen smiled at her grandfather, but to her dismay he gave her only a quick, frowning glance. Once again she had disobeyed his orders.

"The people of Skald are no threat to us, Captain," Pendrake said. "I can assure you these men and women have come only on a friendly errand, and after such a long journey they deserve our hospitality."

"You know I must take the proper precautions, Master Pendrake," said Thorne archly. "My orders come from the Marshal."

"I will personally vouch for Freya Ragnarsdaughter and her companions," Pendrake said. "While they are in Fable they will be my responsibility."

Thorne frowned and looked out over the assembled Skaldings.

"We will give you food and lodging," he announced, "but only on the condition that you surrender your weapons right here and now. Otherwise no Skalding will pass through these gates. As for those Nightbane they brought with them, they will not be setting foot in this city."

The Skaldings parted and in their midst were revealed two alarming-looking manlike creatures with bloated faces resembling those of pigs. Their wrists were bound together with thick rope and another rope was tied between them. They were dressed in the tattered remnants of fancy velvet coats, and filthy white wigs were perched, askew, on their great heads. Their beady eyes darted furtive glances all around, and the fatter of the two began to blubber as if he might burst into tears at any moment. The other, who had a scarred, leaner face, gave him a vicious jab with his elbow.

"These are the Marrowbone brothers, dangerous and bloodthirsty fugitives," Freya said, and Rowen gazed at them with great interest. They were hogmen, a stupid, vicious breed of troll that ate people. The brothers had caught Will in the sewers of Skald with the intention of putting him in a stew. But Will had outwitted them by claiming he was Sir William of the Seven Mighty Companions, a famous hero who had come to challenge them, and while they'd argued over who should accept his challenge, he'd managed to escape.

She caught the rank smell of sweat and fear from the hogmen, and it repelled her, but she couldn't stop looking at them. The scarred one noticed her staring. From what Will had told her about them, she guessed this one had to be Flitch. He gave her a glare filled with hate and she looked away.

Freya quickly described the crimes for which the hogmen had been loathed and feared by the people of Skald.

"After Master Pendrake ended the plague of the werefire in Skald," she continued, "we went hunting for the night-crawlers that had infested our city. These two managed to slip away. Then, on our way here to your country, we passed through the Witchwood, and in the deepest part of the forest we found a tumbled-down old cottage made of gingerbread and sweets. These two were living there, in hiding. Probably hoping to lure lost children . . ."

She broke off and spat at the feet of the hogmen.

"That is utterly preposterous," growled Flitch. "We've never been anywhere near the city of Scorch or whatever you call it."

"Skald," murmured the other, fatter hogman, Hodge. His brother glared at him.

"I met you two, in the sewers under the keep," Freya said, "and I never forget a stench."

Flitch made a puffing sound of disdain.

"You've clearly been clubbed over the head one too many times, girl. My brother and I are honest entrepreneurs, bakers and confectioners who have lately experienced hard times. We found that gingerbread house untenanted and thought it would be perfect for setting up shop to ply our trade. We are legitimate purveyors of sweets and cakes, I assure you. It was nothing less than kidnapping to drag us away from our livelihood."

"Selling sweets in the middle of a trackless forest," Freya shot back. "How's business been?"

"I know about them, too, Captain Thorne," Rowen said. "I was in Skald with Freya when the hogmen captured my friend Will."

Both Thorne and the Marrowbone brothers stared at her.

"You saw them there?" Thorne asked.

"I didn't see them, no, but my friend told me about the hogmen after he was rescued." She stepped closer to the brothers. "And these two fit what he told me."

"That's no proof," Flitch sneered. "It's hearsay. This girl is a friend of our captor. She'll say whatever she thinks will help the Skald woman."

Despite the smell and the hideousness of the hogmen, Rowen again found herself drawn to them. Hodge was still white-faced and trembling with fear, and she almost reached out a hand to touch him. Then she understood what was happening. It was her gift, the *sight*. There was a powerful current of Story around these two frightening creatures, and as she realized this, their story came welling up in her mind.

She saw them as they had been a long time ago. Small, shivering, almost helpless creatures. There were three of them then: she saw a third brother, the eldest. They had left their home in a muddy sty . . . No, their mother *drove* them out to fend for themselves. The elder brother was brave and resourceful, he'd led them through the harsh world, kept them safe. *Tuck*. His name was Tuck. Rowen saw the brothers tramping along the roads, saw them shivering under a haystack in the rain. And then a beast had caught their scent: a wolf. A cold-blooded monster with slavering jaws, nothing like Shade. A creature poisoned and misshaped by the malice of the Night King. They had tried to take shelter in a crude hut of sticks, but the wolf got in easily and killed the oldest brother—*tore him to pieces*—and the other two had fled, always pursued, always in fear.

And then she saw that when they hid themselves in the sewers of Skald, the werefire had changed them, twisted them. Turned them into these foul, hateful creatures, these hogmen. Their story was not meant to turn out like this. It was supposed to end happily, but it had fallen into darkness and horror. Whatever terrible things they had done, the brothers had not always been like this.

Rowen saw all of this in an instant. She *felt* it, as if she had been there when their brother had been torn apart by the wolf. She could not stop it from sweeping over her, and the fear and horror left her shaking.

Before she knew what she was doing she reached out a hand and touched Hodge's sleeve. The hogman gaped down at her in stunned disbelief.

"I'm sorry about your other brother," she said. "And the werefire. But it doesn't have to be this way. You can stop hating, and killing. You can change. If you did, you could be happy again."

Hodge stared at her as if in a daze. His mouth moved but no sound came out.

"*Rowen*," Freya said in alarm, and the spell was broken. Hodge looked fearfully to his brother and Rowen stepped away, dazed, and shocked by what she had done.

"What do these accusations matter anyway?" Flitch said

to Thorne. "We have no interest in entering your city, and clearly you do not want us here, which I assure you we don't take offence at. So in the circumstances letting us go would be in everyone's best interests."

"Indeed it would, sir," Hodge added. "Fable's no place for the likes of us. No more than Skald was."

"*Idiot*," Flitch hissed at his brother.

"We can't let these two wander off on their own," the loremaster said. "I have no doubt Freya Ragnarsdaughter is telling the truth about who they are and what they've done."

"Well," the captain said, eyeing the hogmen with a grimace of distaste, "it seems the testimonies all agree, doesn't it?"

"If we let them go they'll most likely prey on other innocent folk," Pendrake said. "But the people of Skald, who did us all a good turn by capturing these two, are no threat to Fable. Captain, these men and women have come a long way to offer a hand in friendship and they deserve our hospitality."

Captain Thorne appeared to be weighing what the loremaster had said, and then he nodded slowly, though the look he gave Pendrake was anything but agreeable.

"Very well then," he said. "Lieutenant, take the hogmen into custody. I will speak to the Marshal about all of this. And the Skaldings may enter, but let's just be clear that you will be held accountable for their conduct, Master Pendrake." He turned to Freya. "And as I said, your weapons . . ."

Freya nodded reluctantly.

"We'll surrender them," she said, "though if there is need of them, I hope we'll find them in close reach."

Thorne studied Freya for a long moment, and smiled tersely.

"Should there be need of them, yes," he finally said.

Though there was some grumbling, the Skaldings handed

over their swords, axes and bows to Thorne's men, who took them into the gatehouse.

Before he rode off with his men with the Marrowbone brothers in tow, the captain turned once more to Pendrake.

"One of my company, Gared Bamble, is still missing. I was hoping you might be of some help with that, Master Pendrake."

"I'm doing all that I can," Rowen's grandfather said.

"Yes, I believe you are," the captain said icily. "Which reminds me, there's a much-respected mage in town at the moment who has offered us his services in solving this mystery. Ammon Brax, of the school at Kyning Rore. I'm sure you've heard of him, Master Pendrake. We're hoping he'll have better success."

The captain wheeled his mount and rode slowly back through the gates with his riders, the Marrowbone brothers in their midst, still bound together. Hodge glanced for a moment at Rowen with a stunned look still on his face.

"How can he talk to you like that, Grandfather?" Rowen said angrily. "After all you've done for the Bourne."

"The captain and I have never seen eye to eye," Pendrake said. "I was the one who put Finn Madoc forward for apprenticeship in the Errantry. Thorne was not happy about that. He hasn't forgotten it was Finn's brother who killed his apprentice, Lord Caliburn's son. And the story of the golem in the bog, and Finn's ring, has reached him and Lord Caliburn. The possibility that Corr Madoc might be out there somewhere, still alive and unpunished, has stoked an old bitterness. One that Thorne is sure to keep burning in Caliburn if he can."

"But that's not your fault."

"No, but I'm sure that in the captain's mind the fact that Corr remains at large is another of my failures as a loremaster."

"That's ridiculous," Freya said. "Don't they know how you saved Skald?"

Pendrake smiled.

"What matters to them is whether I can save Fable," he said. "With the Marrowbone brothers here now, it might seem that we've come one step closer to the disaster that befell your city."

"I wonder how the hogmen would feel if they knew Sir William of the Seven Mighty Companions was just in Fable," Rowen said, trying to shrug off her dark mood.

Freya laughed.

"I'd forgotten about that tale Will told them. We'll have to make sure they find out."

The Skaldings followed Pendrake and Rowen up the street, escorted by six silent guards on horseback. They were led to a barracks near the wall, that housed soldiers and held provisions during sieges. The barracks was empty at the moment, and the leader of the guards, a woman named Brigid, told the Skaldings that they could stay there for the time being. While the guards waited outside, Pendrake ushered the Skaldings inside. It was a row of low-ceilinged rooms furnished sparsely with narrow bunks, washstands and benches. There was straw on the floor and quite a few cobwebs on the walls.

"You must come and stay with us, Freya," Rowen said. "We have lots of room. We've got so much to talk about."

"You're very kind," Freya said, "but when I've given Father Nicholas the news I bring, I must stay with my people."

Pendrake embraced Freya and held her at arm's length to look at her.

"It is very good to see you again, my dear. Come with us at least for now. You can give us your news at the toyshop, where we can talk freely."

Freya looked around at the other Skaldings, who were busy unloading their gear and exploring their new quarters.

"Go ahead, Freya," said one of the Skaldings, a burly older man.

"Are you sure, Eymund?"

"Your companions will be fine for the moment," Pendrake said, and the man nodded.

Reluctantly, Freya gave in. She went with Rowen and the loremaster up the winding streets of Fable, gazing in wonder at everything she saw. When a messenger wisp streaked past she ducked her head, then laughed. A pair of knights-errant on horseback rode by and Freya followed them with her eyes.

"Is Finn Madoc in Fable?" she asked, her normally apple-bright complexion reddening even more. Rowen felt herself blushing a little in sympathy.

"He's gone north with Will," Rowen said. "We're hoping they'll be home soon."

Quickly Rowen told Freya Mimling's story about Shade, and how Will and Finn had set out to find him and bring him back to Fable.

"May they all return safely," Freya said. The blush had faded from her face, leaving her pale and weary-looking, as if the long journey from Skald had finally caught up with her.

Rowen remembered the samming, the dance of celebration in Skald, after the werefire had been put out by her grandfather, and all the foul creatures that had infested the city, the Marrowbone brothers and many others, were on the run. As they danced together in the samming, Freya and Finn had eyes only for each other. After Will had found his way home, Finn had escorted Freya back to Skald so she would not be alone on the long road. They must have become close on that journey. But once Freya returned to Skald to help her people, Finn had come back to Fable to resume his duties. The two of them probably hadn't seen each other since.

Like Will and I, she thought bitterly. *Something always keeps us apart.*

Back at the toyshop Edweth welcomed them and prepared a meal. They sat together at the table in the library, and at last Freya told her tale.

"Skald is getting back on its feet, Father Nicholas, thanks to you. The nightcrawlers have almost all been rooted out, and many of those who left are beginning to return. Farmers are sowing crops again and there is trade at our market."

"That is very welcome news. And how is your family?"

"Father has been better since he's stopped trying to save all of Skald single-handedly," Freya said with a smile. "Thorri is growing and already talking about coming to Fable some day to join the Errantry."

Pendrake laughed.

"I'm glad to hear it. But I doubt that's everything you came all this way to tell us."

"It isn't," Freya said, and her smile faded.

"What has happened?"

"Earlier this year," she began, "we had the warmest, loveliest spring that Skald had seen in a very long time. There was plenty of sunshine, and rain when it was needed, and the harvest promised to be bountiful. Then came a strange day in midsummer, when a cold fog poured down out of the mountains and hung over the city. Frost grew thick on everything. People gathered in the streets, afraid some new terror was about to be visited on us. Their memories of the werefire were still fresh.

"But nothing happened. The fog lasted all day and into the night. Then, around midnight, a sound woke me. It was hail pattering against the shutters. *Hail*, Father Nicholas, at midsummer. I went outside, and the courtyard of the smithy was covered in a blanket of icy slush. It was as cold as the coldest, darkest night of winter. The air was thick with falling snow. Then I heard a voice. Or it was more as if I felt it, like the way you feel a pounding drum in your bones. It called me by name and I knew it was the dragon. The dragon that lives in the ice. It was Whitewing Stonegrinder."

With a shiver, Rowen remembered the name. On the journey with Will, they had fled the Angel by climbing up onto a glacier high in the mountains. Nightbane had pursued and almost captured them, until the dragon awoke and came forth from his caverns within the ice and routed the enemy. In the battle Rowen had been wounded by a Nightbane arrow, and Whitewing Stonegrinder had healed her with a touch of his icy claw.

"The dragon left the glacier?" Rowen asked. "I thought he would never do that."

Freya nodded.

"I know. I didn't believe it at first, either, but there was no mistaking the voice. His words seemed to come from all around me, though I couldn't see him. And I remembered every word. Every word, as if they had been burned onto my skin with frost. 'Freya Ragnarsdaughter,' he said. 'You came to my home and so I come to yours.'

"'What do you want with me, Old One?' I asked. I don't know why I called him that. It seemed right."

"It was right, Freya," Pendrake said. "That is a term of respect for an ancient power of the earth like Stonegrinder. The long memory of your people was working in you, I'd say."

"I don't know about that, but the dragon didn't seem to mind. 'I have tidings for the keeper of stories, in Fable,' he said. I knew he meant you, Father Nicholas.

"'Why have you come to me?' I asked him. There was something in his voice, a hollowness, as if he had been stricken by some malady or was in great pain. I was suddenly afraid for him. But what could harm such a being?

"'My strength is not what it was,' he said. 'If I go much further from my home, I will not be able to return. You must be my voice, Freya Ragnarsdaughter. Go to the keeper of stories and tell him what he must know.'

"I said I would do as he asked, and then he told me. . ."

She broke off, and looked at Rowen, who was alarmed at what she saw in Freya's eyes. Dread, even despair.

"Told you what, Freya?"

Freya bit her lip, then turned to Pendrake.

"He said that a great darkness was sweeping through the Realm, Father Nicholas. As though the lights of the world were going out, one by one. That is why his strength was failing. He could feel it in himself. The ice of his home was melting more quickly than he had ever known. Servants of the Storyeater, as he calls the Night King, were marching through his domain in great numbers now, defying him. He doesn't have much time left before his guard on the mountains fails. Then he told me . . . he told me the darkness was coming here, to the Bourne."

They all fell silent at these words.

"Coming here?" Rowen finally asked.

"From every direction, he said, creatures who serve the Storyeater are already coming this way. Fable is the place where all will be decided, he told me."

"Then the Night King. . ." Rowen whispered. "He knows. He knows about the Weaving, about the doorway. . ."

"We don't know that for certain," Pendrake said. "Did the dragon say anything else, Freya?"

"He said that he would return to the ice for now and

when he left it again it would be for the last time. Then he asked me to bring you a message, Rowen."

Rowen's startled gaze went back and forth between her grandfather and Freya.

"Me?" she said. "He must have meant Grandfather."

Freya shook her head emphatically.

"'Tell the granddaughter of the keeper of stories that when she has need of me I will come to Fable.' Those were his words. Then he said that snow would be the sign of his coming. That when you saw snow falling, Rowen, you should climb to the highest ground and he would be there."

"But what would a dragon want with me?" Rowen asked breathlessly.

"You were the only one of us whom Stonegrinder touched, remember," Pendrake said. "When he healed your arrow wound."

"I thought of that, too," Freya said.

"An ancient being like Stonegrinder has powers of vision and understanding we can barely imagine," Pendrake said. "I doubt that questioning his message will lead to any answers. You'll just have to wait, Rowen, for snow to fall."

No one spoke for a while. Then Pendrake rose and put his hand on Freya's.

"It was brave of you to come all this way, my dear," he said quietly. "If I could, I'd return with you to Skald and speak with Stonegrinder myself. But that's not possible now."

"I know, Father Nicholas. You're needed here."

"Yes, and something tells me, Freya, you're not planning to go home straight away either. Thorne was right about one thing: you didn't really need an armed band to deliver this message."

Freya took a deep breath. She seemed to be preparing for the loremaster's objections.

"It's true," she said. "We mean to stay as long as we're needed."

Pendrake sighed heavily.

"You should be with your family at such a time, Freya."

"We Skaldings owe you our freedom, Father Nicholas. If Fable is in danger we're here to stand with you, whatever comes."

Rowen could see that her grandfather was not pleased, but the look on Freya's face was so determined that he refrained from speaking his mind.

Now that she had brought the dragon's message, Freya was eager to return to her companions. Rowen saw her to the door. When she returned to the library, she found Pendrake donning his cloak.

"Grandfather?" Rowen said.

"I must speak to the Marshal about Freya's news," Pendrake said distractedly. "I'll be back as soon as I can."

"Why would the dragon say what he did to Freya? What would I need him for?"

Pendrake turned to her, and to her alarm she saw that his face looked much older, as if weighed down with a great sorrow.

"Rowen, if anything happens," he began haltingly, "if anything happens and I'm not with you . . ."

"Grandfather?"

"If I'm not with you any more, find Will. Stay close to him."

Rowen had never heard her grandfather speak like this before, with such sadness and urgency at the same time. She searched his face fearfully.

"What do you mean, if you're not with me any more? What are you saying?"

Pendrake placed a hand on her shoulder.

"I am so proud of you, Rowen," he said, and she felt tears sting her eyes. After all he had said to her lately about her gifts and the threat to the Bourne, of all the grim news and shadowy rumours they'd heard, somehow the way he was talking now frightened her more than anything.

"How can I . . ." she began, choking back her fear, "What if Will is miles away?"

"You'll find a way," Pendrake said. "I know you will."

He took up his staff and hurried from the toyshop, and Rowen sat down heavily in the chair he had just left. After a few moments Riddle slunk in cautiously and curled up at her feet. She reached down to scratch him absently behind the ears, hardly aware of what she was doing. Then she had a sudden thought, and took out the mirror shard again. She looked at the reflection of her face, saw the fear in her own eyes. Was everyone going to leave her? She clutched the mirror shard tightly until she felt it cut into her palm.

"Nothing's going to happen," she said under her breath. "Nothing."

In the main square of Fable, a figure stood alone and still amid the hurrying traffic of a busy day. The figure was dressed in the cloak and hood of a knight-errant, and so it was a familiar sight to most, and for that reason no one paid it much attention.

Getting inside the city had been difficult. The thrawl had been turned away at the gates, and so had to resort to a different method of entry. At night, outside the walls, it had unravelled itself, emptied itself of all the living things it had ingested to give its shape solidity, movement and speech. Then as a ragged veil of the finest gossamer it had let the night breeze catch it and lift it over the walls and into the sleeping city.

From there it had been a matter of regaining its shape. That had not been so difficult. There were many bodies here that would do. It had found one quickly and taken it with hardly a struggle. No one had heard the young man wail his own name as it was torn from him, along with all his memories and his flesh. *Gared Bamble.*

Once the thrawl had regained a form in which it could move, it had traced the thread of the prey to this place, the city square. She had been here, Rowen of Blue Hill. Then her thread had vanished again somehow, but the thrawl still *felt* her presence in the traces she had left among the threads of all these other mortal creatures. Her trail wound away through these busy streets and then . . . there was only rain. But she was here, somewhere.

The thrawl stirred and began to move. It could spin its own invisible threads, too, and it would walk through this unsuspecting city and let threads unravel from itself, threads that would find other threads, those that belonged to anyone the girl knew.

13

Earth said to Sun, Let me lie here and sleep a while, but do not forget to wake me. But Sun saw how beautiful Earth was as she slept, and he wished only to gaze at her loveliness, so he did not wake her. And Earth slept on, and her dreams became the grass and the stones and the animals.

– Legends of the Horse Folk

WILL HACKED AT THE WALL of reeds in front of him until he could no longer lift his arm. He dropped to his knees in the wet earth, panting and struggling to hold back tears. He had led his friends into this place and it had swallowed them alive. He couldn't reach them, and if he stayed here any longer, he was sure to be swallowed up too. No one would ever find out what had happened to him or his companions. And Shade, if he wasn't already dead, might be dying even now. He would never see the wolf again, or his family, or Rowen.

He couldn't give in.

Will jabbed his sword into the ground and used it to push himself up off his knees. With a gasp of effort he lifted his blade over his head.

He paused. He could hear a thrashing sound, faint but growing louder, as if something large was coming straight towards him. With his sword held before him he took a step back.

There was a terrible roar that froze Will's blood, then Balor burst through the green wall, his face contorted and nearly purple with furious effort as he tugged his terrified horse along after him. The wildman's mane of dark hair was matted down with sweat and he was dragging thick braids of reeds twined around his arms and legs that he must have torn out by the roots to free himself.

"We told you to keep going," he bellowed at Will.

"I've found the way out," Will said. "It's not far."

"The way out?"

Finn and the doctor appeared in Balor's wake with their horses. Both of them were frantically hacking at reeds that were clutching at their arms and legs.

"It took my sword," the doctor said numbly when he saw Will, "right out of my hand."

"Let's get out of here while we still can," Finn said, gasping for breath. There was a hissing and rustling and they all looked back the way they had come, to see that the reeds were already gathering and closing in, sealing up the wide swathe that Balor had made. They hurried on as quickly as they could, following Will along what remained of his own narrower trail.

A few moments later they had brushed aside the last of the reeds and stumbled out into bright sunlight, blinking and shielding their eyes.

They were standing at the bottom of a kind of grassy hollow, under a cloudless sky of brilliant blue. Cutter stood nearby, calmly munching the grass. He raised his head when they appeared and gave a whinny of greeting. Stunned and speechless, they all looked back. The wall of reeds stood over them, motionless and silent, looking as though it had never been disturbed by their passage. No one spoke while they plucked the last remaining stalks and tendrils off themselves and the horses.

"So that was a knot-path," Alazar said shakily, straightening his spectacles. "Tell me, Will, are they always so welcoming to travellers?"

"I didn't know that would happen," he muttered as he took Cutter's reins. "I'm sorry."

"No one's blaming you, Will," Finn said. "The knot-paths must be changing along with everything else in the Realm. Darkening and becoming treacherous, as Master Pendrake told us. We escaped unharmed, that's all that matters. Now let's find out where we've come to."

Wearily they mounted their horses again and climbed the gentle slope to the rim of the bowl. Once they'd reached the crest, before them stretched a vast treeless land covered in yellow grass, rippling and whispering in the wind.

"The Great Plain," Finn said. "You did it, Will."

The wind had an icy bite that stung Will's eyes to tears. Other than the grass in the wind, nothing moved under the blazing eye of the sun. A solitary bird, perhaps a hawk, hung in the sky as if it, too, was not moving.

"There's just one problem," the doctor said. "Balor, do you recognize this place?"

The wildman turned this way and that in his saddle. His brow knotted and he frowned.

"Are we lost?" Will asked.

"We're on the Great Plain, that much I'm sure of, and we still know which way is north," Finn said, squinting up at the sun. "But other than that . . ."

"I can just make out a faint line of hills, or maybe mountains," Balor said with a grimace of effort, shading his eyes. Will followed his gaze but couldn't see what he was looking at.

"Since that way is north, those could be the Sand Hills," Alazar said.

"Too far to say for sure," Balor muttered, shaking his head.

"Well, clearly we can't go back the way we came," Alazar said. "So now what?"

"You were certain about this path, Will," Finn said. "Let's assume those are the Sand Hills. If we head towards them, we should come to the Wandering River eventually. From there we can get our bearings."

Will nodded. He looked ahead at the empty vastness before them and hoped that he had been right, that Shade was out here somewhere, not far away.

They rode hard across the plain into the evening, and to Will's surprise it was not the flat immensity he had expected. The land rose to bare knolls and plunged into hollows, and after a while he felt as if they were riding the immense waves of a grassy ocean. The line of hills Balor had seen grew steadily on the horizon, until Will could see them clearly in the slanting light of sunset. They were round with bare grassy flanks and stony summits. From the top of the furthest and highest of the hills, four jagged spurs of rock jutted into the sky.

"Those are not the Sand Hills," Balor said decisively, with a quick sideways glance at Will. "I don't recognize them."

Finn turned in his saddle and gazed long in every direction.

"Neither do I," he said at last. "I don't know where we are."

"I do," Will said.

They all turned and stared at him.

"I've been here before," Will said, shifting uneasily in his saddle. "Sort of. When I was little, my mother used to tell me stories about a boy hero. On one of his adventures he came to a place like this. The Hill of the Teeth."

They were still staring at him.

"You're saying we're in this story your mother told you?" Balor said.

"I don't know," Will said. "If the Realm is the world of Story, then couldn't it be possible? But there's something else, something more important. Mimling said Shade had been burned by lightning, and in the story, Captain Stormcloud sent his Lightning Warriors to battle the hero. I don't know if it means anything, but I've been thinking about that story ever since I first heard what happened to Shade."

He broke off, suddenly aware that what he was saying sounded far-fetched even to him. He glanced up at the hills. The sky to the north of them was dark with bruise-coloured clouds.

"There didn't happen to be a talking wolf in this story your mother told you," Balor said. "A wolf rescued by a small band of brave and incredibly handsome knights?"

"No," Will said. "Nothing like that."

"Well, it must just be a coincidence," Balor huffed. "We shouldn't have come here in the first place. Now what do we do?"

Finn cleared his throat.

"It will be dark soon and we need to find shelter," he said. "It looks as if a rainstorm is coming this way. There's clearly more you need to tell us, Will."

After a short ride they came to the edge of a narrow stony gully. A scattering of stunted willows and spiny bushes grew at the bottom. There had probably been a stream here once, but the floor of the gully was dry now, except for a few shallow pools fringed with sparse grass. They dismounted, led the horses down a slope of crumbling rock and found a place to camp out of the wind, under a thicket of willows. Will hurriedly gathered enough sticks to make a small fire and they ate a quick meal. From time to time they heard a rumble of far-off thunder. The stars were soon blotted out by thick clouds, and though no rain fell, they all felt a heaviness in the air.

"So, Will," Balor said when they'd finished eating. "Why don't you tell us this tale about the boy hero. After all, if we are *in* it now, we should find out what might be in store for us."

Will took a deep breath. He wasn't sure he'd ever told a story to anyone other than Jess, but he had to try. Not only for the others, but for himself, too, so he could sort out whether or not he was right about what he suspected. He looked up for a moment, gathering his thoughts. Through a brief gap in the clouds he saw a few faint stars. To his own surprise it was not his mother's story that came to mind, it was the sight of his father on the back porch with the light behind him. A lump rose in his throat.

"There was this boy," he began quickly, "called Lightfoot."

"A good name for a hero," Balor said.

"He had a pony called Great Heart, and they rode everywhere together, having adventures. Once, Lightfoot came to the great ocean of grass, but it was dry and dying because there was no rain. Captain Stormcloud had it all bottled in his mountain at the end of the world. So Lightfoot set out to steal back the rain. On the way he came to a village of the plains people, who lived in lodges made of animal skins and hunted buffalo, and an old man—"

"What is *buffalo*?" Balor asked.

"Well, they're sort of like cattle, but with thick shaggy coats and bigger heads. A long time ago they lived in great herds on the plains. So Lightfoot came to the village and an old man—"

"Ah, I know what you mean," Balor exclaimed. "The wisent, we call them. You're right, there are a lot of them. You can stand in one place and watch the same herd passing for days. But go on, please."

Will nodded, for the first time experiencing the storyteller's annoyance at being interrupted by those who had asked for a tale in the first place.

"An old man told Lightfoot how to find Stormcloud's fortress," Will went on. "If he rode north he would come to the Hill of the Teeth. And beyond the hill were the barren lands. That's where he would find the—"

"This Lightfoot, was he a knight-errant?" Balor asked.

"Well, in a way, I suppose. He was the one who always solved the problem or fought the monsters or whatever had to be done."

"Then I can see where you got your name, Will," Balor said with a grin. "Though I have to say I've never come across this place in all my travels. I've never heard of this Captain Stormcloud."

"Anyway," Will continued, determined to get through his story now that he'd started, "the old man said there would be many perils on the road through the barren lands. And if Captain Stormcloud discovered that Lightfoot had set foot in his domain, he would send his terrible Lightning Warriors to kill him. So Lightfoot—"

"This is getting better and better," Balor said. "These Lightning Warriors sound like a friendly lot."

Will bit his lip to keep from telling the wildman to shut up. He glanced at the doctor, who was stifling a smile.

"So Lightfoot saddled Great Heart and set out for the barren lands. He had many adventures along the way." Will paused, taking a deep breath. "Many adventures. It took a long time to tell the story and I don't remember all of it. Lightfoot met a grizzly bear at one point, who carried him on his back and fought for him against a stone giant."

"*Grizzly* bear?" Balor asked.

"A large brown bear, with a hump on its back. Very powerful, and bad-tempered."

"I believe I've seen one of those, in the Shining Mountains," the doctor said eagerly. "Magnificent creatures."

"Quiet, 'Zar," Balor said. "Let Will get on with his story."

The doctor sighed and rolled his eyes.

"Why don't you tell us what happened when the boy came to Captain Stormcloud's fortress," Finn said, with a pointed glance at the wildman.

Will was about to continue when a flash of lightning seared the darkness. A crack of thunder followed swiftly after. They all looked up, but from where they sat at the bottom of the gully they could see nothing but the dark sky overhead.

"Lightfoot rode into the barren lands—" Will began, then something made him pause. He looked up again at the rim of the gully, and a moment later another flash of lightning illuminated the night. This time, he saw a shape above them. A small figure crouching at the top of the bank.

The others had seen it, too. They leapt to their feet. Balor drew his sword, but Finn held up a hand, and he lowered it. Finn plucked a stick out of the fire and held it over his head.

"We won't harm you," he said.

A moment later, a boy stepped into the light from Finn's makeshift torch. He looked to be a year or two younger than Will. He was naked to the waist, his upper body and face painted with yellow and ochre streaks. He took a couple of steps down the side of the bank then halted suddenly, holding out a wooden spear in front of him. Will could see the spearpoint trembling.

"Who are you?" Finn said.

The boy opened his mouth to speak, then his eyes rolled back in his head. Before anyone could reach him, the boy's knees buckled and he tumbled down the bank and lay still at their feet.

They gathered quickly around him. The doctor knelt and soon revived the boy with a splash of water to the face from his flask. The boy stared at them all, then his eyes fixed on Will.

"You are the boy from the other world," he said.

Will stared at him, too stunned to speak.

"I ran," the boy said haltingly. "From our camp. You must come with me. The wolf is there."

"Shade?" Will cried. "He's alive?"

The boy nodded.

"Where is your camp?" Finn asked. "How far is it?"

"I ran a long time. You must come with me. The Dreamwalker sent me to find you."

They mounted and set off again across the dark plain, the boy riding with Finn, who took the lead. Will rode alongside on Cutter, and the boy glanced often at him. The look on his face, Will thought, was one of awe or even fear.

"What is your name?" Will asked him.

"Hawk," the boy said. "Of the Horse Folk."

"I'm Will. Will Lightfoot."

The boy stared at him even more intensely than before, and Will looked away.

The land rose gently as they rode on. Finn questioned Hawk about where they were going and who the Dreamwalker was, but the boy would say only that he had been sent to find Will and bring him to his people's camp, where

Shade was. For his part, Will said little. All he could think about was that Shade had survived and soon they would see each other again.

The sky continued to rumble. White flashes and throbs of lightning pulsed within the thick clouds from time to time, but still there was no rain.

Dawn brought a pale, cold light to the plain. The great mass of cloud had drawn off, although the Hill of the Teeth was shrouded from view. Below them they saw a narrow stony valley, with the silver ribbon of a stream winding through it. On the far side of the stream, on a wide space of flat ground, Will saw with surprise a group of lodges, their cone-shaped walls of bleached animal skins gleaming white in the sun. A couple of underfed-looking ponies, one grey and the other dun, were tied to one of the lodge poles. The scene before him was something like what he had imagined when his mother told him the story of Lightfoot, but it was also very different, and he wondered why.

"A Horse Folk village," the doctor said as they drew up on the crest of the hill. "But there's no camp smoke. It doesn't look as though anyone's here."

"And there are precious few horses," Balor said. "Odd, for Horse Folk."

"The people left," Hawk said. "There's only the three of us now."

They rode carefully down the hill, which was steeper and rockier on this side, dotted with strange stone formations: tall pillars of striped brown and tan sandstone, capped with flat rocks. The pillars looked eerily like giant human figures standing in the slanted dusky light. Finn took the lead, and when they had passed between two of these pillars he pulled up his horse suddenly. A girl was crouching in a patch of darkly leaved bushes, picking pale red berries and putting them in a woven basket she carried over one arm. Will and the others drew up behind Finn.

The girl heard the sound of hooves on bare earth and looked up. She was small, probably a year or two younger than the boy. Her long black hair was braided up at the back. She wore a dress of pale animal skin ornamented with tiny shells of many colours.

She looked at her brother and at the strangers, then she rose to her feet, watching them with an intense, unmoving gaze. When she looked past Finn and saw Balor, she slowly began to back away.

"We're not going to hurt you," Balor said quietly.

"My sister," the boy said. "Moon. She will not speak to you."

"We noticed," quipped the wildman. Will thought of his own sister Jess and how quiet she had been after their mother died. Had something like that happened to Hawk's sister? At the thought of his family, he felt keenly how far he was from home and how once again he had run off and left them. And yet somehow here he was, it seemed, in a story his mother had told him. He had come so far, and yet not far at all.

"Why did the people leave?" the doctor asked Hawk.

Hawk looked troubled at the question.

"They fled from the Sky Folk," he said. "My father, the Dreamwalker, would not leave. He said *you*," he looked straight at Will, "would be coming soon, and he had to wait for you. He wanted us to leave with the others, but we stayed with him."

They descended the rest of the way to the bottom of the hill, forded the shallow, rushing stream and rode into camp. There were five lodges in a partial ring, but only two were still wholly covered in animal hides. The others had been mostly stripped of their skins and little more than bare willow poles remained, lashed together at the top with strips of rawhide. There were bare circles in other places with the remains of fire pits, and Will guessed that other lodges had been set up in these spots but had been taken down. As they dismounted and led their horses through the camp, they saw various clay bowls and stone tools scattered on the ground. In the centre of the camp the ashes of a dead fire lay heaped in a pit ringed with stones. Above the fire pit was a rack on which hung a few thin strips of dried meat.

It was obvious that most of the Horse Folk had left in a hurry.

A small dog ran from behind one of the lodges, followed by another, larger one. They were both barking frantically, but ceased when they approached the strangers, and circled them warily.

Finn and the others tied their mounts to a pole nearby. Hawk led them to one of the two lodges that were still intact. He lifted the doorflap and they stooped and went in, with Hawk following. Will looked back as he entered and saw that the girl had remained outside. She was watching the sky.

When he turned from the bright daylight to the darkness inside the lodge, he saw only dim shapes at first, and in the centre the glowing embers of a small fire. There was a large, shaggy form lying on the dirt floor, a form that raised its head as he entered. Behind him, Balor lifted the doorflap higher as he came in after Will, and the light from outside flooded the lodge. Finn and the doctor followed after the wildman.

"Shade!" Will cried.

It was the wolf. He had been lying with his front legs stretched out but climbed to his feet as Will hurried to his side.

"Will Lightfoot," the wolf said. Will threw his arms about Shade's neck and his hands plunged into the wolf's thick, warm fur, and it all came back to him: the feeling of comfort and security the wolf's presence had given him on their long journey together. He had missed that without realizing how much, until now. He felt the wolf's warm life glowing beneath his fur and he closed his eyes and let the tears come.

"You're alive," he breathed.

"I am," Shade said, and his voice was husky with emotion. "It is very good to see you, Will Lightfoot."

"We're glad to see you, too, Shade," Finn said. "Mimling the dwarf brought your message to us."

Will glimpsed bare red flesh along the wolf's flank. He pulled away.

"Are you. . . ?" he asked.

Alazar crouched down beside Will.

"I am a doctor," he said to the wolf. "May I examine your wound?"

"It is healing," Shade said. "The Horse Folk found me and tended to me. There is no longer any danger. The Dreamwalker told me you had come back to the Realm, Will Lightfoot. He said you were on your way here and that I should rest and wait for you."

He turned his head and only then did Will see that someone was sitting at the back of the lodge, on the far side of the fire. He squinted in the dim light and saw that it was a man, reclining against a backrest made of lashed-together bones. His grey hair was twined in two long braids down the front of his buckskin shirt. His eyes were milky orbs.

He was the blind man Will had seen in his dream. And now that he saw him he knew why he had felt no sense of fear or danger. He knew this man was the Dreamwalker the boy had spoken of and that he meant them no harm.

"You and your friends are welcome in my lodge," the blind man said.

"Thank you for helping Shade," Will said.

"He is one of the Old Ones," the Dreamwalker said. "He has always walked in the Dream Country. That is where I saw him, and had him brought here before his enemies found him."

"Do you know who was hunting Shade?" Finn asked the blind man.

"We call them the Sky Folk. They first came to our land seven summers ago, from the north. They came from the clouds, flying on what we thought at first were great birds with white wings, but they were not birds, they were vessels of wood like those built to travel on water. They had strange weapons, and we were frightened because servants of the Storyeater were among them. But they told us they were enemies of the Storyeater, and they would protect us from him."

"*Storyeater* . . . you mean the Night King, Malabron," Finn said.

The Dreamwalker turned his head. He seemed to be pondering what Finn had said.

"I have not heard those names," he said at last. "He is the Storyeater. His servants are at war with the Sky Folk, who have claimed all this land as theirs, from here to the ghostlands in the north, and permit no one to travel across it without their permission."

"The ghostlands. What sort of place is that?" Alazar asked.

"The Horse Folk do not go there," the Dreamwalker said. "Evil spirits walk there, and the land is broken and holds no life."

"Sounds like your barren lands, Will," Balor murmured.

"The Sky Folk dwell there," the Dreamwalker went on, "but there is nothing for them to eat, and that is why they have taken our lands too. They hunt the wisent, killing many more than they take away with them for food. If this goes on, soon the great herds will be no more. And we will be no more. Our young men are in awe of the Sky Folk and their weapons: fine spears, knives of polished metal, strong bows. Too many of our warriors have already gone with the Sky Folk to fight the servants of the Storyeater, and few have ever returned. And now the rain does not fall, and the grass withers, and our hunters search in vain for the wisent."

"But why were the Sky Folk hunting Shade?" Will asked.

The Dreamwalker turned to the wolf.

"He can tell you that."

Shade raised his head.

"I have news of your brother, Finn Madoc."

"Corr?" Finn exclaimed. "What have you heard?"

"After Will Lightfoot had gone home to his world," Shade said, "I went searching for Speaking Creatures like myself. I journeyed far and wide without finding any. At last I came to these lands, and I heard about the Sky Folk, how they were hunting my kin, the wild wolves of the plains, and taking them prisoner. The Sky Folk make slaves of them for their war against the Storyeater's servants.

"I went north then, searching for the Sky Folk, to find these wolves and free them if I could. One night a great wind rose, bringing black clouds that blotted out the stars. There was much lightning and thunder, but no rain. I found a trail of blood in the grass. A man's blood. I thought someone might be hurt and in need of help, so I followed the trail and caught up with the one who had left it, a man stumbling across the plain. His clothes were torn and his bare feet were cut and bleeding. When he saw me he tried to run, but he fell. I told him I would not hurt him and he seemed to understand me, though he could barely speak, and his mind was wandering so that he made little sense, but at last he was able to tell me he was from the Bourne, and he was trying to get back to it."

"Was the man Corr?" Finn said.

"I told him that I had friends in the Bourne, and he asked me to go to the Errantry with a message. He said his name was Yates."

"It must have been Brannon Yates," Finn said, "my brother's right-hand man. He was a knight-errant before he deserted to join Corr's band."

"The man said he had news for the Errantry," Shade went on, "about Corr Madoc. But before he could tell me any more a baying rose above the noise of the thunder. I had not caught their scent but we were surrounded by wolves. The man was terrified. These wolves were not wild. They had been sent to hunt him down. I stood in front of him, to protect him, and their leader sprang at me. He was strong, but too furious and reckless to fight well. I killed him easily."

Shade's lips curled back from his teeth as if he was recalling a distasteful memory.

"His blood tasted . . . like sickness. I think a poison is in these wolves, to make them full of rage and hate. But when they saw what I had done to their leader, the other wolves ran off. I tried to help the man walk, but he was like the wolves, I understood now. The same poison was in him. We didn't get very far when a dark cloud appeared above us, moving against the wind. There was a great flash of light and fire. Everything became darkness and pain. When I could open my eyes again the man was gone. I smelled the wolves, not far away. Now they were hunting me. I tried to run but I could barely crawl. I took shelter in a cave and that's where I met Mimling Hammersong. And that is all I remember, until I woke up in the Horse Folk camp."

"If Yates was running from these . . . Sky Folk, Corr and the others must be their prisoners, too," Finn said. "But why? Corr would've joined forces with them against the Nightbane."

"The Sky Folk do not befriend anyone," the Dreamwalker said. "They only take."

Finn said nothing. Will could see that the young man was far away in his own thoughts.

"We don't know for certain what's happened to your brother," Alazar said, studying Finn with a look of concern. "The truth is he may be . . ."

"He's alive," Finn said.

"We shouldn't be making any plans until we know more."

Finn nodded slowly, but he wouldn't look at the doctor. Shade turned to Will.

"You must return to Fable, Will Lightfoot," the wolf said. "The Sky Folk are still hunting for me. If they find you here they will take you, too. They take the young and strong, to fight in their war."

"I'm not leaving here without you, Shade," Will said.

"Then we will go together. I am strong enough now that I can walk, but I will be slow, so we must leave as soon as we can."

"If these Sky Folk come back," Alazar said to the Dreamwalker, "you and your children will be helpless."

"Now that you have come, we will leave this place and follow after our people. The Sky Folk do not take the blind or the very young."

"Still, perhaps there is another way," Finn said. "Alazar, Balor, we need to talk."

The three Errantry knights excused themselves and left the lodge. The Dreamwalker turned to Will again, raising a hand to beckon him closer.

Will went to the man's side. The Dreamwalker reached up and took Will's hand in his thin, leathery hand. Will was surprised at the urgency of his grip, as if the Dreamwalker was trying to see him through touch rather than sight. Will felt a surge of fear and almost pulled his hand away. A moment later the Dreamwalker let him go.

"I have walked far enough in the Dream Country to have learned that the world my people know, the world of grass and earth under the sky, is not the only one," the Dreamwalker said. "There are as many worlds as the sky holds stars. You are from a world stranger than any I have ever walked in. You are the boy who is light of foot, and yet you are not."

"You . . . *know* about Lightfoot?" Will asked.

"I dreamed of him many years ago. Long before the Sky Folk came to our lands and claimed them as their own. I dreamed of his travels and his brave deeds, and I wondered why I saw this boy from far away in the Dream Country. When the Sky Folk came with their lightning and their weapons, I thought, *now is the time when that boy will walk among us.* And then you came in search of your friend, and you are called Lightfoot, but you are . . . not him. I did not see this. You are Will Lightfoot, the pathfinder, and you have a different task. You must find a path for someone else."

"What do you mean?"

"You are close to one who will walk where others have not gone. She is the weaver of worlds. You must help her find the way."

"I don't know anyone like that."

"I have seen her with you in the Dream Country. A young girl with hair the colour of fire. She does not yet know all that she will become."

"Rowen!" Will exclaimed. He felt a sudden longing for

her that set his heart pounding. "It must have been Rowen. What did you see? Do you know if she's all right?"

"I saw that you had been with her not many sunsets ago, and you wish to be with her again. That is your greatest desire."

"It is. Why did you call her the . . . weaver of worlds?"

"Very soon she will make a long and dangerous journey, to the place on the far side of all the worlds. I see beings there who wish her harm. They hate and fear her for the great power that she will find within herself. The power to weave new worlds, new dreams."

"Are you saying this is something that's really going to happen?" he asked breathlessly. "That it's not just a dream?"

"What you and your companions call Story, my people call Dream. She will make this journey, to the land of the one who devours stories. And there she must make a new story, as the weaver weaves the threads and her own life together to make a new pattern in the cloth. This she must do for the sake of every being in all the worlds. This is her task, and only you can help her accomplish it."

Will shook his head. He understood very little of what the Dreamwalker was saying, but still he felt fear for Rowen clutching at his throat. The one who devours stories had to be Malabron, the Night King. If the Dreamwalker was telling the truth, Rowen would be going to the Shadow Realm. But why?

"Do you know where Rowen is now?" he asked.

"She is still where you last saw her, in her grandfather's house. She has not yet left on her journey, but very soon she will. And now that you are here, I see that you must go with her. The road will be long and there will be many dangers. She will falter and lose her way. You must help her find the path. And you must stay with her, or she will surely fail in her task and be lost for ever. And darkness will come to all the worlds."

"Of course I'll stay with her . . . but can I get back to Fable in time, before she leaves? It's so far away."

To Will's surprise the blind man smiled.

"Is it?" he said quietly.

"What do you mean?"

"You already know there are other paths through this world than the one we tread with our feet. You *can* find her before it is too late, Will Lightfoot, but not by turning around now and going back. You must go further on this journey you've already begun. Lightfoot was meant to journey to the ghostlands and bring back the rain. Then the grass would grow again, and the wisent would return. And the Sky Folk might see their folly, before it is too late. That was his journey, and it must become yours."

Will swallowed hard. He turned to Shade, who sat, calmly waiting.

"I came for my friend," he said. "That's all. I'm not the one you've been waiting for. You said so yourself."

To Will's alarm the Dreamwalker's sightless eyes seemed to fix on him, and see him.

"Have you not heard me, Will Lightfoot? Only by keeping on, not going back, can you return to the weaver of worlds in time to help her. How that can be, I have not dreamed. But it is so. Lightfoot was meant to find the Sky Folk, and so must you, if you wish to help the weaver of worlds. The dream of my people and your own story must meet and walk together. And your friend the wolf must go with you."

Will turned to Shade.

"I can't ask you to do that, Shade," he said. "The Sky Folk want to capture you. If they do they might poison you like they did those other wolves."

"I will go with you, Will Lightfoot," Shade said, rising stiffly and limping over to Will. "Rowen of Blue Hill is my friend, too."

Will hung his head, unable to speak. After a long time he took a deep breath and looked up.

"I'll go," he said. "I'll find these Sky Folk, if it's the way back to Rowen. But if I'm not the one you've been waiting for, then I can't bring back the rain."

14

In the sky a great flock of birds appeared. They were very large, with black wings and sharp talons. None could say what sort of birds they were, for such creatures had never been seen before in that land, but all who saw them knew fear.

– Tales from the Golden Goose

WHEN HE STEPPED OUTSIDE the lodge with Shade, Will found Finn and the other knights arguing. They broke off when he appeared. Finn turned to him with an impatient look, as if he had been wondering what had taken Will so long.

"Will," Finn said, "you and Shade will return home to the Bourne with Balor and Doctor Alazar. I'm staying with the Dreamwalker and the children. I'll accompany them until they find their people. Then I'll be setting out on my own, for the ghostlands."

Will shook his head urgently.

"No," he said. "I have to go with you, Finn. And Shade too."

They all turned and stared at Will in surprise. Finn frowned.

"I'm afraid not, Will. It's too dangerous."

"But the road home will take too long. We won't get

back in time, before Rowen leaves Fable. The Dreamwalker said I—"

"You are a knight-apprentice of the Errantry now," Finn interrupted him sharply. "Your duty is to obey your superiors. I told you when we started out that I would order you home when I judged it was unsafe to keep on. That time has come. Your part in all of this is over."

Anger boiled up inside Will. Finn was so concerned about his brother that he couldn't see or hear anything else. But Will had to make him see . . .

"Yes, it is unsafe to keep on," Alazar said suddenly. "For any of us, Finn, including you."

"I'm not turning back when I've finally come this close," Finn said. "Think of what Shade told us, about Brannon Yates. On the run and half-dead because of these Sky Folk, whoever they are. Who knows what's happening now to the rest of Corr's men? I will not go back to Fable and wait while Caliburn and the Council debate what to do . . ."

He broke off. His fists were clenched so tightly the knuckles were white. Will had never seen him like this, and he was suddenly afraid for Finn as he never had been before.

"Finn won't be alone, 'Zar," Balor announced. "I'm going with him."

"No you're not, Balor," Finn said. "You will accompany Will, Shade and the doctor back to Fable. They will need you on the road."

"You need me, too, Finn. You know I'm worth any three other knights put together."

"This is no time for your stupid swaggering, Balor," the doctor snapped. "I don't agree with this at all, Finn. This party of ours is small enough as it is, in a huge and dangerous land. We don't even know how far we are from the Bourne. And now you want to split us up."

"I don't want to, but there's no other way," Finn said. "Balor, Will is your apprentice. Your duty is to stay by him, no matter what. I shouldn't have to tell you that."

Balor glowered, his face turning redder than it normally was. He appeared to be about to respond with angry words, then he sighed and nodded.

"Yes. Yes. Of course. But what about your duty, Finn? You know this is foolishness. It's against the code of the Errantry. Return to Appleyard with the rest of us. Don't do this."

"I'm sorry, Balor," Finn said, turning away. "But I have to find Corr, and nothing is going to stop me."

"Then you're more like him than I thought," the wildman muttered.

Finn froze for a moment but he didn't look at Balor. Instead he turned to Will and put a hand on his shoulder.

"Tell the Marshal what we've discovered," he said. "There are many families in Fable who've been waiting for this news."

Will was about to protest, but the steely look in Finn's eyes silenced him. Somehow he and Shade would have to find a way to give Balor the slip on the road home. But for now it was best to act as if he had given in.

"Let's see to the horses," Finn said, and turned away.

Will noticed that Balor was studying him, but he avoided the wildman's gaze. Then he saw that Hawk had been standing in the doorway of the lodge, watching them with wide, frightened eyes.

"If he goes in search of the Sky Folk," Hawk said to Will, "he won't come back. No one ever does."

It was decided that before everyone departed it would be good to have a quick meal. Balor got a blaze going in the fire pit near the Dreamwalker's lodge, took out his cooking gear and got to work making a soup with some of the food he carried in his provisions. Shade hunkered down beside Will, who sat on a log and said nothing, keeping his anger and frustration held tight. Hawk and his sister stood nearby, watching everything in silence. Will looked up at them and saw that they were frightened by all that had happened, and probably hungry. All this time they had been waiting for him, for the one who would bring back the rain. His anger faded.

"Come on," he said, beckoning them closer. "There's plenty for everyone."

Shyly, Hawk and his sister came forward and sat beside Will on the log. The girl fixed her solemn gaze on Balor, and it wasn't long before the wildman noticed. He served out the soup to everyone in tin mugs, then sat down to drink from his own, avoiding the girl's eyes.

"Would your father like to join us?" Alazar asked the boy.

Hawk shook his head.

"He has gone into the Dream Country. He walks there almost all the time now. He's looking for the Sky Folk, to see if they're coming this way."

Will glanced over at the Dreamwalker's lodge. The way Hawk spoke about his father's journeys in Dream, it almost sounded as if the boy believed he was actually travelling in some other land.

Finn had been packing his gear, and now he came over and sat down without a word. The small fire fluttered like a rag in the wind.

Balor cleared his throat. As he lifted the pot to pour himself another mug of soup, the girl leaned towards her brother, her eyes still fixed on Balor, and whispered something. Hawk nodded.

"What did she say?" Balor asked.

"She said . . ." Hawk hesitated, biting his lip.

"It's all right," Balor said, "I have a thick skin."

"To go with your skull," the doctor murmured.

Balor ignored him. He smiled at Hawk.

"Come on, lad. I won't be angry, I promise."

"She thinks you are the bear," the boy said.

"A bear?" The wildman shrugged. "Huh. I've been called worse things."

"She said you must be the Great Bear."

"Really? Well, that's even better."

"The Great Bear who protects Lightfoot."

"Protects Will? Of course I would, if it came to that."

"It will. Father says that you will battle the stone giant."

Balor scowled.

"Stone giant? What stone giant?"

Hawk was about to reply, but his eyes went wide, gazing at something behind the wildman. They all turned.

The Dreamwalker stood near them. Will stared in disbelief. He hadn't heard a sound, and he'd had the Dreamwalker's lodge in view the entire time they'd been sitting at the fire. He was sure he had not seen the blind man come outside.

Hawk jumped up and took his father's arm. Will looked at his companions and saw that they were as stunned as he was, but no one said anything.

The Dreamwalker lifted his head towards the sky to the north, into the thickest of the clouds. Will watched Hawk looking at his father with an intense, unbroken gaze.

"We are too late," the blind man said. "They are coming." He turned to Shade. "They have picked up your trail."

Everyone rose to their feet.

"How much time do we have?" Finn said.

"They will be here very soon," the Dreamwalker said. "There are caves on the hillside not far from here. Places you can hide. My son will guide you there."

"Father . . ." Hawk began, but the Dreamwalker raised his hand.

"Take your sister with you. When the Sky Folk come I will tell them I am alone here."

"If they bring their wolves, they will track our scent to the caves," Balor said.

"I will deal with the wolves if it comes to that," Shade said.

"You must go. All of you," the Dreamwalker said. "The caves will conceal you, and if the wolves come, you will be able to hold them off better there than here."

Balor threw sand on the fire and started packing up the cooking gear. Alazar gathered the horses. Finn buckled on his sword.

"Balor, take everyone to the caves," he said. "Keep them safe. If you can get away, head south for the Bourne."

The wildman stared at him.

"Finn?"

"I'm staying with the Dreamwalker."

"That's madness."

"Go with the others, Balor. They'll need you."

The wildman glared at Finn, but then his shoulders slumped. He sighed, turned and came over to Will and the doctor.

"Let's go," he muttered.

"This is wrong, Finn," the doctor shouted over the rising wind. "You're endangering all of us. If they find you here, they'll suspect there are others nearby. If they search, they'll find the caves."

"There's no time for this, Alazar. *Go.*"

At a shout from Hawk, they looked skywards to where he was pointing. Amid the broil of clouds there was one darker than the rest, moving distinctly on its own towards them. It was descending, and was holding its shape while all around it the other clouds were roiling and shearing apart in the wind. From within its blue-grey depths came a dim pulse of lightning. Will stood, transfixed. If these were the Sky Folk, what should he do? He was supposed to find them, and here they were, but they were after Shade.

"Come on, Will," the doctor shouted. Will stirred and looked around. Shade was standing near him.

"Let's go to the caves," Will said. He couldn't let them take the wolf. He would help Shade escape now, if he could, and go after the Sky Folk when he knew his friend was safe.

Hawk helped his sister onto the dun pony and led the way from the camp. Balor and Alazar followed with the horses, and Will walked beside Shade, who was still limping but able to keep up. When Will looked back, Finn was standing in the middle of the camp, watching them go. The Dreamwalker stood next to him.

They climbed the grassy slope nearest to the camp. Hawk led them over a rise studded with boulders, and down the other side, into a shallow, stony ravine that might once have been the channel of a stream but was now dry and overgrown with tall grass. Ragged clumps of brambles grew in crevices of the rock. Hawk pointed to a darkness under the brow of a jutting slab of rust-coloured stone.

"That is the largest of the caves."

They all dismounted and led the horses. The camp could not be seen from within the ravine, but they could still see the dark cloud. It was much closer now and seemed to have slowed until it was hanging almost motionless overhead. The sun had been blotted out, as if dusk had fallen in a moment.

The cave entrance was large enough for the two ponies

to be led unwillingly inside, but there would not be enough room for all of them and the horses, too.

"We'll set them loose for now," Balor said. "They'll run from whatever's inside that cloud. We can find them later."

Hastily, he and Alazar removed the tack from the horses and set them running with shouts and slaps to the flanks. Cutter and the other horses seemed to understand what was needed of them. They set off together at a gallop down the hillside and away from the camp and the approaching storm. Moments later they were out of sight.

"Into the cave," Balor shouted. With the two ponies, they all crowded into the dark, cramped space under the stone slab. Shade hunkered down beside Will. Hawk came in last and sat closest to the entrance, watching the sky. The rank smell of the terrified ponies filled the small space.

The wind was fierce now. Leaves, grass stalks and even small branches flew everywhere. The ponies whinnied and rolled their eyes in fear. Hawk held their rope bridles and spoke softly to them. A deep, low rumbling began from within the cloud and the earth shuddered. Pebbles danced crazily across the cave floor. All at once white fire stabbed out of the gloom beyond the cave. For an instant everything blazed like bright midday. Will ducked his head as the earth seemed to tilt under him and a tremendous roar filled his ears.

When Will looked up again, the wolves were there.

There were six of them, all with dark, matted fur and red-rimmed eyes. They had arranged themselves in a semi-circle near the mouth of the cave and stood motionless, watching. Hawk, who was crouching closest to the entrance, rose and backed up slowly into Will, who clutched his arm. He could feel the boy shaking.

"What are they doing?" Balor said. "Why haven't they attacked yet?"

"Because of me," Shade said, and before Will could stop him, he pushed forward between Will and Balor and limped out of the cave.

"*Shade,*" Will breathed desperately. "They can tell you're wounded. They'll attack."

Shade did not reply. He walked slowly towards the wolves until he was only a few feet from them, then he halted and made no other move. One of the wolves, the largest, bared his fangs and growled warningly. Shade gave no responding growl but stood still as a statue. The large wolf crouched as if he was about to spring at Shade, who remained still. Just when Will was sure the lead Sky Folk wolf was on the brink of leaping to the attack, Shade moved.

He moved faster than Will would have thought possible. Silently, with a great bound, he leapt at the lead wolf and an instant later had him on his belly, pinned and writhing. The other wolves flinched and backed away. Some let out anxious whines.

Shade, his paws on the lead wolf's chest, made a sound then, something between a growl and a bark. It was a short, harsh sound that startled Will and made him flinch like the wolves. Will had never heard Shade make such a sound. It was a statement of who was in command.

The lead wolf scrambled out from beneath Shade and crawled away to rejoin his fellows. Shade paced back and forth in front of the wolves, who whimpered and ducked their heads.

"They will obey me, for now," Shade said to Will. "If their masters come I do not know what will happen, so I will lead them away from here, northwards."

"But Shade," Will cried, "how will we find you?"

"I will find *you,* Will Lightfoot," Shade said. "No matter what happens, we will be together again."

Suddenly he gave a loud yip and sprang away out of the ravine, and without a moment's hesitation the wolf pack bounded after him, eager and panting, like submissive dogs following their pack leader.

"That's it, then," Balor said. "Shade's given us a chance. Let's find the horses and make a run for it."

"Wait, where's the boy?" Alazar shouted.

Hawk was no longer beside Will. Moon was still cowering at the far end of the cave beside Balor. Will darted out of the cave just in time to see the Horse Folk boy disappear over the rim of the ravine in the direction of the camp.

Will called his name, and ignoring Balor's shouts for him to come back, he scrambled up the side of the ravine. At the top of the hill he paused. He could no longer see Hawk, but only a short distance away the dark cloud had touched the earth, its edges creeping like tentacles over the ground, almost surrounding the camp. The Dreamwalker and Finn were visible as tiny figures for only a moment, before they vanished in a sweeping curtain of cloud. For an instant Will had a glimpse of a huge dark shape within the cloud, something descending to the earth, but it was gone again before he could tell what it was.

A moment later Hawk appeared again below Will, from out of a fold in the hillside, running for the camp. Will shouted at him to stop, but the shrieking wind swallowed up his voice.

A flash of lightning struck so close it made Will stagger and fall to his knees. As he picked himself up, he saw a tall figure in a dark grey cloak appear out of the mist, moving towards Hawk with a net in its hands. Another cloaked figure emerged from the mist on the other side of the Horse Folk boy, and another followed swiftly behind. All the Sky Folk were masked to the eyes in grey, and the second and third each carried a long metal stave topped with a black sphere.

The sky will come to earth, Will thought suddenly. The second part of the shadow's message.

Hawk saw them. He halted for a moment, then dashed on again. Will saw the first of the Sky Folk lift his net, its edges weighted with what looked like dark metal discs.

But Will did not see him throw it. At that moment he heard the doctor's shout behind him.

"Will! Run!"

Will whirled to see two more cloaked Sky Folk advancing on him. One had a net and the other carried one of the metal staves. There was no sign of the doctor or Balor. Desperately Will sprinted away, down the hill in the direction Hawk had gone, reaching for the hilt of his sword as he ran. Before he could draw it, there was a blinding white light all around him and something struck his body a painful blow that sent him sprawling. He lay for a moment, dazed and thoughtless, his skull seeming to crawl with a cold fire, then he staggered shakily to his feet and tried to run. To his horror his legs would hardly obey him. They had gone numb, as had his arms.

He had staggered only a few steps when dark shapes loomed out of the fog, moving swiftly towards him. Will stumbled away from them, but something caught at his feet and he fell, tangled in strange wet strands like ice-cold webbing.

15

... I will speak a word of darkness in your ear...

– The Kantar

THE MARROWBONE BROTHERS HAD spent a long night in their locked room high up in the Gathering House. No one had come to speak to them or bring them anything to eat since they'd been given some thin broth and hard bread the evening before. Flitch was sitting hunched on his narrow bunk, his eyes boring holes in the floor, while Hodge stood at the window, his enormous face squeezed between two of the bars.

"More riders are leaving, brother," Hodge said excitedly. "That's the third party this hour. I wonder where they're all going."

Flitch said nothing.

"Oh, wait," Hodge said, straining on tiptoe. "There's another rider, coming in through the gates. Riding fast. His cloak is all muddy. Looks like he's ridden a long way. I wonder where he's come from."

One of Flitch's eyes twitched.

"What do you think's going on, brother?" Hodge asked.

"In your head, you mean? Not very much," Flitch snarled, "as usual. And if you don't come away from that window I'm going to maim you in a number of highly original ways."

Hodge turned to his brother with a hurt look.

"Please don't be that way, Flitch. I'm only trying to keep busy. Trying to make the best of it."

Flitch glared at him but said nothing.

"At least we have a window," Hodge said. "We never had a window before, in any of the other places we lived."

"We're prisoners, you dolt. We're not living here. We're trapped here."

A tremor of panic rippled across Hodge's face.

"What do you think they'll do to us, brother? Maybe . . . maybe they like bacon for breakfast . . ."

"I already told you, they don't kill their prisoners, and they don't eat them."

"But why not? Not that I want to be eaten, of course, but I don't understand why they haven't killed us already and strung us up in a smokehouse somewhere."

"Because they're *noble*. They have this ridiculous code of honour that only allows them to kill to defend themselves. Idiots. Eventually they'll have to let us go, or even better, their little country will be overrun by *his* armies and then we'll find a way to turn things to our advantage, like we always do. And when we do, I'm going to find that Skalding witch, that Freya Ragnarsdaughter, and . . ."

His enormous hands reached out like claws, as if he saw Freya in front of him.

"And eat her?" Hodge said cautiously.

"We wouldn't be eating her, not right away. No, we'll pay

her back first. She was the one who led that little wretch's friends to our lair."

"You mean Sir William of the Seven Mighty Companions?"

"Don't call him that. He was no *Sir William*. He was a scrawny nobody with powerful friends. He would have been ours, if it hadn't been for her. The blacksmith's daughter brought the one who doused the werefire and drove us out of Skald. So when we see her again, dear brother, and we will, we're going to make her suffer. We'll lead her on a chain through the dirt like she led us. We'll see how she likes grovelling for her life. Oh yes, she shall grovel, and feel the whip . . ."

"Then we'll eat her?" Hodge breathed.

Flitch nodded, his eyes half closed and his hands still outstretched, as if he was gripping an imaginary neck.

"Yes, then we'll eat her," he murmured.

Hodge summoned up a smile, but there was no delight in his voice as there might once have been.

"Well, that's good, then. Now all we have to do is get out of here."

Flitch's eyes opened. His hands dropped to his sides. He looked up at his brother with hate-filled eyes.

"You have to spoil everything, don't you?" he muttered. "Even my daydreams."

He looked more closely at Hodge and his eyes narrowed.

"What's the matter with you?" he said. "You've been more gristle-brained than usual since we got here. It's that red-haired little snitch, isn't it? The old man's granddaughter. What did she say to you?"

Hodge was about to reply when they heard the sound of a key in the lock. Flitch stiffened, and Hodge backed away into a corner.

The door swung open. Two knights of the Errantry, armed with swords, stood in the doorway. A man in a long burgundy cloak strode into the cell. His face was flat, his eyes narrow. It was the kind of face that gave nothing away.

Hodge whimpered.

"Please, my good sir, remember your code of honour," he snivelled. "You don't eat your prisoners."

The man's thin lips parted in a faintly mocking smile.

"No fear of that," he said. "I'm only here to talk."

He raised a hand, and a moment later a short, stout man in a cook's apron wheeled a small wooden cart into the cell. On the cart was laid out a heaping platter of steaming, juicy-looking cuts of meat, fresh breadrolls, a huge wedge of cheese, and a large wine bottle and two silver goblets. Hodge and Flitch stared at this unexpected bounty, hunger and suspicion playing across their faces. The man in the apron eyed them with obvious disgust.

"Waste of my efforts," he muttered as he left the cell.

The man in the burgundy cloak gestured to the platter.

"Please," he said to the hogmen, "help yourselves."

"Is this all for us?" Hodge asked, glassy-eyed.

"It is," the man said.

"It's not . . . our last meal, is it?"

The man smiled.

"I'm sure there will be many more such meals for you, my friends."

That was good enough for Hodge. He lunged at the cart and began stuffing handsful of meat into his mouth. Flitch stayed where he had been sitting, his cold eyes fixed on the man in the cloak.

"Who are you?" he asked bluntly.

"My name is Ammon Brax," said the man. "I'm a mage in the service of the Errantry." He gestured again at the heap of food, which Hodge had already considerably diminished. "Please, feel free."

"I don't, at the moment," Flitch said. "What do you want with us?"

"Straight to the point. I like that. Well, then, I understand you dwelt in Skald before you came here."

Flitch's eyes narrowed. It was clear he suspected a trap. There were many people in Skald who wanted to see the Marrowbone brothers pay for their crimes.

"And if we did, what of it?"

"It was our home," Hodge blurted out, spraying spittle across the cell, "and we were driven from it most cruelly."

Flitch glared at Hodge, who was too busy with his meal to notice. He let loose a thunderous belch and dived back into the food. A sneer of repulsion curled Brax's lip but a moment later his face had recovered its mask-like impenetrability.

"I have heard something of your ordeal there," Brax said. "And I can assure you that if you help me, you will face no such oppression in Fable. In fact it is in my power to have you released from this cell."

"Really," Flitch said guardedly. "And how can we help you?"

"I would like to know more about how things were, in Skald, before you were . . . exiled. The more you can tell me, the more I can do for you."

"How things were?" Flitch asked. "What do you mean?"

"Fings weren't so bab," Hodge mumbled through a mouthful of gristle. "We had a lovely sewer to ourselbes and lobs of peeble to eat—"

"*Shut your hole,*" Flitch hissed.

But Hodge was now so involved with his meal that he was beyond his brother's threats. A gobbet of stringy fat hung from his lip. He sucked it up like a noodle and smacked his lips.

"Will there be dessert?" he asked.

"I'll see what I can do," Brax said. "But for the moment, I'd like to hear more about Skald, and what happened to you there. I understand you lived in the sewers under the keep."

"It was pleasant enough in the sewers," Hodge said, licking the grease from his fingers. "I liked it there. I liked it very much. Except for . . ."

He glanced fearfully at Flitch.

"Except for what?"

"The fire," Hodge said. "The werefire. I mean, the fire was one of the reasons things worked out so well for us at first. The Skaldings were so busy fighting off the nasty things the fire brought to their city that they didn't have time to bother with us. But the fire . . . it *hurt* us. And there was something in the keep, where the werefire first broke out. A terrible thing. Its screams . . . it's like they were inside your own head. Screams like razors. *Brrr*. We stayed clear of the keep. Anyhow, despite that we were doing all right, you could say, we were getting by. But then the werefire was put out, and the Skaldings weren't busy with all the nasties any more and they came looking for us."

Brax nodded.

"I see. How unfortunate," he said, leaning forward. "But it's a fascinating story, really. I'd like to hear more. In particular, I would like to know everything you can tell me about this strange fire."

"Oh, good sir, I'd rather not talk about it if it's all the same to you," Hodge said quickly, a strip of meat hanging forgotten in his hand. "I really don't want to remember the fire. It's a bad thing. A terrible thing. That girl knows. She knows how it hurt us."

"Girl," Brax echoed, his brows knitting together. "What girl?"

"The old man's granddaughter. Sh . . ." He swallowed hard and his eyes became watery. "She was sorry about our brother, Tuck."

He wiped his eyes, then glanced warily at Flitch, who was staring at him in speechless amazement. Brax's eyes were fixed on Hodge, too, but they were the keen, cold eyes of a hawk whose prey has just come into sight.

"What are you babbling about now?" Flitch snarled.

"It's true," Hodge said miserably. "Ask her, good sir. I don't really know how I know it, but she *saw* everything that happened to us ever since we left home. She . . . she *felt* it, and she felt sorry for us. It's true she looks like nobody important, just a skinny scrap of a girl, but she understands about the werefire. And a lot more, too, I'm sure."

"Does she indeed," Brax said with the faintest trace of a smile. "Please, my friend, tell me more about the girl, and what she knows."

Edweth had never seen the morning market so busy. In addition to the usual crowd of locals there were so many outlandish folk in Fable these days, all of whom had apparently decided to visit the market at the same time. Still, she never tired of Storyfolk-watching, and today was certainly providing a bumper crop of notables. But each time she made it through the press of bodies to one of her favourite stalls, she found the wares already mostly picked over. Usually Edweth would fill her basket quickly and then take some time to chat with any acquaintances she might run into. But today she had been here far longer than usual and had only managed to salvage half a dozen eggs, a couple of loaves, and some rather forlorn-looking apples. Not only that, but people seemed to be on edge, impatient, easily offended. There was even an angry scuffle over who had laid first claim to a juicy-looking ham. Edweth had never seen tempers flare like this at the market before, other than her own the time a shifty baker had put only ten hot-cross buns in her bag instead of the dozen she'd paid for.

If homeless Storyfolk kept on streaming into Fable in such numbers, she wondered, what was going to happen? Would the city walls burst at the seams?

Clutching her basket, she shouldered her way through the crowd, eager to get back home and put breakfast on the table. If she couldn't keep the Master from taking Rowen into that frightening place, she could at least make sure the girl was well-fed. She was so thin.

Edweth came to a sudden halt. A couple of rough-looking characters were arguing with each other in some incomprehensible language, right in her path, and neither of them showed any inclination to move. As she searched for a way around them, she glimpsed the grey of an Errantry cloak nearby. On closer inspection she saw to her disbelief that the owner of the cloak was just standing there, in a shadowy corner of the market, with his hood up and his head down. *Look at that,* she thought. *Pandemonium breaking loose and he's not doing a blessed thing. What is this city coming to?*

When Rowen got up, she found Riddle curled at the foot of her bed. He lifted his head when she approached, his eerie eyes fixed on her.

"Good," said Rowen. "You're awake."

"Riddle is always awake."

"Don't you ever sleep?" she asked, surprised.

"*Sleep*. Funny word. *Sleep. Sleep.* Riddle has seen creatures in the forest do that. Bat sleeps in the daytime. Bear sleeps all winter. Riddle doesn't sleep."

"Never?"

"Never. Riddle just waits here for Rowen. Watches her. Listens to her talk."

"Talk?"

"Rowen talks while she sleeps. Riddle thought she was talking to him, but when he spoke back she didn't answer. So Riddle knew she was talking to someone else."

"What did I say?"

"You said the boy's name. Will. You sounded happy, and you were saying, 'Will, Will.'"

"Oh. I see."

To her annoyance Rowen felt a blush spread across her face.

"What shall we do now?" Riddle asked.

"I'm not really sure. Let's go and talk to Grandfather."

They found him in the kitchen, sitting alone at the table peeling an apple with a penknife and munching on the slices.

"Edweth has gone to the market," he said. "I can make you something for breakfast."

Rowen shook her head.

"I'm not hungry."

"You should eat. It might be a long time before you get the chance again."

"Why?"

"The dragon's message means we have far less time than I had hoped. We're going back into the Weaving today. There is a lot more you need to learn, and soon."

Rowen swallowed.

"What about Brax? What if he comes back to see you?"

"I'm told he's riding with Thorne this morning, inspecting Fable's defences. They've become fast friends, those two. Which gives us some breathing room, I think."

"Good."

"We're going now, to the place where things become other things?" Riddle asked as they left the kitchen.

"Grandfather and I . . ." Rowen began, "we think you came from the Weaving."

"From the rain place?"

"We think so. You . . . *feel* like that place feels. And you change, like the Weaving changes."

"Riddle already told you that," the cat mumbled, with a hint of rebuke in his voice.

"Yes, you did," Pendrake said. "We just didn't think it was a good time to bring you with us."

"So now is a good time?"

Before the loremaster could answer, they heard a knock at the front door. Rowen looked at her grandfather.

"I'll answer it," he said. "You stay here." He strode off down the hallway and returned a few moments later with Freya. He ushered her and Rowen into the library.

"What is it, my dear?" he said to Freya. "What brings you this early?"

"I didn't want to bother you, Father Nicholas," Freya said, her face pale and tense. "Captain Thorne has been back to see us. He says he has orders from the Marshal to have the Skaldings out of Fable by tonight."

"What? Why? He agreed you could stay."

"Yes, but that sentry who went missing has never been found."

"Gared Bamble. Surely Thorne hasn't accused you of his disappearance?"

"Not in so many words. But he doubled the guard on us, and now he says we must leave."

"This is absurd," Pendrake said angrily. "I will speak to the Marshal."

He turned to Rowen.

"Our business will have to wait," he said. "Freya, will you stay with Rowen? I don't want her to be alone."

"Of course, Father Nicholas."

Pendrake took up his staff.

"I will return as soon as I can." He turned to Rowen. "Don't leave the toyshop, and don't go . . . anywhere else."

Rowen shook her head.

"I won't, Grandfather."

He glanced down at the cat.

"Riddle, remember what we talked about."

"Riddle remembers."

He hurried out of the room and a moment later they heard the front door shut. Freya sank into a chair.

"You have your cloak on," she said to Rowen. "Were you going somewhere?"

"It's hard to explain," Rowen said.

"We were going to the rain place," Riddle said.

"The rain place?" Freya echoed. Then she seemed to notice the troubled look on Rowen's face. "Well, it's none of my affair."

She glanced over at the dented, rusting suit of armour that had stood in the room as long as Rowen could remember.

"Is that Father Nicholas's armour?" she asked.

"It was. He hasn't worn it for many years."

"I didn't know he had been a knight."

"He wasn't, but he fought in some battles a long time ago, when he was very young," Rowen said. "He doesn't talk much about it." She turned to Riddle. "What did you and Grandfather talk about? What does he want you to remember?"

"The toymaker said that if someone tries to harm Rowen, Riddle must protect her."

"Does this have something to do with the sentry who disappeared?" Freya asked.

"I don't know," Rowen said. "I'm just supposed to stay in the toyshop. It's the safest place in Fable."

"Why is that?"

"That's also hard to explain," Rowen said, smiling in spite of herself. "There's something here that keeps our enemies from finding us."

They heard the front door suddenly open, and both started and glanced at each other. Freya half rose from her chair.

"Rowen?" called the housekeeper.

"I'm here, Edweth," Rowen shouted, relieved.

The housekeeper bustled into the library a moment later, carrying her market basket.

"Good morning, Freya," she said cheerily. "Will you be joining us for breakfast?"

"I don't think so," Freya said. "The loremaster will probably be back soon and I should return to my friends."

"You have friends here, too," Edweth said, arching an eyebrow. "I ran into the Master on my way here, and he told me to feed you both well. So you just sit there and gossip and I'll have something ready in no time at all."

"We'll join you," Rowen said. "It's warmer in the kitchen."

They left the library and followed the housekeeper down the hall into the kitchen. Rowen stoked the fire in the stove while Edweth marshalled her pots and pans.

"My word, you should have seen the market this morning," the housekeeper said as she cracked eggs. "Utter madness. Folk nearly coming to blows over fish and bread. And there was a knight-errant there, but he wasn't doing a blessed thing to keep order. I gave him a sizeable piece of my mind, let me tell you, but he just stood there like a post, not saying a word. Apparently they don't teach manners up at Appleyard any more. And strange-looking? I thought that ogre or whatever he is, Balor Gruff, was the most outlandish of the whole crew, but this one truly gave me the shivers. Looked like he'd just crawled out of a grave, he did. Not a spot of colour in his face. Where the Errantry is doing its recruiting these days, I don't know. I mentioned it to the Master when I passed him just now, and I hope he'll take my complaint to the Marshal."

They heard the front door swing open slowly on its hinges. Edweth glanced up with a frown.

"Your grandfather back already? He must have forgotten something. Here, Rowen, look after these eggs for me."

The housekeeper wiped her hands on her apron and hurried from the room.

"With your housekeeper here, I don't think you need me to stay with you," Freya said with a grin. "She could take on just about anything."

"I know," Rowen said. "But I'm glad you're here. I hope Grandfather will convince the Marshal to let you stay. I'm sure it won't be long before Will and Finn come back with Shade."

Freya smiled shyly. She was about to reply when from the front hall they heard a piercing scream, followed by what sounded like a body hitting the floor.

"Edweth!" Rowen cried. She and Freya rushed out into the corridor.

Someone in a cloak of the Errantry stood at the far end of the hall, leaning over the housekeeper, who lay prone on the floor.

"Edweth!" Rowen screamed.

The cloaked figure stood and turned to them. It was a young man, or at least resembled one. His skin was bone-white, his eyes dark holes. He carried no weapon they could see, but a chill seemed to radiate from him.

"Rowen of Blue Hill," he said, in a voice like a buzzing of many insects.

"Who are you?" Freya cried.

"I've seen him before," Rowen said. "He's . . . he's the sentry who went missing. Gared Bamble. But he's not—"

"There's something wrong with him," Freya breathed. "He's not alive."

"What do you want?" Rowen said, backing away.

"Rowen of Blue Hill," the young man repeated, and they saw that his mouth did not move as the words came out. He stepped over Edweth's body and came slowly towards them.

Freya clutched Rowen's arm. "Follow me!"

Rowen obeyed, dashing after Freya into the library. Riddle came bounding after them. Freya ran to the suit of armour and slid the sword from its scabbard.

"Still sharp," she muttered, testing the blade with her thumb. "This should do."

A moment later, the thing in the shape of Gared Bamble appeared in the doorway.

"I am here," said a voice. Rowen and Freya turned to see another Rowen standing near them.

"Riddle?" Rowen whispered.

"I am Rowen of Blue Hill," said the other Rowen.

The thing hesitated, then strode swiftly towards Riddle, who darted away and sprang for the door faster than Rowen herself could have moved. One of the thing's arms shot out from its body like a whip and wrapped itself around the other Rowen.

"Riddle!" Rowen screamed.

The other Rowen gasped and struggled as the thing pulled her towards itself. Then she seemed to melt, and a snake appeared where she had been, and slithered out of the thing's grasp. A moment later Riddle took cat form again, and crawled away, whimpering.

The thing watched Riddle for a moment, then turned to Rowen.

Freya strode forward and swung the sword. The thing's head slid away from the neck, hit the floor and rolled along the wall. The cloaked body stood wavering for a moment, as if it might topple over, then it took a slow step, and another, and then it was advancing on Rowen again. As she watched in horror, slits opened on its arms and naked chest, like wounds cut by an invisible knife. Then she saw that they were not wounds but mouths. Mouths all over the thing's body, splitting open, gasping, muttering. As it walked slowly towards her, something like spider's threads whipped out of the hole in its neck and swiftly coiled themselves into the shape of a head.

Freya levelled the sword at the creature and stood in front of Rowen.

"When I tell you to, *run*," Freya whispered.

At that moment the loremaster appeared in the doorway.

"Grandfather!" Rowen screamed.

Pendrake strode into the room. He threw his staff aside.

"You are a walking spell, thrawl," he shouted at the creature in a commanding voice. "Your name is your power. Speak it to me and fulfil your task."

The thrawl was still facing Rowen, but its features suddenly sank back into its face, reappearing where the back of its head had been. Its limbs twisted around and now it was facing the loremaster.

"You will say your name to me, thrawl, not to her," Pendrake said. Slowly he began to move into the library, and the thrawl's head turned as it watched him.

Rowen saw that her grandfather was drawing the creature's attention away from her, leaving an opportunity for her to reach the doorway and escape.

"You are nothing but your master's voice," Pendrake said to the thrawl. "You live only to speak your name. Speak it now and die!"

The thrawl hesitated, its many mouths silently opening and closing, then it turned away from the loremaster and headed once more towards Rowen and Freya.

"Run, Rowen!" Pendrake cried. "To the Weaving! You'll be safest there!"

She could not move. Pendrake's eyes implored her, then he turned and lunged at the thrawl, grasped its arms. The creature thrashed and struggled against his grip but could not free itself.

"Speak your name!" Pendrake cried. "Speak it to *me*!"

Finally all of the thrawl's mouths gaped open at once, and a sound came from it, a cry, a shriek, a word that was hate and horror and despair.

Rowen covered her ears.

The thrawl began to come apart, like a skein of thread swiftly unravelling. It coiled itself around the loremaster as if wrapping him in a cocoon. Rowen darted forward, screaming for her grandfather. She clutched at the tightly coiled threads, desperately trying to tear them apart, and then suddenly they fell asunder in her hand. The cocoon shape collapsed like an empty cloak. The lifeless threads fluttered to the floor.

Her grandfather was gone.

16

No one knows when the loremasters first came to Fable, but many generations of them have lived here, quietly going about their work of helping others, though few ever realized who they were, or know it even today. As far as can be determined, the loremasters always lived in the house at the end of Pluvius Lane, a narrow, out-of-the-way little alley known only for the curious fact that it so often seems to be raining there, or about to rain.

– The Secret History of the Bourne

"I TRIED TO STOP IT," Edweth said tearfully. "I tried. It brushed me aside like a feather. I've never felt a touch so cold."

Rowen sat beside the housekeeper, who lay on the settee in the library. Rowen and Freya had helped her there after the loremaster had vanished. Riddle crouched on the rug beside Rowen, his tufted ears laid back against his head. Edweth was weak and shaky but otherwise unhurt.

"Just rest," Rowen said as soothingly as she could. The housekeeper only shuddered and covered her eyes. Then she looked up again at Rowen, her face stricken.

"The Master . . . what's happened to him?"

"Grandfather . . . he's gone," Rowen said, her voice breaking.

"He's *dead*?"

Rowen shook her head, knowing she did it to convince herself as much as to comfort Edweth.

"I don't know where he is," she said, fighting back her own tears. "That thing vanished and so did Grandfather."

"Vanished?"

"I've searched the whole house. He's not here." Then a new thought occurred to her. "The . . . the thrawl. That's what he called it. The thrawl spoke my name. It must have been sent to find me."

"To kill you?"

"I don't know. Grandfather kept it from reaching me. He said something like *you will take me, not her.*"

"Take him . . . where?"

Rowen's heart went cold.

"To *him.*"

Edweth covered her mouth with her hands.

"Oh, Rowen, no . . ." she sobbed.

Rowen's shaking hands knotted into fists. All at once a terrible rage boiled up inside her, drowning her grief and fear. Nightbane had killed her parents when she was a child. Her grandmother had gone into the Weaving for her sake and had never returned. And now her grandfather was gone, too. The Night King had taken everything from her.

The rage was like a burning knife in her heart, a knife she wanted to take in her hands and turn on someone else. On *him.* She had never felt such hatred before, for anyone or anything. She wanted to scream and strike out at the one who had done this to her, but he wasn't here. She had never seen him. Ever since she was born he had struck at her from the shadows, hurting everyone who loved her, but he had never shown his face. It would not happen again, she would not let it. She would find him somehow, and she would hurt *him.* She would make him pay.

"What about Freya? Is she all right?"

The housekeeper's voice seemed to come from far away. Rowen gasped for breath, pulled back from the terrible place she had been. She groped for an answer to Edweth's question.

"She ran to Appleyard . . . to tell the Errantry what's happened."

Edweth took a deep breath and seemed to gather herself together.

"Well, I'm not going to just lie here . . ."

Rowen put a hand on the housekeeper's shoulder.

"No, Edweth," she said. "Please don't get up. I'll make some tea, while we wait for Freya to get back. Riddle, stay here with Edweth."

"Riddle, go with Rowen," Edweth commanded. "Don't leave her side, do you hear me, cat?"

"Riddle hears," the cat said, lowering his head.

Rowen went to the kitchen with the cat beside her.

"The small loud one is right," Riddle said, as Rowen moved about the kitchen. Boiling water and spooning out the tea leaves gave her something to do, kept her thoughts from that terrible place inside, where the rage still smouldered, waiting for her to give in to it. "Riddle is supposed to keep close to Rowen. The toymaker said so."

"Grandfather told you to make yourself look like me, didn't he, if anyone tried to harm me. That's why you did that, isn't it?"

The cat nodded his head slowly.

"Then Riddle was supposed to run away, so the bad things would follow him and leave Rowen alone. Riddle tried to do what the toymaker said, but the thread-thing was too strong. Riddle is sorry."

"Don't be. You did your best."

She brought the tea things to Edweth, who had already risen from the settee and held out her hands to take the tray. Rowen let her take it, and sat down slowly in a chair. Her heart had gone cold, as if the knife of rage had turned to ice. She looked around the room like someone in a trance. There was her grandfather's staff, lying on the floor where he had cast it. She bent to pick it up and saw something else under the table. She reached for it. Her grandfather's spectacles.

Rowen folded the arms of the spectacles and slipped them into her pocket. Edweth set down the tray and put her arms around her.

"Lord Caliburn will help us, love," the housekeeper said. "I'm sure he'll send a troop of the Errantry's finest to search for your grandfather and bring him back."

Rowen shook her head slowly. She knew what she had to do, and it seemed to her that she was already far away, walking that strange road into the unknown.

"It would be no use," she said. "The Shadow Realm is not some place riders can get to, like the Forest of Eldark. Grandfather always told me it's another Perilous Realm, a shadow version of this one, on the other side of all that is. You could ride all the way across the Realm and you'd never find it."

"Then, is there any way . . ."

There was an urgent knocking at the door, then a familiar voice called to them from the front hall, and Freya rushed into the library.

"I went to Appleyard and told them everything," she said breathlessly. "I brought back someone who can help."

Behind her came the mage, Ammon Brax. Rowen's first urge at the sight of him was to shout at him to get out of her house, but she forced herself to keep silent. Then she saw the look on the mage's face was one of pain and concern for her, and for a moment she felt her hopes lift. Maybe she had been wrong about him. He might really have come for her sake. Maybe he could even help her find her grandfather . . .

"Your friend Freya told me what happened," Brax said to her in a voice hoarse with emotion. "I have heard of these creatures, these walking spells. We will find your grandfather, Rowen. We will find him and bring him home. I promise you that."

He placed a hand gently on her shoulder. She wanted so desperately to believe him. Maybe Grandfather was wrong about this man. Maybe he had changed. And if she confided in him, told him what she knew about the raincabinet and the Weaving, maybe they could search for Grandfather together, and the task wouldn't seem so hopeless.

Then she glanced up at his face and saw his dark, narrow eyes searching coldly around the room, taking in everything, appraising it all like someone planning to move into a house that was not yet his.

At that moment she saw him for what he was and the anger blazed up inside her again. Brax didn't care about Grandfather. This was simply the opportunity he had been waiting for. The secrets of the great loremaster, Nicholas Pendrake, were almost within his grasp. And she had been about to give them to him.

She bit her lip to stop a scream.

"Captain Thorne wants you to come to Appleyard, Rowen," Freya said. "He says you'll be safer there."

"I agree with the captain," the mage said, and his hand lifted from her shoulder just in time, before she was about to push it away in disgust. She knew she couldn't speak without the bitterness and anger spilling out and so she said nothing. She wouldn't give anything away. She had to think now, to come up with a plan.

"The most important thing is to keep you safe," Brax

went on. "And then you and I can work together to solve this. I know we can."

"The Master always said the toyshop was the safest place in Fable," Edweth said, studying the mage with a suspicious look.

"Is that so?" the mage asked casually, as if the housekeeper's comment barely interested him. "I wonder why. But I'm sure the captain knows best."

"The Master has his reasons," Edweth said. "There's something about the toyshop that—"

She broke off and looked guiltily at Rowen.

Rowen took a deep breath and stood.

"I will come to Appleyard," she said to Brax. "But I need to gather my things."

It was weak, she knew, but it was all she'd had time to come up with. Her eyes locked with the mage's for a long moment. She could see he was calculating whether he had the power yet to force her to his will. Finally he nodded and looked away.

"Of course," he said obligingly. "I'll wait for you here while you get ready."

"Could you please," she said, trying to still the tremble in her voice, "return to Appleyard now and tell the captain I'm on my way?"

"I really should accompany you," the mage protested in a tone of quiet reason. "For your safety. I don't mind waiting while you prepare."

"Freya's here," Rowen said. "She'll bring me to Appleyard. And I . . . I need to say goodbye. I need a moment by myself. This is the only home I've ever known."

The mage looked to be about to protest, and she wondered if she had overdone it. Anger and suspicion flickered across Brax's sharp features. Then he inclined his head.

"Very well," he said. "I will return soon."

The mage made them all a slight bow, turned on his heel and strode from the room. As soon as he was out of the toyshop door, Rowen rushed to lock it behind him.

"Don't let him back in, Edweth," she said. "No matter what."

"If only I hadn't said anything," the housekeeper said, shaking her head angrily. "Now he suspects we're hiding something."

"He already suspected that," Rowen said. "The only reason he came to Fable in the first place was to find Grandfather's secrets. But he mustn't learn anything. He mustn't find out about the raincabinet. We have to keep him out of here."

"What about the Marshal?" Edweth said. "He wants you in Appleyard, too."

"I'm not going," Rowen said. "I have to stay at the toyshop. It's what Grandfather would want me to do."

"I thought the mage wanted to help," Freya said with a scowl. "I shouldn't have brought him here."

"He would have showed up soon enough anyway," Rowen said bitterly. Then she had another thought. "Freya, what did the Marshal say about you leaving Fable?"

"He was busy and wouldn't see me. But Captain Thorne still wants us out of the city by evening," she said numbly. "Rowen, you should come with us. What if another of those creatures comes looking for you? Now they know where you are."

"I think that is best," Edweth agreed. "And I'll come with you. For all we know, more of those horrors may be on their way here right now. And I know some folk in other parts of the Bourne who can be trusted. They'll help us, and keep quiet about it. We'll find somewhere you can be safe . . ."

"For how long, Edweth?" Rowen cried. "I'll be hunted

wherever I go, and anyone who hides me will be in danger. Here I've got the only chance of finding out what happened to Grandfather."

"You mean . . ." Edweth began, her eyes filling with fear. "You're thinking of going back *there*. Oh, Rowen, no. *No*."

"Grandfather told me that everyone has a thread in the Weaving. The thread of their own story. Maybe I can find his thread. Maybe I can reach him before he's taken into the Shadow Realm."

Freya pursed her lips, nodding to herself as if she had made up her mind about something.

"I'll stay here with Edweth," she said to Rowen. "I'll make sure Brax doesn't get through that door."

"But your friends, Freya," Rowen protested. "You should be with them. Captain Thorne won't do anything to me, but he could have you locked up if you stay."

"Father Nicholas risked everything for my people," Freya said quietly. "And now at last there's something I can do to repay him. I don't understand where it is you're going, Rowen, to search for your grandfather, but at least I can stand guard here while you're gone."

Rowen nodded.

"Thank you," she said. She took up her grandfather's staff and headed for the corridor.

Edweth gaped at her.

"Now?" she said. "Already?"

Rowen halted in the doorway.

"It can't wait," she said. "Brax will return, and he might bring some of Thorne's men with him, to make sure he gets his way this time. If he tries to force his way in, tell him I ran away. Tell him . . . tell him I took Grandfather's book of secrets and ran off with it."

"Book of secrets? What are you talking about?"

"There isn't a book of secrets, Edweth. But tell him that. Maybe it'll throw him off the trail."

She hurried along the corridor to the stairs. Edweth and Freya followed her, and Riddle came padding after. At the bottom of the stairs, Rowen stopped once more. She saw Riddle and a faint flicker of hope rose in her.

"You're coming with me," she said to the cat.

"That is what Riddle told the toymaker he would do."

Rowen hugged Freya, then Edweth. The housekeeper held her tightly as if she would never let go.

"I will come back," Rowen said. "I promise."

"Be safe, child," Edweth whispered.

Rowen dashed up the stairs with Riddle close behind. Reaching the top floor, she hurried to the door of the rain-cabinet, paused a moment, then opened it. She looked into the rainy darkness, and her grandfather's words came back to her. What he'd said to her after Freya had brought them the dragon's warning . . .

If I'm not with you any more, find Will. Stay close to him.

"Are we going in there at last?" Riddle asked.

"Yes, we are. If you really did come from the Weaving, maybe you can help me find my way."

But her thoughts were still with Will. How she wished he was here with her. He must be miles away by now, she thought, and Shade needed him, too, even more than she did. She couldn't do what her grandfather had asked. She couldn't set out to look for Will now. It was too late for that. She was alone, and there was only one path left to her. A path through the Weaving that she was certain would lead her to the Shadow Realm.

17

Ashes fall upon the earth like snow,
the stars no longer know their names.
And men, it must always be so,
tread the dark road to the flames.

– Legends of the Northlands

WILL WOKE UP WITH A CRY. All around him was darkness and the creaking of wooden timbers. He felt a hand on his shoulder. Doctor Alazar was crouching beside him.

"It's all right, Will."

"Where are we?" Will asked groggily. He was lying on a rough blanket in a small room. The wind was shrieking outside. A candle lantern with a smoky glass cover gave off a dim yellow glow, by which he could see that the walls and the floor of the room were made of wooden planks crossed with thicker beams. The whole room seemed to shudder with the force of the wind's blows and Will even felt the floor beneath him heave. He caught the faint acrid smell of something like burning tar.

"The Sky Folk have taken us prisoner. We're aboard one of their ships."

"Ships . . . ?" Will echoed, bewildered. Then another fear seized him. "Where's Shade? Did he get away?"

"I don't know. He may have. I hope so."

Will took a deep breath. If Shade had at least escaped the Sky Folk, not everything would be lost.

"And Finn and Balor . . . ?"

"They aren't here. But I saw them catch Balor in one of their nets. And there was a second ship. They may be on it."

Will clapped a hand to his belt. His sword was gone, of course. He squinted in the gloom and saw someone lying on another blanket nearby.

"Hawk," Will said. "Is he hurt?"

"He's asleep. I finally got him to rest. He's exhausted."

"They took him, too?"

"But not his father or sister. The Sky Folk left them alone."

"The Dreamwalker said they wouldn't take the young. Why did they take Hawk?"

"The Dreamwalker was wrong, it would seem," the doctor said. "These people must be losing their war if they're looking for children to fight for them."

A door suddenly opened in the dark wall before them. Will saw a narrow flight of wooden steps and a figure blocking the light, solid and broad-shouldered, the lower half of his face masked like the Sky Folk that had attacked the Horse Folk camp. The figure pulled down its mask, and for one glad moment Will thought it was Balor. Then he saw that this silhouetted face was not that of the wildman.

Mordog.

Will cried out and shrank back. The mordog's beastlike face bore livid scars. He remembered the mordog that had pursued him in the mountains the first time he came to the Realm. They were brutes, killers . . .

"He won't hurt us, Will," the doctor said.

"The boy is awake, good," said the mordog in a throaty rasp. Will gaped in surprise. He had thought these creatures were incapable of speech. The mordog thrust a small clay bowl into Alazar's hands.

"Give him some broth," the mordog said, and turned to climb the steps, shutting the door behind him. When he was gone, the doctor set the bowl down on the floor.

"Don't eat or drink anything they give you," he said to Will. "There's something in it. I don't know what. I had some of this broth earlier and it made my thinking foggy. It might be the same poison that Shade said was in the wolves, and Yates."

Will looked around the room. The timbers of the walls rattled as the wind buffeted them.

"You said we were on a ship," he said. "How can that be? We were in the middle of the plains . . ."

"Can you get up?"

"Yes."

"Then I'll show you. We're not locked in here."

"Why not?"

"You'll see in a moment."

Will rose unsteadily to his feet. Together he and the doctor left the room and climbed the steps, which led out onto the long, narrow deck of a ship. Will shielded his eyes from the sudden painful light. A huge white sail towered above him into the sky, bellied out in the wind and straining against its rigging. The mordog who had brought the broth was near the hatch they had just come out of. He stood at least a head in height over the doctor, and held a thick stave tipped with an iron sphere. One of those lightning staves, Will thought. He remembered what it had done to him in the camp and he shivered. Over his mail, glittering with water droplets, the mordog wore a long dark grey cloak of some slick, oily-looking cloth.

Will gazed across the deck. The wind shrieked and the air was wet with a fine streaming mist that beaded on his face and eyelashes. He could see nothing on either side of the ship's low bulwarks but churning billows of cloud. Where was the river or sea they were sailing across? Several figures were moving about the deck, some climbing the weblike rigging of the sails. Others were hurrying along, carrying ropes with grappling hooks on the ends. All of them wore the same dark, slick cloaks as the mordog. Some of the ship's crew were human, Will noted with surprise, but not all. Will glimpsed another mordog, and several others who were strange to him, and who he guessed were Storyfolk of one kind or another.

At the far end of the ship, a large metal cylinder protruded from the deck. Dark smoke was streaming from its upper end, and Will realized the cylinder must be venting some kind of furnace or boiler below the deck. That must be where the smell of burning tar was coming from.

The light brightened suddenly, and Will saw that the clouds around them were thinning. Patches of blue sky appeared here and there.

"Where are they taking us?" Will said, bewildered. "And how did we get out on water?"

"We're not on water," the doctor said, beckoning him to the rail. Will stepped up beside him and looked over. Below them plunged the curving hull of the ship. And far beneath the ship, hundreds of feet below, was the earth. A few small clouds drifted past in the gulf between. Will pulled back dizzily at the sight.

They were sailing through the sky.

After a moment he looked down again. They were passing over a grey, lifeless landscape of broken and tumbled rock, riven in many places with dark chasms from which steam was rising, and pitted with pools of what looked like bubbling mud. A sulphurous reek rose to Will's nostrils and stung his eyes. Far ahead in the distance, in the direction that Will guessed to be north, the lifeless plain vanished into a wall of dark cloud.

"These people call themselves Stormriders," Alazar said. "Not Sky Folk. But I'm guessing these are the barren lands from your story, Will. Or the ghostlands, as the Dreamwalker called them."

"Stormriders," Will echoed, and he thought again of Captain Stormcloud and his Lightning Warriors.

He watched the shadow of the ship ripple over the stones far below. It would be nearly impossible to travel over such broken, treacherous terrain on foot. And there was no way off this ship unless you jumped over the side.

"Do you remember anything else from your mother's story?" the doctor asked.

"A little," Will said. "Lightfoot was captured as soon as he set foot in Stormcloud's kingdom."

"Just like us, then."

The ship shuddered as if something had struck it from below. Will gripped the rail and peered anxiously over the side.

"It's those steam vents we're passing over," Alazar said. "The heated air makes for rough sailing."

"How can this ship fly?" Will said to himself, but the mordog overheard him and grunted.

"The Sky Lord can do anything, boy," he said, then his gaze moved past them, and Will turned to see what he was looking at.

Before the ship and somewhat below it, a great squarish mass of dark stone rose from the plain, its summit hidden among shreds of dark cloud. Will thought it was a mountain at first, then he saw battlements and deep-set windows. If it was a mountain, it had been shaped and tunnelled into a fortress. But some disaster seemed to have befallen it: the fortress's vast bulk stood tilted forward, as if an earthquake or some other titanic force had cracked and collapsed its foundations. Just beyond the walls of the fortress the land fell away sharply into a wide stony valley obscured by roiling plumes of steam and black columns of smoke.

"The home of the Sky Folk, no doubt," Alazar said. "Who turn out to be only men, allied with Nightbane."

"We are not *Nightbane*," growled the mordog. "That is your name for the Storyeater's slaves. We are slaves no more. I am Grath, and I serve the Sky Lord and fight for my freedom, as you will."

Will and Alazar glanced at one another in surprise but said nothing.

The ship was somewhat higher than the fortress, but as it neared its destination it began to descend and come around to the side that leaned out over the valley of smoke and steam. As they came closer, Will saw that whoever inhabited this fortress had carved and shaped it *after* the disaster that had caused it to lean out so alarmingly. New battlements and walkways had been constructed that were parallel with the earth rather than the tilt of the walls, and huge stone buttresses shored up its northward face.

On this sheer side looking out over the valley, narrow tongues of stone jutted out from the wall, and after a moment Will realized they were docking platforms for the ships. Two other skyships, their sails furled to bare masts, were moored by thick cables from one of these docks.

The ship approached the fortress at about its mid-point, and slowed. Now Will saw figures clustered at the mouth of one of the docks. It was here that the ship came to rest, without the merest bump or jolt that he could feel. Three of the ship's crew slid out a gangplank and the Sky Folk on the dock caught it and secured it into a groove in the stone.

There was a sound of scuffling behind Will and he turned to see Hawk being hauled up out of the hold by another grim-faced mordog. When the boy saw Will he twisted free and ran to him, clutched his sleeve.

"Don't worry," Will whispered to him. "Just stay close to me."

The mordog gestured to them and they climbed onto the gangplank and descended. Will looked down once into the gap between the hull and the dock. He caught a dizzying glimpse of the land dropping away below the fortress wall into the smoke-shrouded valley. A dull hollow booming sound seemed to be rising from below, though he couldn't tell for certain where it was coming from.

They were almost across the plank when there was a shrill cry of warning from one of the crew still on the ship. Will heard a cracking sound and looked up to see a slab of rock the size of a large door break away from the wall and plummet past him. It had come within a few terrifying feet of the gangplank. Will saw the slab strike the earth in a cloud of dust and a moment later the deep boom of the impact reached his ears. A belated shudder passed through him.

The mordog named Grath cursed and kept them moving forward.

They passed through a long chamber with a high vaulted roof, then Grath and one other mordog herded Will, Hawk and the doctor down a long descending corridor. Glowing coals set in iron baskets gave off a dim red light that wavered on the polished stone walls of the passageway. At one point the corridor became a gallery that wound around an open shaft plunging into darkness. From far below came a loud metallic clanging, like the striking of many hammers. And then he caught another sound that stopped him in his tracks and made his heart race.

The howling of wolves.

"Keep moving," Grath rasped, prodding Will in the back with the end of his stave. Will felt an electric jolt stab through him. He stumbled forward and kept walking.

"You keep wolves here?" Alazar asked.

"We breed them," Grath said. "Make them stronger. Make them fighters."

"You're making monsters," the doctor said angrily.

"To kill monsters," the mordog growled with a grimace that might have been a smile. In his desire to boast he had clearly forgotten the task at hand. "We just caught the biggest, strongest wolf of them all, not far from where you and your friends were netted. Been hunting him for a long time but we finally brought him down. You're lucky we Stormriders found you before he did. A born killer, that one. Tore the throat right out of our fiercest pack-leader."

"Where are you keeping him?" Will asked quickly, certain they must be talking about Shade. But Grath recollected his duty and shoved Will forward so that he stumbled and nearly fell.

At the end of the corridor they came to a door of iron, guarded by two men with lightning staves. One of them unlocked the door and Will, Hawk and the doctor were prodded through, into a dim stone chamber with high walls. The door slammed shut behind them.

Finn and Balor rose from where they'd been sitting on a wooden bench bolted to the floor. Finn was pale and had a cut over one eye. Balor's hands were manacled.

"You're alive," Balor shouted, lurching towards them. "It's good to see you, Will."

"And I'm doing well, too, Balor," the doctor said.

"They wouldn't tell us anything," Finn said. "We didn't know what had happened to you."

"We're all right," Will said, glancing at Hawk, who had stayed close to his side. "Before you were captured, did you see what happened to Shade?"

"No, but we've heard wolves since we've been here," Finn said. "They're keeping them somewhere in the lower halls of the fortress."

"I think they must have Shade," Will said. "We have to find him."

He looked around the stone chamber and his hope fell even further. There was a round wooden lid in one corner, over what he guessed was the latrine. The walls were bare stone stained with damp and the only light came from a small barred grate near the ceiling. The room smelled of long neglect.

"The fact that we're still alive suggests these Stormriders want something from us," Finn said.

"To fight for them, that's my guess," Balor said. "Like they took the Horse Folk warriors. Well, they'll have a fight on their hands all right, when I get these manacles off."

"Did they give you anything to eat?" Alazar asked.

"Some thin soup," Balor said. "It had a nasty aftertaste. Gahh. Nightbane food."

"They've drugged or poisoned it with something," Alazar said. "Did you notice anything else, other than the taste?"

"Come to think of it, I felt a little . . . odd afterwards," Balor said. "I thought it was because I was still hungry. When you're this size, broth doesn't get the job done."

The floor began to shudder under their feet and they braced themselves against the chamber walls. For a moment it seemed as if the entire fortress was shaking itself apart. Slowly the tremors lessened, then finally stopped.

"This place is falling apart," Balor said. "Bits and pieces of it have been breaking off ever since they brought us here. And the way it leans. You'd almost think someone picked the whole blasted thing up and dropped it."

The wildman turned suddenly to Will.

"That story your mother told you, Will," he said, "about Lightfoot and this Captain Stormcloud. How did it end?"

Will touched his hand to the cold stone wall.

"It didn't," he said.

They sat waiting in the cell for what seemed like hours. Every now and then they would hear rumbling, and feel the stone shudder beneath them. At last there was a sound of feet in the corridor outside and the door was unlocked and groaned open. This time there were four other mordog besides Grath, and the two door sentries. The prisoners were marched out of the cell, Balor still manacled. One of the mordog took Hawk and began to lead him away from the others.

"Lightfoot!" the boy cried, struggling against the mordog's grip on his arm.

"Where are you taking him?" Will shouted.

"Let the boy stay with us," Finn said.

The mordog did not reply, and Hawk was hurried out of sight. The last Will saw of him was his frightened eyes.

Will and the others were herded along another narrow, winding corridor that rose steadily upwards, then out onto a staircase that was open to the air because part of the wall had crumbled away. They were looking down into the inner part of the fortress, Will realized. As with the chambers and corridors, the tilted courtyard had been reshaped into a series of terraced spaces connected by staircases. The sun was setting in a haze of smoke and dust, but shed enough light to bathe the upper walls in a warm amber glow.

The stairs led back inside the fortress and to another short corridor. At the end was a doorway flanked by two more sentries, and inside it a spacious hall. At one end of the room a large arch-shaped opening looked out into the sky, with a narrow lip of stone that jutted out like one of the mooring platforms, but smaller and probably meant as an observation deck. There was nothing to see through the archway but dark churning cloud, though Will knew that they must be facing the smoke-filled valley.

A tall figure wearing bright mail and a dark red cape stood at the archway looking out into the gloom.

"My Lord," Grath murmured.

The figure raised a hand but did not turn. All of their escort except for Grath bowed and left the hall.

"Unbind the wildman."

"Yes, Lord."

Grath took off Balor's manacles and shoved him forward.

"That's more like it," Balor growled, rubbing his wrists. "Maybe some of you *aren't* cowards."

The figure at the archway turned and looked at each of them. He was a tall man with dark hair, but they could not see his features well in the fitful light. A mask of leather covered the left side of his face. He took a few steps forward, and Will saw that his gait was stiff and laboured. Around his neck, on a thick chain, hung what looked like the iron tip of a spear, or an arrowhead, of dull black metal.

"You've come a long way, travellers," the man said in a rough, rasping voice. "To the end of the world, in fact."

Finn stepped forward.

"My name is Finn Madoc. My companions followed my lead, and they are blameless in whatever it is you have held us for. Let them return home."

"Home," the man said with what sounded like scorn. "And where would that be?"

"Far to the south."

"A country with no name, then?"

Finn stayed silent.

"Perhaps you'll tell me what brought you here."

"Your men did," Balor said, stepping forward. "I assume we have the pleasure of addressing the mighty Sky Lord. We had no dealings with you and our business was our own, and yet your skyship crew took us captive."

"You are strangers, found among those whom we protect. It was the duty of my Stormriders to bring you here. And now I would like to know what you were doing in our lands."

"We were on a scouting mission," Finn said. "Rumours of war in the north reached our country, and we were sent to find out what we could."

"A scouting mission," said the Sky Lord in a sceptical tone.

"We are knights of the Errantry," Balor said loudly before Finn could stop him. "My name is Balor Gruff. Remember it. I come from a land called the Bourne. The boy is my apprentice. He was supposed to return home with the doctor here. Let him go, and the other lad as well, the Horse Folk boy. They're no warriors."

"Knights of the Errantry," the Sky Lord said, his eyebrows rising. "I never would have guessed."

"You've heard of us, then," Balor said. "Which means you know what we're capable of."

"*Balor,*" Finn said warningly.

"Oh, I know it all too well," the Sky Lord said with what sounded again to Will like a hint of scorn. "I also know that you didn't come here on any scouting mission. I think you were searching for someone."

No one spoke.

"The others came with me out of friendship," Finn said at last. "I came seeking news of a man named Corr Madoc. He left the Bourne ten years ago, but we found out only recently that he may have come this way with his followers."

The Sky Lord nodded.

"I see. And what was this Corr Madoc doing here?"

"He was hunting a band of Nightbane who raided our land and killed some of our people."

"So he was seeking vengeance."

"It was a reckless action, not condoned by the Errantry. He had fifty men with him, and not a word has been heard of any of them since. Their families don't know if they're still alive."

"So this Corr Madoc, this hunter of Nightbane, if he returned home, would he be hailed a hero?"

"He wounded a young man on his way out of the Bourne, a young man who tried to stop him from taking horses that belonged to the Errantry."

The Sky Lord was silent for a long moment.

"The young man lived?" he said at last.

"He died later of his wounds. When my brother returns to Fable, he will have to face the consequences of that act. I would expect no less of him. He was always impulsive and angry, but I know he would wish to do what's right."

The Sky Lord turned back towards the archway. He clasped his gloved hands behind his back.

"Perhaps after ten years, one's idea of what's right may change," he said.

"Do you know what happened to him? Is he here?"

"The man you seek, the one called Corr Madoc, is dead. You've come here in vain."

Finn hung his head for a moment, then raised it again.

"Can you tell me how he died?"

The Sky Lord reached up, undid the buckles on his mask. He turned to them again and Will saw his face was that of a man of thirty or so. A deep, livid scar ran down the left side of his face. His left eye was an empty socket.

"Corr Madoc put on this mask," the man said. "That is how your brother died, Finn. And how the Sky Lord was born."

18

There are fires that wander, and fires that shoot like an arrow to their goal.

– Sayings of the Hidden Folk

ROWAN WALKED WITH RIDDLE through the dark. A few faintly glowing droplets of rain came out of blackness above and fell away into blackness below her feet, so that it seemed she was walking on nothing but darkness. The droplets fell with a soft patter on her cloak and hood. She should have been in complete darkness, but the raindrops seemed to cast a faint light as they fell.

"Will we find the toymaker here?" the cat asked.

"I don't know," Rowen said, clutching her cloak tightly around herself. She was not cold, but the emptiness and silence had been working on her, making her more uneasy with each step. When she stepped into the raincabinet she had expected to walk through the slashing curtain of rain in an instant, as she had before. But this time there was only the darkness, and these few drops of rain. It was as if she had passed through the curtain and come to . . . *nowhere*. She was only certain she was still in the Weaving at all because there was the same wavery, fluid quality to this place, like walking underwater.

"Grandfather never had the chance to show me how to find someone's thread in the Weaving," Rowen said, more to herself than to Riddle. "There's supposed to be more than just rain."

She realized she needed to hear her own voice, to be certain that she was still herself, that she wasn't about to stumble into a story again, with glass slippers or wicked stepmothers or worse things. Her grandfather had told her the Weaving changed according to what a person was thinking and feeling. She wondered now if this place was so dark and empty because that's how she felt inside.

"I don't even know what I should be looking for," Rowen went on. "Grandfather said it was like footprints in sand. But there's nothing like that here. Nothing."

She halted suddenly. It seemed foolish to keep walking through the dark when she had no idea where she was going, or if she was going anywhere at all.

She had a sudden thought, and looked down at the cat.

"Does this place seem familiar to you?" she asked.

Riddle gazed around, his yellow eyes wide.

"Riddle walked in dark like this before," he said slowly. "A long time ago. But . . ."

"But what?"

"When Riddle walks backwards in his mind, backwards as far as he can go, he comes to this dark."

"Backwards . . . you mean when you remember. This is the first thing you remember?"

"Yes. Now that Riddle is back inside the dark he remembers there was something before it. There was light before the dark, and Riddle was warm."

"Do you remember anything else about the light?"

"It was all around Riddle. It was like the colour of *this* one," he raised one of his tawny paws, "only more so."

"More so . . ." Rowen murmured. "You mean brighter?"

"And darker, too."

"I don't understand. The light was brighter and—"

"Like this one, but brighter and darker. And all around."

"I don't know what that means."

"That was Riddle. That *is* Riddle."

Rowen sighed. She closed her eyes, raised her face to the rain. The droplets fell like cold needles on her skin.

Then she looked at the cat again.

"Wait. You're saying that this light and dark . . . that this was *you*?"

"Riddle doesn't know."

"Can you show me? I mean, can you change into whatever it is you remember?"

The cat lowered his head.

"Riddle can try, but . . ."

"Just try. Show me what you remember."

The cat raised his own head, as Rowen had done a moment before. His eyes blinked in the rain. Then suddenly he was on fire.

"Riddle!" Rowen cried.

Bright yellow flames were leaping and snapping all over him, seeming to grow out of the orange and brown bands on his fur, but his face remained as calm and inscrutable as possible. Rowen gaped at him, horrified.

"It does not hurt," he said.

Slowly the flames died down and suddenly went out.

"That is all," Riddle said.

He lifted a furry paw and licked it.

"I see," Rowen said. "I still don't know what it means."

Disheartened and suddenly aware of how exhausted she was, she leaned on her grandfather's staff. She had carried the staff with her into the raincabinet along with his spectacles, though she wasn't sure why. Perhaps only to have something of her grandfather's when she returned without him to this strange, frightening place. In her imagination she could see him as clearly as if he was standing beside her, walking along at his usual brisk stride, staff in hand, and there she was herself, following along, pestering him with questions. *When, how, why* . . . They had taken so many walks like that together.

Whenever they were about to set off somewhere he would tap his staff once on the ground. She couldn't help but smile at the thought of that age-old habit of his. The sound of that tap on the tiles at the door of the toyshop was one of her earliest memories. It meant an adventure might be about to begin.

She held out the staff in front of her now. There was no ground under her feet that she could see, only more blackness with rain falling into it. But with a sudden impulse of hopeful defiance she thrust the staff downwards. With a crack it struck something hard and unyielding, and at the same instant a room took shape around her, just for moment, then sank into darkness.

Riddle said, "Oh."

Rowen tapped the staff again, harder this time. The room reappeared and this time it stayed, though as with everything else in the Weaving, the walls and the furniture and the rugs upon the floor all shimmered slightly with that disturbing uncertainty, as if things were not entirely there until she turned her attention to them. But despite that strangeness she knew this place very well.

It was the library in the toyshop.

"This is the last place I saw Grandfather," Rowen said, her heart pounding with new hope. "Maybe that means . . . this is the beginning of his thread. Wherever the thrawl took him, maybe the trail begins here."

There was something else odd about the room, other than the shifting quality of the edges of things. It seemed smaller, or the ceiling seemed closer than she remembered. And then she understood: *this was the room as her grandfather knew it*. He was taller than her and she was seeing the room as it appeared to him. She touched her hand to the oak table in the middle of the room. It felt smooth, cold to the touch. So solid and real.

"The toymaker *was* here," Riddle said. He was sniffing cautiously at one of the armchairs near the fireplace. "But Riddle doesn't see any threads."

"I'm not looking for a *real* thread," Rowen said. "When Grandfather used that word he meant someone's path through Story. Their life's story, I guess. The places they'd been, and where they were going to. All of that is supposed to be here in the Weaving."

"So this isn't what you're looking for?" Riddle asked, and Rowen turned to see what he had found. The cat had wandered away from the armchairs and was sniffing something lying on the floor near the doorway. Rowen bent down beside him for a better look.

It was a small tangle of bone-white thread.

She found one end of the thread poking out of the tangle, but the other end . . . There was no other end. The thread snaked away from the tangle and she followed it with her eyes, seeing that it ran across the floor to the wall.

With true catlike curiosity, Riddle plucked at the tangle of thread with a claw. Like a tendril of white smoke, the thread parted at the touch and then slowly came back together.

"Don't," Rowen said sharply. The cat stared at her with unblinking eyes.

"We shouldn't disturb it," Rowen said in a softer tone. "I think we have to follow it."

"But you said—"

"I know what I said, but . . . I think we should follow this. I think it is a little bit of the thrawl. It's the trail it left. And if it came from the Shadow Realm, then maybe this will lead us there, to where it took Grandfather."

"It's made of nothing," Riddle said.

"No, not nothing. It's like . . . a shadow of what was. It will show us the way."

She wasn't sure how she knew this, but all at once she was certain of it.

She stood up.

"Come on," she said to Riddle. "Let's go."

Rowen walked across the room, following the thread at her feet. When she got to the wall she kept going and as she had suspected would happen, the wall gave way like the thinnest lace curtain. She felt something cold rasp faintly against her skin as she passed through and for a moment she could see nothing but vague shadows, then she found herself in the street. Although it had been the middle of the day when she went into the Weaving, here the light was dim and grey.

"Where are we?" Riddle breathed. She looked down to see he had followed her.

"I'm not sure," she said.

This was Fable, but not the Fable she knew. The deathly silence, the sickly pale glow of the lamps lining the street, the grey vagueness of the buildings on either side . . . this was how her city would look, she suddenly understood, through lifeless eyes. She looked for the thread, but it was no longer beneath her feet. It was hovering above the ground at about the height of her breastbone, a faint white ribbon, so thin as to be almost invisible, but still it was *there*, snaking away into the dark.

"This way," she said to Riddle, and started forward again.

The thread did not lead her along the street but instead took its own way through whatever lay in its path, and so she went with it, through walls and lampposts and wagons, and everything parted to let her pass as if the whole city was made of nothing but mist. She saw people, too, but they were only dim, wavering shapes that swam up momentarily out of the gloom and then vanished again. For a moment she was terrified that they were all ghosts and that somehow everyone in Fable had died, but then she remembered where she was and what her grandfather had told her about the Weaving. This was not the real Fable that lay outside the door of the toyshop, it was more like a dream of Fable.

But that thought was no less terrifying.

As she walked it seemed to her that she was covering more ground with each stride, so that in a matter of moments she had come to the wall of the city itself and had passed through it and was moving swiftly across a dim land of bare rocky hillocks, stagnant pools of water and withered trees. This was not the Bourne. They had already left her own country behind.

One tree stood taller than the rest, though it was dead, too, and covered in rags of cobweb that stirred listlessly in the chill wind.

Standing under the tree was the thrawl. The thread led straight to it. The creature did not move as she approached, it only stood under the tree and watched her with the lightless holes that were its eyes.

"Rowen must not go there," Riddle whined, plucking at the edge of her cloak.

"I have to."

She walked slowly towards the thrawl, and when she was only a few steps away, she stopped, and raised her grandfather's staff, though she knew it would not help her.

"Is this the Shadow Realm?" she asked, her voice sounding thin and fearful to her own ears.

"This is the Weaving," said the thrawl in its chilling voice like the drone of flies.

"Are you . . . *real*?"

"I come from the Shadow Realm."

"Where is Grandfather? What did you do with him?"

"He lives. I will bring you to him."

"Why aren't you attacking me, like you did in the toyshop?"

"This is the Weaving. The place of all that is or might have been. I am not the thrawl that was sent to find you. That one spoke its name and is gone, but the memory of the thrawl persists here, like an echo. That is what I am. An echo of the voice that spoke me. My only task is to take you to your grandfather."

"Why are you telling me this? You could be lying."

"You carry a piece of the Mirror Samaya. The Mirror of Truth. One such as I cannot speak lies in the presence of the mirror. But even if I could deceive you, I would still tell you the truth."

"Why?"

"Because my master wishes it."

"The Night King?"

"You seek your grandfather. He is alive, and in the Shadow Realm. That is where I will take you. There is no purpose in lies. You will join your grandfather and come to the Lord of Story, as you were meant to. Even if you do not follow me now, you will come to him soon enough."

Rowen took a deep breath.

"Very well, then," she said. "I'll follow you."

The thrawl turned away and began to walk slowly through the marsh. Its steps, Rowen noticed, did not disturb the water.

"Rowen must not do this," Riddle hissed, and he plucked again at her cloak. She turned to him.

"I'm not asking you to come along, Riddle," she said. "In fact, I don't want you to. Maybe . . . maybe on your own you can find out who you were and where you came from."

"Riddle does not want to be alone," the cat moaned. "Riddle will stay with Rowen."

She could not tell how long they followed the thrawl. They soon left the marsh behind, but the country they came to after that was even more dim and insubstantial. After a while they seemed to be passing through a great city, but it was silent and empty of people. They crossed deserted squares, descended into tunnels and came out again, crossed slender stone bridges over dark abysses. Everything had the same shimmering edges she had seen elsewhere in the Weaving, but whenever she touched one of the walls it felt all too solid.

"What is this place?" she asked the thrawl.

"It was once a great city. Many Storyfolk lived here. They thought themselves powerful and important. Now this is all that is left. Soon it, too, will vanish and be no more."

Eventually they left the city and came out again onto a wide plain under a grey sky. After a while Rowen became aware that the gloom around her was not as empty as she had first thought. Out of the corner of her eye she glimpsed movement, and she turned and saw something that she felt certain was not just drifting mist. It was a dim figure, walking slowly in the same direction as she was, on a faint, winding path. And further away was another one, also walking the way she was going.

Riddle hissed, and Rowen turned to her other side, where the cat was staring transfixed into the gloom. There were shadowy figures walking on this side of her, too. She turned. There were more behind as well.

"These others around us," she said to the thrawl. "Are they following you, too?"

"No, but they are going to the Shadow Realm," the thrawl said without turning to look at her. "And we are almost there. From here all roads become one."

"Who are these others?"

"Those whose stories are over."

We're all going the same way now, she thought.

They walked on again in silence, then Rowen heard a faint sound that startled her in this lifeless place. The sound of trickling water. The hard, stony earth began to slope downwards. In a short time the sound of water grew louder, and out of the mist a great dark shadow appeared, becoming more solid.

A river, wide and dark, with shreds of mist drifting across it. The far shore was a pale band of grey that was only slightly less dark than the water.

The thrawl stopped here and turned to her.

"I am fading and cannot take you any further," it said. "From here you may cross on your own. You will find what you seek on the other side."

"Wait," Rowen said quickly, as a new thought came to her. "You said you have to tell me the truth. Tell me, then, is there a way I can free Grandfather from the Shadow Realm?"

"There is not. Once you reach the other side of this river

you will become as I am. You may resist a short while, because you wear the Mirror. But it will not protect you for very long. Soon you will know only the Lord of Story and you will serve him."

"There has to be a way to escape," Rowen said desperately. "*Tell me.*"

"There is no escape."

The thrawl began to unravel, like an unwinding spool of thread.

"Wait," Rowen cried, but already there was no one for her words to reach. The thrawl had become a loose swirl of threads that were swiftly plucked away on the wind. Rowen gazed at them until they vanished into the grey shadows, and then she turned to Riddle.

"I'm going now," she said.

"Rowen must not do this."

"There's no other way," she said, almost unable to speak through the fear and despair rising in her. "If you can, Riddle, find your way back to Edweth. Tell her where I went."

The cat hunched himself into a trembling ball of misery.

"Riddle will wait here, for Rowen to come back."

"I . . . may not come back."

She turned away quickly from the cat, afraid that her resolve was about to crumble, and walked down to the shore. The water was dark, almost black, and flowed very slowly, as if it was not water but some thicker substance, like obsidian. She gazed across, looking for the far shore, hoping that she might see her grandfather there, but she saw nothing.

Weeping, she waded into the stream up to her waist. It was cold. Colder than anything she had ever known. A cold that soaked through her clothing in an instant and then into her body and even into her mind. She knew then, as her veins turned to ice and her heart shrank within her, that the thrawl had told her the truth. By the time she got to the other shore, there would be little left, if anything, of who she was.

The river looked slow, but the current was very strong, and as she took her next step she lost her footing and fell, and the water closed over her head. She came up gasping, with a feeling as though a blade of ice had stabbed her in the heart. She could not see, she could not remember anything except that she had to reach the far shore, and even the reason why she must reach it was beginning to fade.

Then something tugged at her cloak and pulled her back, choking and gasping, dragging her out of the water.

A moment later she was lying on the shore, and there was a flickering light around her. She raised her head.

It was Riddle, on fire. He was still a cat, but he was larger now than he had been. He was so close to her, and the fire that played over him was so bright that she flinched and shaded her eyes.

"That was not a good way," he said, and his voice was deeper and filled with a calm certitude she had never heard in it before. "Riddle knows the way."

"There's another way to the Shadow Realm?"

"Follow," said the cat, and he turned and bounded away.

Rowen hesitated a moment, then she climbed to her feet. To her surprise, her clothes were dry. She had no time to wonder about this, because the cat was almost out of sight. She started after him, calling for him to slow down, but he stayed always ahead of her, a flame-like blur just visible in the gloom.

She ran after him, and it seemed to Rowen that the darkness grew somehow even darker around her, or that maybe the blazing comet that was the cat threw everything else into a sharper blackness as it passed. She could almost feel this blackness as a thickness, an utter lack of light turned solid, closing in upon her. She was sure it would have smothered her so that she was lost for ever, if it wasn't for the cat burning a fiery passage through it for her to follow. And so she followed, for that was all that she could do.

As she ran, her eyes fixed on the flaming firebrand that was Riddle, she had the dizzying feeling that they were not running along some flat, featureless ground any more but plunging, diving through the darkness, down and down, and it seemed that her sense of how long she had been following Riddle was being swiftly left behind as well, as if time itself was being swallowed up in the blackness.

She ran, or plunged, or soared, after the cat, until she became aware that something other than utter darkness was taking shape around her. The wildcat's fiery, rippling form lit up what they were passing through, and Rowen saw she had come to the midst of a thick, silent wood, though there was still that breathless sensation of plummeting downwards at tremendous speed. And as if his brightness kindled the world around them, Rowen saw that everything, the trees with their strangely large, drooping leaves, the grass and the flowers, had begun to give off their own soft, warm light. She didn't know why, but she suddenly felt safer here than she had since she entered the Weaving.

Then Riddle disappeared.

She was alone in this eerie, glowing forest.

"Riddle," she called. "Where are you?"

With the cat gone, the solitude of this dark, silent world suddenly descended on her. She had felt an ever-present fear simmering inside her from the moment she stepped into the raincabinet, expecting dangers that she couldn't even imagine, and now that fear threatened to boil up into panic.

There was a sound from the darkness nearby, a faint

rustle. She turned in the direction of the sound and saw two catlike eyes take shape out of the blackness.

"Riddle," she said. "Why did you run away?"

The undergrowth moved, and the eyes seemed to float towards her. Then the cat's body came out of the shadows, but it was no longer a small striped wildcat. Like a smoky flame, a large, sinuous form flowed out of the forest.

A tiger.

"Riddle," Rowen said, backing away. "That's you, isn't it?"

The tiger's banded gold and black body was like a bright fire flickering with sharp shadows. The closer it came the fiercer it blazed, so that she almost had to turn away. And yet she could not turn away. She had never seen anything more beautiful and at the same time so terrifying.

"This is what you remembered, from before the rain," she whispered. "This is what you really are, isn't it?"

The tiger gazed at her impassively, with no recognition in its eyes.

"Say something," Rowen said, growing angry. "This is no time for your games."

The tiger fixed her with its unmoving gaze a moment longer, then it turned and flowed back into the forest. As it disappeared, something her grandfather had said, a story he had told about the night her mother was born, came back to her. How he had listened to someone sing a song about a woman who wove a tiger, and with the tiger had come a whole world. And then he had taken a piece of wood and carved a tiger.

Her heart began to beat faster. She pushed through the leaves and clinging branches, the big cat's fiery shape flickering just ahead of her as it made its way through the dark undergrowth. As she hurried along, the light around her grew. Shafts of bright, glad sunlight shot down through the leaves. Rowen increased her pace, barely aware of the branches that snagged her clothing and scratched her face.

She burst out of the trees into an open glade. The tiger was nowhere to be seen, as if it had melted into the sunlight.

"Riddle?"

The glade rose in a long grassy slope before her, to a cottage of whitewashed stone with a thatched roof and a chimney of red brick. The front door, with a small round window of blue glass set in it, stood slightly ajar. Beside the door hung wind chimes that made a soft ting-a-ling as they stirred in the warm breeze. To one side of the house a small garden plot was laid out and fenced off with wattles. At Rowen's feet lay a path that wound up the slope to the cottage, a path set with flat stones of many colours.

Before she knew what she was doing, Rowen stepped onto the path and began to climb. Her feet seemed to know these stones, as if she had walked this path many times before. Her breath quickened and her heart was pounding now. Each step she took was like remembering another note from a long-forgotten melody.

Then she knew this place, and she felt her heart might burst with joy and grief.

This was Blue Hill. Where she had lived with her mother and father. She had been born here. This was her home.

She paused on the path, scarcely able to breathe. Only once since her grandfather had taken her to live in Fable had they gone back to the hill. He had taken here there because she had hoped that seeing her childhood home would help her remember her parents. That visit was already many years ago, and even then the thatch had been falling in, the whitewashed walls cracked and peeling, the untended grass growing up to the windows. She had wandered around the hill then, and sat in the silent, dust-shrouded cottage, but the memories did not come.

Before her now was the cottage as it once must have been when she lived there with her mother and father, the walls brightly gleaming in the sun, the thatch fresh and clean on the roof, the garden tended. But how could it be here? Someone had done this, woven this place out of the past . . .

For her to find.

Rowen quickened her pace. She reached the open door. She halted, and peered in.

"Is anyone here?" she said in a trembling voice.

When her eyes had adjusted to the dim light inside, she saw that the interior was very small. At the far end was a fireplace with coals glowing in it, a pot on the hearthstone, a broom leaning in a corner. The room was filled with the warm, comforting scent of freshly baked bread. Near the fireplace stood a large wooden object like a strangely complicated bedframe. It was a loom, she realized a moment later, and beside it stood a spinning wheel. A tapestry was stretched upon the loom, but the woven pattern was somehow hard to see, and many of the threads hung in tatters, as if they had fallen or been torn out.

There was a stillness in this place that startled her after the shifting restlessness of the Weaving. No one was in the cottage, but someone had just been here, she was sure of it.

Rowen heard a noise behind her and turned.

The tiger stood in the doorway. It was no longer a blazing creature of fire, it was just a tiger, but even that was a frightening and awesome sight.

"Riddle?" Rowen whispered. "Why don't you speak to me?" Her voice broke, but she struggled on. "Is this the place you came from? Who lives here?"

Even as she spoke, another figure appeared in the

doorway behind the tiger. A slender older woman in a green wraparound dress, carrying a clay jug on her head. Her hair was dark and streaked with grey.

"What is it?" she said softly to the tiger. Then she saw Rowen. Slowly she set the jug down on the floor.

"Who are . . . ?" she said, then she caught her breath and stood staring. Her eyes filled with tears. "You," she breathed.

"Grandmother," Rowen said.

And then she fainted.

19

The traveller stood before the tall iron gate of the emperor's palace and gazed through the bars in wonder.

"The lord of this place," he said to a ragged old beggar sitting outside the wall, "must have a lot of gold."

"I am sure he does," the beggar said. "More than anyone could spend in a lifetime."

"I wonder where he keeps all of that gold," the traveller mused, dreaming of vast underground vaults piled to the ceilings with shining nuggets and ingots and crowns.

"I couldn't tell you that," the beggar said, as he gazed up at the forbidding walls topped with sharp spikes that surrounded the palace. "But I think I can tell you where all that gold keeps him."

– The Cabinet of Mysteries

"CORR," FINN SAID, STEPPING FORWARD. "Corr, it's really you . . ."

"That name has not been spoken for a long time," said the one-eyed man, setting the mask aside on the table beside him. "But yes, it's me, Finn. Your brother. Or what's left of him."

"Corr . . ." Finn said again, his voice breaking.

The brothers embraced, then Corr held Finn at arm's length and shook his head slowly.

"Look at you," he said, breaking into a smile. "My little brother, a man now. And a knight of the Errantry.

I suppose I shouldn't be surprised. You never did listen to anything I told you."

"Corr, how can this be?"

"You expected to find me dead?"

"No, I never believed that. Never. But all of this . . ."

"All of this," Corr echoed, nodding. "It's not what anyone would have expected when we set out from Fable all those years ago, least of all me. But tell me, Finn, when did you join the Errantry?"

"Not long after you went away," Finn said, and for a moment he sounded like an eager boy instead of the serious young man Will knew him to be. "I ran away from the farm and came to Fable. When the Errantry took me in I trained hard, then I looked for you. Everywhere they sent me, I looked for you."

"And what of Mother? Is she well?"

"She . . . died three years ago, Corr," Finn said.

"Ah. I see."

"Before she died, I promised her I would find you."

Corr looked away for a moment. Then he nodded slowly and put a hand on Finn's shoulder.

"I'm sorry you won't be able to bring her the news. It shouldn't have been that way."

"I also made a promise to the Errantry, Corr. I came looking for you to bring you home. And all of the Bourne folk with you."

To Will's surprise, Corr broke into a laugh.

"Bring us home," he said. "That will never happen, Finn. This is our home now."

"When I took the oath of the Errantry, I swore I would find you, and bring you back to Fable, to judgement."

"I wonder who made you swear such an oath?"

"Lord Caliburn."

"Of course. To *his* judgement, then. Not difficult to imagine what that will be. And the sentence carried out by his faithful dog Thorne. Did you know it was Thorne who decided I wasn't fit for the Errantry all those years ago? But never mind that. Tell me, what were your orders if I refused to return to Fable? What then, I wonder. Were you to bring the Marshal my head?"

"No, Corr. I knew it would never come to that. I knew that if I found you and asked you to come back with me, you would."

Corr gazed at Finn for a long time.

"I'm afraid you were wrong, brother. Much has changed since I rode from home that day. Nothing will undo what I've done, or bring back the boy I killed. But here . . . Here I can do some good. For all of us. For the Bourne as well. Going back to Fable would only mean abandoning our mission."

"And what is that mission?" the doctor asked. "Beyond terrorizing the folk of the plains?"

"You're the doctor?" Corr said to Alazar with obvious interest.

"I am," Alazar said, in a cold voice.

Corr turned to Will. His eyes narrowed.

"You're not long from the Untold, are you, lad?"

Will shook his head. Something in Corr's voice, as friendly seeming as it was now, held a threat. He wondered how Corr could tell he was not from the Realm.

"I have to wonder what you're doing with this search party," Corr said to him. "But that tale can wait until there's more time."

Balor stepped forward again.

"What about Hawk, the Horse Folk boy? Where did your Nightbane friends drag him off to?"

"He has not been harmed. Forgive me, I should have told

you. There are other Horse Folk among our company, so I had the boy sent to them. I thought it would help to lessen his fear if he saw that his own people are with us."

"Did you kidnap them as well?" Balor growled.

Corr took a deep breath and his face darkened. It was clear to Will that Balor was close to pushing Corr's patience to its limit.

"How can all of this be, Corr?" Finn said. "Nightbane as allies, the flying ships . . . What happened to you?"

Corr smiled and for a moment Will saw a much younger man appear in that scarred, weathered face.

"So much has happened, my brother," Corr said. "But it is a long story and I must meet with my lieutenants now. A place has been prepared for you and your friends to rest and refresh themselves. You are my welcome guests. We'll meet again soon and all will be explained. And I promise you, there will be no more manacles."

Will and his companions were escorted, this time by unarmed attendants, to a room deep within the fortress, without windows, but with beds, a coal brazier for warmth, and a bath. Like everything else here, the walls had been carved or shaped out of the rock itself after the fortress had been damaged, because the ceiling still sloped at one end. The wooden beds were narrow with no pillows and only one thin woollen blanket each.

Balor surveyed the room with a scowl.

"You'll notice they haven't given us our weapons back," he said.

They took off their travel-stained clothes and changed into fresh clothing that had been set out for them.

Balor tore the tunic he was struggling to put on.

"They don't seem to have my size," he said, tugging at

the too-short sleeves. "Which suits me fine. I have no intention of fitting in here."

"Have you noticed the colours?" the doctor said. "Black and silver. Errantry colours."

Balor nodded.

"I guess he's not above borrowing a few ideas from us."

Will washed his face in the basin and dried it on a rough cloth, then sat on the edge of the bed he had been assigned. He studied Finn, who had withdrawn into his own thoughts. His eyes were shining and it was clear he was overjoyed to have found his brother at last, but he was troubled, too, and avoided looking at anyone. Will, Balor and the doctor exchanged glances but they said nothing to Finn.

A chill grew in the room that suggested evening had fallen in the world outside. Will shivered and drew closer to the brazier to warm his hands. He gazed into the glowing coals, wondering if Shade was all right, and thinking about Rowen, too. Shade was still in danger, after all that Will had tried to do, and the same was probably true of Rowen. The shadow of things to come had brought him a warning in time, but it had been in vain, as far as he could tell. And the Dreamwalker must have been wrong. There was no way he could get back to Rowen now.

The door opened suddenly and three Stormriders came in, two men and one mordog. As far as Will could see they were not armed. One of the men announced that the Sky Lord had invited them to dinner, and Will thought quickly: if he stayed behind, maybe he could slip out later and search for Shade. He considered trying the excuse that he felt sick, but he hesitated too long and the Stormriders began herding them all out of the room. It was clear that the invitation was one they were not meant to turn down.

They were led along the same corridor by which they'd

come, then up a flight of stairs to a circular chamber with a lofty domed ceiling. There were heavy wooden chairs here, arranged in a semi-circle in front of a huge round stone table that looked as if it had grown out of the floor like a giant flat-topped mushroom.

Corr was there already, seated in a chair, speaking in low tones with someone sitting near him, an old man, white-bearded and very small, who Will realized after a second glance must be a dwarf. With his gaunt, narrow face and sunken eyes he did not look much like Mimling Hammersong. He wore an iron band around his forehead, a coat of dark mail, and had many unornamented iron rings on his long, bony fingers. Grath, the mordog, stood to one side of the table, impassive.

There was meat and fruit and bread already laid out on the table, along with decanters of water and wine. Corr had clearly touched none of it, nor had the dwarf. When Finn and the others came in, Corr stood and greeted them, then invited them to sit. The old dwarf did not rise from his chair.

"This is Nonn," Corr said, gesturing to the dwarf, who surveyed the new arrivals with a cold, unwelcoming look. "He and his brethren are my allies in the battle we wage here. Now, please, sit and eat. You all look a little thin."

"Not much to eat on the plains these days," Balor muttered. If Corr heard him, he made no sign.

As they approached the table, Will remembered the food they had been served in the cell, and he looked at the doctor.

"It's perfectly good," Corr said, noticing Will's glance and clearly realizing what it meant. "I'll join you if that will help."

He poured everyone a goblet of red wine and raised his own.

"To the downfall of the enemy," he said.

"And the recovery of what has been stolen," the dwarf

said, his voice low and rattling, like chains being dragged across a stone floor.

"We were served food on the ship," Finn said, not touching his goblet. "The doctor seemed to think there was something—"

Corr raised his hand.

"My apologies. The mordog's fare is not to everyone's taste, is it, Grath?"

The mordog grinned.

"It's *gaal,* isn't it, Corr?" Finn said. "Fever iron. That's what's in your Stormriders' food and drink."

Corr stared at Finn and slowly set down his goblet.

"It is. We salvage what little we can from the rocks around the fortress. The metal has properties no one in Fable ever guessed, Finn. Nonn and his artificers have put it to incredible uses. It's *gaal* that keeps our skyships in the air."

"It's also a poison," Alazar said. "It drives men mad."

"Men it may, if they use it recklessly," said Nonn sharply. "Not dwarves."

"Our mordog allies grind it into a powder that they ingest with their meals," Corr said. "It makes them fiercer warriors, nearly impervious to pain."

"And your own men, too, I imagine," Alazar said. "Do they also take this powder?"

"Those who wish it."

"But it must be killing them slowly. Surely you see that. Like that poor wretch—"

He broke off and glanced quickly at Finn.

"Whom are you speaking of, doctor?" Corr asked.

"The . . . Horse Folk told us of a man wandering the plain," Finn said quickly. "He was sick and delirious, but he told the Horse Folk he had news of you, for the Errantry."

"Ah, Brannon Yates," Corr said. "That was unfortunate.

Yes, he took too much of the *gaal*, and it . . . affected his mind. After all we had been through together. He disappeared, but we found him, fortunately, and brought him back to the fortress. He is in a bad way. Perhaps, doctor, you could look in on him later."

Alazar was about to speak, but he pursed his lips and only nodded.

"Now, please," Corr said, raising his hands, "help yourselves. I assure you there is no fever iron at this table."

They sat down and ate and drank sparingly. Corr joined them, taking a small amount of food for himself. Will noticed that he hardly ate any of it. The dwarf ate nothing.

"How can you have fare like this, Corr, in such a place?" Finn asked.

"The Horse Folk supply our provisions, in return for the protection we give them," Corr said, and Will wondered if Finn would challenge this statement, which must be a lie if the Dreamwalker had been telling the truth. But Finn said nothing.

"They would have fled long ago, or become slaves to the Nightbane," Corr said, "if we had not been here. The people bring us what they can, and often their young men and women join our cause."

"The plains are dying from lack of rain," Alazar said. "The animals have fled and the people are hungry. It doesn't seem right to ask them to supply your needs."

"Without us, they would have nothing at all."

"But what about the drought? Is that somehow your doing?"

"The *gaal* gives us power even over the weather. You must have seen the rods on the rooftops of the fortress when you were brought here. With those rods Nonn's folk have bottled the clouds up here in the ghostlands, to harness the lightning. Regrettable, but necessary."

"Regrettable?" Balor muttered.

"When the clay giant came to us," Corr went on, "I knew it must have been you who had sent him, Finn. I didn't know how you'd done it. But I hoped some day you would follow."

"Ord the golem found you, then," Finn said. "I was right about where he was going."

Corr took out a green stone from his pocket and set it on the table.

"This is yours," he said to Finn. Will remembered the ring with the green stone that Finn had worn on their first journey together. How Finn had set the stone into the forehead of the golem to save them from the storyshard they were trapped in.

"So you call him Ord, do you?" Corr said. "He came striding out of the south one morning. Ploughed through a throng of our strongest mordog like a pile of dead leaves. Didn't hurt any of them, not badly anyway, but they couldn't stop him. He broke through the gates and just kept going, up through the corridors, no matter what we threw at him. Nothing, not even the lightning, slowed him down. He tore through a door of solid iron to get into my chamber. I thought I was finished, but then he just stopped. Just stood there, like he'd turned to solid rock. Then I saw the green stone in his forehead, and I remembered the ring I had given my brother . . ."

He slid the stone across the table to Finn, who caught it and picked it up.

"That belongs to you, brother," Corr said, "but if you have no objection, I will keep the golem. He has his uses."

Finn closed his fist around the stone. No one spoke.

The doctor finally broke the silence.

"I don't understand how all of this happened. The fortress, the army of Stormriders, the flying ships . . . you left Fable with only a small band of men."

Corr picked up his goblet.

"There were only fifty of us," he said with a nod. "But we acted with one thought, one goal: to find the beasts that had slaughtered our people, and rid the Realm of them.

"We rode for days and days, following the trail of the Nightbane west and north from Fable," he continued. "After many weeks we caught up with a band of mordog, part of the larger force that had raided the Bourne. That night we encircled their camp under cover of darkness and attacked. We killed them all, except one. He became our unwilling guide, but he led us true, many leagues north into wild, dangerous lands, by little-known paths. We found the rest of the raiding party and finished them. And then . . . well, we kept on. Battle after battle, year after year. Other men joined us, outlaws and exiles, soldiers, mages, warriors, men with no homes, no kingdoms left to defend."

"Some of the Bourne folk in your army must have wanted to return to Fable, to their families," the doctor said.

"Whoever wished to leave us was free to go. A few did, but clearly none found their way home. I am sorry for that. Most of the men who left Fable with me stayed, though, gladly. There was much for us to do. We learned that well-armoured companies of Nightbane were coming and going from these ghostlands, as the Horse Folk call them. So we tracked the Nightbane here and discovered their stronghold in the valley below."

He paused, and smiled bitterly.

"Our victories had made us reckless," he said. "We attacked too soon and the Nightbane came forth in greater numbers than we had suspected and scattered us easily. Many men died. I lost my eye in that battle, and took a blade of fever iron in the chest. The Nightbane hung me from a dead tree over a stinking hole in the earth and left me to rot."

Will looked at Corr's hand, gripping his goblet. The knuckles had gone white.

"Nonn's people found me," he said. "I was nearly dead, but they brought me to the fortress and healed me. In time my men gathered together again and rejoined me. We learned that Nonn's folk had taken refuge in the ruins of this fortress many years ago, after the Nightbane drove them from their home in the valley of fire. Ages ago the dwarves built a city in that valley, delving into a crater left by a great iron stone that fell from the sky. It was a city of many levels descending in concentric rings into the depths of the earth, and they called it Adamant. The dwarves had lived there for longer than even their own tales could reach back. They mined ores and precious metals, refined them, shaped them into beautiful things, ingenious things."

"The Sky Folk dwelt here, too, in the kingdom above the clouds," the old dwarf said. They looked at him in surprise. He had said nothing for a long time, and now his guttural voice broke harshly on their ears. "This land was peaceful then. The valley of fire was green with growing things. We traded with the Sky Folk, crafted many treasures for them. Jewels, weapons. And when we discovered the properties of fever iron, as you call it, we built flying ships for the Sky Folk, so that they could travel from the heavens to the earth more quickly."

Will suddenly remembered Mimling's tale.

"You're the Elders. The Ironwise. Someone . . . another dwarf . . . told me about you. He always wondered if you were only a legend."

"So some still remember us," Nonn said, fixing Will with his cold gaze. Will noticed that the dwarf's skin had a pale blue tinge and was pocked and pitted with many tiny scars, as if some burning thing had once exploded into fragments in front of him. Which, Will considered, was very likely for someone who worked with fire and metal.

"We are not what we once were," the dwarf added. "The war against the Night King brought much ruin. The kingdoms in the sky fell, and the earth was broken and heaved up so that rivers of molten rock burst forth and engulfed our city. Most of our people were swept away like dry leaves in a fire. The valley was burned and blackened, and has gone on burning ever since. Those of us who survived hid in the deepest tunnels beneath our city, taking refuge from the Nightbane and from the ghosts that wandered these wastes, the shades of the dead that the Night King had once enslaved. That is why the Horse Folk call these the ghostlands and do not come here."

"Fetches," Corr said. "They have no will of their own. After Malabron was defeated they were like puppets whose strings had been cut."

"Yes, and we discovered we could make them serve us," the dwarf said. "The ghosts were drawn to the *gaal*, like shivering wretches drawn to a fire in the cold. We found that we could seal them inside armour made of an alloy of *gaal* and ordinary iron, and they would do our bidding. Much as the golem serves the Sky Lord. Without the armour they were mindless, weak, insubstantial as mist. Sealed in the armour they could carry, and lift, and tunnel as we bade them. And unlike men or dwarves, they would never tire, or rebel against their masters."

"You made slaves of the fetches?" Finn asked.

The dwarf scowled and shook his head.

"How can one enslave that which has no mind, no will of its own? With their ceaseless labour, we began to rebuild our ruined city, and our fortunes. But it did not last. The fetches, as you call them, began to refuse our commands. Soon we realized they served the will of another, but it was too late. Before we could destroy their armour and render them helpless, they took up weapons and drove us from our mines and foundries. Then the Nightbane returned in great numbers, with fell beasts and the flying worms. They guarded the city while the forges were relit and the great hammers rang once more. We believe the fetches are making more armour, to capture and hold more shades of the dead. The *things* we created are making more of themselves."

"They're forging an unstoppable army for the Night King," Corr said. "Malabron's strength is not yet great enough to control thousands of fetches by his will alone, but with the armour he can do it. The *gaal* in the metal binds the fetches to him and they move as one."

"Those of us who were not killed by the armoured fetches took refuge here," Nonn said, "in the ruins of what had once been a shining citadel of the Sky Folk, before the kingdoms above the clouds crumbled and fell. And here we waited, doubting we would ever take back what is ours. Until Corr Madoc came to these lands and it seemed to us that the Sky Lord had returned."

"When I hung on that dead tree, over the pit," Corr said, "something happened to me. The *gaal* seemed to sharpen my vision and I saw . . . more deeply than I ever had before. I saw what had once been. I saw the lost sky kingdoms as they had once been, glorious and powerful. I saw the skyships that were rotting now like bones on the valley floor . . . I saw them soaring through the clouds, lightning flickering along their masts, and I knew they could soar once again. And I saw that a great lode of ore lies beneath the ruins of Adamant. Enough of the *gaal* to raise a fleet of hundreds of skyships. If we can take the city back from the Nightbane and the fetches . . ."

He paused, and lifted the black metal spearhead that hung around his neck.

"This is the shard of *gaal* that cut away my old life and gave me a new one. You see, doctor, I wear the fever iron around my neck and it has not poisoned me. The truth is, it has given me greater strength and deeper sight than I ever had before. I have brought the people of these lands together in a great cause, and we will not fail."

"But you have Nightbane—mordog—for allies, Corr," Finn said. "How can that be?"

"They have thrown off the yoke of the Shadow Realm. When we first came to the ghostlands we found Grath and his companions hiding in the hills, hunted by their own kind. They had rebelled against their master, but there was nowhere else they could go where they would not be hated and feared. They renounce the name we've given their folk, Nightbane, but that is how they would be seen anywhere else in the Realm. So they have stayed here, in the hope of one day driving out Malabron's forces and making a homeland for themselves."

"We saw that the armoured fetches had risen up against their masters," Grath said with an unexpected fierceness. "Then we knew we no longer had to be slaves, either. We will not be the enemy in someone else's story. We are free folk. We are Stormriders."

"But none of this explains why everyone calls you the Sky Lord," Balor said.

"He *is* the Sky Lord," Grath rumbled.

"I died," Corr said simply. "I died with a shard of fever iron in my chest, and the Sky Lord was reborn."

Balor snorted.

"I don't ask you to believe it," Corr said. "But you can see for yourselves what we have accomplished here. Without our ships and our lightning, the lands to the south would have been overrun long ago."

"Your brother wields the lightning," the dwarf said to Finn. "As the Sky Lord once did."

"The Horse Folk fear you, Corr," Finn said. "They flee from your Stormriders. And the wisent herds have been driven away. The people are hungry."

Corr smiled bitterly.

"They owe us what peace they have, yet some are ungrateful. That is always the way of it. The defenders, the ones who get blood on their hands, are scorned and feared. And we need more defenders. We always need more defenders. It is what commanders in time of war have always done. If they will not send us their young and strong willingly, we are forced to take them."

"Like you took us," Balor muttered.

"The ship's crew had no idea who you were. They were only doing their duty. We take the young and we train them to defend themselves. They become strong, protectors of their own people. Most come in time to thank us for it."

He turned to Alazar.

"You have skills we need, doctor, and I must repeat my request. Will you go to the infirmary, to look at Yates and some of the newly wounded? Nonn's healers are overwhelmed."

The doctor took a deep breath.

"Where is the infirmary?" he said quietly.

"Grath will show you the way. You have my thanks."

Alazar followed the mordog out of the room. There was a long silence. Corr took a drink of wine and set the goblet down heavily. Will noticed that Balor had been quietly fuming since the doctor left. Finally he could no longer contain himself.

"When 'Zar is done, we're leaving, Finn," the wildman said. "Unless you'd like to join the fun here. I'm sure they'd be happy to have you."

"Would I be pleased to have my brother fighting at my side?" Corr said, with a look at Finn. "Of course. But that is his choice."

They all looked at Finn, who gazed down at the table without speaking.

"I don't see that you are defending anything here, Corr," Finn said slowly.

The Sky Lord gave a soft laugh of surprise.

"Are you sure you know what you're talking about, little brother?"

"This is a siege," Finn said. "Nonn's folk want their mines and forges back. You want that precious, deadly ore because it keeps your skyships in the air, and there's almost none left, is there? Except in the deeps where Nonn's people lived."

"Of course we want the *gaal*," Corr said with a shrug. "Without the power it gives us, the command of the air and the lightning, there is no way we can hold these lands against the Night King's forces. You don't understand yet, Finn. You don't see the greater purpose in what we do, and how much we have sacrificed . . . the men who have died." His voice grew hoarse as he spoke the last few words.

"Well, I think *I* understand," Balor said, rising from his chair. "I hope you're giving us the same choice you're giving your brother, Corr Madoc, because if it's all the same to you I choose to leave."

Corr and the dwarf exchanged a quick glance.

"I cannot allow that," Corr said. "My lieutenants have informed me that the Nightbane are massing in the valley of fire, beneath the outer walls of the dwarves' city. The watchtowers have reported dragon sightings. We believe they are preparing an assault by air and land, and our ships cannot be spared to return you to the plains. You will have to remain here, for your own safety, for the time being."

"For our safety?" Balor thundered. "We're prisoners here. You have no intention of letting any of us leave. Alazar's too useful to you, and Finn and I, we'll make handy fighters, won't we, in your quest for fever iron? That's been your plan all along, hasn't it?"

"*Balor,*" Finn said warningly, also rising from his chair.

"I don't know if you've noticed, *Sky Lord,* but your fortress isn't exactly up in the sky, is it?"

"It will be," Corr said. "When we have enough *gaal* to raise it again. Nonn's people are building a forge like those on board our skyships. When it is ready—"

"Oh, yes, the *gaal,*" Balor boomed. "That wonderful harmless stuff that's clearly driven you mad. How much fever iron have you been sprinkling on your morning porridge, Corr Madoc? This is sheer lunacy."

Corr's scarred face shook with fury. He slammed a fist down on the table.

"*Enough,*" he roared. "You are not going anywhere, wildman, and if you cannot govern your tongue, you will be locked up."

Balor turned to Finn, his own face darker than Will had ever seen it.

"It looks like you won't be bringing anyone back to Fable, my friend," he said.

Finn lowered his head, then looked up at his brother.

"Corr, listen to me," he said. "Let my friends and the Horse Folk boy leave, and I will stay here. I will join you."

"Finn, *no,*" Balor said.

At that moment a horn sounded. Corr sprang to his feet.

"The assault has begun," he said, and there was a new tone in his voice now, of excitement, even eagerness. "This discussion will have to wait. It's best that all of you come with me now."

20

. . . know that you have come to the end of all things,
and that those who dare tread here soon find
how many ways there are for the bold to die . . .

– The Kantar

WILL AND HIS COMPANIONS followed Corr and the old dwarf through the corridors, several armed Stormriders falling into step behind them, to the observation chamber where they had first been taken to meet the Sky Lord. Torches on poles blazed along the rim of the archway that looked out onto the valley of fire. Outside in the dark, rain was falling at a slant in the wind. More of the valley was visible now, as the wind had sheared away the steam and smoke, and Will could see further than he had before. The faint glow of distant fires glimmered at the edge of sight, and he wondered if they marked the rim of the unseen city of Adamant.

Two Stormriders in dark red capes stood on the platform, one a tall, bearded man and the other a grey-haired mordog with one missing hand that was capped with an iron spike.

Will guessed that they were two of Corr's lieutenants. The tall man was peering into the darkness through a spyglass. When Corr arrived, he bowed his head and handed his commander the spyglass. Corr stepped onto the observation platform, into the streaming rain. He looked through the spyglass a moment then lowered it and continued to gaze out into the rain. Three of the skyships, their hulls just visible in the red torchlight, were launching from platforms further above in the fortress wall.

"Report, Alfric," Corr said.

"Dragons," the bearded lieutenant said, with a quick, curious glance at Will and his companions. "They're motherworms, Lord. Two for certain, perhaps more. And something's happening below. The scoutship sighted Nightbane marching in columns to the rim of the valley, on both sides of us. Hundreds of them. Some are hauling heavy wagons. We can't tell what they're carrying: the loads are covered."

"Why two columns?" Corr murmured, leaning out over the platform edge. Will followed his gaze for a while, then looked up again to watch the ships fade into the darkness.

"Where are the ships going?" he asked.

"They'll rain lightning down on those columns," Corr said. "They'll break and scatter them."

"What about these motherworms, Corr," Finn said. "Are they a danger to your ships?"

"If they get too close, yes. But the lightning should prevent that."

They waited in silence. Before long Will could see flashes of orange light in the distance.

"The motherworms," said the mordog lieutenant. "They're circling the ships now. Moving in."

Flickering tongues of fire spouted here and there, then scattered into sparks and faded away, like a burst of fireworks. As if in answer, a jagged blade of white light stabbed the dark. Moments later thunder cracked and boomed. The darkness throbbed with light again, then several bolts shot out all at once, from one ship or several, Will couldn't tell. For an instant night became day and they could see the dark hull of a ship and a huge winged shape above it, descending through the cloud and smoke. All went dark again. Then another lightning bolt flashed at the same instant that a second burst of many writhing flames rained down on the ship.

"No," the bearded lieutenant said, his voice hollow.

The ship erupted into a blazing ball of orange light, blooming in the dark like a hideous flower. Swiftly the fireball shrank and darkened, became a roiling mass of red flame and billowing steam that slowly tumbled out of the sky. Moments later they saw it erupt again as what was left of the ship struck the unseen earth. Gouts of flame shot up and fell in a shower, burned for a short time and flickered out.

"There were Bourne folk on that ship," Alfric said, turning away from the platform.

"Send out more ships, then," Nonn said. "Send all of the ships."

"Never mind the men on them," Alfric muttered.

"Signal the captains to keep going, and send the rest of your men out on foot," Nonn said to Corr, in a peremptory tone that made Will wonder who was really in command here. "They can flank the Nightbane and crush them. This is our chance."

Corr peered out into the rain, then shook his head.

"We'll wait for now," he said. "Your people have braced this fortress to withstand the shaking of the earth. It will withstand their assault. The Nightbane will break on it like waves against a cliff, and when they do we'll come forth and scatter those that remain."

"But the *gaal* is out there," the old dwarf rasped, thrusting a pointing finger into the dark. "That is where we must take the battle, to *them*. We've hidden in these crumbling halls too long already. If we do not seize this chance, we will lose everything."

Corr did not look at Nonn but gazed out into the dark, straining forward as if the dwarf's words were like a goad he could barely resist. At last he straightened, and shook his head.

"No," he said hoarsely. "It's too soon. I won't make that mistake again."

The dwarf was about to reply when someone cried, "*Worm!*"

Through the rain and smoke Will had a brief vision of a vast black form rising like a dark planet from the smoke below, a gaping mouth brimming with fire.

"Everyone get back!" Corr shouted.

Balor pulled Will away from the platform's rim just in time. With a roar the mouth vomited a ball of bright flame that flew apart into many smaller blazing snakelike shapes. *Dragons*, Will thought as the wildman's huge arm came around him and pulled him to the floor. As he fell he saw one of these small fiery dragons scrambling up the wall, another scuttling across the ceiling, spitting gobbets of flame. Then black smoke seared his vision and a stench of burning tar filled his nostrils. When he could see again, through watering eyes, a few sullen scraps of flame were flickering here and there on the walls and floor, as if the small fire-dragons had quickly burnt themselves almost to nothing. One of Corr's men, clutching his blackened tunic sleeve and gasping in pain, was being helped from the chamber by another. Will heard a hissing sound and turned to see one of the dragons writhing on the floor near his feet.

One of Corr's men kicked it over the edge of the platform and it fell, crackling, into the rain.

Corr was brushing at his singed cloak and already striding back out onto the platform. The old dwarf cowered against one wall, his sunken eyes bright with fear.

"Where did the motherworm go?" Corr said. "Did anyone see?"

"It dropped," someone shouted. "To the base of the walls. And there was a second one. I saw it."

Corr leaned forward and peered over the side of the platform.

"Can't see anything," he growled.

"They were carrying something in their claws," Alfric said.

"Chain," Finn said. "I saw a coiled length of thick chain. And there was a rider on the first worm, I'm sure of it. Or more than one."

"The motherworms never come this close to the walls," Alfric said. "What in all the hells are they up to?"

"The chains," Corr said, snapping shut the spyglass and turning to face his men. "They're bolting chains to the sides of the fortress. Those wagons that the Nightbane were hauling were carrying winches."

"For what purpose?" the mordog lieutenant said.

"To bring the fortress down," Corr said.

"Is that possible?"

"I don't intend to find out. Send a ship down to the base of the walls. Nonn, some of your folk must go as well. Those chains must be cut and the worms driven off."

The dwarf climbed unsteadily to his feet.

"But there are two worms, Lord," the mordog lieutenant said. "The crew won't have a chance."

"Send a ship now!" Corr roared. "And send another to

those columns with a full contingent of men, and the wolves, too. Tell the captains to find the winches and destroy them."

"My Lord, the wolf-keepers say that the new one, the big wolf we just brought in, is causing trouble. He won't obey the keepers, and the others are following his lead."

"Has he been fed the *gaal*?"

"Yes, Lord, but there hasn't been time to give him enough. He's still resisting."

"Then give him more."

"But . . . it is too soon. The keepers say that more *gaal* now will burn him up too quickly."

"We don't need him to last long. Have him given twice the dose."

"No!" Will shouted. Finn gripped his arm to hold him back.

Corr stared at Will, his eyes narrowing.

"You don't want the big wolf harmed. Why not?"

"He's my friend," Will said desperately. "If you hurt him, I'll . . ."

"Your friend," Corr said, his eyebrows rising. "So that's why you're here. You came looking for him. That's what this whole expedition of yours was about, Finn. Now I see. The wolf is very important to you."

Nonn was studying Will now, too, with a look of interest.

"Tell me, boy," the dwarf said, "does the wolf understand our speech?"

Will said nothing.

"He does, doesn't he?" Corr said. "Then I think we've found a better way to ensure his cooperation. You will tell him that he will fight for us, if he wants his freedom, and yours."

Will shook his head slowly.

"I won't do it," he said.

Corr gazed at Will for a long moment.

"No, you won't, will you? Very well. Commander, you have your orders. Make sure the keepers double the wolf's dose of *gaal*."

Will tore his arm out of Finn's grasp.

"No!" he cried. "Please, don't hurt him!"

Corr signalled to two of his men. They came forward and held Will's arms.

"Corr, this is wrong," Finn said. "You can't."

Corr turned to his brother.

"If this fortress comes down, we will all die. The Nightbane will break through our defences and overrun the plains and then they will come to the Bourne. Make no mistake about that. You said you would stand by me if I let your friends go. I give you my oath that when this battle is over, I will let them all return to Fable. The wolf, too, if he's still alive."

"When this battle is over, there will be nothing left!" Balor roared. "We should get everyone on board the ships and head south while we still can."

Corr glanced darkly at Balor, then gestured to one of the guards who had followed them to the observation platform.

"Escort the wildman and the boy back to their quarters, and make sure they stay there."

"Finn!" Balor shouted, as he was surrounded by four tall guardsmen with lightning staves.

Finn turned to Balor. His face was stricken and pale.

"Stay with Will," he said. "Keep him safe."

21

The truth was proclaimed in a thousand tongues, it was heralded by blaring trumpets and written in fiery letters in the sky. But only when it came as a whisper in the darkness did I hear it and answer.

– The Great Forest Book

"I KNEW WE WOULD MEET AGAIN," Maya said.

They were sitting together in the little cottage. Rowen was at the table, numbly sipping a cup of tea but barely tasting it. Her grandmother was working at her loom, slowly unwinding a skein of thread that was wrapped around a short, sword-like wooden stick. As if in a dream, Rowen watched her grandmother's hands working. She knew there were terrible things she still had to do something about, but for the moment, while her grandmother's hands moved back and forth across the threads, those things seemed to be far away.

"I wish I could remember," Rowen said. "I mean, remember . . . you."

"I'm not surprised you don't," Grandmother said with a quick, smiling glance. "You were so young when I left. There's no reason to feel bad about that."

When Rowen had first recovered from her faint, Grandmother had led her to a chair, made her some tea, then listened to her rushed, jumbled tale of everything that had happened that had brought her here. Rowen told her of the journey with Will, and the warning Freya had brought from Whitewing Stonegrinder, and the mage Ammon Brax. Rowen took out her grandfather's spectacles. She gave them to her grandmother, who looked at them wonderingly, with fear growing in her eyes. Haltingly, Rowen told how Grandfather had been taken by the thrawl. Maya listened, holding the spectacles in shaking hands, and then she wept. Rowen wept with her, but she felt strange, sharing her grief and fear with someone she didn't remember. And it pained her when the old woman took up her weaving while they talked, as if the tapestry mattered as much as everything they had to say to one another.

"How long *has* it been?" Grandmother murmured now as she worked, shaking her head slowly. "I do lose track of time . . . sometimes."

"You've been gone for more than ten years," Rowen said. "Grandfather told me that you went into the Weaving not long after my mother and father . . ."

Grandmother's hands halted in their busy work. She closed her eyes a moment, then looked up at Rowen.

"That long," she said in a trembling voice. "But of course. Look at you now. A young woman. And so beautiful." She smiled, nodding at the plate of little honey-coloured cakes beside the teapot. "Eat something. You need to recover your strength."

Rowen picked up one of the cakes, but didn't put it in her mouth. She glanced around the interior of the cottage again. There was the old wooden washbasin, hanging from a peg on the wall. Her father's flute rested on the mantel.

"It's just as I remember it," Rowen said, her heart full.

"When I first came here I needed something familiar," Grandmother said, "to keep me from losing my way. So I made this cottage in the likeness of your home on Blue Hill. I stayed there for a time after you were born, to help your mother. It was the happiest place in the world to me then."

"So we're still in the Weaving," Rowen said. Everything was so much like her memories that she began to wonder if they had somehow returned to the original Blue Hill. "But . . . the house looks so real and solid. As though it's not about to vanish, like everything else here does."

"We are deep within the Weaving," Grandmother said. "Deep within the past. Things are not so uncertain here. I *told* this house, and the forest around it, from the fathomless fire. Then I told him." She gestured to Riddle, who was lying on the woven rug in front of the hearth, lazily running his tongue over his paws. In the firelight his striped form seemed to ripple like slow waves.

"He doesn't seem to know me any more," Rowen said.

"He remembers what he is now. I suppose that means he has no need to speak. He has become once more what he always was: the fathomless fire."

"Riddle is the *fire*?"

"He is one face of it, as is everything here. It may look as if he's just lying on a rug napping, but he's also out there, with the sunlight, the trees, the birds and the creatures in the grass. You called him Riddle, did you?"

"He gave himself that name. He didn't know who he was or where he had come from."

She looked again at the tiger, lying sleepily on the hearthrug.

"That's why you couldn't stay in one shape for long," Rowen said to him, suddenly understanding. "Because you never were *someone* . . ."

"That's a good way to put it," Grandmother said. "The fire never stays still, not for a moment." She paused, and her brow wrinkled. "I should have realized," she said at last, "what might happen when I sent him to . . . to your grandfather."

"You sent him?"

"He was supposed to find Nicholas and show him the way here, to me. That's why I gave him the shape of a tiger, like the toy that your grandfather carved the night . . . the night your mother was born. I knew Nicholas would see the tiger and understand I had sent it, and follow him back to me. But something must have gone wrong. Riddle, as you call him, went astray."

"What do you think happened?"

"I can't say for certain, but I wonder . . . When I sent Riddle to find your grandfather, I hadn't been here long and I didn't understand the fathomless fire as I do now. I think it was wrong of me to confine Riddle to one shape, when change is his nature. That must be why he lost his way. He tried too hard to become *something*, so hard that he forgot what he really is. Which is all of this."

She raised her hands, gesturing to the room and what lay outside it.

Rowen nodded silently, overwhelmed by all the feelings rushing through her. She was glad to be here and have all of these strange things explained, but there was still something missing, something she felt as an ache deep inside her. This woman had loved her since the day she was born, but they didn't know one another. She didn't remember her.

Fighting back tears, she looked down at the little cake in her hand, then without thinking dipped it in the tea and took a bite. As the taste of the cake and the tea mingled in her mouth, she was startled by a memory that came sharp and piercing, like a pain and a joy all at once. She dipped the cake again in the tea, took another bite. Yes, now she remembered. A long time ago she had eaten cakes like this, dipped in tea. She had done this before, when she was very small. Sitting like this with someone nearby working at knitting, or was it at a loom, dipping cakes in tea . . .

She looked at the old woman, who had stretched a length of thread taut between her fingers and was examining it closely.

"You made these cakes for me," she cried. "When I was little. I remember. I remember eating them, with the tea."

The old woman looked at her in surprise, then nodded her head.

"Yes, I did," she said eagerly. "I had forgotten that."

"I remember you now," Rowen said excitedly. The taste of the little cake had brought back so much, like an immense book opening to her gaze. That washbasin: her mother had bathed her in it. And the flute: she and her mother had danced while her father played. And there was someone else there, just on the edges of the memory, someone singing and clapping her hands while Rowen danced. A kind voice, laughing eyes.

Tears slid down Rowen's face.

"You were there too, Grandmother. I remember . . . standing in the doorway, crying. My parents had gone somewhere and left me at home. I was sad and scared. I wondered if they were coming back. And then . . . you were there, and you brought me tea and cakes, and showed me how to dip the cakes in my teacup. You told me . . . 'It makes them taste much better.' I remember you saying that. Then I felt safe, and warm."

"We spent a lot of time together, you and I," the woman said softly. "Your mother was often away with the Errantry.

I'm so happy you remember, and that we can be together again, but . . ." A look of pain or fear crossed her face. "You cannot stay here much longer."

To Rowen's dismay, Grandmother turned back to the tapestry.

"So much to do," she murmured. "Hand me that comb, will you?"

There was a basket near Rowen's feet with several balls of thread and oddly shaped pieces of wood piled in it. Hurt and bewildered, she picked out the object that looked to her like a comb and handed it to her grandmother, who took the white thread she had been pulling from the sword-like stick and began to work it with the comb into the already woven tapestry threads. As the white thread was woven into the design, Rowen was able to see more of it, as if the new thread had illuminated the other threads around it. There was a pattern there, but as soon as Rowen thought she had grasped it, seen what it was, it seemed to change, become something else that eluded her effort to give it a name.

"What are you making?" she asked, surprised at the anger in her voice. What was so important about this tapestry?

Her grandmother looked over at her and a sudden understanding came into her face.

"I'm sorry, Rowen. You've probably been wondering why I insist on sitting here at the loom when we have so much to say to one another. If I could, I would set aside these tools. But it's too late for that now. This tapestry is the Weaving. And I am one of its weavers."

"But I thought all of this . . ." Rowen gestured around the room and out of the open door. "I thought all of it was the Weaving. I thought we were inside it."

"We are. Everything is. And the Weaving is inside us. The Weaving is as small as a grain of sand and wider than the sky.

It's the tiny spark in the dark of your mind that grows into a world. Don't try to think your way around it. No one can. Only when you simply allow it to *be so* will you understand."

Mystified, Rowen studied the tapestry again. She noticed that many of the edges were ragged, and that there was a tight tangle of thread in the centre, a knot of darkness that seemed to have drawn many of the threads towards it, leaving gaps and holes where the weave had been pulled out of shape.

"You're repairing the tapestry," Rowen said.

"Attempting to, yes. But one story is growing so powerful that it's changing and warping everything, even the past. That knot at the centre is Malabron's story, and he is bending all his powers now upon Fable. If it falls, the tapestry will tell only his story everywhere and for ever. No one will remember there was ever anything else before, or imagine that things might be different. There will be no more beginnings or endings, no more princesses or brave knights or woodcutter's sons. Or tigers, for that matter."

Rowen's heart went cold.

"Those holes in the weave," she said after a long silence. "There was a rift, an empty place that Balor Gruff of the Errantry stumbled into, near Fable. When Grandfather found it, the rift was already almost sealed up again. Was that you?"

"I have repaired many holes in the weave, so it may well be. I rarely leave the loom any more, but despite all I do the darkness grows and is already beyond my power to heal. And it is spreading faster now than ever, as if it has woven all of its long-prepared threads and is moving them at last, to seize its prey."

"Prey . . . you mean Fable, and the raincabinet?"

"And you, Rowen. I think that when you stepped into the

black river, the Night King saw you clearly for the first time, saw what you could become, and that is another reason for his sudden haste."

"Can't anything can be done to stop him?" Rowen cried. "What about the Stewards? Grandfather said you went into the Weaving to find out what had happened to them. Did you find them? Can they help us?"

Grandmother pulled the comb away from the tapestry and turned to Rowen.

"I have learned much about the Stewards here," she said. "I know now that they did not begin the Realm, as we once thought, they only shaped and tended what was already there. The Weaving, the fire, has no beginning. Stories come only from other stories. And now the story of the Stewards is over, it is a part of the ancient past that the Night King has almost completely consumed, so that few remember it. Now it is the task of others to save the Realm, if they can."

"You mean me," Rowen said heavily, and the doubt and fear she had set aside settled on her again like a terrible weight. "Maybe . . . I can stay here with you, and help you with the tapestry. Maybe if we work together . . ."

"That cannot be," Grandmother said. "If one stays too long in the Weaving, one can never leave it. One cannot weave without being woven. In a way, you could say I have become the Weaving."

"Then that means . . . *you* can't leave here," Rowen said in anguish. "Why not, Grandmother? I don't understand."

It seemed for a moment that her grandmother hadn't heard. She was looking down at her hands lying in her lap, as if they were now empty of something she had once been carrying. Then suddenly she raised her head and gazed long at Rowen, her eyes filled with love and sadness.

"I came here . . . because I saw that one day you would

be more powerful than any loremaster who has ever been. I knew you would have a great gift, and a great purpose, and that this would put you in terrible danger. I wanted to help you, protect you, by bringing back the secrets of the Weaving. But I discovered I could do more for you if I stayed and worked at the loom, even if it meant I could never return. That was my choice. To leave you, when you were a child, so that I could help you when you were grown. And that was the hardest thing I've ever done . . . leaving you."

"Grandmother . . ." Rowen said, her voice breaking. "I didn't know."

Hesitantly the old woman reached out and gently brushed back some stray locks of Rowen's hair.

"My child," she said softly.

Rowen threw her arms around her grandmother. They held each other for a long time. Then Grandmother took a deep breath and sat back so that she could look into Rowen's eyes again.

"I did what I could here for you, such as it was," she said. "The snugs in the forest, the knot-paths . . ."

Rowen stared in wonder. She couldn't help looking at her grandmother's hands. They looked so frail. An old woman's wrinkled, almost translucent hands.

"*You* made those things?"

"I wove them into the world, yes."

Rowen remembered the cosy snug they had stayed in on their way home to Fable. As always when they stayed in one of those mysterious little rooms, she had wondered why they were there and who had prepared everything in them for weary travellers.

"But Grandfather said the snugs and the knot-paths were made by the Stewards," she protested, "ages and ages ago. They've *always* been there."

"From this place, I discovered, I could reach into the way things were, even the most ancient times, and weave them anew."

"You mean you . . . changed *the past*."

"Here in the Weaving one learns that time is . . . well, it's not something we *have*, it's what we are. We weave with it, and are woven by it. And now I have become part of the past that I wove. That is why I cannot leave. But at least I have been able to change a few things for the better, though I had to be careful. Too much meddling with stories and one starts down the road to becoming another Malabron. But I knew that one day you and your grandfather might have need of safe refuges, or secret ways to flee far from danger. And so I came up with the idea of the snugs, and the knot-paths. And once I'd woven them into the past, it was as if they'd always been there, since the beginning."

Rowen thought of Will then, and how he had saved them from the Angel by finding one of those mysterious paths. She had never known, never suspected that the path was only there for Will to find because of her grandmother.

"You were right about us needing them," Rowen said, then a strange new hope came to her. "If you can change the past like that, what about the future? Couldn't you just make it so that Malabron will be defeated in the end?"

"I cannot. The past is all I dare weave, and that is dangerous enough. But even were it possible for me to change what will be, I would not do it, Rowen. The future is that part of the weave which is yet unwoven, ever unfinished. Only fools and tyrants say 'this will always be so.' We stand against Malabron for that very reason: if he conquers all, he conquers time itself, and there will be no past or future, only a dead *now* where nothing changes and nothing new can ever come to be."

Rowen shook her head slowly.

"It all seems so hopeless," she whispered bleakly. "The dragon, Whitewing Stonegrinder, he warned us that the Night King's armies are marching on the Bourne. Malabron knows about Fable being the crossroads. The key to all stories. The Errantry won't be enough to withstand him. Then he'll have the raincabinet, and the past and the future and everything . . ."

Grandmother put her hand on Rowen's.

"I see the future in you, and what I see fills me with hope. I am the past, I've done what I can. This, now, is your time, Rowen. The power you need to defend Fable is in you. Never doubt that. But you will not be alone in this task, for I've also made sure you would have allies. The folk of Story are coming to the Bourne. They are coming from lands far and near to Fable, to fight for it."

"You called the Storyfolk? Or warned them. How?"

"Into as many stories as I could I wove a rumour, a legend, a prophecy, of a time when darkness would fall across the Realm and all free folk would rise to defend it. And now the darkness has come, and everywhere the legend is being remembered, the prophecy has been spoken again, only now as a dire warning. The folk of Story are awakening. Many of them are already on their way to Fable to stand with you and the Errantry in the hour of need."

Rowen lowered her head. She felt as if her heart would tear in two. Her grandmother had done all of this for her, to help her, and now she had to tell her what she had chosen to do.

"I'm not staying in Fable," she said. "I can't, at least not now. I have to find Grandfather and bring him back. That comes first, before anything."

Grandmother's eyes filled with pain and fear.

"Rowen, no. You cannot go to the Shadow Realm. You don't understand what awaits you there."

"I do, Grandmother. I'm sorry, after all you've done for me, but I have to go."

"Nicholas would not want you to do this."

"But he's alive. I know he is. He needs me and I'm going to find him. I won't let . . . *him* take anyone else I love. I couldn't bear it if I knew that Grandfather had become like those others . . . the ones I saw walking to the Shadow Realm."

"Oh, my dear one, I know how much you want to bring your grandfather home, and I want that, too . . . but Malabron is still searching for you. Other than the rain-cabinet itself, you're what he most desires to find and make his own. The moment you set foot in his realm, the moment you cross into his nightmare, he will know it. He will see you at once, and take you, and you cannot defend yourself against his power."

"That's what the thrawl told me, but I'll find a way," Rowen said, struggling against despair. "There must be a way."

Grandmother gazed at her in silence for a long time, her face stricken with pain. At last she drew a deep breath, and bent to search in her basket of weaving tools.

"If you do this, then my heart will break," she said, "but I won't stop you. All I can tell you is that you will have to find a hidden, secret way into his realm, or it will be over for you in a moment. And for that, you will need some help. A pathfinder, perhaps, like your friend, Will Lightfoot."

"Will," Rowen cried. "If only I could see him again before I go. But he's so far away."

Then she remembered the mirror shard and drew it out.

"Will gave me this," she said. "Maybe I can use it to find him, like I used Grandfather's staff to find his thread. But . . .

he may still be searching for Shade. If he is, I can't ask him to come with me."

Grandmother took Rowen's hand.

"The Weaving is not only a tapestry on a loom. It is in you, too. In all of us. But you have a gift few have, to sense the threads as they weave and unweave. Look inside yourself. Your friends are there, too. What do you see?"

Rowen went still and closed her eyes. She opened them a moment later. The truth had been there for a long time, but she hadn't seen it.

"He's found him," she said. "Will is with Shade. They're together . . . but they're in danger."

"You must find Will. I think only he can help you now. Ah, but wait, there is one more thing I have to give you. Something I've been preparing for a long time. How could I forget? I sent Riddle to your grandfather so that when he found me, he would take *this* back to you. But now I can give it to you myself."

She reached into the basket at Rowen's feet and lifted out a tiny golden ball, little bigger than her own thumb. She held it out in her palm and after a moment Rowen took it, felt how light it was in her hand, almost not there at all. Looking at it closely, she realized the ball was made of tightly coiled, finely-spun golden thread. She turned it over but could not see an end to the thread, if there was one.

"What is it?" she asked.

"Scarcely more than a thought as yet," Grandmother said. "Or a breath. I spun it from what has been lost and forgotten. But it is strong, the strongest thread there is. Once you weave with it, the thread can never be broken."

"But I'm not a weaver like you, Grandmother. What do I do with it? How do I use it?"

"You must find that out for yourself, Rowen. You will

know what to do when you see what has been unwoven and needs to be mended."

Rowen gazed at the ball of thread, mesmerized by its fine golden sheen. Then she slipped it into her pocket.

She stood, took a deep breath and looked away, out of the cottage door. The clearing was bright with quiet sunlight. It was so peaceful here, but inside her a storm of doubt and fear was raging.

"The raincabinet," she said. "I left the door open. If that mage, Ammon Brax, finds it, he'll find the Weaving. Grandfather said that mustn't happen."

"Then you must go back there, before you do anything else. Find a way to stop him, or hide the raincabinet from him."

"I'll try," Rowen said.

Grandmother dropped her weaving comb into the basket and rose from her seat.

"It's getting late," she said. "Let's join Riddle outside."

Rowen glanced over at the hearthrug. The tiger was no longer there. She was about to say something, but Grandmother was already going out of the door. Rowen followed, and squinted as she came back out into the sunlit glade.

The tiger was there, standing at the edge of the woods, eyeing them askance as if wondering what had taken them so long.

"Go with Rowen," Grandmother said to him.

The tiger's lithe feline shape began to dissolve and come apart into sinuous flames. Then each flickering tongue of fire sped off in a different direction and swiftly vanished in the bright sunlight. Rowen wondered why Riddle had disappeared, then she saw that one of the flames had remained, hovering near her. As she watched, it settled at her feet, growing and unfolding into his familiar tawny wildcat shape.

"Riddle is still here," the cat said. "Riddle will . . . *I* will go with Rowen on her journey."

"Thank you."

Rowen turned to her grandmother. They threw their arms around each other, and tears came again for both of them.

"How I wish I could keep you safe with me, my dear one," Grandmother whispered.

"If the Night King isn't defeated . . ." Rowen began fearfully, "if everything is swallowed up, even the past, what will happen to this place? What will happen to you?"

"The Weaving cannot be utterly destroyed, even if it is woven only with darkness for a time. Something of me will always be here, Rowen, working at the loom."

22

. . . on that day even the earth will rise up against you . . .

– The Kantar

THE DOOR OF THEIR ROOM slammed shut and Will threw himself against it, hammering on it with his fists. Then he heard the lock click, and he backed away and sank down slowly on one of the beds. Balor stood staring at the door, then began to pace back and forth.

"What in all the Realm is Finn thinking?" he muttered after a long silence. "Why would he join that madman?"

"They're going to kill Shade," Will said, shaking his head.

Balor halted and scowled.

"No they're not," he said. "We'll stop them."

The wildman staggered forward as the stone floor shook underneath them. Dust drifted from the walls. They could hear the tread of many hurrying feet in the corridor outside.

"We must get out of here . . ." Balor growled, then his eyes brightened. "I have an idea. Will, hide under one of the beds. I'm going to make the guards open the door."

"How?"

"Wait and see. This will work, I'm sure of it."

Will shook his head doubtfully, but did as the wildman asked. He dropped to the floor and crawled under one of the beds. When Will was out of sight, Balor strode up to the door and pounded on it.

"Hey, you out there!" he roared in a voice that seemed to shake the very walls and made Will flinch in spite of himself. "I'm starving to death in here and I've decided I'm going to eat the boy. After all, I'm . . ." He took a deep breath. "I'm an *ogre*, and that's what ogres do. Just thought I'd let you know, because you'll have to answer to the Sky Lord's brother for locking me in here with his friend."

A few moments later the lock rattled and the door creaked slowly open. Two guards stood in the doorway, both holding lightning staves levelled at Balor.

"Where is the boy?" one of them asked, his face turning pale. "Did you . . . ?"

"There he goes!" Balor shouted. "Catch him before he gets away!"

Both guards turned and the wildman lunged at them. He brought one down with a fist to the jaw and took off out of the door after the other, who had dashed away with a shout. Will slid out from underneath the bed and climbed to his feet, just as Balor returned, dragging the other guard, limp and senseless, by his arms.

"It actually worked," Balor said. "The fever iron must dull their wits. They'll both have splitting headaches when they wake up, but we'll be long gone."

"We must find Shade. He's somewhere down in the lowest part of the fortress."

"But we don't know where exactly."

"I know but we have to get to him before they . . ." Will

broke off. "If we can hide him somewhere, maybe we can find Finn and he can convince his brother to let Shade go."

"I think Finn's brother is beyond convincing of anything. But what choice is there? Ah, just a moment."

Balor picked up one of the guards' staves.

"This might be useful."

They set off down the corridor, reached a narrow flight of stairs and descended. At the bottom they came to a meeting of three wider corridors. Balor sniffed the air.

"Straight on, I think," he said.

They kept going, stopping whenever they heard voices or sounds. The corridor led to another descending flight of stairs that Balor said they should take, but halfway down a bald, burly man, armed and cloaked, suddenly appeared before them, climbing upwards. He had no lightning stave, but when he saw them he drew his sword and advanced slowly.

"You are not supposed to be down here," he said warningly.

Balor stepped forward and pointed the lightning stave at the man, who lunged out of the way.

Nothing happened. The man stared at Balor and the lightning stave.

"Oh, never mind," Balor said, and he dropped the stave and charged at the man, slamming him against the wall before he could recover and raise his weapon. The man slid to the floor, unconscious, and Balor stepped over him, picking up the stave.

"Nothing like the traditional methods," he said, and he led the way down the stairs. At the bottom there was another meeting of corridors, each of which plunged steeply downwards. From one of them came a stinging smoke and the ringing of hammers on metal. While they hesitated here for a moment two dwarves appeared from the smoky passage, younger than Nonn but just as gaunt and grim-faced, carrying between them a leather sling filled with blades and axes. At the sight of Balor they dropped the sling and backed away down the passage.

"Come on," Balor said, leading Will to one of the other descending passages.

At the bottom they came to a long, narrow chamber lined with iron cages, most of which were open, and empty.

"They've already taken the wolves," Will said. "But where did they . . ."

Just then they heard a commotion in an adjoining chamber. It sounded like the crack of a whip, followed by a low, warning growl.

Will darted for the other chamber, and came through the door to see three short, stocky Stormriders with thick leather gloves and masks, surrounding Shade, who was backing with a limp into one corner. The chamber stank of dung and rotting meat. Two of the keepers had whips and one was lifting a net with barbed knots. A fourth keeper stood nearby, brandishing some kind of spear with a tip that tapered to a needle-thin point.

"Get away from him!" Will shouted. The four keepers turned at the sound. Before they could do more than stare in shock, Balor barged into the room and raised the lightning stave on high.

A crackling tendril of white light erupted from it, its searing brightness filling the chamber and blinding Will. When it had passed, three of the keepers lay on the floor, groaning, their clothing burnt and smoking. The one with the spear had vanished. Balor stood staring at the lightning stave with a dumbfounded look on his face. It was clear he had no idea why the stave had worked this time.

Shade lay in the corner, not moving. Will hurried to his side and knelt beside him.

"Shade?"

The wolf stirred, then suddenly sprang up, jaws snapping. Will fell back with a cry.

The wolf snarled savagely, his teeth bared, then sank back down, panting. His eyes rolled back in his head, and slaver dripped from his jaws.

"Shade, it's me," Will said, wiping away the tears that clouded his vision. "I'm here. What have they done to you?"

The wolf's head came up. His eyes darted about wildly, then he seemed to see Will at last.

"Will Lightfoot. I am sorry. They put their poison into me. There is a . . . fire in my blood. I cannot see or think well."

"We're getting you out of here," Will said. "Can you walk all right? Did they burn you with the lightning again?"

"They did not. When I saw that the Sky Folk had caught you, Will Lightfoot, I let them take me," Shade said. "I wanted to go where they were taking you. I was hoping I could escape and find you, but they gave me their poison and I forgot everything."

"That keeper will bring others back," Will said. "Maybe if we can get to one of their ships . . ."

"We can try," Balor said.

Will helped Shade to rise, then the three of them hurried out of the chamber together. After a short dash they came to a meeting of two dim, narrow passages. Down one they glimpsed a flicker of torchlight and heard the heavy tread of booted feet. They took the other passageway and followed its slowly winding rise until they could feel cooler air on their faces. Around a corner their flight came to a sudden end. A gate of thick iron bars blocked the corridor. Will looked around in panic, before noticing a crack in the wall to his left, a narrow fissure running from the roof to the floor. It had probably been caused by the tremors that had shaken the fortress, and was wide enough for him to see a pale light and drifting cloud through it.

"What's on the other side of this?" he asked himself aloud.

"Maybe nothing but a hundred-foot drop," Balor said. "But if there's a walkway or a battlement . . ."

"It's better than being trapped here."

"Stand back," Balor said. "Let's see if I can get this thing to work again."

He aimed the lightning stave at the fissure. The tip of the stave glowed a brilliant white, and a bolt of lightning burst forth and flew at the wall. There was a roar and a rumble of falling stone. When the choking clouds of dust settled, they saw that the gap was twice as large as it had been before.

"You did it, Balor," Will shouted.

"Yes, but . . ." the wildman began. In his hands he held the two broken halves of the stave.

"I'm not sure what I did wrong," he muttered, dropping the broken stave. "And I know what I said about magic weapons, but this really came in handy while it lasted."

"Come on," Will said. He ducked and climbed through the hole, with Shade and the wildman following quickly after. They found themselves on a narrow stair without a railing, running along the base of the wall Balor had just blasted open. The cloud-cloaked sky was a pale grey, and Will realized that dawn was not far off. Far below them lay the dark earth, veiled in smoke and lit here and there with sullen red fire. The stair they were on climbed along the wall to a landing, and what looked to be an archway to another part of the fortress.

"Up that way, I think," Balor cried above the roar of the wind. "We can't stay here."

"Shade, can you climb?" Will asked.

"I am staying with you no matter what, Will Lightfoot."

"If those motherworms find us out here, we're done for," Balor said, then added in an undertone, "nothing motherly about them, if you ask me."

They climbed slowly up the stair, constantly watching the sky and the wall below them for any sign of the dragons. When they were almost at the landing, Will suddenly stopped.

"What's that?" he said, pointing downwards.

In the dim light they could see a long column of dark armoured figures, climbing up the rim of the valley. Will followed the line of their march to its origin and saw that the figures were filing out of one of the black fissures in the earth. The column, hundreds or maybe even thousands strong, was marching south, but away from the fortress, not towards it. They were not marching to the assault, Will realized, but leaving the valley. Perhaps marching out of the ghostlands altogether.

"Where are they going?" Balor shouted. "The battle is here."

Will had no answer, but as he gazed down at the column, he felt a cold wave of dread pass through him. There was something in the way these dark figures moved perfectly in step, as if each was exactly the same as all the others, that was familiar to him in a terrifying way.

"It's the fetches," he said. "The armoured fetches Nonn told us about."

"Why aren't they attacking the fortress?" Balor said. "Well, never mind that now, we have to keep moving."

They started climbing again. A short time later they reached the landing and hurried through the archway, which gave onto a wide circular platform of stone, surrounded by columns, some cracked and fallen over. There were black scorch marks on the flagstones, and on many of the columns. Far above, a thin ray of morning light had pierced the smoke and cloud, and the naked stone of the towers high above glowed a pale red.

"This is a training ground if ever I've seen one," Balor said. "Probably where they practise using the staves."

"Will Lightfoot," Shade said warningly, and Will turned to see what the wolf's watchful eyes were fixed on.

A tall figure stood at the edge of the ring. At first Will thought he was clad in some kind of dull-grey armour, then he saw that the armour was in fact the figure's flesh, and that it was not metal but clay.

"The stone giant," Balor muttered, then he grinned. "I'd forgotten about that. And I'm the bear. Well, let's not disappoint the Dreamwalker's children."

"That's Ord, the golem," Will cried. "The one we met in the bog. He didn't hurt us then. Maybe if we just walk away . . ."

"He's the Sky Lord's servant now, remember?" Balor said. "Mark my words, he's been sent to find us and bring us back. Will, take Shade and get out of here."

"You can't fight him, Balor," Will said. "He's too strong."

"We'll see about that," said the wildman.

The golem was much as Will remembered him. Silent, impassive—then suddenly he was moving towards them like the stone of the fortress itself come to life.

Will could feel his heavy tread underfoot. He backed away with Shade, and watched in fear as the golem advanced slowly, inexorably on Balor, who had yet to move. Ord approached the wildman with arms at his sides and eyes fixed as if unseeing. At the last moment the golem's arms rose and reached for Balor, who braced himself and grasped Ord's wrists. It was clear to Will now that the wildman had waited for his moment, in the hope of throwing the golem to the ground, but although he strained with all his might and grew purple in the face, the golem did not move.

Finally Balor let go and staggered back, his face gleaming with sweat.

The golem came at him again, as slowly and unrelentingly as before.

"I will help Balor Gruff," Shade said, but Will clung to him tightly.

"You're hurt, Shade. Please stay here."

This time when Ord reached him Balor ducked under his outstretched arms and threw himself at the golem's midsection. He dug his feet in and shoved. Now the golem actually moved backwards a step or two. Then his arms reached around the wildman. At the last moment Balor dropped and rolled away. Will understood what would happen to him if the golem got Balor in his grip, and the wildman seemed to know it, too.

The golem came at Balor again and the wildman swung one of his huge fists and struck Ord full in the face. The golem's head and torso jerked back with the force of the blow, but his feet, Will saw with astonishment, did not even move. He righted himself just as Balor struck again, with a blow that Will thought would have been enough to floor an elephant. And again the golem's upper body was thrown back, but he was not budged the slightest from where he stood. Again the golem righted himself and came on.

Balor seemed to understand clearly now what he was facing. He backed away and began to circle his adversary, his eyes never leaving the stone giant's. The golem followed Balor, his slow, steady pace unchanged, unhurried.

Suddenly the wildman bent forward as if exhausted or in pain. As Ord approached and reached for him once more,

Balor sprang up, grappled the golem from below and succeeded in lifting him off the ground. The strain on Balor's face was terrible to see. He was only able to lift the golem's feet less than a hand's breadth from the stones, but it seemed as if he were lifting a mountain. Balor's brawny arms were around the golem's midsection, shaking as the wildman squeezed his opponent, but there was no apparent effect on Ord. With a cracked roar, Balor heaved the golem away from him. Ord struck the floor, rolled once in the dust, then climbed to his feet and started towards Balor again as if nothing had happened.

Will could see that Balor had little strength left. The wildman didn't back away again, but his chest was heaving and as he came on, he tottered for a moment as if he might fall. As the golem came past the place where Will was watching, Will saw that instead of the green stone from Finn's ring, the golem had set in his forehead a dull black disc.

"Balor, his forehead!" Will cried.

Balor shot a puzzled glance towards Will, who touched his own forehead.

"The disc in his forehead!"

Balor's eyes widened with understanding and he nodded, just as the golem's arms reached for him once more. He batted them away, struck the golem a blow to the chest and pulled his fist back with a grimace of pain. Then he clutched at the golem's forehead with his other hand. His fingers scrabbled desperately for a moment, before he pulled his hand back as the golem reached for him, but it was too late. The golem's arms were around him now and his hands locked together, imprisoning the wildman. Balor struggled, growled, hammered the golem on the back with his fists as he was lifted easily off the ground. For a moment it seemed as if nothing was happening, but Balor's face darkened, his features contorted, and Will knew that the golem was slowly squeezing the breath out of him.

A friend will fall, Will thought in horror.

"He's killing him," he breathed desperately.

Shade pulled away from Will's side with a growl and leapt at the golem. His jaws closed around one of Ord's wrists and his head wrenched to one side. The golem's grip loosened just long enough for the wildman to free one of his arms. But the golem flung the wolf away in the next instant and regained his crushing hold on Balor.

Shade hit the stone floor and rolled. He was up a moment later and Will was by his side.

"Shade, wait—" Will began, but Shade was already running at the golem again. Then suddenly he stopped.

Out of the shadows strode Corr Madoc, followed by Finn and a small party of Stormriders carrying torches. One of them seized Will by the arm and another pointed a lightning stave at Shade.

"Enough," Corr said, and Will realized he was speaking to the golem.

Ord let the wildman go, as if he was suddenly forgotten. Balor tumbled to the floor, gasping for breath. The golem stood over him, unmoving, not even looking at the adversary he had bested, as if waiting patiently for his next task.

Finn hurried to Balor and crouched by his side. The mordog who was holding Will back released his grip, and Will darted to Shade's side. Finn turned from examining the wildman.

"He's still breathing," he said. "We need to get him to Alazar, Corr."

"Your friend the wildman isn't dying," Corr Madoc said. "The golem does not kill. We've seen it many times already, when we send him against our enemies. My mages tried to change that, but they weren't successful. It makes the golem less useful, perhaps, but still, he's practically unstoppable, and quite intimidating in battle."

Finn stood and faced his brother.

"Did you order this attack?"

"I ordered the golem to find your friends and hold them," Corr said, returning Finn's steady gaze without expression. "It was for their own safety. The Nightbane have been driven back from the walls for now, but they are regrouping and the assault may begin again at any time."

"You did this for our safety, Corr?" Finn cried, his eyes blazing. "Look what's happened to Balor."

"He will live to fight another day."

"The question is," said a voice from beyond the circle of men, "will any of you?"

Doctor Alazar made his way through the press of Stormriders, followed by a man Will had not seen before. He was older than Corr, his hair thin and greying, his face pale and deeply lined. There were dark rings under his eyes.

Alazar hurried to Balor's side. The wildman groaned and raised his head.

"'Zar, good to see you," he said groggily. "Did I beat that thing?"

"To a standstill, my friend," the doctor said.

Balor grinned and closed his eyes. The golem still stood where it had dropped the wildman, as lifeless as a statue.

"Is he . . . ?" Will asked the doctor, tears welling in his eyes.

"He lives," Alazar said. "He's just passed out, Will."

The words came to Will again: *a friend will fall*. Balor fell to the golem's strength, but he will live, Will thought with relief. And if all of the shadow's predictions had come to pass, did that mean Rowen and Shade and Will's other friends were safe now? Desperately he hoped it was so, but deep down he felt a faint dread still churning inside him.

"Yates," Corr said to the man who had come with Alazar, "you should be resting."

"I've been asleep long enough," the man said in a hoarse voice. "I'm done with all of this, Corr. If you won't let me go, you'll have to kill me."

Corr's gaze locked with Yates's for a long moment.

"Go where you will, then," Corr said at last, turning away from him.

"He should be free of this place," Alazar said. "You all should. I know now why the *gaal* is so important to Corr's men, Finn. I know why they're so desperate to drive the Nightbane from the dwarves' city. They *need* the fever iron. After they've taken it a few times, their bodies crave it and sicken without it. Over time they need more and more of it to gain the fierceness in battle that it gives them. But the more they take, the more it poisons their bodies and minds."

They all looked at Corr, who glowered at the doctor, then turned to Finn with a shrug.

"There is always a price to be paid," he said.

"I saw it in the wounded," Alazar went on. "They're barely aware of their injuries. I asked them about returning to their homelands some day, and they no longer care about that. All they wanted to know was when they were getting their next ration of the *gaal*. Yates here is one of the few who fought against the craving that was killing him. That's why he tried to get away. Nonn and his folk knew about this, they must have known, but they kept it secret from you and your men, didn't they Corr, until it was too late and you needed the *gaal* as much as the dwarves needed your swords."

"Are you . . . taking the *gaal*, Corr?" Finn asked.

"We all are, brother," Corr said. "You are, too. It's in the air here. There's a fine, almost invisible dust from the smelting of the ore. It's everywhere. You're all gaining strength from it right now. Just think: you've all gone without sleep for hours, you've hardly eaten a thing, and yet none of you feel tired or weak, do you? You already see what the *gaal* can do. Think of that, and perhaps you will judge us less harshly."

"We saw the armoured fetches marching below," Will said. "They're heading south, out of the valley. There are hundreds, maybe thousands of them."

"We've seen them," Corr said. "We will respond when the time is right."

"There is no time left," Finn said. "Clearly, they've been building up their numbers and their strength for this day, while you thought you were keeping them boxed in. The dragons' attack, the chains, it's all a diversion to keep you busy, Corr, while their main force escapes the valley, probably to attack the lands to the south."

"We don't know that," Corr said. "It may well be a feint of another kind, to draw our attention while they launch a greater assault on the fortress. These armoured fetches are just puppets. Their helmets have no visors, no eye-slits. They're walking blind, mindlessly, where they're bidden. Their purpose may only be to draw us out, so that the Nightbane can finish us."

Helmets without visors, Will thought, and then he remembered Rowen's dream.

"I know where they're going," he cried. "They're marching on the Bourne. Rowen saw it, in a dream she told me about. Armoured figures without faces. They were hollow inside. They had Fable surrounded. She saw this happening. They're going to attack Fable."

Corr turned to Will with a dubious look.

"Someone, *not you*, saw this in a dream?" he scoffed. "I

will need more proof than that, boy, before I believe such an unlikely tale. Of what possible interest would Fable be to the Night King?"

"I don't know, but Rowen is a loremaster, descended from the Stewards," Will said. "She can see such things. Finn knows her, too."

"It's true, Corr," Finn said. "Rowen is the granddaughter of Nicholas Pendrake. She has a gift of seeing into the weave of the Realm. I don't pretend to understand it, but I wouldn't dismiss anything she says."

Corr smiled.

"Pendrake is a good man. One of the few in Fable I ever trusted. But Finn, if I had listened to all the prophets and soothsayers over the years who warned me to turn back, the Bourne probably would have been overrun long ago. Will here is desperate to get home. To see the girl again, no doubt."

"I'm not lying," Will cried. "You have to believe me!"

"You promised you'd let my friends go if I stayed with you, Corr," Finn said. "Let them return to Fable now, to warn the Errantry about the host coming south. Even if Fable is not their destination, our people should know about this so they can prepare for the worst."

Corr looked up into the dawn sky, then at his brother. For a terrible moment Will thought he was going to refuse. Then he sighed and put a hand on Finn's shoulder.

"So be it," he said. "I have no time for your friends and their foolishness. It's better they were out of here than spreading their wild tales among my men. Yates, are you well enough to pilot a skyship?"

"I am, Corr. The doctor has helped me get back on my feet."

"I questioned the dwarves' healer," Alazar said, "and he finally admitted to me that his people know of a herb that can be brewed into a medicinal drink. It helps the mind and body resist the fever caused by the *gaal*, and takes away some of the craving for it. The healer was reluctant but in the end he gave me a small amount of the dried herb. It has helped Yates already, and it can help the rest of your men, Corr. The healer wouldn't tell me where to find more of the herb, but perhaps if you ask Nonn—"

"My men do not need medicine, doctor," Corr broke in harshly. "They need victory. Yates, you may leave if that is what you wish. Take the boy, the wildman and their wolf friend back to the Bourne, or as close to it as you can. We've never flown the ships such a distance, and I don't know for certain if they can even make it that far, but it's the only way you'll cross the plains in time to bring your empty warning to the Errantry."

"Thank you, Corr," Finn said.

"You're staying here, Finn?" Will said sadly.

"I am, Will. You've saved Shade, and I know Balor will get you back to Fable safely."

"All of us should leave," Alazar said. "You and all your men, too, Corr. Give up this hopeless siege and bring all your ships south. If Will is right we will need your help to defend the Bourne."

Corr smiled bitterly.

"I tried to defend the Bourne once before, doctor, if you remember. But the Errantry didn't want my help. And you said it yourself, my men need the fever iron. Without it, we cannot help anyone, least of all ourselves. There is nowhere else for us to go, now. This is where we make our stand."

"Then I'm staying too," Alazar said. "I'm needed here. More of your men, Corr, are likely to die from the wretched state of your infirmary, than in battle."

"Alazar, you can't," Finn cried. "You must go with Will and Balor. They need you too."

"If 'Zar wants to stay, let him," the wildman said, and they all turned in surprise to see that he had woken and was struggling to rise. "Someone needs to watch out for you, Finn, since clearly you've abandoned all sense. I will get Will home safely."

"Balor, you're in no condition—" the doctor began.

"I'm fine," Balor rumbled, climbing stiffly to his feet. "It takes more than some walking mudball to put a crimp in my step."

"Very good," Corr said. "I'm glad to see you suffered no worse damage, wildman. You fought like no one I've ever seen, and I wish I could keep you here. You'd be of much use in this battle. But enough. Take a ship, Yates. One of the scouting skiffs. That's all I can spare, and even that is more than we can easily do without now. Go, before I change my mind."

"Wait," Will said, stepping forward. "One more thing. The Horse Folk boy, Hawk. Let us take him back to his people."

The Sky Lord turned to Will.

"Why do they matter to you?" he said. "You're not even from this world, boy."

"It matters because I'm like you," Will said, refusing to back down from the Sky Lord's steely glare. "The Dreamwalker, Hawk's father, believes I'm a hero returned. He thinks I'm the one who will bring the rain back to his lands. He's looking to me to make things right again for his people and I know I can't do that, but maybe I can bring him back his son."

Corr studied Will for a long moment, and Will saw something in his cold eyes change.

"Very well, Will Lightfoot," he said. "Take the boy home to his father. And we shall see about the rain."

Corr swept away with his men, and the golem turned and followed ponderously after him, as silent and impassive as always. The doctor stood apart, waiting for Finn, who watched his brother stride away.

When they were alone, the doctor took Finn's arm and said to him in a low, urgent voice, "Nonn is using your brother for his own ends. He has some kind of power over him. Surely you can see that?"

"I've seen it," Finn said sadly. "That's why I have to stay."

He turned to Will. "Take care of yourself. Once you warn the Errantry, don't remain in Fable. Leave with the loremaster and Rowen. Find a refuge, or get back home if you can."

"You don't have to stay here, Finn," Will said. "He would let you go, too, if you asked him. I'm sure of it."

"Very likely," Finn said. "But I lost him once, and I'm not going to abandon him now." He turned to the wildman. "Get Will home, Balor. That's all I ask of you, old friend."

"And what do you want me to say when I return to Appleyard?" Balor asked him. "About Corr, about all of this?"

"You can tell Lord Caliburn that I still intend to fulfil my oath. I will bring my brother home. It just might take a while longer."

"I think you've sniffed too much *gaal* already, 'Zar," Balor said to the doctor. "But if you're hellbent on tending to these madmen, just don't try to be a hero. That's my job."

"I agree," the doctor said with a thin smile. "And this way I won't have to listen to your singing all the way home."

He turned to Will and handed him a small cloth pouch.

"Take this, Will. It's some of the dwarves' herb. Brew it in boiling water when you get the chance and drink it. Make sure Balor does too. He has a habit of not listening to his doctor. Farewell for now."

"Goodbye," Will said.

Finn and the doctor turned away and followed Corr. Will watched them go. They disappeared into the haze of bitter smoke drifting along the walls.

23

Master: Where have you been?
Apprentice: I climbed to the top of the mountain.
Master: Did you find anyone there?
Apprentice: I found no one there.
Master: Then you have not been to the top of the mountain.

– The Enigmatist's Handbook

AS ROWAN STEPPED OUT of the raincabinet with Riddle at her side, she heard raised voices coming from below. Edweth's she recognized, arguing heatedly with someone. The mage, she guessed, had returned and was demanding entrance.

Rowen looked back into the darkness of the raincabinet. She thought for a moment of her grandmother, and the impossibly vast world that lay within that darkness. How had her grandfather hidden it? What had he done to make it look like an ordinary broom cupboard?

You take what is, and you nudge it a little, with what might be.

Rowen looked down at her feet. A small puddle of water from the endless rain had formed at the sill of the doorway. Just as it might in a cupboard with mops and buckets. She closed her eyes.

"Be hidden," she whispered desperately. The voices below were getting louder.

The sound of the rain faded. Rowen opened her eyes. She was looking into a small cupboard with dark stone walls. A broom and mop stood in the corners. A bucket with a rag draped over its rim sat in the middle of the puddled floor.

Rowen took a step into the cupboard. She reached out a hand and touched the back wall. Her palm pressed up against cold, solid stone. She gave a push. The wall did not move.

"It will have to do," she whispered. She turned from the raincabinet and hurried downstairs with Riddle at her heels.

She found Edweth and Freya in the front hall, facing three of Thorne's guards. To Rowen's dismay the mage Ammon Brax was there, too, standing to one side and smiling indulgently like someone waiting for a troublesome obstruction to be cleared out of his way. Edweth had a large iron frying pan in her hand that she had raised menacingly. Freya was not armed, but looked grim-faced and ready for a fight.

"You were telling me," the mage said to Edweth when he caught sight of Rowen, "that Master Pendrake's granddaughter had run away. Clearly she didn't get far."

Rowen looked at the housekeeper, who returned the silent urgency of her glance. She knew that Edweth wanted to hear what had happened to her in the Weaving, and Rowen wanted more than anything to tell her she'd found her grandmother, but this was not the time. Instead she summoned up all her outrage and strode forward.

"What are these men doing here?" she demanded.

"They think they're going to throw us out," Edweth cried. "Out of our home."

"Our orders come from the Marshal himself," one of the guards said. "You're to come with us to Appleyard immediately. All of you."

"What about Freya?" Rowen asked. "She's done nothing wrong."

"Those are my orders, miss."

"I know who you are," Edweth said to the guard who had spoken. "You're Hutch Kenning, the miller's son. I don't think your father would approve of this sort of conduct."

"My orders, ma'am," the guard said with calm resolve.

"Lord Caliburn would never agree to this," Edweth said. "He is a good friend of the Master."

"But Master Pendrake is not here," Brax said. "The city of Fable has lost its loremaster, and as unworthy as I am, the Marshal has appointed me to take his place, at least until he is found or returns on his own."

"So you're taking his place and his house as well?" Edweth snapped.

The mage took a deep breath, and Rowen saw with a kind of bitter gladness that the housekeeper had finally begun to fray his careful self-control.

"Lord Caliburn has asked me to search the toyshop for any clues as to what happened to Master Pendrake. And he wishes the two of you to be safe, which this house clearly no longer is. Surely, madam, you can see that the girl needs protecting. What if more of those spell-creatures find their way here?"

"The loremaster told me this was the safest place for Rowen to be," Edweth protested, but Rowen could see that the mage's last argument had carried some weight with her. She folded her arms across her chest, but there was doubt in her eyes.

"It may have been once," the mage said, turning to Rowen. "Believe me, if it was my choice I would let you stay. After all, you've lived in this house most of your life. You know it better than anyone, I would imagine, and you might notice things I wouldn't. You might be able to help me find your grandfather. I will speak to the Marshal when I can, and perhaps he will relent."

The way he looked at her sent a chill through Rowen. He *knew.* Somehow Brax had worked out that she was only pretending to be ignorant and uninterested in her grandfather's secrets. He wanted her to see him as the only hope she had, so that she would give in and confide in him.

She was struggling for a reply that would give nothing more away, when the guard named Kenning cleared his throat.

"The Marshal is waiting," he said to Edweth. "You're to come with us willingly to Appleyard, otherwise we'll have no choice but to drag you there."

"You wouldn't dare," Edweth said. The guard's face darkened and he moved towards the housekeeper.

Rowen was about to step in the way, when she looked past the mage into the street outside. Flakes of snow were drifting slowly down through the evening shadows.

Snow. It was late summer and the days were warm and sunny. There was never snow in Fable at this time of year. The guards had seen it too, and were gazing out of the doorway in wonder.

All at once she knew, and her heart leapt. It was the dragon. Whitewing Stonegrinder had come, as he had promised.

"We'll go," Rowen said quickly. "We won't give you any trouble."

Freya stared at her in surprise, but when she caught Edweth's eye a wordless understanding passed between them. The housekeeper had known Rowen since she was a mischievous little girl who used to sneak into the kitchen to steal cookies. Edweth could always tell when she had something up her sleeve.

"Rowen?" Freya said. "We're just going to let them . . ."

"We can't do anything about it now," Rowen said. "At least at Appleyard we can talk to the Marshal about all of this, like Master Brax said."

"Very well, then," the housekeeper said with a heavy sigh that was almost too theatrical, then she pointed a finger at Brax. "I am serving you a warning, Mister mage. If anything of the Master's is disturbed or broken or missing when I come back, and I *will* be coming back . . ."

"I shall give you no cause for grievance, madam," the mage said with an exaggerated bow. Then he turned to Rowen with a look of feigned pity and understanding that she wanted dearly to wipe off his face with a slap.

"I know this is hard for you," he said to her. "But it's what your grandfather would have wished."

Why are you talking about him as if he's dead? Rowen wanted to scream, but she held tightly to her anger. It would have to wait. She had one last chance now to throw him off the scent before the toyshop was his. If he already suspected how much she knew, then she could use that to her advantage. She had to make him think she was not troubled about leaving, then maybe he would wonder if she was walking out of the door with the very thing he was desperate to find.

"Thank you for helping us, Master Brax," she said, and she smiled. It was a false smile, but that was what she wanted him to see. The smug grin of someone getting away with something.

And for a moment suspicion and doubt flickered across the mage's guarded features. It had worked. He wasn't so sure of his victory now. She hoped the doubt would gnaw at him, keep him preoccupied, until she could find a way to return.

Then before he might see the calculating in her own eyes,

she scooped Riddle up in her arms, turned quickly and went out of the door, followed by Edweth, Freya and the guards.

As they walked up the silent, white-shrouded lane she turned to look back. Through the falling snow she saw Brax standing in the doorway, a dark figure against the light from within. As she watched, still unable to believe that this was really happening, he slowly shut the door.

When they arrived shortly afterwards at the Gathering House, the guard named Kenning showed them to the small, tidy room that would be theirs for the time being. Then he nodded to the other two guards, who stood on either side of Freya. One of them took her arm.

"Come along," he said.

"Where are you taking her?" Rowen asked.

"Captain Thorne wants to question her further about what happened to Master Pendrake," Kenning said, "then she'll be escorted out of the city with her friends."

"Don't worry about me, Rowen," Freya said as the guards took her away. "I'll tell the captain everything I know about Brax."

Kenning ushered Rowen and Edweth into the room.

"You aren't prisoners here," he said in an effort to conciliate Edweth, who was still smouldering with anger. "The door will not be locked. But for your own safety you should stay here. We'll be keeping watch."

As soon as he'd shut the door behind him, Rowen set Riddle down and ran to Edweth. She threw her arms around the housekeeper.

"I met Grandmother," she whispered. "She's alive. Oh, Edweth, there's so much to tell you, but there isn't time now."

That was true, but Edweth tearfully insisted on hearing

more about Maya. So Rowen quickly told her as much as she could of what had happened in the Weaving and how she had met her grandmother at the cottage. Throughout the tale Edweth laughed and wept and held Rowen's hands.

"You found her," she kept saying in wonder. "If only Nicholas could hear this."

"I have to go now, Edweth," Rowen said, gently pulling her hands away. "The snow means that Whitewing Stonegrinder is here. The dragon. He told me that when I saw snow I should climb to the highest place and he'd be there waiting for me. The highest place around here is Appleyard Hill."

"Yes, yes," Edweth said, wiping her eyes. "That must be the place. I see now. That's why you let them take us here."

"In the meantime, keep demanding to see Lord Caliburn. If you get to talk to him, tell him that Brax is only after Grandfather's secrets."

"I will, Rowen. Now you go. Find the dragon and bring him here to terrify some sense into these stupid men."

Rowen nodded, and kissed Edweth on the cheek. The housekeeper looked at her, startled, then understanding came into her eyes.

"You're not coming back, are you?"

Rowen leaned forward and Riddle jumped into her arms again.

"I need to find Will," she said, "then I have to get back to the raincabinet somehow, to search for Grandfather."

"Very well," Edweth said, brushing back Rowen's hair. "You're not a child any more, are you? You're a young woman. Do what you must, my love. I will take care of things here. Yes, I will raise such a commotion . . . They'll regret bringing *me* to Appleyard, make no mistake."

They rose from where they were sitting, and Rowen

opened the door. A guard stood in the corridor. He was unarmed, but older and dour-faced.

"We demand to speak with the Marshal," Edweth said imperiously.

"He's got no time to chat with women and children," the guard said coldly.

"I am going to see him," Edweth said, striding past the guard into the corridor. "I have important news that he *must* hear."

The guard moved in front of her.

"You can't go marching around the Gathering House as you please," he said. "Stay in your room and I will send someone with a message to the Marshal."

While the guard was blocking Edweth's path, Rowen turned and began to walk the other way. The guard noticed and shouted after her, "Where do you think you're going?"

"I don't feel very well," Rowen said in a weak, submissive voice. "I need some fresh air. I won't go far, I promise."

"And in the meantime," Edweth said hotly to the guard, "I'm not waiting for someone to deliver my message whenever it suits them. This is a matter of grave importance. I am going to see the Marshal."

The guard looked from Edweth to Rowen and back again. Clearly he decided the housekeeper was the bigger problem, because he turned his back on Rowen. The last thing she heard as she hurried along the corridor was Edweth using several impolite words that Rowen hadn't been aware the housekeeper even knew.

The two sentries at the doors of the Gathering House were busy sweeping snow from the stairs. They gave Rowen suspicious looks as she passed, but when she turned and walked away from the gates, they said nothing and let her go. Once around the corner of the building, she let Riddle go and they hurried up the stone path through the apple groves. The trees were all white-headed from the snow. They almost seemed to be glowing with their own light in the thickening gloom.

By the time the two of them were nearing the crest of the hill, the snow was up to Rowen's ankles and Riddle was ploughing gamely through it, sending up puffs of powdery white with each bound. Ahead of her Rowen could see two sentries at the top of the beacon tower, scarves around their heads, huddled around a brazier for warmth.

She and Riddle passed under the tower, trying to go quietly, though her shoes made what sounded like a terribly loud squeaking in the fresh snow. But the sentries didn't seem to notice.

They came to the low wall where Rowen had sat with Will only a few days before. Below her, Fable was almost hidden by darkness and flurrying flakes, though she could see a few of the blue lamps gleaming dimly. She turned away from the sight and gazed around the shrouded hilltop. The only sound was the soft whistle of the wind. She looked at Riddle, and he looked at her, but said nothing. The cat seemed to have become very quiet since he'd returned to the place he came from. She found she missed the talkative Riddle, just a little bit.

Rowen stood still, and her attention was caught by one of the thousands upon thousands of tiny white flakes fluttering down out of the sky. It whirled and spun as it fell, and landed on the sleeve of her tunic. She had seen many snowflakes, and had always marvelled at their perfect shapes, like tiny crystal flowers, or stars. But she had never seen a snowflake like this. It pulsed with a faint blue glow, and it did not have petals or rays, like most snowflakes did, but was shaped more like a leaf. *Or a scale,* Rowen thought excitedly. *A dragon scale.* The snowflake rested on her sleeve only a moment, not melting as other snowflakes would, and then it lifted off again and joined all the others whirling around her.

"Whitewing Stonegrinder," she said quietly, scarcely daring to speak. "Are you here?"

Rowen of Blue Hill. I have come.

She gasped as the voice, seeming to come up from the earth, thrummed in her bones. She glanced at the sentries in alarm. They were still huddled over their fire and hadn't noticed anything. Perhaps the voice had truly only sounded in her bones and nowhere else.

"Where are you?" she asked. "I can't see you."

You see me all around you, the dragon's voice said, and Rowen now heard what Freya had heard in it: a great struggle being made, as if the owner of this voice was sick or in pain. *This is all that I am now.*

For a moment she thought she saw a huge shape forming in the flurrying of the snow before her eyes, then it was gone, scattering into countless whirling flakes.

"I don't understand. What happened to you?"

The river of ice was my home for longer than you small beings with two legs have crawled upon the land. In truth I was *the ice. I could take any form that water shapes itself to. From ice as hard as stone, to snow and rain, to the thinnest mist. But no longer.*

"Why not?"

The ice high in the mountains has been melting. My home is dying, more swiftly than I would ever have thought possible. The world is unweaving once more. I can no longer defend the high places from those who would defile them. The slaves of the Storyeater are pouring through the high passes in great numbers. They are coming here, to destroy this city. And so I have come to defend it.

"But how did you know about us?" Rowen asked. "How did you know that Fable was in danger?"

When I healed your wound, a memory awoke in me. Long ago it was foretold that I would leave my eternal home to protect a city of mortal folk I had never heard of. I would forsake the ice for one such as you, a mortal child whose fate and that of all the world were bound together.

"Grandmother's message," Rowen murmured. "It came to you, too."

I am here to do your bidding, granddaughter of the keeper of stories, with what strength remains to me. Speak, and command me.

Rowen hesitated. Her first impulse was to ask Stonegrinder if he would drive Ammon Brax from the toyshop. Still shaken by the dragon's presence, she had no doubt that even in his weakened state such a task would be a trifling matter for him. But it was that sense, the awe she felt for this ancient, powerful being, that kept her from asking such a thing. Dealing with Brax would have to be her own concern. There was something else, something only the dragon could help her with.

"I need to find someone," she said, her mind made up. "My friend, Will Lightfoot, of the Untold. You met him when we came to the ice, when you saved us from the Nightbane."

I remember him.

"He's far away. I don't know where, but I need to find him quickly."

You have something with you that can help you find him. Something of the Fair Folk. And I can bring you to where he is.

Rowen took out the mirror shard. She looked into it, saw her own face.

"Is it true?" she said. "How do I use it?"

Carry it with you, and I will carry you. The shard will seek out its other half.

The ground lurched under her feet and she gasped and flailed her arms, afraid she was about to fall. But somehow the flurrying snow held her and she did not fall. She felt herself held, buoyed up, and after a moment she was able to hold out her arms for Riddle, who sprang into them and nestled tightly against her. Then they were rising from the ground, lifted on a swirling cloud of snow.

Rest now, mortal child, the dragon's voice said. *You will need all of your strength for the task that lies ahead.*

And in the midst of a white storm that howled in her ears as she rose into the sky, Rowen felt herself cradled, safe and warm.

24

... without stitch or seam
in the space of a breath
one tale becomes another ...

– The Kantar

MOON, THE DREAMWALKER'S DAUGHTER, was the first to see them coming.

After Hawk and the others had been taken, her father returned to his lodge. He had walked into the Dream Country. She sat and waited alone while he walked there, in the place where she could not go. When he came back at last, after a long time, he told her they would leave the camp now and go in search of the rest of their people.

"I have seen your brother," he told her. "I have spoken to him. He knows he should not look for us here."

She hadn't wanted to leave in case Lightfoot and his friends brought Hawk back.

"He is with Lightfoot," her father said. "We will go to our people and Lightfoot will find us there."

She knew then for certain that this would happen. She

knew that what her father saw in the Dream Country was as true as the earth under her feet.

So they had set out walking across the plain, and the sun had crossed the sky and gone down. Then they had rested for a while and when the sun returned they walked on. The sun climbed to the top of the sky and seemed to halt there. The dry grass hissed in the hot wind and once Moon saw a snake slither away under a stone. Nothing that lived wished to be out under the eye of the sun, but her father walked on and she followed. They had a little water in a skin and when it was gone her father led her through a narrow canyon of red rock, where they came upon a spring trickling into a small pool. It was so shallow she could see the colours of the smooth stones on the bottom. There was only enough for them to quench their thirst and refill the water skin.

That day they found Lightfoot's horse and those of the men who had come with him. The horses did not shy away when her father approached them, and after he had spoken to them in their own language they had followed him. When the sun was low again in the west they had come to the rim of a wide valley, and there on the flats below were trees and the silver ribbon of a river and the white lodges of their people. They climbed down into the valley and walked into the circle of the lodges. The people came hurrying to greet them. They were home.

Then Moon had eaten well for the first time in days, and that evening she had been given a warm robe to sleep in, but she hadn't slept. She'd stayed awake that night and before dawn she had climbed to the edge of the valley and stayed there, watching the northern sky, which was starry and cloudless.

That was why she was the first to hear the distant rumble of thunder and the first to see the great bird coming on the wind. All the dogs in camp barked wildly and the people came running out of their lodges with terrified faces as she ran to warn her father. He joined her outside and turned his face to the north and put his hand on her shoulder and she had known that this time there was nothing to fear.

It was Lightfoot returning, as her father had dreamed. He was returning her brother to his people, and with him the rain.

Will stood at the prow of the ship with Shade and Hawk, the Horse Folk boy, gazing in awe at the earth as it unrolled beneath them. The skiff was much smaller than the other skyship he'd been on, the one that had taken him to the fortress, and when the wind struck it, the little ship was buffeted and pitched about like a boat tumbling over rapids. Will hung on to the rail, knowing he should be exhausted by now but unable to rest, as Balor had urged him to. The wildman was hunched on a thwart in the middle of the ship, looking pale and unwell. He was not finding the ride in this smaller vessel to his liking. At the stern, Yates stood in his oilcloth cloak, his hand on the iron tiller of the ship. Some colour had returned to his face, and his eyes gleamed. Everything about him spoke of a man who was sailing from bondage into freedom.

Will didn't fully understand how the skyship stayed aloft. He knew there was some kind of furnace set into the hull that contained *gaal*. When Yates wanted the ship to rise, he worked a foot-treadle beneath the tiller that fed into a bellows to make the *gaal* burn hotter. Another treadle cut off the air, to cool the *gaal* and make the ship descend. Eventually the fever iron would burn itself out, and then the ship would begin to fall out of the sky. Will hoped that would not be for a long time yet.

They had been sailing for hours through a day and a

night, out of the ghostlands and across the empty windswept plains, leaving the marching army of faceless soldiers far behind. The moon had appeared, pale and metallic in a haze of cloud, and in its light the earth was silvered and dreamlike. And even then, when the wind died down and the ship's motion had lulled Hawk into a fitful sleep, Will's eyes refused to close. He stood with Shade at the ship's prow, and it seemed to him that he was waiting for something to appear out of the dark, though he didn't know what it was. He was also troubled about Shade, and glanced at the wolf often, almost certain he was not imagining the alarming change he found in his friend. It seemed to him that Shade had grown *larger* since they'd come to Corr Madoc's fortress. His grey fur looked darker, too, and more bristled, as if he was tensed constantly against unseen threats. Will guessed that all of this had something to do with the *gaal* Shade had been given, but he said nothing about his concerns, hoping that as the fortress was left behind the changes in the wolf would fade.

Then day had come, and the sun flooded across the plains and revealed a different world. They passed over deep winding canyons of banded reddish rock, and wide, treeless uplands dotted with huge boulders, as if giants had smashed a mountain to bits and scattered the pieces. There was water, too, at least a little, as Will realized when he saw a few pools dotting the landscape and flashing like coins in the sun. Then Shade's keen eyes had spotted a small herd of dark, shaggy-coated animals gathered in a narrow, shaded canyon.

"The wisent," Hawk had cried, clinging to the rail and watching the animals until they were out of sight.

Buffalo, Will thought to himself in awe.

"They're not all gone," the boy had said to Will, his eyes

shining. "I will remember this place. I will bring the hunters here."

From that point on he wouldn't leave the ship's prow but stayed there, tirelessly scanning the earth below.

Finally he gave a great shout and pointed.

"There!" he cried. "My people are there. Where Father told me they would be."

A wide valley opened before them, with the wrinkled seam of a nearly-dry riverbed running through it. On the far bank of the riverbed, close to a grove of poplars, stood a ring of many gleaming white Horse Folk lodges. By easing off the treadle and working the rigging, Yates brought the ship lower and lower until it was hovering just above the ground, at the top of a gentle rise above the Horse Folk village.

Yates uncoiled a rope ladder from the side, and Will climbed down with Hawk.

"Lightfoot," Hawk said, and he threw his arms around Will. Will hugged him back.

"They call me Lightfoot," Will said, "but that's you, Hawk. You ran all the way from your camp to find us and bring us back. That's something I wouldn't have been able to do. And now you can help your people. You can lead them to safety."

"I am not Lightfoot," Hawk said.

"You will need to be. Those warriors without faces are coming. If they keep on the way they're going, Balor says they will pass through this valley. You and your people mustn't stay here."

The boy nodded, then turned away. Will watched him walk a short distance and then break into a run down the slope. Several figures came from the circle of lodges, walking quickly towards him. Among them Will saw Hawk's sister, Moon, leading their father. With an ache in his heart he thought of Jess and Dad.

Then he saw the horses—Cutter and the others—on the edge of the Horse Folk herd. A young man had a rope halter around Cutter's neck.

"Should we take the horses back to Fable with us?" Will called up to Yates.

"I advise against it," Yates said. "Horses don't do well on the flying ships, and I doubt that we have enough *gaal* left to reach the Bourne anyway. But don't worry. The horses will be well looked after among these folk."

Will turned back to see that Hawk had reached his father and his sister. And he took another look at Cutter. *Goodbye,* he said under his breath.

Will climbed back into the cloudship and rejoined Shade. The ship rose again and as it sailed out of the valley, Will looked back and saw a towering column of dark cloud coming from the north, dragging a long grey curtain of rain. With relief and gratitude he saw that the cloud would sweep across the valley, filling the dry river, and fall upon the camp of the Horse Folk.

Will thought of his mother then, and wondered what she would think of the ending he had found to Lightfoot's story.

They travelled through the rest of that day until evening began to descend and the shadow of the sail stretched out like a wing across the plain. Then a wind rose from the west, and icy rain slashed across the ship's deck. While they crouched in the stern, out of the wind, Will saw daylight between the planks and heard them rattling as the wind buffeted the hull.

"The skiff is breaking apart," Yates said, when Will showed him what he had found. "I've seen this before, when we take the ships out onto the plains, far from the ghostlands. It may be that the magic the dwarves use in the crafting of these vessels loses its power over long distances. Whatever the reason, I can barely control her any more. She's beginning to drift."

"How close are we to the Bourne?" Will asked.

They looked over the side and studied the landscape. To the south, through the rain and the falling gloom, Will could just make out a dim line of hills. On one hilltop he could see the faint suggestion of towers and battlements.

"I think those are the outer hills of the Little Kingdoms," Balor said, shaking the rain out of his eyes. "If so we're not far now, less than two days' march from Annen Bawn. If you can keep this flying bathtub up in the air a little longer, Yates, we should be able to land it right on their doorstep."

But Yates was now struggling to steer the collapsing ship where he wanted it to go. They all watched in frustration as they were shoved and bullied eastwards by the wind, away from the hills, until at last they could no longer see the towers.

"If we drift much further in this direction," Balor said, "we'll be over the Screaming Wastes. We don't want to touch down there, believe me."

"Why not?" Will asked.

"Unpleasant things live there. Things that hunt at night and have lots of sharp teeth."

Without thinking Will touched the hilt of the sword at his side. Corr had returned their weapons to them, but the grim look in Balor's eyes told him they would be of little use.

"I should bring us down now, then," Yates said. "While I still have some say in what kind of landing we make."

As it turned out, there was little else he could do. The wind had grown stronger and began to tug at the sail so fiercely he could barely control it and was forced to furl it most of the way, which started the skiff on a sudden descent. The hull groaned and shuddered as they rode down through the churning air, and Will wondered whether at any moment the bottom would give way underneath them. The tiller had become useless, too, and as they dropped, they were nudged mile by mile further east by the wind. The land beneath them grew stony and barren. Jagged pinnacles of rock rushed all too closely beneath them.

"The Wastes," Balor said with a scowl. "We were closer than I thought. The ship's going to land right smack in the middle of them."

"The *gaal* is burned out," Yates cried. "We're going to hit the ground hard. Hang on."

The ship was dropping faster now, plunging through the air like a falling arrow. Will clung to Shade, who seemed best able to stay balanced against the pitch and roll of the deck. The wolf planted his feet firmly against the shuddering planks and lowered his head. Then he raised it again.

"Will Lightfoot," he said, "you are glowing."

Will glanced down at his breast pocket. There was a white light pulsing through the fabric. For an instant he had no idea what this could be, then he knew and pulled out the mirror shard. Peering into the glass he saw his own reflection as a vague shape, and behind it a small but bright star shining in the dark.

"What is it, Will Lightfoot?" Shade asked.

Will didn't answer. He turned and searched for the star in the clouded night sky. He found it at once, a glimmering pinpoint in the darkness, the only star to be seen. He watched as it grew brighter and larger, and then suddenly it was gone. The dark had filled with whirling flakes of snow, like a moving, flurrying wall of white.

Then Will noticed that the ship had stopped shuddering. All was so still and quiet amid the swirling, streaming snow that he couldn't tell if they were still falling through the air or had already landed. And the wind had dropped from a shriek to a whisper.

Will climbed to his feet, the planks creaking softly under him, and Balor and Yates did likewise.

"What is this now?" the wildman groaned.

"I think," Will said, gripping the mirror shard tightly, "it's a rescue."

He looked towards the bow of the skiff. Out of the streaming white wall a small figure in a red cloak appeared, stepped down lightly onto the deck, and pulled back the cloak's hood. It was Rowen.

Will hurried to her. They took each other's hands. Rowen's face was so pale and careworn that he was startled and frightened, but her eyes lit up with happiness as she looked into his.

"I found you," she said.

Blue Hill, the *real* Blue Hill, was a day's walk north-east of the Bourne. The little thatched cottage was half buried in tall grass. Mice ran in and out of the cracks in the walls. Even so, Rowen couldn't help hoping her grandmother would suddenly appear to greet them.

Whitewing Stonegrinder had set the skiff down in the unmown meadow at the edge of the woods, his strength almost exhausted, and they all climbed out and took what shelter they could find in the cold, dusty cottage. Then the dragon, or the snowstorm, as he appeared to be, had flown to the top of the hill and settled there, a blanket of shining white against the stars. Stonegrinder spoke once more, and this time not only Rowen but all of them heard his voice like a deep drumming within them. The dragon told them that he must sleep for a time, but he would wake again when he was needed.

The fireplace was cleared of the straw and earth that had filled it over the years, and soon a fire was burning and they were huddled around it, warming themselves and sipping the medicinal tea brewed from the herb the doctor had given Balor. Only as the drink warmed him and calmed his racing thoughts did Will finally realize how powerfully the *gaal* had been affecting him. He felt his exhaustion now, but it was a true feeling, his body's own wisdom telling him it was time to rest and restore himself. He felt a great weariness, and sadness. While they were still in the skiff Rowen had told Will what had happened to her grandfather, and now he sat and looked into the fire with a heavy heart.

A friend will fall, the shadow of things to come had told him. What had the old man been if not one of Will's best and most trusted friends? Now that he was gone Will understood how much his hope and courage relied on knowing the loremaster was there, and believing he always would be.

Will sensed that Rowen had more to tell him but she was holding back in the presence of Yates and the wildman, neither of whom she knew. For his part Yates said very little. He seemed stunned by the strangeness of their rescue, or by the fact that he was back in his own country again after so long. Whatever the reason, he soon left the fire and stood by the door, looking out with bright, watchful eyes. It was clear he could hardly wait to set off again, to find whatever friends and family had been waiting and hoping all these years for his return.

Balor did most of the talking, describing for Rowen what they had gone through and how they had found Corr Madoc and all that had come after. When he had finished, he glanced at both Will and Rowen, who had hardly spoken, and understanding dawned in his face. He gave a great yawn, got out his bedroll and dropped it in a straw-filled corner, announcing it was time to catch up on a little of all the sleep he'd missed over the past few days. Yates left the doorway then and went to another corner, where he hunkered down, wrapping himself in his cloak.

Without having to speak, Will and Rowen rose at the same time, and went outside together. Riddle followed them, picking his way carefully through the thickly drifted snow. The air was still and cold. Far-off lights of other farmhouses gleamed like fallen stars through the icy fog that hung in the air. Will looked up at the silent white hilltop, marvelling once more at the thought of the strange, powerful being that had brought them to this place and now lay slumbering there.

"This is where you lived?" he said. "It must have been a peaceful place."

Rowen put her hand in Will's.

"I think it was," she said. "I remember more about it now."

Then she told him about meeting her grandmother and all she had learned from her, about the Weaving and what she must do, how she would have to find a hidden way into the Shadow Realm. She showed him the ball of golden thread Grandmother had given her, and like her, when she first saw it, his eyes were drawn by its fineness and shimmer. He asked her what it was for.

"I don't know yet," she said. In her inward vision she saw the ball of thread uncoiling, spinning out into the dark, a spidery strand of gold so fine it was almost invisible, so gossamer thin it seemed as if a breath would part it. But she couldn't see what had brought this about, or what the thread would weave, or mend.

When she had told him all there was to tell, Will said, "I'm coming with you."

"I've seen you, in the story," Rowen said. "I saw I couldn't find the way without you, but . . . I don't want you to come with me. I don't want anyone I care about going into that place. You don't know . . . you can't imagine what it will be like."

"We'll do this together," Will said firmly. He was about to tell her what the Dreamwalker had said to him, that he must stay with her or she would fail and be lost for ever, but he held back. Her task seemed hopeless enough without that prophecy to weigh her down. And there was much the blind man had told him that he didn't understand. Rowen was going in search of her grandfather, but the Dreamwalker had spoken of a great task that lay ahead for her, something she must do to save all the worlds of Story. Will knew he would have to tell her what he'd learned from the Dreamwalker, but he couldn't bring himself to lay this new burden on her shoulders. Not now, not yet.

"When I left the Realm the first time," he said at last, "I told you that this was my story, too. That's why I came back. I came back . . . for you."

"I know, Will, but you're in the Errantry now . . . they will need you in Fable."

"I don't care about that. You can't . . . I'm not letting you do this alone."

"I won't be alone. I'll have Riddle with me."

Will glanced dubiously at the cat.

"Rowen . . . can you really trust him?"

"Riddle knows what he is now. I *need* him with me."

Will stood in silence for a while.

"I'll help you find a way to the Shadow Realm," he said at last. "But I'm not leaving you to go there alone. That's the end of it."

Rowen was about to speak again, but she fell silent, slipped her arm through Will's, and rested her head on his shoulder. Arguing was pointless: she knew he was right.

She had foreseen enough of their journey already to know that he must come with her. Ever since she returned from the Weaving she had been aware that her gift of sight had grown, sharpened, to the point that now it was always *there*. She no longer had to search for the Story in things, she felt it shimmering all around her at every moment, and through her, too, the same humming life she felt when she'd held Riddle in her arms, the quivering, dancing movement of countless threads of possibility coming together, branching apart, joining together again to make the world. The weave of all that was and would be.

This endless, intricate dance was what she really was, what they all were, a ceaselessly moving and changing tapestry in which they lived and breathed and had their being. Grandfather had tried to show her this in the Weaving, she remembered, and she realized now that she had not really believed him. Or maybe it was that she hadn't known *how* to believe him. But now she could feel the truth of it. Each thread was unique and unlike any other yet the tapestry was somehow a seamless whole, so that the deeper she looked the less able she was to tell where she ended and everything else began. That included Will, and because of it she knew in her bones that he would come with her, that it had to be.

They turned at the squeak of snow softly trodden upon and saw that Shade had come out of the cottage to join them. The wolf and the cat glanced at each other warily, and Will remembered that Shade had met Riddle once before, too, in the forest. He had been tricked by this creature just as Will and Rowen had been. It would take a while, he thought, before they all learned to trust one another.

"I will go with you, Rowen of Blue Hill," the wolf said.

"Oh, Shade," Rowen said, throwing her arms around his neck. "You're the bravest, most loyal friend anyone could have, but you can't come with us. What they did to you with the fever iron . . . if you went to that place it would only get worse."

She clung to him, wondering how she could tell the wolf what she'd seen when she first climbed aboard the skiff, the terrible, undeniable change in him, and what she felt now as her hands sank into his warm fur. The poison was in him still, but it would fade in time and he would heal, unless he came with them to the Shadow Realm. If Shade set foot there, she saw now with horror, the power of the fever iron would grow stronger in him. The deeper he went into the nightmare that was the Night King's story, the harder it would be for him, even with his great heart, to resist. And if he faltered, if he lost the struggle, that story would transform him for its own purpose, misshaping him in anguish and rage into a creature of the oldest, darkest fears. A beast rising like a mountain against the sky, a monster with blazing eyes and vast gaping jaws, and a name of terror prepared for him in ages past: the Devourer.

She let go of the wolf and looked into his eyes, and she knew that he had guessed something of what she had seen. And Will had, too. His sad, troubled look said as much. But only she knew how great the danger really was, and how dire the consequence. No, she could not tell them that. She couldn't bear to see what little hope they had for this journey die in their eyes.

"I am stronger than I was," Shade said. "My eyes, ears and nose are sharper and my legs can run further. The poison has done this, I know, but while I am still able, I will stay with you and help you."

Unable to speak, she buried her face in the wolf's fur.

"We'll find your grandfather, Rowen," Will said. "We'll bring him back."

Rowen turned to him.

"When we do, we'll be coming back to a war," she said. "We've both seen it, Will. Grandmother says that Storyfolk from all over the Realm are on their way to defend Fable. But I don't know . . . I don't know if it will be enough."

"What about the Fair Folk?" Will asked. "They're Malabron's greatest enemies. Will they be there, too?"

"The Tain Shee," Rowen said with a surge of hope. "Maybe they can help us find Grandfather. Some call them the Hidden Folk because they're masters of concealment and illusion. No one sees them if they don't want to be seen, and Moth said they know all the hidden paths."

Will understood.

"If anyone knows a secret way into the Shadow Realm," he said, "it'll be the Lady of the Shee."

"But first we have to find them, if we can," Rowen said. "And to do that we need to get back to the raincabinet and look for their thread. There's no time to set off searching for them out here. Only the Weaving can bring us to them before it's too late."

Will and Rowen stood together for a while longer, both eager to set off right away, but the night was cold and they were hardly able to stand for weariness. Finally they turned to go back inside the cottage, Riddle and Shade following them. First thing in the morning they would set out for Fable together. The return of Brannon Yates after ten years would be news indeed, and Rowen hoped it would overshadow everything else, so that she and Will could slip unnoticed into Fable and Ammon Brax would not hear of it. Somehow she had to get back into the toyshop, and into the Weaving, without the mage finding out. If he had discovered the raincabinet, then maybe they were already too late.

She went inside, her thoughts troubled, and Will

followed her, but in the doorway he paused and looked out at the moonlit clearing that sloped down to the dark wall of the trees. He was reminded of the woods behind his house, the woods he had walked through to get to the Realm. Suddenly a strange feeling came over him that his own world was very close, that after his journey hundreds of miles across the plains and back again through the sky, he had not gone very far at all. It seemed to him he needed only to walk a short way through those trees and he would see the back porch light burning and be home. But with that feeling came the certainty that what he and his friends did here, in the Perilous Realm, mattered there, too. In the cold and silence of the night both worlds waited for him, and for what tomorrow would bring.